More Books
by Stephen T. Vessels

The Mountain and The Vortex (2016)
The Door of Tireless Pursuit (2017)
The Ruptured Firmament (2020)

FALL OF THE MESSENGERS

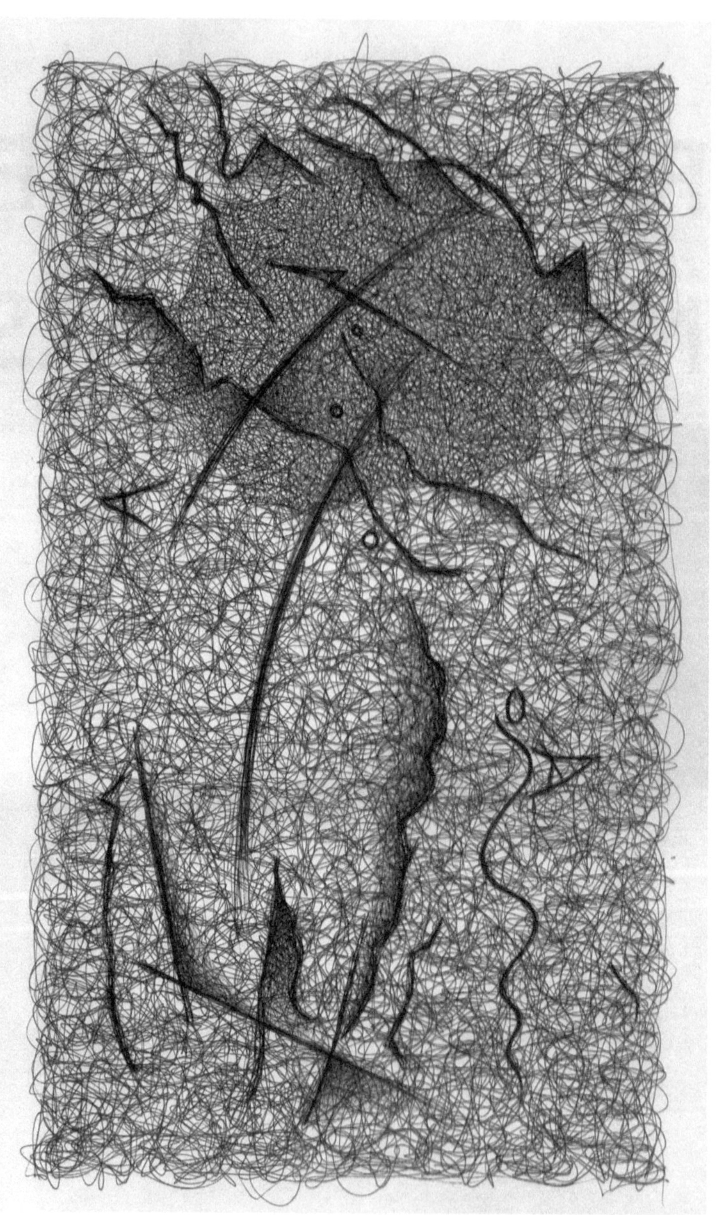

FALL OF THE MESSENGERS

STEPHEN T. VESSELS

2022

Fall of the Messengers
/ Stephen T. Vessels
ISBN
978-1-954397-04-0 (pbk)

Frontispiece and Author's Page Art
by Stephen T. Vessels

Cover Art and Interior Illustrations
by Alan M. Clark

ShadowSpinners Press

FALL OF THE MESSENGERS

Chapter One

The messenger arrived on Earth in the worst body he'd ever made and searched the woods for his partner. Like leaves from a tree of indecipherable symbols, shapes poured in a torrent through the branches overhead. Beyond the hill the city teemed and milled, its multitudes unaware of what would soon befall them. The messenger had never been alone before. Frisa was nowhere to be seen. The world was ending and there was nothing he could do about it without her.

A path wound up the hill. The sky, mangled with clouds, bore a golden hue. The messenger watched the shapes. They'd been drawn, as he, to the imminent disaster. There was no time to reach out to them. He knew some of the names of things. His clothing: a 'tweed walking suit' and 'bowler hat.' He wondered what would become of the trees, and what their names were; looked, again, for his partner.

Bare branches, spread like blast patterns, here and there a leaf clinging. Most of the shapes would die. He wanted to go to the top of the hill; she might be on the other side. He was too fouled in the time stream, could be destroyed himself.

They had never gone to a planet separately before. She must be playing with him. That was what he'd told himself, when he woke to find himself alone. The call had seized his attention—another species in peril. Then he saw that she was gone. The vaults of space were too empty.

But no, she was playing with him. He would indulge her, pretend surprise when she appeared.

Leaves on the ground picked up, tumbled, resettled, all without sound. He realized that he was deaf. At least some measure disconnected. The rudimentary body he had assembled possessed limited faculties. He could not feel the air on his skin, or smell the forest. His only adopted sense was sight.

He worked his fingers, clenched them. He could feel himself. He touched his face. In the center was a single eye; the rest was featureless. There should have been openings, in some configuration, to breath through, smell through, hear through …

He had been clumsy. Frisa would laugh. No sooner did he think that he should concentrate, and put his one eye to good use, than the sky went white. Beyond the hill, a fireball rose like a molten fist. Trees along the hilltop were blown flat, the tops of those about him burned. His hat flew off.

What was it called? A departing shape limped by, low to the ground. He reached out. It stared up at him, bewildered and ill, slow to understand. London, it answered. Yes, London was gone.

He took a last look around. Frisa must have been there somewhere; they both needed to imprint the event. But he could not sense her, not the faintest trace. He experienced an emotion (he could evade it no longer) that was new to him. Not new, perhaps, to the many beings whose lives he had lived and left behind but new to *him*, his core, original self, that had been there from the start. Uneasiness—the apprehension that a terrible vacancy had infiltrated his existence. There was nothing to do but move on. He stepped away, as light, or in his case shade, leaves a meadow, and the world receded. The embers, the whole murderous cloud, sank to an anvil of smoke, then a scorched mote, bleeding grey on the turning land.

A year later, in New York, everything seemed calm. Cars and pedestrians blurred and flickered past. This was how the worst things happened: without warning.

He was sobered now, more focused. Frisa's game had gone too far. They should imprint at least the second event together. Again, though, there was no sign of her. He had entered the stream correctly, at least. Time was mullioned, as it should be, counterbalanced, arrayed in staircase fashion. His dress was out of date but it did not matter. He was high in the time stream, too quick to be seen. Distant as the shapes were, he knew more of the names of things. The people here were markedly placid with the destruction of London so recent. That was how the mind adapted, carrying on with banal concerns so that horrors did not overwhelm. Every act was movement away, creating the past, displacing the prospect of its repetition.

He walked to the nearest intersection, looked four ways down the defiles of skyscrapers. The shapes amassed, more densely here, a quivering veil upon the sky, an oscillating tumult through the canyon streets.

Frisa—He needed a mouth to say her name.

The event approached. He turned to face it and went deep in the time stream. Cars and pedestrians came into focus, froze in mid-step, crept across asphalt. The brightness of the explosion seeped through the sky; the blast wave radiated slow havoc. Only he had the luxury to appreciate its beauty, the exquisite symmetry of destruction. He skipped over the shockwave, felt it tug at him—a soft, magnetic pull. With reluctance, he leapt high above the city, and witnessed its full collapse. Everything was wrong, now. He bore only half of the message. It had been made to be delivered whole.

He took to the shallows and let time race. Seventy years passed in a blur before the ruined metropolis that had been New York began to reconstitute in another form. The messenger knew only one rationale for action, only one path to pursue. He could not search the galaxy for his partner. If she was gone she was truly gone. Uneasiness turned to dread—no, he would not think that way. He had missed her somewhere, that was all. They would find each other. He let another fifty years spill by, until the changes below settled into a pattern, then went deep again, waited for the sun to sink beneath the edge of the world, and headed back down. Again he looked for Frisa to arrive at his side. She did not.

It was a less organized place than it had been. The old grid of streets had been smashed; those that replaced it wandered more fluid routes. The ruins of the city that had been coexisted with the one it had become. There was something unique in that. Lights were sparse.

With the population much diminished, it was not difficult to find a discrete spot to enter the collective present unobserved. He descended to a broad, triangular intersection that was paved in an evenly laid mix of broken bricks, masonry, and fragments of concrete. Ovoid lights, affixed at regular intervals to exterior walls along both sides of three converging streets, formed warm zones of illumination, lent height to shadows and darkness.

The surrounding buildings were a mish-mash of damaged structures and trackless amendments. Additions both graceful and awkward—bulbous, curved, angular, many precarious—protruded from and connected the ruins, in places held together by undisguised tangles of cables and supports. It was not restoration which had occurred, here; what was ruined had been stabilized, without any effort to disguise its state, and built upon unmatched. The ordered world had been forsaken for a mosaic realm of functional randomness. He sensed release in that, humility and acceptance. A peace had been forged between catastrophe and perseverance.

It was the time he sought.

Only one street crossed the intersection; the other two ended where they met with it, both from the left, the nearer more or less at a right angle, the other obliquely, some distance off. The way roads curled about, now, he could not see far down any of them. Directly ahead, the connecting street tunneled through a section of a toppled building that had survived its fall intact. It looked like it had been renovated on its side. Mounded structures bulged from the ends, on his right swept up into an angular, multi-sided edifice that joined irregularly with broken walls at street level.

Like a bubble popping, his hearing awoke. He heard Frisa call his name, but that was in his mind, too, the voice she had worn on the last world they visited, where the buildings walked and trees flew. He stood still, listening to the night. Sharp, animal sounds echoed up the street to his left, became squeals, fell silent. There was a pervasive background hum, a clatter and hiss of mechanical activity. Far away someone shouted.

Several stories overhead, in the windows of a beak-like addition cantilevered from a maw of twisted beams that crowned a once taller building, lights came on. The messenger saw a woman come to the center window—a female figure in silhouette. It called to his loneliness.

Chapter Two

Out of the ambient background noise a loudening whine became distinct. A mechanical object drew into view—ovoid, like the lights—rounding the visible bend in the near intersecting street. It was suspended like an ornament from a metal arm that rode a track secured to the walls of buildings, cement towers supporting it across gaps. The messenger recognized that it was a transport of some kind. The track wrapped around the corner of the beak-crested high-rise. The transport would pass above him. He withdrew to the opposite side of the intersection and backed into the deeper darkness of a recessed doorway.

The transport was large enough to accommodate maybe six passengers, brightly lit inside, flat on the bottom, with windows facing four ways. This one had only one occupant. A man with dark hair and a rugged, square face looked down in the messenger's direction as the transport turned the corner and went by. Whatever the man saw did not seem to startle him. The transport picked up speed where the street went straight, slowed and passed from view around the far corner.

The woman withdrew from her high window; the lights went out. The messenger could detect no other presence that might observe him. He returned to the center of the intersection. A transient breeze blew through. He lifted his hand to hold his hat, remembered he'd left it behind. Above the crumpled skyline a few shapes drifted.

It was always Frisa who initiated contact. He did not know how the shapes would respond to him on his own. They would know that he was incomplete. His makeshift body was a mimicry of form, a mere impression cobbled together from transient matter, devoid of life. He reached out. He could withhold nothing; any effort at concealment and the shapes would reject him. They halted their movements, regarded him with curiosity. There was a hesitation in their reaction that mirrored his own incertitude. Nevertheless they came, and soon others joined them. If he faltered now, they would not trust him again; the call had been answered, the quest begun. He opened his mind and reached out through the city.

What began as a gathering grew to a throng. They came and they came, the shapes of this world, ethereal, semi-transparent, each unique, geometric and hard-edged, symbol-like, fluid and undefined, hundreds, thousands, glowing faintly with myriad colors—they swirled about him in an excited multitude, hesitation relinquished as they read him and understood his purpose. He raised his arms and invited them to commune, and share, with him, their signature. They lifted away and drew together, surrendered their boundaries, their colors, their distinguishing characteristics, and coalesced into an immense grey sphere. This they did without awkwardness or resistance, swiftly and efficiently, as if it were a simple thing, in their nature to effect with ease. The messenger knew otherwise. They came back down to him.

The sphere was half as broad as the intersection, many times the messenger's height. A good gathering. It had an oscillating, liquid-like surface. The messenger touched it, allowed himself to be taken inside—to be, in effect, absorbed—surrendered dummy imposture to the training of life. So began the transformation, the learning of what it was to be human. The passions, the pains, the limitations and treasures of this particular flesh—he wrapped himself in them and embraced them as he could, in all with a sense of void. He had never submitted to the process alone, and never in uncertainty; perhaps because of that the connection went deeper than any he had experienced before. He let go of comparisons with the scores of other sentient beings he had been, accepted mortality, and became, except in the one immutable way, a man.

The names poured through him, associations, styles, customs, languages and beliefs of the day. With the aid of the shapes, he undertook the careful process of fashioning a persona, a personal history, an identity and an appearance—with the right number of eyes, and a full complement of senses and facial features. The tweed walking suit was exchanged for black trousers, thick-soled black boots, a black, lead-lined greatcoat that was surprisingly light, a collarless blue shirt. The shapes became playful and made him handsome, lean, fair-haired.

He grew impatient; this was not theater. He needed to find Frisa. The shapes quit their fussing. He was about to leave their sphere when he sensed among them a question unlike any he had ever encountered. A number of their fellows—a great many—had gone missing. They had no explanation for it, and were concerned. The hesitation in their initial reaction to him had been caused more by this than his own misgivings. They were in the same predicament as he, it seemed.

Long ago the messenger had learned to mistrust coincidence. His instinct was to suspect a meddlesome influence, whose he could not imagine. He saw, then, that on this world, another first, he would have more than one objective. In addition to the mission with which he had come, he must solve the mystery of Frisa's disappearance, and that of the missing shapes.

He solicited an amendment to his identity. The shapes concurred and became more serious. They aged him a bit, darkened his hair, weathered his greatcoat, pants and boots, swapped his pressed blue shirt for a rumpled grey one, gave him a scar on his chin that he had earned falling down a stairwell drunk. They provided him with a badge—yes, he might well need authority to seek answers.

He stepped out of the sphere and it burst apart, a dispersing flock of innumerable species. The street was still empty. He stood, watching the shapes fly off, waited for a direction to take him. Five of the shapes stayed, intent on assisting him. Two were amorphous and multi-hued, one looked like a calligraphic symbol that wavered between red and orange, one was an irregular dodecahedron, bluish-green, and one resembled a silver spoon. He had never had a retinue before. He did not like it. Given the strange circumstances, he supposed they might prove helpful.

They wanted to name him, though. He told them that he had a name. ¼=ca.85 would not do, they objected. No, but he always introduced himself to the recipient by his birth name. It was a point of honor. But he had not yet chosen a recipient, they persisted. What if he had to introduce himself to someone else? There should be a name on the badge, they pointed out. He would choose a name when the time came. That was how he had always done it.

He still was not sure which way to go. Filtered through the senses of another species, the call, for him, was reduced to a vague impression. Until he located a recipient, his impulses possessed an illusory character, as easily attributable to imagination or random curiosity as to any authentic reaction to stimuli. Frisa never had this difficulty. She always knew—*Go this way*—and he followed. She teased him about it—*For a future to be possible, it must first be imagined.* Yes, from a certain perspective, ¼=ca.85 knew that to be true. Then again, things happened all the time without anyone's imagination being the least bit involved.

Witness his current predicament.

He set off toward the tunnel. That seemed to suit his inclinations. Nearing the fallen segment, he saw through the windows that flooring had indeed been installed to agree with its post-cataclysm horizontal orientation. The tunnel, lit by ovoid lights, was unfinished, the entrance ragged, the interior wall-less. Naked braces to either side of the passage gave onto unreclaimed voids heaped with bricks and debris.

¼=ca.85 wanted to hurry but there was no place yet to hurry to. He wound his way along the road beyond the tunnel. Flotsam architecture lined his route—non-repeating variations of jumble-walled high-rises. Mound-like dwellings formed slouching pyramids. Some stretches were unlit, bordered by scaffolding.

No two worlds alike, he thought, except in suffering. A memory rose to cut him:

Do you think about it, that we cannot have children?

What do you mean? We've had hundreds.

And never one of our own.

They have all been ours ...

The notion was ridiculous to him, that their makers had left them unfinished. They had been given a purpose; that was enough. But now he saw why the thought had come to preoccupy Frisa so, and how it must have worn on her. To bear child after child, impregnated by her recipients, but never by him. Never giving birth from her original flesh, for that flesh was wombless. She could never honor their parents with a descendant in their image. He had been guilty of insensitivity to a degree of which he had assumed himself incapable. She would not leave him for that, would she? Where would she go? Nowhere among the stars were there others like them. She might go to Ixil; he supposed they would understand her there. And treat her like an oddity, a conversation piece, one with which they would soon grow tired. She would be more alone there than adrift in the deeps. ¼=ca.85 shook his head. Their shared purpose would draw her back to him. She was somewhere ahead, waiting, looking for him as he was for her.

Or behind. He stopped and looked back.

What about Gascot? the shapes asked him. Wouldn't that do? That was what Frisa called him, wasn't it? Yes, and no one else, he responded. Aeons ago, Frisa and he had given each other private names. They did not suffer others to use them. He moved on, past a truncated row of high-rises that had fallen against each other. A web-work of beams and cables stabilized the parts that remained intact.

He did not like even the shapes using the name he had given his partner. They should use her birth name, _=ca.110. He did not convey the thought. Nevertheless the shapes read it, and were offended. Not offended—offence was beyond them. But they were hurt, according to their respective capacities for emotion. ¼=ca.85 shook his head again. The exchange skirted absurdity. Arches spanned some of the rooftops overhead. Bridges? The indigo black of the sky was pale in contrast to the night black of the buildings, or was it the latter's crenelated starlessness? He had not yet accustomed himself to the spectrum of human vision. Maybe he should name the shapes; perhaps that would mend their spirits. The idea shocked them. We do not have names. We are what we are. Yes, and by your own appointment what you are is my assistants. I need a way to address you. Not so, they countered. They would discern his needs without prompting. He named them anyway. The two amorphous ones he would call Morph and Morpho, though he doubted he would ever tell them apart. The calligraphic shape he would call Graph, the dodecahedron Twelve, and the spoon, well, Spoon. The shapes did not respond, though ¼=ca.85 sensed that the conferrals pleased them.

There was another possibility, more terrifying to consider. The thought infected his companions with fear. Gascot tried to convince himself that Frisa would not harm herself. No—they had stood before the Galactic Council together, and she had defended their calling more staunchly than he. She might leave him, for a time, out of pique; that he could understand, now. But she would never abandon him to the certainty that he was alone in the universe. It would mean the end of their mission. How could he carry on? No—it would be tantamount to genocide on a scale beyond reckoning. He shook his head a third time. Of suicide he had to believe her incapable.

But what must immortality look like, knowing your dearest wish can never be fulfilled? And so he knew the wish must be—dearest—harbored in secret for thousands of years. It was in her voice when she spoke of it. He had pretended not to understand. Yes, pretended, for he did understand. He *did*. Though he denied it to himself, as if evasion could dispel her inconvenient pain. "Frisa—" He stopped again and searched the stars. It was a terrible thing, how eternity could shrink to the confines of a moment. For all his great knowledge, he was a fool. He had never known this misery of doubt.

The shapes reminded him that he was speculating. It made him angry. But they were right; he was scaring himself. A firmer sense pulled at him. He took breath and moved on. He needed truth, not mad imaginings.

He heard voices ahead, laughter. He arrived at an irregularly shaped park upon the perimeter of which five streets converged. The buildings that surrounded it were the tallest he had seen— historicity, he imagined. Street lights encircled the park but the interior was dark.

A group of men sat and stood around an outdoor table, some distance in. They watched him as he drew near. They all wore hats, mostly flat caps, though two wore bowlers—still in fashion, evidently. ¼=ca.85 nodded, affected an attitude of belonging. Invisibility was his special art. A couple of the men kept their eyes on him, though. The community was close-knit; they spotted newcomers. ¼=ca.85 drifted by. The grass was patchy, its blades flattened. The trees were saplings—except for one, an ancient pine near the far end of the park, with upper branches dead and bleached, pale in street light. ¼=ca.85 veered toward the old tree, overheard conversation—

"They need to lift the ban on hovers."

"Too many unstable buildings."

"I know."

"They need to distribute the pods better."

"They're expanding the bays fast as they can. We have to be patient."

"I waited on the platform an hour, yesterday ..."

Pods—that was what the ovoid transports were called. ¼=ca.85 attended the texture of the exchange more than its content. The sublimation was there, the background resignation. He'd already been sure, but it further confirmed that he had found the right time.

A small person sat on a low branch in the old tree. A boy, ¼=ca.85 made out. The boy watched, too, more keenly than the men had. ¼=ca.85 stood still. For a moment recognition was strong between them. He might have mistaken the boy for Frisa's recipient but he was too young.

Someone behind ¼=ca.85 shouted. A man emerged from an alley, ran across the park to the table where men were gathered. He spoke urgently, pointing back the way he had come. Those sitting stood up; they all hurried toward the alley. ¼=ca.85 followed them.

The alley was narrow, serpentine, paved with irregular cobbles. Holographic signs hovered above doorways—a market, an electronics store, clothing, wine—all closed at this hour. Other signs, not above businesses, were symbols ¼=ca.85 could not decipher. They had no meanings, Graph explained. They were reminders of the limitations of language.

The alley straightened startlingly. Without deviation it stretched to the limit of sight. *"An aisle far as the eye can see, and none to come in search of me—"* An Earth rhyme from Graph, gesture of sympathy. Not helpful. Up ahead, a crowd had gathered, beyond which gyrating blue, white and red lights swept the walls. ¼=ca.85's attention was drawn to the entrance of a bar. Above its red door a holograph of an olive skewered by a burning toothpick hovered. Something there—the track led there. But ¼=ca.85 wanted to know what was going on.

He pushed through the crowd. He did not like to become involved in anything before the message had been delivered. But anomalous occurrences could not be ignored in the present situation. The shapes all settled on his shoulders. He was glad, now, for their company. His new brain had not had time to cross-reference the information he had absorbed. He would need help to communicate convincingly.

"Make … way, I'm a … police … officer;" he tried out his new voice. His speech lacked cadence and his pronunciation was off. But they let him through. At the front of the crowd he encountered two officers keeping people back. They wore the dark blue jumpsuit uniforms and helmets of patrol cops. Behind them their patrol vehicle hovered, its roof strobes flashing. Between the hover and the officers a body lay sprawled on the ground.

¼=ca.85 flipped his badge open and shut—too quickly, he hoped, for the officers to notice that it bore no name.

One of them frowned at him. "I don't know you," she said.

Answering a question required connection, acknowledgment, recognition of directed inflection. Planchette glanced around, avoiding eye-contact. "I transferred … from … The Angels—" the opposite side of the continent, where records were kept by hand. Morpho's idea, and a good one. ¼=ca.85's vocal delivery still sounded contrived. The officer was too shocked to notice.

"The Angels!"

He nodded. "Got in … this evening. I'm just … looking … around but—" he nodded at the corpse.

She looked at it too. "It's a homicide. You have experience?"

He smirked—his first reflexive facial expression. "You might … say that."

"Want to take lead?" It was clear she was eager to unload the responsibility.

He shook his head. "I'm not … logged in. Mind if I … have a look anyway?"

"Go ahead."

He stepped past her, crouched by the corpse. Male, it was, cut deep across the throat. The head, a peninsula in a lake of blood, was almost severed, the face caught in a rictus of incomprehension. The man was familiar. Which was impossible, until ¼=ca.85 placed him. A cold presentiment scaled through his new body, down his spine to the tips of his extremities. It pooled within the core part of him that was not human.

No, never trust coincidence. The victim was the man he had seen go by in the elevated pod, just hours ago that same evening.

Chapter Three

Another police vehicle, larger than the patrol hover, descended into the alley. Its passengers disembarked and it auto-parked above the first one. The new arrivals were clad in white coveralls and carried equipment cases. Crime scene techs. ¼=ca.85 gave them space, returned to the young female officer. She and the other uniformed cop had moved the onlookers back and stretched a tape barrier across the alley.

"Witnesses?" ¼=ca.85 asked her.

The officer nodded. "A woman." She raised her chin toward the bar entrance. "She's in there."

¼=ca.85 headed that way.

"You going to interview her?"

"Before she's too drunk to talk, yeah." He had the cadence, now.

"Shit, I didn't think of that. Hey, what's your name?"

¼=ca.85 ducked under the tape. The gawkers made way. At the red door he paused. The pull was strong, here, like something tugging at his gut. He held the handle, confused by his hesitation. The shapes pressed at his back.

He went into a short entry hall. On the left was a coat check room. The young woman behind the counter got wide-eyed, stuttered about taking his coat. He ignored her and went to the end of the hall. The lounge was done in golds and browns, with indirect lighting. Low black tables, big cushions for seats. The bar was low, too, the bartender's dog-run sunken. The place was near empty, though there were unfinished drinks on several tables. ¼=ca.85 guessed they belonged to some of those out rubbernecking the crime scene. Two women sat in the far corner on his left. They stared at him. The bartender stared too, runt-like in his pit. The only other occupant was a woman in a rust-colored pants suit, who sat on a cushion at the bar, facing away.

Even from behind, he recognized her. A warmth rose in ¼=ca.85 that was unmistakable; she was his recipient. The sight of her both reassured him and increased his anxiety. He wasn't ready to talk to her. There was a restroom to the right. He told the shapes to wait outside, went in and splashed water on his face, leaned on the sink. He studied himself in the mirror, rubbed the scar on his chin. He needed a shave. He looked at his eyes. The organs of sense never ceased to impress him, no matter what creature they served. Those related to vision were the most mysterious. The irises of these were deep blue, with a pale brown fringe.

He could feel himself becoming more human with every movement, every breath. The way he thought was changing. The person he and the Earthly shapes had invented was coming into focus, his core nature receding into dormancy. There came a point, following a transformation, when it felt like reality became slippery and indecipherable, the ground unstable underfoot. He and Frisa had always sought quiet places to wait out such spells but this night afforded no opportunity for that.

He dried his face, kneaded the paper towels in a wad, looked around. The tile work was blue mosaic. The sink had been reassembled from a shattered state. The urinal and toilet were mismatched, the latter blue, the former white. 'Restroom—' it was a sanctuary with a time limit. He did not know where his actions would take him. The unknown, as ever, was never the same.

He ran his hands through his hair and went back out, drew scrutiny from the bartender and the two women again. The coat check girl peered around the corner of the entry hall. But the recipient still did not look at him. He sat down on the cushion next to her, opened his badge on the bar top, said nothing. She had red hair, styled in a tapering, shoulder-length wave. Her outfit was business cut. Under her jacket she wore a pearl-colored blouse that was stiff in the bodice—lead-lined, probably.

She looked at the badge—"You're a cop."

He nodded.

She frowned. "You got a name, Detective Blank?"

¼=ca.85 squinted at the badge, feigned confusion. "I'm not logged in." Irrelevant but she wouldn't know.

"What's that mean?"

"I guess that this is informal."

"Great. I hate formality. Still don't know your name."

"One quarter equals circa 85," he said.

She stared at him with her chin pulled in. "You're kidding." Her eyes were amber-colored, one eyebrow shaved and replaced by a tattoo of a stylized flame. Face a bit elongated, small nose, pleasant mouth. She was the recipient; everything about her was pleasant.

"It's an aleatoric musical time signature in a dead language. Roughly translated it means a quarter note gets about 85 beats in a measure of arbitrary duration."

Her head sank another increment. "Your parents must have been a riot."

"I'm the offspring of millions of souls yearning to heal. I am a hope and a prayer."

Her eyes lost the shine of interest. "Listen to *you*." She finished her martini and raised her glass at the bartender. Post-cataclysm glass, made of fused shards. ¼=ca.85 caught the bartender's eye. The man surreptitiously added water to the shaker, refilled her glass. She drank, murmured, "I guess that's all of us," looked at ¼=ca.85 again. "If you're talking like that to put me at ease—" she held the martini up—"my fourth. Mission accomplished."

The urge to have sex with her and convey the message welled up with such force that it hurt, like an omni-directional blow delivered internally. Everything was happening too quickly, off kilter and out of sync. It had to be her idea, her choice, her decision, and she showed no sign of recognition. Maybe it was the alcohol, maybe shock of the killing, but she was blind to him. The lens of her will was opaque.

¼=ca.85 had never known fear of failure. His tongue felt sticky and large in his mouth. He surrendered to his human persona, put what faith he could in profession, consulted Twelve, brushed the shapes away, thumbed the sensor on his badge. His new name appeared. "Here's what I go by." He showed her.

"Planchette Chron," she read, mispronouncing his surname 'Krawn.'

"Chron," he corrected. "The 'o' is long." He could relate to her only through his persona. Desire became an unrequited ache.

"Planchette—is that one of those utility names?"

"It isn't, no."

"I had a plumber named Spigot—"

"I'm not a Utilitarian."

"Can you predict the future, Detective Chron?"

"I make an effort to influence it. What did you see?"

She laughed, afflicted by transient cynicism. Then paled. "I saw *her.*"

"The killer was a woman?"

She started to answer but winced at an inner vision. She gripped her glass with both hands. "Know it still happens but ..."

"It's different seeing it first hand."

She nodded, shook her head. "More than that."

"Let's start with the easy part," he said gently. "What's your name?"

"Claire Fontaine."

Graph touched Planchette's hand. "The writer?" he asked.

She nodded.

"You write art and music reviews for the *Times.*"

She nodded again.

"You're a good writer."

Her eyes scrolled ceilingward.

"Why did you come here tonight?"

"Worked late. Felt like a drink."

"Do you come here often?"

"Not really. Once in awhile."

"No special reason tonight?"

She shook her head.

"Did you come straight here from your office?"

"I work at home." She anticipated him and gave her address; "And yes, I came straight here."

Morph prompted him. "That's a long way. You took a pod?"

She nodded.

"When did you get here?"

"Don't know. About an hour ago, maybe. Wasn't watching the time."

"Tell me what you remember. However it comes to you. Don't worry about getting things in order."

She closed her eyes, breathed deeply.

"Take your time."

She'd ridden a pod to the park platform. She'd wanted to get away from familiar surroundings—that counted as a reason, she guessed. She was near the bar entrance when she saw a man coming the other way. She didn't know him, but they smiled at each other. He trotted over to get the door for her. Their attention was drawn by a sound—she couldn't remember what it was. They looked back and saw a woman walking up the alley from the direction the man had come. She didn't seem to be heading to the bar—didn't look at them. There was something strange about the way she moved. Her clothes were strange—a gown-like confusion of mismatched veils or scarves that hid her figure. She wore no shield garment, unless it was under the gown. The man seemed surprised, as if he knew the woman but hadn't expected to see her there. He let go of the door and went toward her. That was strange too—the way he went to her, like he was taken by an impulse. The woman still didn't look at him. She kept her gaze fixed ahead, down the alley. When the man got close, the knife came out—a long, slender blade, like a short sword. The woman cut his throat with a single, quick slash, without ever looking at him. Claire went blank, and sometime later found herself alone in the alley, still standing by the door. The murdered man was dead on the ground, thirty or forty feet away. She had a weird image in her mind of the killer bursting into hundreds of brightly colored scarves that flew off into the night.

"You passed out?"

"I don't know. Didn't fall down."

"Were you dizzy?"

Claire shook her head. "She was so absent, the way she killed him. Didn't seem human."

Planchette digested what she had told him. The account was disturbing in several ways.

Claire frowned at him. "That it?"

"You didn't recognize the woman? You've never seen her before?"

"No."

"But you'd know her if you saw her again."

"Won't forget that face soon."

Something in his mind clicked and Planchette 'remembered' that he needed a description. "Age?"

"Mid thirties. Maybe older."

"Length and color of hair?"

"Shoulder length. Dark."

"Skin color?"

"White. White-white. Really pale."

"Weight? Height?"

"Weight I don't know because of that gown. She might be fat. Height fairly tall, five-eight, five-ten." She rubbed her eyes and raised her hand for another drink.

Planchette shook his head at the bartender. "You need sleep," he told Claire.

She grunted. "If I *can.*"

"I'll have a hover take you home. You want someone to stay with you?"

"No."

"Tomorrow we'll need you to come to the station to make a statement, and help us put together a facial composite. The earlier the better." Morph and Graph conveyed a procedural matter. "I'm afraid they'll need to take your clothes before you go, too, and scan your exposed skin for blood spatter. They'll provide you with coveralls."

She stared at him.

"It's just to eliminate you. We have to do it."

She nodded but he could tell he had scared her.

"Wait here. I'll have someone come get you." He stood up.

"Hey."

He stopped.

"You're either a really weird cop or a really good one."

"How about both?"

That earned him a faint smile, and for an instant it was like she recognized him. She might never know how much that meant to him.

Outside, the cruisers were stacked six high, now, the C-techs' hover at ground level behind them. Flood lights had been set up around the crime scene. Uniforms were questioning people in the crowd. The young policewoman came over.

"No one's taken charge?" he asked her.

She made a helpless gesture. "Me and my partner. No one with rank has shown up."

Planchette sighed. It was the height of absurdity, what she expected of him. With irony he reflected that this was the first human, the first person on this world, with whom he had communicated directly. His memory of her, of the expression on her face when he told her that he came from afar, would never fade. He saw her, now, defined by the moment, how she wanted to be significant, how she cared about life and people and sought to be true and good, how she hurt, sometimes, to be alone, and wondered if she were loveable. Her eyes widened in the path of his scrutiny. There was no time to argue with his worries, or let the internal shifts he was experiencing quiet down. A non-human agency was behind this intrigue; however humans might be involved they were pawns. It appeared that he would have to investigate the latter to get to the former. He would have to be what he seemed to be, which, irony of ironies, was exactly what he was.

"All right," he said to the young officer, "the victim says the killer was a white female—"

"You mean the witness?"

"What?"

"You said 'victim.'"

"The witness, yes. White female—ultra-white, note that—middle-aged, long dark hair, tallish, possibly heavy-set, wearing some kind of multi-colored gown. Pass that description around. Have Processing put out an alert. There were some guys in the park when I walked through—they came in here. Yeah, they're still here." Planchette pointed them out. "They might have seen the perpetrator exit the alley."

The young officer straightened, lifted by his trust. "I'll make sure they're questioned."

"Get someone to take the witness home. Claire Fontaine— she's circling the drain at the bar. C-tech will have to look at her, first. Whoever takes her stays with her. If she doesn't want them inside her place I want them outside the door." Planchette wondered why he was acting like he was in charge. He wasn't, and didn't want to be.

"I'll take care of it. Let me see your badge again."

He held it out. The young officer ran a pen-like instrument over it.

"Make sure we find out which of these people were in that bar when this happened," he said. His persona was asserting itself, becoming reflex. "And there are people inside that need to be questioned. Especially the bartender. We want to know what our witness said when she first went in." Yes, this was who he was; this was what he did. It was like waking up in a foreign country to remember that he had been born there. The world grew firmer underfoot.

"I'll get on it." She pointed at his shirt pocket. "Answer your sheet. The captain wants to talk to you."

Planchette looked down. The end of a similar pen-like instrument clipped to his pocket flashed red. He got another quick tutorial from Twelve, pulled it out, removed a soft piece from the bottom end and put it in his ear. His hands shook. The earpiece customized itself to the opening. He pressed a bump near the flashing end of the 'sheet' and a small holoscreen dropped down lengthwise. Planchette found himself confronted by a broad-faced, stolid-seeming individual with short dark hair and a bushy moustache.

"You, uh," the man looked away, "Krawn?"

"Chron—" Spoon tapped Planchette's knuckles—"Sir."

"I'm Captain Hasker, Chron. Your badge is from The Angels. You're not logged in for New York."

"I'm aware of that, sir." As aware as he could be.

"Says here," Hasker looked away again, "the dump from your badge says you trained at The Angels Memorial Academy?"

"That's right, sir." The rest of the shapes settled on Planchette's shoulders again. Story-telling time.

"Good school. Problem is I need a hard copy of your file and I don't have one. I don't even have a transfer request for you."

Planchette feigned incomprehension. "I'm sorry, sir. I was told everything was in order." He hated lying. It was the part of his lives that he never got used to. It separated him from everyone. Except Frisa.

"I'm not going to look a gift in the ass, Chron; I can use you. I want you to have 'em call me. Now, I mean. I'll give 'em a secure link and they can transmit your file."

"I can't do that." That much, at least, was true.

"Why not?"

Morph, Morpho, Twelve and Graph concocted a plausible tale. "They don't have that sort of communications capability where I was posted. There's still a lot of mistrust of technology out there."

"You guys make the stuff."

"That's up north, sir. Down south it's mostly small towns."

"You're coming to me with village experience?"

"It's broader spectrum than you might imagine, Captain. We're spread pretty thin out there. My circuit was eight, sometimes ten communities."

"Huh. They must miss you."

"They got a replacement for me."

"So you decided to try the big city, huh? We've got 300,000 people. Think you can handle it?"

Planchette didn't like where this was going. "I'm interested in what you're doing here, Captain. I think I'm qualified."

Hasker considered. "Well, your badge checks out. I guess I can go ahead and log you in. We'll deal with the file-work later. Dunn tells me you've got homicide experience."

"Dunn?" The policewoman raised her hand at him. "Oh. She and her partner did a good job securing the scene."

"Noted. Is she right, you have experience?"

"You might say that." It was like watching the inescapable clomp toward him.

"Say it, then."

"I have experience."

"Good. My homicide 'squad' right now is two guys. Schnitke's investigating what looks like sabotage at a Transit bay. Perls is on my shit list and I want to keep him there for awhile. If you want to get your feet wet, like I said, I can use you."

"I wouldn't want to step on anybody's toes, Captain."

"Trust me, they won't care. You want lead, it's yours."

The identity that had seemed like an advantage was turning

into an impediment. He didn't want to head a murder investigation. He didn't even want to find out who the murdered man was, much as he expected he needed to. It was too late to back out. "Well, that's what I'm here for, Captain."

"Right. You got a sidearm?"

Planchette noticed a big man weaving his way through the civilians and the cops questioning them. The man showed a badge to a uniform standing post and ducked under the tape. He was plainclothes something-or-other, clad in a pale gray greatcoat and wide-brimmed fedora. Dunn intercepted him.

"I—I didn't go through any processing, Captain. I wasn't planning to go on duty tonight. I just arrived."

"Well, you hit the ground running. Have Dunn issue you an O-bow. I don't want you chasing a killer unarmed."

The newcomer brushed past Dunn, came close enough to violate Planchette's comfort zone and stared down at him without expression. It was a ruse—his eyes seethed with ill will. He was about six inches taller than Planchette. He had a massive jaw.

"Excuse me, Captain." Planchette was tempted to give the lantern-jawed man a glimpse of who he was dealing with and let him run home to try to put his mind back together. But it would further nothing, and it was not Planchette's way. It was an indication of how off balance he was that the urge surfaced. "Do I have a problem with you?" he asked instead.

The plainclothes cop opened his badge. 'Perls,' it read. No first name.

Planchette held the big detective's gaze. "Captain, Detective Perls is here."

"I'll talk to him when we're done."

"He says he'll call you in a minute," Planchette told Perls.

Perls stared at him a beat longer and drifted away. He said something to a couple of uniformed cops that made them laugh.

"Chron?"

"Yes, Captain."

"I'll send someone who knows the terrain to assist you."

Planchette watched the young policewoman pass his instructions to another officer. He'd dealt with enough strangers for one night. "What about Dunn?"

"You like her that much, she's yours."

"I'll take her." Spoon rapped his knuckles again. "Thank you for the opportunity, sir."

"I want a briefing at 8 A.M. You won't be getting much sleep."

"I'll be there."

"Welcome to the New York City police force, Detective Chron."

The holoscreen cut off. Planchette saw Perls' sheet flash, watched him click it without taking it out of his pocket and speak to the air with his hands on his hips. The exchange was brief. Perls clicked his sheet again, went back under the tape and left without giving Planchette another glance.

Two hours on the planet and he'd made an enemy, something else ¼=ca.85 had never done before.

Chapter Four

An 'O-bow' was a sonic pulse weapon, named for the ring-shaped burst it fired and a resemblance it bore to a musical instrument. So Twelve explained while Planchette secured the one he'd been issued in a newly-donned shoulder holster. Planchette did not like weapons. He pulled his greatcoat back on.

"We have an ID on the victim?" he asked Dunn.

"Victor Friedman. He's a professor at Columbia College. Was."

"Professor of what?"

"His ID doesn't specify. He had a membership card for the Physics Club."

A scientist, then, as Planchette had feared. With the 'coincidences' piling up, it was a near certainty that the dead man was Frisa's recipient.

"You want to get out of that fish suit?" Planchette had always had a taste for jargon. It served to steady him.

Dunn took a moment to work out what he meant. "Sure!"

"You're with me, then. Tell your partner."

"He'll be jealous."

"Explain something to me, why is this alley so straight?"

She looked where he looked, smiled. "It's an illusion. Some artist did it. If you go down there it turns right."

"Come find me after you talk to your partner."

Planchette went toward the illusion. Med techs had bagged the body and were loading it into an ambulance. The crime scene people had spread out. Planchette stepped around them, mindful of their perimeter. His eyes still said that the alley went on; even knowing the impression was false he couldn't tell where it began.

A vague, crooked line in the sky, about four stories up, could have been the top of a camouflaged wall. Planchette almost walked into the mural before he saw it. Even up close it looked real, an orderly row of tenements, extending without end. Lights concealed in nooks and crevices in the adjoining wall illuminated it. The painted surface was smooth, and had some kind of finish that canceled glare. Planchette registered, then, what it was: an homage. Such a street had no place in the city that existed now. Above the tromp-l'oeil skyline the wall was painted black and dotted with stars. During the day the fantasy would be obvious but at night it acquired the aura of resurrection. And yet nowhere in the image was a living person depicted.

The alley dog-legged to the right. The mural extended far enough to sustain its deception until one reached the corner. Past the turn the way was less inviting. There were no holograms or lights. Planchette ventured to the next bend left, beyond which darkness was near absolute. He made out trash cans and stacked boxes.

Dunn came up behind him. "He was jealous."

"He'll get over it. Let me see your torch."

"Torch? Oh." She passed him her flashlight.

Something caught Planchette's eye. He shined the light on it. A piece of fabric clung to a pole sticking up out of a trash can.

"Get a pair of gloves and an evidence bag from the C-techs."

Dunn hurried off. The pole was wooden, the protruding end broken. A mop handle, maybe. Planchette examined the cloth fragment. It was white, with splotches of pink and green. It drooped like it was wet, though it appeared dry. He played the light about the walls, down the passage, up at the sky. There was no way of knowing how long it had been since the last call, how long Frisa and he had drifted through the void this time in their crystalline sleep. It might have been a thousand years or more, as humans measured time. The ninety-eighth species to receive the message, if he could deliver it.

Memories crashed down; Frisa was everywhere. What was he doing here, on yet another ruined world, pursuing a mystery he feared to solve? His body was new but he felt old.

"Detective Chron? Are you all right?" Dunn had returned.

"I'm tired. Get the gloves?"

She gave them to him and he pulled them on. He gave her back the flashlight. "Shine it on this." Planchette picked the fragment off the broken pole and laid it in his hand. It relaxed across his palm and retained no wrinkles. The weave was very fine. The fabric had the texture of flesh. Planchette put the fragment in the evidence bag.

"The killer came through here," he said. "I want this alley gone over."

They returned to the crime scene and Planchette gave the cloth fragment to one of the C-techs. Dunn led the tech back to show him where it had been found. Planchette tried to reconstruct what had happened. A woman came up the alley from the direction of the mural. Like stepping out of the past. She wore a 'gown,' possibly composed of the curious fabric he had just discovered. Her way of moving was 'strange'—what did that mean? *She might be fat.* The 'gown' must have been voluminous in some way. Planchette looked back toward the bar entrance. Friedman saw the woman, went to her. Planchette flexed his arm, his hand, made slashing movements, right and left. A single cut nearly took his head off?

The medical examiner was over by the ambulance, making notes on his sheet. He was a skinny person, middle-aged, with hair that seemed prematurely white showing beneath the sides of his flat cap. His ID was clipped to his coveralls: 'Clarence Tythe.' Planchette introduced himself.

Tythe scrutinized Planchette's badge like it was a dubious hors d'oeuvre. "You're new."

"I am. What can you tell me?"

The M.E. shrugged. "He's dead."

Planchette looked away. "I wasn't sure. Could the wound have been made by a single cut?"

"It would seem unlikely. On the other hand the cut is very clean."

"Thank you."

When Dunn got back Planchette commandeered her cruiser. He left her partner in charge of the crime scene. Dunn drove. They backed out and the other cruisers dropped down in unison to fill the void. The alley sank away.

"Where to?" Dunn asked.

"The victim's residence. Has anyone contacted his family?"

"Processing hasn't come back with any known relatives."

"He lived alone?"

"Apparently."

"Have Processing send a locksmith, or find someone who can let us in." They passed over the park. Planchette looked for the boy in the old tree but couldn't see him.

"Door'll probably be open, Detective. People don't lock much around here."

"Let's not wait to find out. And I want C-tech ready to go in."

Dunn clicked her sheet, contacted Processing, made the requests.

They flew in silence. The city rolled below, a dark, weary beast, slumbering amid the remains of its former might. Planchette tired of the conflict in his thoughts. He could not dismiss the possibility that Frisa had murdered her recipient. Neither could he believe she had done so. He would welcome the shame he would feel when he found the true culprit.

His thoughts distressed the shapes. Now he regretted letting them accompany him. If their fellows found Frisa before he did, and knew what he suspected, he feared what they might do. I would ask, he conveyed, that we keep my thoughts to ourselves, until we understand fully what has happened. Planchette suffered, awaiting their answer. Loyalty was a strained prerogative along such untested lines of allegiance. We are here to assist you, they responded at last. So long as you need us, we are with you. He let out a sigh.

"You can doze off, if you want," Dunn said. "I'll wake you when we get there."

"I'm okay."

Friedman lived near the outskirts of the new city. Beyond the perimeter of re-colonization the old one was a dark expanse of ruin, embraced by ink-black rivers. The lights of behemoth scrubbers made slow passage through the rubble. The machines worked day and night, back and forth.

They parked in front of what had to be one of the tallest buildings in the city, now. It went up twenty floors. The roof and something like half of the exterior, along an uneven height-wise diagonal, was brick reconstruction, the foot and the other half a multi-faceted assemblage of glass. A man with a tool case waited by the entrance. His face was deeply creased and he had a goattee. He wore the square-and-compass emblem of the Utilitarians pinned to the breast of his grey coveralls.

"Locksmith?" Planchette asked.

The man nodded. "Pick Sutton." He held out his hand.

Planchette experienced his first contact with human flesh, incipiently moist, sensed apprehension, maintained hold until Sutton frowned. Longer than customary, Spoon conveyed. Planchette let go and introduced himself and Dunn. The three went in. The lights in the lobby were off, the space bathed in pale streetlight, carved into eccentric angles by massive beams and their shadows. They boarded an elevator with walls a jigsaw of brushed steel. Dunn pushed the button for the seventeenth floor.

"You got here fast," she said to Sutton.

"I live nearby."

The elevator was slow and quiet. Silence, to Gascot, was companionship's deepest realm. Frisa and he never needed to talk much. It was foolish to think she would judge him for his worst moment.

"Only about two percent occupancy in here," Sutton said.

Dunn looked up. "I don't like tall buildings."

The walls of the seventeenth floor hallway were tea-colored, the carpet warm grey. Ribbon lights inset along the baseboards and ceiling joints softly lit the passage. The doors broke uniformity, all recycled salvage, variously repaired.

Friedman's door, dark wood with metal patches, was unlocked, as Dunn had predicted. Nevertheless Planchette asked Sutton to wait. He stopped Dunn from turning on the lights, put his hand on her shoulder and moved in front. The living room was dimly illuminated by holographic art—male and female nudes, bodies in peak condition. Chairs, low tables, a counter. The wall ahead was part brick, inset with frame windows, part plate glass, divided along a steep diagonal. The amorphous city slept beyond.

Dunn came up behind him.

"Sometimes I notice things in the dark," Planchette said.

She surprised him: "I know what you mean."

Planchette had no sense that Frisa had been here. Something else, though …

Dunn and he saw it together, light seeping under a door at the end of a hall to the right. Planchette went down and listened, heard faint electrical sounds. He put his hand on the door, sensed something he couldn't identify. The shapes felt it too.

Planchette knocked. The door was metal; it sounded solid. "Hello? Is anyone in there? This is the police." He tried the knob. It wouldn't turn. "Let's have the lights."

Dunn switched them on, came back. The door had an electronic lock, with a keypad and a sensor.

"Get the locksmith."

Pick Sutton crouched down and examined the lock. He got some tools out of his kit and pried off the cover. There were no visible wires or circuits, just seams that outlined solid components. He took readings with an oscilloscope, consulted his sheet, hummed in surprise. He knocked on the door, as Planchette had, then on the wall to either side of the frame. He sat back on his haunches, hummed again.

"What?" Planchette asked.

"I can't open this."

"We need the code?"

"That and the dead guy's hand. At body temperature. Even with that I'm not sure. You might have to burn through." He looked up at Planchette. "Take some doing. You use this kind of mechanism for a vault. There could be bolts running the perimeter of the frame."

"Can you tell who manufactured the lock?" Dunn asked.

"There's only a couple of places that make stuff like this. But I don't think that's going to help you."

"Why not?"

"It's been modified. This lock's one of a kind."

Planchette and Dunn looked at each other. "Does the department have someone for something like this?" he asked her.

"Something like what?"

Planchette put his hand on the door again. He recognized what he was sensing, and wondered why he hadn't before. And why the shapes hadn't. "Let Processing know what we've run into," he told Dunn. "We'll have to get someone up here with a cutting torch. We need this door open."

She nodded.

Planchette told Sutton to put the lock back the way he'd found it. "What time is it?" he asked Dunn.

She checked her sheet. "Almost three."

"Anything from the witness's description?"

She shook her head. "The alert went out."

They had a look around the rest of the apartment. Not a Spartan environment. Chairs in the living room large and overstuffed, the sofa bed-like, all upholstered in deep blue fabric with gold piping. The walls were a light olive-brown. Aside from the holograms, the only other decorative element was a painting over the sofa of a necropolis under a yellow sky. More holograms in the bedroom, some ancient-looking books lined up neatly on a shelf. The kitchen was a study in chrome and black mosaic. Planchette shook his head. The place was more conceptual than hedonistic. The man who lived here didn't have a home; his life was behind that door. Planchette was keen to know what that life was. "Let's get out of here. We'll come at it again in the morning."

They met two C-techs and a uniformed cop in the hallway. Planchette apologized to the techs and told them they would have to come back later. Dunn frowned at him. "I don't want anything touched until we've gotten into that room," he told her. Which was no explanation but she seemed to accept it. The C-techs, however, were unhappy.

"Anything you *would* like us to do, now you've got us out of bed?" said the senior of the two, a person about Planchette's height with tousled brown hair. 'Randall Fry,' read the ID clipped to his jumpsuit. He indeed looked under-slept.

"Go over Friedman's office at Columbia College. You might have to find someone to let you in—"

"We know how to do our job, Detective." Fry and his colleague departed.

Planchette recognized the uniformed cop from the crime scene. 'Officer Baranski' was overweight and past his prime. He looked tired, too. "How long have you been on duty?" Planchette asked him.

"Since yesterday morning, Detective. I've had some homicide experience. Processing called me back in."

"Think you can stand watch until I get someone to relieve you?"

"No problem."

Dunn started to contact Processing but Planchette stopped her and told her he would take care of it. They returned to the street and said goodnight to Sutton. Planchette asked him to keep himself available.

Dunn went around to the driver's side of the cruiser. "Where are you staying?" she asked.

"You go on," Planchette told her. "I'm going to walk. I need to think."

"Do you even know where you are?"

"I'll be all right."

"Sir, this city is real easy to get lost in."

"Get some rest, officer Dunn;" he started away. "Briefing at eight. Lose the fish suit." He waved goodbye.

He kept going until she'd left, then turned back.

Officer Baranski was sitting on the floor. He stood up when he saw Planchette.

"You can go home," Planchette told him. "I'll wait for your replacement."

Baranski looked worried. "I can wait, Detective."

"Your day's been long enough. I want to have another look around."

When Baranski had gone, Planchette went to the locked door, put his hand on it again and reached out. The connection was faint. The shape on the other side seemed debilitated in some way. With the help of Morph and Morpho he managed to get the code. There was a vocal element—a word he didn't recognize. None of his assistant shapes recognized it either. He let them connect with his core. They merged around his thumb, then latched onto his throat. He keyed in the numerical code, placed his thumb on the sensor. In the dead man's voice he said, "Apophasis."

The lock disengaged. Planchette heard bolts retract around the door's edge. He pushed the door open slowly. The room beyond was dominated by numerous holoscreens, ranging from a few inches to several feet in size. Ahead and left, vertical shutters ran the periphery, all of them closed, except for a gap on the left, where a potted coleus stood on a small table. A peculiar little doll sat beside the plant.

The larger holoscreens were covered with handwritten equations. An interface gauntlet and several stylus wands lay on a glass-topped desk. On some of the screens number and symbol groups changed intermittently. Programs were running. Planchette looked for the shape he had connected with through the door but did not see it. He noticed that his assistants had gathered around the doll.

Planchette had never seen a shape adopt the appearance of its parent species. He had not even known it was possible. The effort involved must have been considerable, rudimentary though the result was. In unmistakable mimicry of a human body, the shape had manifested pseudopod-like arms and legs, extending from a torso, as well as a semblance of a head. It even had eyes, which on closer examination proved to be spiraling fractals. A vague indentation in its 'face' implied a mouth. The shape was very old, and terribly depressed.

Morph and Morpho settled on the table to either side of the strange shape. The shape knew that Friedman was dead. That was why it was so sad. It had formed an attachment to the murdered physicist.

Planchette's throat and thumb were sore. He might be hoarse for a couple of days. He sat down at the desk and surveyed the holoscreens. His capacities were oriented towards emotions. Much of the math was beyond him, and none of his assistants could help. Frisa would have understood all of it, probably. As near as he could make out, Friedman had been attempting to characterize certain energies inherent to the void.

It did not seem a remarkable vein of inquiry for a physicist to pursue. Yet Friedman had kept this research hidden. The doll-like shape was traumatized and uncommunicative. It took hundreds of years for a shape to develop such a complex identity. At this late remove in its existence, this one had tried to take on human form. It was too weary and disheartened to explain itself. Planchette scanned the holoscreens. It occurred to him that shapes were composed of energies like those with which the physicist had been preoccupied. He rolled his fingers on the desk. Something very strange had occurred in this room.

There seemed no more to learn here now, and it would be unwise to linger. He contacted Processing and requested a replacement for Baranski. A last try at the old shape yielded only an impression of loss. Instead of answers, Planchette had found more questions. At every turn was he more embroiled. He was halfway out the door when a voice said, "He knew I was here."

Planchette snapped about and gaped at the old shape in astonishment. It had not actually spoken but its 'voice' had so stimulated the nerves of his ears that he had registered its words as speech. How the old shape had labored to make itself heard!

"He talked to me," the shape said. "He couldn't hear me but he talked to me. He called me 'Goethe.'"

With that, the old shape died. It lost its humanoid appearance and diminished into a dark pool, and farther, until it was barely a mark, a mere smudge. Any clarity Planchette had retained about his purpose on this world was in tatters.

Chapter Five

Destruction and deterioration. Tangled, mutated flora, dead where the scrubbers had passed, sand in slow migration where nothing had grown, torn slabs of concrete bloodied with a hundred years of rust, saw-toothed vestiges of fallen towers gaping at vacant heights.

No one to give it meaning.

The taxi flew over the 'veldt,' as it was called, the debris field that extended beyond the limits of re-colonization. A waning moon hung low in the sky to the east. The ruins of the old city passed below, bleached in the undercarriage lights of the hover. Some places looked like jungle, others desert. Fifty to a hundred sweeps by the scrubbers were required before construction crews could move in.

¼=ca.85 was inured to the panoramas of apocalypse. He had beheld similar sights on close to a hundred worlds. Nothing he could do would prevent them. His concern was with what followed. He saw no graveyard amid the ruins. He did not imagine the legion dead haunting their descendants. Guilt and blame were irrelevant. For him it was all a failure of theories and an opportunity for consciousness to evolve.

It was the way he was made.

Gascot had never reflected much on how alone he and Frisa were with their vision. He did not know what it would mean if he could serve that vision no longer. His value on this or any world would be reduced to insignificance. He didn't want to investigate a murder and hunt for a killer. He wanted Frisa to come back and tell him that everything was all right. He wanted to get started living another finite life, and help raise their children. He wanted to travel with Frisa and take in the sights of another wounded world on the mend. He wasn't made for this work.

He'd had many jobs in the lives he had lived, to satisfy his identities. Such occupations could not sustain him. Merely filling whatever mundane function availed itself on one crippled planet after another, knowing it would have no impact on the fate of the inhabitants. The impotent among the despairing—and he would outlive them all.

The driver was watching him in the rearview mirror. "You're new here, aren't you?"

Planchette nodded.

"You're not wearing a hat, that's how I knew. You should get a hat. 'Lead Head's got the best selection. Are you taking the supplements?"

"I didn't know about it."

"Take them. It's important."

Planchette nodded. "Where are we going?"

The driver looked back at him. "Insomnia."

"That's a place?"

The driver smiled. "It's a club zone, out in the veldt. Not strictly legal but nobody cares."

Planchette noticed a stationary cluster of lights in the distance. "Over there?"

"Yeah." The driver rummaged in his glove compartment. "Here—" he passed a pill container back to Planchette.

"These are the supplements?"

The driver nodded. "You can keep those. I've got more."

"Thanks. What do people do out here?"

"Watch old movies, listen to old music. Get drunk."

"It's a brothel district?"

The driver shook his head. "The sex zone's inside the rim. You can't have a sex club in the veldt. That is *strictly* illegal."

"Because of the radiation?"

The driver nodded. "You don't want a snag-tail getting knocked up where the level's over the bar."

Planchette had more questions but fell silent. The shapes weren't paying attention to him. He left them alone. They were in mourning. He was not comfortable with the sacrifice they had made for him.

They had not informed their fellows of the death of the old shape, whom Morph had identified as the Station of Futures, one of the Stations of the Close, the council of elders within the shapes' collective. The remains of one so venerable should have been shared with a great gathering. But Planchette's assistants would not have been able to keep from their fellows, in such a communion, what they knew of Planchette's fears, and so had honored their agreement with him, and divided the remains privately, among themselves. Unasked, without rebuke, while Planchette bore solemn witness.

The sympathy that showed in the face of the young officer who came to relieve him at Friedman's apartment no doubt reflected the shock in Planchette's own. Planchette managed a nod, gestured at a position by the door, made his exit without speaking. He had not meant to enter the veldt. He left the building in a daze, wandered until he found himself at the end of a street, beyond which lay the wilderness of ruin.

Several taxis were parked in a graded lot nearby. The driver of the one nearest lowered his window, asked, "Insomnia?" Planchette misunderstood the question. He got in the cab, surrendered to chance, having lost all sense of direction.

The clustered lights were below them, now. The driver brought the cab down in a disembarkation area, a divot of space in the wreckage about fifty feet square. Planchette passed him his badge to scan for payment.

"You're a cop?" The driver was surprised.

"Anyplace you recommend?" Planchette asked.

Eyebrows high, the driver scanned the badge, passed it back.

"I'm not a masochist, so I don't go for movies. If you're into that, a lot of people go to the Grist Mill. For music, I like the Goodbye Room."

"Where's that?"

"Go left on the main path over there, and stay on it. You'll run into it."

Planchette got out. "How do I get back?"

"There's usually somebody here. If not, you're a cop."

Planchette looked away. "Thanks for the pills."

The path led, ravine-like, through the maze of wreckage. Some plant life survived, here: paint-splotch thistles with leaves flattened against the surfaces they clung to, stubborn shrubs more branch than foliage. The ubiquitous ovoid lamps lit the way. Here and there a gap in the rubble gave entrance, cave-like, to a club. Recorded noises issued forth—music, voices, sound effects. Some of the clubs had holographic signs above their entrances. Planchette wandered in under one that read 'Post-cognition.'

The passage tunneled down through the rubble. Nothing was shorn up. Broken concrete slabs, twisted beams and rods, pipes, crushed unidentifiable materials, encroached on both sides. The footing was precarious.

He entered a small space set with tables and chairs. The ceiling was a cracked tent of concrete, stabilized by wedged beams. The "screen" was a rectangle of white paint on a wall. Currently projected was a montage of damaged film segments that had been digitally scanned and spliced together. Sound was garbled and intermittent.

In a dark, rundown warehouse, two men in long coats stood over a body. One reloaded his gun. "Frog One is in that room," he declared defiantly, and ran toward a doorway. The next clip was black and white. A white-haired man stood in an empty courtroom with a book in each hand, as if weighing the two against each other. He slapped the books together and exited the picture with them under his arm. The image bubbled away to a wide view of a regal wedding.

The patrons of the club were fixated on the projected images. There was no pleasure or curiosity in their eyes; their attitudes were grim and resigned.

Planchette went back outside and continued along the path where the cab driver had directed him. He did not like this place. These 'clubs' were sepulchers of bygone creativity. Obsession with pre-cataclysm life had been a heart-blow to the arts of this world. Little new art was produced that did not serve architectural ornamentation or assemblage building design. Music had been reduced to synthesized, narcotic reiterations of harmonic over-tones, or collages of recorded noise. No one wrote songs, anymore, or played instruments. They didn't tell stories, either, let alone write any down, or translate them into theatrical presentations. Fiction was dead.

Other lighted paths met, here and there, with the one he was on. He did not venture down any of them. The vegetation became thicker, as he went along. Creepers and grasses competed with taller thistles. There were even a few trees, twisted and cankerous, with irregular leaves. Species uncertain. The path skirted a vast mound of bricks that had nearly greened over. A crumpled church steeple sprawled atop it.

The path straightened toward an overpass that was heaped with rubble. The space under the bridge was walled up with pitted sheet metal, the side of an old cargo container, a bill board on which could still be made out the pale, shredded vestiges of a woman's face—all snugged in place with cinder blocks, bricks and chunks of concrete, the overall assemblage centered by glass double-doors. A handwritten sign taped inside the left door identified this to be the Goodbye Room. Planchette looked through scarred glass on a space many times larger than Post-cognition. No music was playing. People sat at tables, not talking, preoccupied with private reflections. It would be the same in all of these clubs. This was where the city's inhabitants came to vent the depression they pushed down and locked away at home and at work. They were in there together but all leagues apart, alone as they would be on private islands. A vanquished cosmos rode their shoulders.

It was oppressive. Planchette turned away. Left of the overpass was a hard-packed rise of earth about thirty feet high. He climbed it. From the top, the veldt stretched away more or less at eye-level, beneath the stardust river of the galaxy. To the south, the new city was a dark, hunkered mass, pin-pricked with lights. A scrubber lurched along about a mile distant to the northeast. The air smelled of green life, dust and dryness, and the ghost putrefaction, like rotten stone, unique to areas where nuclear weapons had detonated. Riding the low, distant rumble of the scrubbers, the sounds filtering out of the various clubs made an accidental composition. Planchette could understand why someone might want to record such phenomena. Capturing chaos both contradicted and clarified its truth. He realized that he had not been paying attention to a feeling he'd had since arriving at Insomnia, an irritating peripheral awareness of a certain familiar presence. It had been muffled by the moribund ambience of the place and his own dark musings— too, by the deeper extent to which his core self had withdrawn inside his human consciousness. But now he identified who and what it was that he sensed, and much that had been mystifying became clear. He was not the only outsider on this world.

The alien was somewhere off in the ruins to the northwest. Planchette climbed back down to the path and continued along it, leaving behind the Goodbye Room. A few hundred yards on, where the bottom three floors of a blown-down tower, overgrown with vines, marked the corner of a former intersection, an impression of an old avenue survived, extending west. Miles off, in that direction, two more scrubbers labored. The avenue was rubble-strewn, buried in sand and soil drift, and choked, not far along, with vegetation. But its line was still perceptible, even in the filmy light of a hangnail moon. Scratchy orchestral music issued from a club on the ground level of the erstwhile corner tower.

The defunct old avenue was unlighted. It would be a hazardous passage in the dark; but that was where Planchette's senses directed him, so he turned down the ruined way that people once traveled to schools and offices and homes. The lamps of Insomnia, at his back, were more hindrance than help, casting long shadows that confused the lay of the ground. Planchette was reduced to testing each step. The mutated flora that encroached upon and then overwhelmed the avenue made going worse. He fought through vines and foliage he could hardly see and discovered a path. Sorting crews had been through here, separating bricks, concrete, metal and other materials into piles. Wild plant life encircled the mounds.

A light came on ahead.

Chapter Six

Haliel waited on the far side of a narrow clearing. He had followed ¼=ca.85 and _=ca.110 to seven worlds, now, having been assigned by the Galactic Council to monitor them. Planchette always forgot about him until he showed up. He had never seemed important before.

In the center of the clearing stood a small radiant stove, on which rested a conical pot. Haliel had fixed himself some hot drink, which he sipped from an ornate cup.

"Hello, Eighty-five." Haliel smiled in greeting. "What do you think of my construct?" He held his arms out, the cup dainty in his left hand, swivelled side to side. The Ixilian's retinue of shapes, identical pale white ovoids, hovered behind him in equidistant formation. They were fewer than Planchette remembered, only thirty or so. "I'm getting better at this, don't you think?"

As ever, Haliel had copied ¼=ca.85 in assuming the likeness of a male of the planet's cognitively dominant species, and, as ever, had done it badly. Not through any failure of accuracy but by excess of perfection—a quintessence of form and feature that might result from an ideal blending of human racial variations. With a tangle of misshapen foliage for a backdrop, Haliel emanated an aura of mythical ancestor, a first father, come to dispense redemption upon his sullied descendants. His skin fairly glowed.

"Where is Frisa, Haliel?" Planchette's assistant shapes flitted among the Ixilian ones, scrutinizing them, trying to make contact. It would never happen.

"Who?"

Planchette assumed Haliel's confusion feigned, then realized he had used his private name for his partner. He did not correct himself.

"You mean One-ten? Is that the name she's using here? You're saying she's missing?"

Haliel even had the language down, better than he ever had before, every syllable enunciated with crisp precision.

"You've taken her somewhere, and I think you know who killed her recipient, if you didn't do it yourself. We can argue about whatever's behind this later. Right now I want to see her."

Haliel was a portrait of bewilderment. "You think I—I don't know what you're talking about!"

"Don't treat me like a fool." ¼=ca.85 had to rely on bluff with Haliel. He'd never been Ixilian so he couldn't tell when one was lying.

Haliel stared at him. His eyes tracked in thought. "What happened?"

Planchette turned to go. "I'll find her myself. If you think you can keep her from me, you're mistaken."

"Eighty-five!"

Planchette stopped. "I hate mendacity, Haliel." He wanted Haliel to reveal his intentions.

"You lie more than I *ever* have!"

"About ephemera, in service of truth. Never to discourage or pervert."

"I'm not aware of having done differently."

Planchette remained impassive.

"You might tell me what you think I've done before assuming that I'm guilty."

Planchette narrowed his gaze.

Haliel raised his hand for patience. "Let—let me ask you something." He sat down on a weather-worn chunk of concrete. "How long have we known each other?"

Planchette had no idea. The question was irrelevant.

"You don't know, do you? It's been over ten thousand standard galactic kerns since you were summoned before the Council. That's about fifteen thousand years on this world. These humans probably hadn't figured out how to make fire. Ever since then I've been assigned to you. Me—no one else. Here I am again. That doesn't strike you the least bit curious?"

Haliel always underestimated other species. "I suppose you'll tell me why it should."

"What's the longest life expectancy among the sentient species you've encountered?"

"Haliel—"

"Indulge me. Guess."

"I don't know, maybe three, four hundred kerns. Make me believe this is going somewhere."

"Something less than ten thousand, then."

Planchette saw Haliel's point, and it gave him pause. It was true; he never much considered the passage of time. From his perspective it was an abstract. The past was an empty stage, the present a perceptual continuum he could quicken as he pleased. He had begun to fear the future, but that was new. "You're telling me that you're a manufactured entity."

"No, *you're* a manufactured entity. I gestated in my mother's womb, the old-fashioned way. And before you ask, yes, Ixilians are quite long lived, by galactic standards. The oldest on record lived about eleven hundred kerns."

Planchette became interested in spite of himself. He sat down, alert for subtext.

"You're the oldest living creature in the galaxy, Eighty-five. Maybe the universe. You might even be immortal. And it never enters your mind. All those ministers who sat on the Council when you and One-ten went before it are long dead and forgotten. You live out a life on some planet, go to sleep until the shapes of another world scream out in terror and wake you up. Would you like to know what happens on Ixil when you come out of hibernation? Actually, the Council doesn't convene on Ixil anymore. They've eco-formed an entire planet for the purpose. Galaxy Prime, they call it—not very inventive. The beacon that monitors you sends out a signal. And somewhere, in the office of some minor functionary, in some forgotten annex of one of Galaxy Prime's vast administrative complexes, the message is received. A light blinks, a line of text flashes on a screen; the functionary has no idea what it means. He consults with other functionaries, and they others, and eventually they find their way to a forgotten archive, and then another forgotten archive, and so on, until, very eventually, they find me, tucked away in an increasingly antiquated stasis chamber. They wake me up, dust me off, and subject me to a very long process of reverse de-briefing, during which I explain, over and over, who I am and who and what you are to a series of functionaries and bureaucrats and administrators, on up the strata until I stand once again before the Council Major, none of whose members are remotely familiar to me, nor I to them. I keep a copy of my original commission in the stasis chamber with me so that I can verify my identity and assignment. The Council members argue and deliberate but it always comes out the same. They send me off again to watch you because it becomes inescapably obvious that I am the only one who has any understanding whatsoever of who you are and what you're up to. That used to be the case, anyway.

"Everyone I knew when you and I first met, my friends, my family, they've all been dead thousands of kerns. The graves that held their remains don't exist anymore. I don't visit my home world. There's nothing there I recognize. The only ones left with whom I have anything resembling a relationship are you and One-ten."

Planchette gave himself a moment to reflect. The sounds of Insomnia filtered through the night. "You describe a lonely existence." There was a poignant irony in Haliel's tale but it failed to inspire Planchette's sympathy.

Haliel shrugged. "I chose it. I didn't think through what I was doing. I thought they were wrong. I thought you should be stopped."

"You've changed your mind?"

"Everything's changed, my mind included. You have enemies you don't know about, Eighty-five, that you've never had before. If they are interfering with you, and it seems they are, you need a friend."

Planchette regarded Haliel with undisguised skepticism.

Haliel bristled. "You are the most myopic person I've ever known. All you think about is your precious message." He scoffed. "You never think about what's going on in the galaxy around you. We've identified thirty-nine planets you visited. You and I both know that's not all of them. Do you ever wonder what's happened on any of those worlds, since you left? You think all those species just flourished in your wake?"

Planchette had had many arguments with Haliel but none had taken quite this turn. Then again, Planchette wasn't sure what he and Haliel had discussed in the past. He had never paid much attention to him. Or thought he hadn't, or imagined that he thought he hadn't.

"They haven't all been successes, Eighty-five. Some of those species died off in spite of you. Ah, I have your attention."

"You're lying."

Haliel' expression sagged. "I shouldn't have told you that. But this ridiculous notion that I'm you're enemy, you can't afford it any longer. You need my help."

Planchette harbored disdain for Haliel. The environment of Ixil was so agreeable that consciousness and intelligence among his kind had been nearly beckoned to evolve. Neither Haliel nor any of his ancestors had ever suffered or struggled for anything. The very air they breathed and water they drank provided them with all the nutrients they needed to sustain life, health and longevity. They were incapable of understanding the species ¼=ca.85 sought to aid.

He was through listening; he would find his answers elsewhere. He would not permit the legitimacy of his mission to be denigrated by the likes of Haliel.

"There's no connection between us, Haliel. There never has been." Planchette stood up. He gestured at Haliel's false body. "That's not a construct, it's a costume."

"You flatter your disguise!" Haliel called after him.

"Have it your way."

Planchette fought back through the dense vegetation, returned down the defunct old boulevard. He had the uncomfortable feeling that he'd cut Haliel deeper than he'd meant to. Difficult to imagine any Ixilian guilty of murder. They were non-violent to a fault; it was a near organic characteristic of their species. Planchette couldn't worry about it. The idea that his efforts had failed was a swarm of hot knives. He wouldn't believe it. Haliel was trying to discourage him. Which did not make his claims false. It could be a ruse, a distraction, likely was, and a good one, for it targeted ¼=ca.85's blind spot with terrible accuracy. His children, all of whom he had loved and loved still, crowded his memory. He had abandoned them and their descendants to oblivion.

Planchette faltered against a broken wall. Many of the beings he had been secreted fluids in response to emotion. But Gascot had only done so out of joy or gratification. Now, for the first time in the unnumbered aeons of his existence, he cried in anguish.

"Frisa!"

Their children were dead. All of them. He had never thought about it. He'd loved them with devotion, every one! How many could he be asked to outlive? His mission had always called him away from such reflections, held his attention pinned to the future. Myopic indeed!

It was the shapes who steadied him. They cradled his mind with pleas and assurances. You are a hope and a prayer, they reminded him, not a promise. It was our predecessors, who, like offspring trapped in a burning house, called out to you, not knowing if you or any of your degree existed. However uncertain the help you offer, it is help we lack and welcome. Spoon answered Planchette's need the clearest. You are better to mistrust your doubts, the shape of etiquette conveyed. Think of all that has gone well, and confirmed, to you, the rightness of your quest. Perhaps you may learn from this trial. It would contradict both ethics and aesthetics, to say nothing of the intentions of your creators, for the lesson to be one of futility.

Planchette nodded. He was trying to escape his fears, and feeding them thereby. It was an integral component of the message he bore, fear's propensity to inflate when avoided. Time, it seemed, to apply that understanding himself. A question had been raised that he could not answer. The void it created could only be accepted.

It occurred to him that he had been infected by the very inclination to despair that he had been created to redress. There was design in that; whether Haliel's or some other's, there was design. Planchette straightened and steadied himself, became more a man than he had been, more a human than he had ever been anything other than himself.

Clouds had gathered in the south. A wind picked up. The sounds and odors and funereal malaise of Insomnia eddied about him. It would not do. It would not do at all. He went back to the Goodbye Room.

A police cruiser had parked in a nook in the rubble, a distance down from the earthen mound he had climbed. Planchette went inside the club; he did not know why. A few patrons glanced his way, returned to private reveries. A jazzy, instrumental piece was playing. The walls and ceiling of the club were festooned with a chaotic assortment of pre-cataclysm artifacts, no doubt collected from the veldt. Parts of cars and appliances, tattered clothing, broken musical instruments, fragments of sculptures, all manner of signs, scorched picture frames that housed blackened canvases, a plethora of minutia—pens, toothbrushes, combs, glasses, flat-ware, dolls, disintegrating books, bottles, cans, fragments of photographs, pottery shards, and on—shrouded the room in loss. A section of the wall to the left was covered with hats.

There were a few shapes in the club, old ones, indolent and listless. They took no notice of Planchette or his assistants. The music ended. Seated before a holographic computer screen on a raised platform at the front of the club, the DJ, haggard and sallow-faced, scrolled through files, more as if searching for a different life than another piece to play. In front of his platform was an open area, presumably reserved for dancing. No, it was a memorial—forbidden ground. People avoided crossing it when they went to the bathroom.

Two men and a woman moved among the tables to take orders. Most patrons shook their heads. Planchette heard someone ask for coffee. It would be dawn, soon.

"Here's something more from the new batch of stuff we got from the Continental Archive," the DJ said. He peered at his screen. "Not sure what this is. I guess it's a song, uh, by a musical group called, uh, it's another one of those peculiar ones, 'Fine Young Cannibals.' That's uh—yeah, I uh—yeah—well, I'll just play it."

The music began, with pumping rhythm and biting guitar notes. The club's patrons exhibited no reaction. Their spirits were hunched so far down inside of them that it might have been static playing. Except for one: a woman with red hair and a tattooed eyebrow who sat with a police officer at a table near the DJ's platform. She was clad in C-tech coveralls, now. Her eyes were closed; she moved her head and foot in rhythm to the music.

At the sight of Claire Fontaine a physical certainty flooded Planchette. He'd done enough thinking for the time being. Of all the limbs he had worn, he'd known none that did not want to move. The shapes settled on his shoulders but he didn't need them. He'd had scores of lives to prepare for this. He strode to Claire's table, cutting straight across the dance floor. A gasp went through the crowd. He stepped before her and extended his hand. Her eyes fluttered open—startled, shocked—"What?"

The cop with her was one of those who had laughed at Perls' joke at the crime scene. He shot to his feet. "Detective! She said she'd come on her own if I didn't bring her—"

Planchette withdrew his hand and extended it again. Recognition arrived—not the kind he wanted, just one person knowing another. "Detective Chron?" She saw what he intended but didn't believe it.

The music was too low. It wasn't meant to be played like that; it was meant to blow through restraint. Planchette pointed at the gaping DJ, bellowed, *"Turn that shit UP!"* With the disoriented haste of a schoolboy caught napping, the DJ obeyed.

Planchette did a full turn, his greatcoat flaring out like a cape, planted his foot on the downbeat, extended his hand a third time. "Dance with me." Mesmerized and confused, Claire took his hand. He yanked her to her feet, led her through a turn, pulled her close. She knew no steps but followed, eyes wide, breath catching in her throat. Someone shouted, someone clapped, someone fled in terror. Planchette sidestepped Claire across the virgin dance floor, pulled a fedora from the wall of hats, slapped it twice against his thigh to knock the dust off, rounded it onto his head, tilted it low, gave her a spin.

The singer from another time sang, *"I'm not the man I used to be—"*

People cheered and sobbed. The old shapes bounced about the relic-burdened ceiling; Planchette's assistants spun like dervishes. A fat man with a pony tail and a door-knocker beard fell to his knees with his fists clenched to his breast, growled and babbled like one possessed.

It was breaking apart in the Goodbye Room, the weight that held them. Claire saw him better, now; but she was still blind. Her will might never clear. It did not matter. With or without Frisa, whether or not Claire ever recognized him, Planchette would fulfill his mission, and be damned to any who stood in his way.

Chapter Seven

The relationship between memory and estrangement acquires a cosmological bearing when one considers the hyphenated, aeons-long history of Hirolyte and Krymsala, who in their final days were known as Planchette and Sibyl.

—Kum Laret, *The Fortieth Visitation*

The briefing was held on the third floor of the municipal police force's main central station, in a large room, with light grey walls and a dark grey floor, reserved for extreme crime investigations. About thirty uniformed officers sat on chairs and desk edges, and stood around the room's periphery. Clarence Tythe and three C-techs were there. Perls stood to the left, in front. At his side, another plainclothes detective, a short, grim-faced person Dunn had identified as Schnitke, leaned against a column. The captain was speaking. Behind him an array of holoscreens displayed images of Victor Friedman, alive and dead, the crime scene and environs, a map of the area, forensic shots of minutiae. The latter included the scrap of fabric Planchette had discovered and the broken pole on which he had found it.

He knew that he should have been in front, too, but Planchette kept to the back and waited to be asked forward. He was having difficulty concentrating, partly because of the room's eccentric geometry—a product of two towers having met each other's fall, and the surviving, truncated ruins having been stabilized and joined. An irregular placement of vertically askew and perpendicular columns confused sight lines. None of the walls were parallel or equal. The ceiling was several feet higher in the near right corner than it was on the far left. The west wall, to Planchette's right, leaned outward, perforated by a slanting row of plate glass windows that looked onto other, counter-slanting windows a few feet distant. The cumulative asymmetry lent the floor a pronounced optical tilt.

Planchette was afraid that when he was called on to speak he might break down. Weep, throw a fit, he didn't know what. The shapes shared his concern. They saw clearer than he the dimensions of turmoil at work in him.

He was having to examine his mind—something else he had never done—to understand what was going on. The problem, or *a* problem, had something to do with his memory. There were fissures in his fledgling human consciousness, mnemonic faults disrupting his perceptions. He was bedeviled by intermittent impressions that his fellow officers had the wrong number of limbs, lacked fins, had too little hair, or too much. Perls should have had a carapace. They all smelled wrong. There didn't seem to be words in any human language for how they should have smelled—not, at least, in the languages that he knew.

"This is bullshit," Dunn muttered at his side.

Planchette forced himself to focus.

"… so Detective Perls will take lead, as of now," the Captain said. "But I want to thank Detective Chron for helping—filling in on short notice. Not the—not the sort of welcome he should've received, so let's everyone give him a better one." The Captain clapped. Officers turned to applaud Planchette. Perls patted his fingers together a couple of times, under Schnitke's wry surveillance.

Planchette contrived sincerity, smiled and nodded. His perplexity increased at the same time that his disorientation subsided. They were taking the case from him? Why?

The Captain yielded the floor. Perls drew a circle on the holo-map with a wand. "Canvas the area—everyone living in a half mile radius from the crime scene. Our witness will be in later to give us a composite. Soon as she gets over her night out." Laughter skittered through the room; a few officers glanced at Planchette. "But we've got a description and for now go with that. Sweat the sockheads. We've got seven black holes in the city; pull them in. I want to talk to them. Work your way through the buttons. Reds, blues, and, yes, if we're still not getting anywhere, start looking at the yellows." A collective groan went up. "Okay, just everybody shut it. This is a homicide investigation and this is how we do it. I know some of you've got blisters in your pockets. That includes me, and I'll submit to questioning with the rest of you, if we get to that."

Planchette parsed his way through the jargon. 'Sockhead' was a euphemism for sociopath—that he followed. But his memory was stuttering. The colors and buttons were words without anchors. The Dissociative Apperception Test, Graph supplied— Planchette shouldn't have needed that. Yes, he remembered, everyone had to take the DAT, the test the Psychology Council had developed to identify persons with sociopathic tendencies. He would probably have to take it himself, at some point. He wondered how his persona would score. He'd encountered similar practices on several worlds. Here, if you failed, you were assigned a color, and had to carry a button with you that you were required to produce when asked. Black was the most severe. 'Black holes' had to wear their buttons visibly displayed whenever they were allowed off of their reservations, and black buttons were equipped with tracking devices. Yellow was the mildest. Maybe half the general population carried yellow buttons, disparagingly referred to as 'blisters.' Police couldn't question somebody just because they had a blister until they'd eliminated from their inquiries the yellow button holders in their own ranks.

"Okay, I think we'll split this down the middle," Perls said, "put half of you on door-to-door. Sergeant Robles—" he pointed the wand at a stout woman with close-cropped hair—"will make the assignments—"

Planchette noticed the Captain signaling Dunn and him. The Captain gestured for them to follow him and headed towards a door at the opposite end of the briefing room. Dunn went ahead of Planchette, through the middle of the room. Perls misinterpreted their approach. "Oh, Detective Chron, you have something—" He looked at the Captain, who over-the-shoulder met his gaze. "Sorry, Chief." Perls focused on Clarence Tythe. "What do we have from autopsy, Clarence?"

"My unyielding support," Tythe replied.

More laughter—with an edge of artifice. It was in the human character that mirth veiled despondency. Even in his fractured state, Planchette read it. The eyes of several officers, male and female, lingered on Dunn as she passed. She had on an olive green jump suit that revealed her figure. Planchette understood, conceptually, why she drew attention; but viscerally, in that moment, it was beyond him. He followed her through the door, down a zig-zag flight of stairs, into a hallway. At the end was the Captain's office. The Captain waited behind his desk, watched them come in. A pinned-up collage map of the city dominated the wall behind him. The desk was half wood, half metal, spliced together, stacked with files, a holoscreen open, left of center. Friedman's ID showed in oblique reverse.

"Close the door and sit down," the Captain said.

Planchette pulled the door shut. He looked at his hand. He was shaking again. But it was a human hand. Dunn and he sat down.

"House cleaning," the Captain said. "It was an error in judgement on my part, Chron, to assign you fresh on the ground, so I take responsibility for any mistakes that were made. That being said, why the hell didn't you record your interview with the witness? You had a sheet."

Planchette shifted in his seat, muscled emotions into abeyance. The shapes hovered about him, anxious to help, unsure if they could. "It would have been illegal, Captain. I wasn't logged in." He had grown a bit hoarse, as he'd thought he might. But his speech still had cadence and personalized inflection. He was holding together.

"Then you shouldn't have interviewed her."

Dunn, with a quaver in her voice, spoke up. "That was my fault, Captain. I let her go in the bar. Detective Chron rightly guessed that she would start drinking, so he went in to interview her while she was still … interviewable."

"That the way it happened, Chron?"

Planchette looked at Dunn. She had defended him. His sense of kinship with her, that they were both human, strengthened. She was his workmate, his … partner.

"Chron?"

This was who he was; this was what he did. "Judgement calls, Captain. I don't think Officer Dunn should be faulted for the way that she handled things."

The Captain sat back and smirked. "Don't fall in love too quickly, you two. So what's this business at the end of your report—'verbatim account?'"

"I have an eidetic memory, Captain."

"Come again?"

"Total recall. My transcription of the interview is exact."

"That's handy. Sort of hard to prove, ain't it?"

The question, banal to the Captain, presented Planchette with an existential conundrum. Who could verify that his old memories were accurate? Only one, and she was absent. The rest were dust. Planchette shifted again. "Point taken, Captain."

"It's 'Chief' or 'Boss' to you; dump 'Sir' and 'Captain.' Amend your report. Next item: evidence moved before being photographed in situ." The Captain slipped on an interface thimble and tapped his holoscreen. An image of the cloth fragment from the alley behind the crime scene came up. The Captain looked pointedly at Planchette.

"You said it yourself, Cap—Chief. I hit the ground running."

Haliel was familiar with part of his history, it occurred to him. It became a comfort, albeit an odd one, to know that he was around.

The Captain's expression soured. He rolled his fingers on the desk. "Next item: I don't know how you do things out west but around here we don't worry about upsetting people's beauty sleep when we're investigating a homicide. Door-to-door should've started last night."

Planchette nodded. He watched the Captain roll his fingers on the desk again. Something about that peripheral, semi-conscious gesture bothered Planchette.

"Why'd you keep C-tech out of Friedman's apartment?"

Planchette opened his mouth, said nothing.

"Another judgement call, I take it."

Planchette shifted, looked away.

"Right. Less judgement and more procedure, pretty please. Which brings us to your early morning antics. Insomnia, you couldn't have known, is illegal. We let it slide but one of these days we're going to have to shut it down. The scrubbers have to work around it, and those people—I know I've got cops going out there—whatever they're doing, they're endangering themselves. It's way, way over the bar out there. That whole area's hot as fresh stew."

Planchette nodded.

"How'd you know the witness would be there?"

"I didn't."

"Coincidence kind of dogs you around, does it? I got a report from Officer Mubarak, here, that says, uh—" the Captain tapped his holoscreen again—"I, uh—is this right? You *danced* with her?"

"It's … hard to explain."

The Captain laughed. Again, with that insidious veil, the masked faintness of hope. "Yeah, I'll bet. And then you, uh, took her to *church?*"

Planchette sucked his teeth—a reassuringly reflex reaction. "She was in a traumatized state."

The Captain nodded, peered sidelong in bemusement. "Interesting investigative style you got there, Chron, I gotta say."

"Captain—Chief—"

"No, I like you better schtum."

"Am I off the case?"

The Captain inhaled sharply, shook his head. "No. This thing's weird, and we need all the experienced hands we can get. You're weird, too, but clearly experienced. So you're in. But you take your orders from Perls. And forget what I said about him; he's a good cop."

Planchette hated politics. It washed through him again, all the dead he'd outlived. Sordid intrigues afforded ill comfort.

"You all right, Chron?" the Captain asked. "You don't look so great."

Planchette flexed his lips. "Permission to speak, Chief?"

The Captain cleared his throat. "Go ahead."

"No, I'm not all right. I'm tired and I'm pissed off. You throw this thing at me and snatch it back—that stuff upstairs was humiliating." It alarmed the shapes but it felt good to assert his persona. The churning in his core abated.

The Captain's features flattened with anger. "Noted." He pointed at the door. "Get a shave and get back to work. Stay where you are, Officer Dunn."

Planchette was happy enough to go. He paused in the hallway, wondered if he should wait for Dunn. Other passages fogged the one he was in: warrens, vestibules, colonnades, aisles, some plain, some ornamented. He squeezed his eyes shut, blinked. His vision cleared. He wanted something to focus on.

Framed photographs lined the walls—the station in various states of completion. The last picture showed a complement of officers posed on the front steps of the finished facility—a vaguely conical structure, attached by webs of cables to superstructure-like wings that curved in about it on both sides. Buildings were entities, too; they had characters and souls. The buildings of this city were trying to tell him something that he didn't yet understand. Planchette studied the faces in the photo. All these people craved mystery, pined for answers. In the former regard they were a minority, in the latter like everyone.

His memories were layered, he perceived. Ninety-eight lives—ninety-nine, including his first—deposited one on another, all that knowledge and experience, like sedimentary strata. Some function in him, some neurology, some energetic—it was impossible to classify the organs of his innermost self—some mechanism had ceased to function. The thing that held his old memories quiescent and constrained them to serve, with autonomic proficiency, immediate questions and circumstances, had failed—partly failed, it could get worse—and the memories were on the loose. He saw no way to return them to their rest. He could only ignore them, which was onerous and appalling. He would have to remind himself, divide his attention, decide over and over to focus on current reality, the way a recovering addict has to decide again and again to resist cravings. Minute to minute, hour to hour, day to day—

Frisa's absence had driven him to think back more than he ever had. That, and Haliel's questioning. The two events together didn't seem adequate to create such breakage. Some other agency had to be involved.

Another unanswerable question, another coincidence. And the only way forward was to do his job.

He headed back upstairs. The shapes wanted reassurance. I am afflicted, he conveyed; it will run its course. The briefing room had cleared out. A few uniforms lingered at desks. Perls and Schnitke stood together discussing something. Schnitke noticed Planchette, nodded towards him. Perls turned.

"The Captain says I take orders from you," Planchette told him.

"He kept you on?" Perls was startled—shocked.

"That would be why I am here."

Schnitke chuckled, shaking his head. "I told you it wasn't over, Nate." He strolled away, with a fingery wave. "I'm back on the Transit thing. Call if you need me."

"All right, Al." Perls regarded Planchette. His gaze drifted up. "Listen," he sighed, "if I came off, last night—however I came off, it wasn't about you."

"No, it wasn't."

Perls gave Planchette an appraising look. "So we're working together. What do you have for me?"

"Been to Friedman's place yet?"

Perls shook his head.

"More like a front than a residence. Whatever was important to him is in that locked room."

Perls nodded. "The City Engineer's office is sending someone to cut through the door. I'm heading over there in a little bit."

"What do you want me to do?"

Perls pursed his lips, looked down, tapped his foot a couple of times. "Go to the college and snoop around, question Friedman's students, anyone who might be relevant."

Planchette nodded. "Faculty, administrators, staff—how many students? The Captain lets me keep Dunn, that's two people."

Perls shook his head. "Friedman had seven doctoral candidates he was advising and wasn't teaching classes this term. I'm going to check out his apartment, lean on the black holes and talk to forensics. I get done I'll meet you over there."

"All right."

"I don't think he'll take Dunn from you. If he does, pick someone else. I'll authorize it."

Planchette glanced around. The pickings were getting thin.

Perls turned sheepish. "You really get here last night?"

Planchette grinned sourly.

"You want to take a break? Get some rest?"

"Ask Tythe if the wound was made with a single cut."

Perls frowned. "Why?"

"Look at it. One cut? A woman? That's someone with unusual strength or unusual skills. Or both."

Perls' eyebrows went up.

He left. The brute mass of the man was more impressive from the back. He'd parked his adversarial attitude, at least. No doubt with reservations. *The enemy of my enemy is my friend*—another Earth quote from Graph. Hardly the first world on which Planchette had encountered that sentiment.

The college was the next place he'd wanted to go, anyway—things had worked out well enough, for the present. He reviewed the material displayed on the holoscreens. The memory storm quieted, he noted, as he returned his attention to work. His senses became less inhibited, better attuned to matters at hand. Several interface gauntlets hung from a rack on a nearby column. Planchette slipped one on, took a wand off a desk. By Friedman's ID photo he wrote:

ISOLATED
SECRETIVE
SINGLE

He stepped back and stared. How well those words applied to him. How well to everyone.

Chapter Eight

"We are not the inheritors of reasons; we are inheritors of the result."

Through the passenger window of the hover, Planchette watched a team of grazers make inching, deliberate progress across the upper floors of a crumple-faced high-rise. The robots looked like giant, gravity-defying pill bugs. These were about hat-sized; some that operated at street level were big as hovers. A legion of the mini-scrubbers tirelessly scoured the city's skin, spraying out and vacuuming up surfactants and solutions of eccentric salts, bathing every brick and window in counter-active particle rays and microbial agents, collecting and carting off the dust and sand that perpetually blew in from the veldt. Neutralizing radioactivity was slow work. In fifty years or so the city's inhabitants might be able to relinquish their shield garments.

"Our reading today is from the Common Litany, beginning with the Commentary on the Cities. Gather ye faithful and attend."

If medicine had not advanced, no one could live here. Seventy-two percent of New York's populace had cancer, in one form or another. No comprehensive cure had been found, but treatments had been developed that greatly ameliorated the disease's impacts. Cancer had been, in effect, domesticated, like a wolf turned into an unaffectionate but docile dog. Humanity had adapted, once again. Cold comfort to the residents of a poisoned realm, who knew that the poisoning had been done by their forebears.

"Our ancestors warred upon each other, and many great cities fell."

Dunn drove east toward Columbia College. Small clouds floated here and there, becalmed in a lucid sky. In the distance ahead, the recolonized city extended to the far side of the East River, connected by foot bridges and ferries. Beyond that, and northward, ruin-strewn landmass, patchy with green life, stretched to the hazy boundary of the ocean. Planchette's old memories had subsided, for the moment. It seemed that he would be all right, as long as he focused on his job and didn't have to contend too much with peripheral concerns. So he told himself. The shapes were unconvinced. He watched the city pass below. Its denizens might imagine themselves ants in a labyrinth but never numbers on a grid. In the light of day, New York resembled a whorled accumulation of flotsam left by an eddy in an erstwhile flood. Cranes and scaffolding were ubiquitous. Where skyscrapers fifty to more than a hundred stories tall had once crowded the topography, now only a handful rose above ten, and those twenty at most. Pedestrians streamed along the winding streets, crowded together at transit platforms. Planchette noticed a lot of bridges and catwalks getting heavy use. Tunnels too, Morph conveyed; they serve as short-cuts across the city's gridless layout. Pods tracked above and below the foot traffic, stacked up at platforms. Here and there a surface flashed with a nacreous sheen, an effect of the engineered micro-organisms dispersed by the grazers. A hawk, the first bird Planchette had seen, circled down to perch on a bent beam that stuck up like a beckoning finger from a spindly high-rise.

"And many who had not begun the conflict joined it, and were also warred upon, that they might not find supremacy in an aftermath without victors. And more great cities fell."

Something about the scene below bothered Planchette. In some essential way, it didn't match up with any of the recovery efforts he had seen on other worlds. He didn't want to dwell on the matter for fear it might provoke another memory fugue. Perhaps you simply require additional data, Twelve suggested, and the nature of the incongruity will become clear without rumination.

Planchette did not respond. His assistants were growing tiresome. They weren't helping things with their fretting. What he needed was the other half of his mind. A brief consultation with Frisa and he could have worked out what he was sensing. Planchette spotted the church to which he had escorted Claire after they left the Goodby Room.

"The great systems upon which our ancestors relied did fail. It was seen that self-sufficiency is a myth, and among the cities which escaped bombardment were the majority abandoned."

It had been clear that their departure from the club marked, for the other patrons, the culmination of a singular event. Everyone stood when Claire and Planchette moved to leave. Planchette returned the old fedora to the wall. Some clapped—haltingly, unsure it was appropriate—others thanked them, conveyed gratitude with looks and nods. A minority reacted with less appreciative scowls and muttered chastisements. Still others wept, whether from grief or gladness it was impossible to tell.

Officer Mubarak took them back to the city. They rode most of the way in silence. Claire leaned against Planchette, holding his arm. They were near the residential tower where she lived when she said, "I want to go to church."

She did not meet Planchette's questioning look. "Which one?" he asked.

Mubarak echoed Graph and Morpho: "There's only one."

"There followed the time of darkness, when our ancestors set upon each other in the manner of beasts. Famine, pestilence and brutality diminished humanity to the verge of oblivion."

So it was that they came to the Catholic Sanctuary of Religious and Cosmological Cooperation, an imposing structure both austere and Baroque. Architecturally it was an amalgam of curves and angles that seemed to move in place, or suggest an inherent potential for change. It was six or seven stories tall; the random placement of windows gave no indication of levels. The entrance was a lofty gothic arch, perhaps fifteen meters high. Its perimeter was embedded with fragments of sculpted brick, stone and terra-cotta salvaged from the ruins of other churches and temples. Saintly and angelic faces, geometric and graphical symbols clustered in collective incoherence. Overall the entrance gave a wound-like impression, as if a woody trunk had been wrent from the church, and a knurled scar developed around the resulting hollow.

It was cool inside. A narrow, elevated aqueduct centered the nave, its walls encrusted by a mosaic of salvaged materials similar to those that embellished the arched entrance. Water coursed its length with a soothing murmur. Congregants dipped their hands, touched their heads and hearts. No one spoke. The vault of the nave was soaring and undulate. Except in height, it echoed no architectural precursor. Quasi-ideographic holograms drifted through it—more indecipherable non-symbols, like those near the crime scene. The vault was tiled with a dark mosaic that glistened in candlelight emanating from a multitude of un-matched candlesticks and chandeliers. The floor, laid in a polished material of variegated opacity, mirrored the ceiling. The latter had been fashioned, Spoon explained, from bricks and masonry vitrified by the atomic blasts. Around the periphery were a number of entryways, above each a sculpted symbol or figure relating to a pre-cataclysm faith. There was no raised dais at the front, only a simple lectern of unembellished concrete.

The pews were curved, formed of concrete, joined to the floor, and encrusted, back and sides, with more mosaic work. Their arrangement was irregular, confounding any impression of regimentation. Claire took a seat near the entrance and Planchette sat beside her. When all of the congregants had chosen places, a wizened, bespectacled woman went to the lectern, turned on a holoscreen, and began to read. Planchette felt uncomfortable at religious gatherings. He was an outsider to all of them, and yet his history often echoed legendary and mythical figures that peopled their theologies, and his message almost invariably dispelled mysteries that those theologies held sacrosanct. But he was neither a hero nor a saint, and most certainly no deity-dispatched redeemer. He was a manufactured entity with a purpose—a servant, nothing more. In many ways he was merely a highly advanced type of scrubber. He had given up wondering, long ago, if he had a soul.

"… A silence came upon the minds of our ancestors," the old woman read, "and they looked upon the void, and witnessed as one the enormity of the unknown, which they had veiled with policies and beliefs. The natural world proved more resilient than had been understood, and humanity suffered mercy, and was given to endure. And the keepers of knowledge emerged from their places of shelter, and went once more among the people, and a way beyond the past was forged anew. It was seen that people needed faith, and so it was that the Church of Cooperation was formed, and a place given where life itself might be revered, without compensation or clarity. Here, therefore, do all people have a place, whatsoever they believe, and place is kept, without cause or exception, for the absent member. It was seen also that belief is a choice. Here, therefore, do all of the old faiths also find a house, and any who have need of worship, prayer or contemplation, of whatever design, may come beneath this roof and honor that purpose."

There was much wisdom in the creed of this religion, Planchette thought. His assistant shapes objected that it was nihilistic and moribund. Planchette had no answer for them. Each species had to find its own way past its burden of wounds. It seemed to him that a step had been taken, here, in a constructive direction.

It was then that he noticed the ghosts. It struck him that the church seemed fuller, and he realized that many in attendance were not human.

The old woman turned off the holoscreen, and spoke directly to the congregation. "As members of this church we have only two aspirations. The first is that we care, the second that whatever we do for ourselves, in like measure we do for others. Personally, I am heartened that so many voluntarily conduct their affairs to reflect these aspirations. There is no perfect way to do so, and each of us must discover our own ..."

He recognized his children among the congregants, and realized that he was hallucinating. The apparitions turned to look at him. He seized Claire's hand, which was a violation. She was the one who needed strength and stability from him, not the other way around. She wiped the tears from his eyes and leaned against him. How he longed to open himself to her.

"Let us now extend to each other gestures of fellowship and goodwill, and observe a moment of silence for the past, and the multitudes resting in its lost domain."

The congregants stood and shook hands with those about them. Planchette resisted the urge to reach out to his children. He shook hands with an old woman, a child, a young man. The phantoms of his offspring faded from view.

People resumed their seats and fell silent. Planchette struggled with emotions. He pushed the hallucinatory experience from his thoughts, told himself it was a transient neurological reaction to the peculiarity of his circumstances. "Any who adhere to the old faiths," the old woman resumed, "are invited to proceed to the denominational sanctuaries and perform such rites and obser- vances as you require. Those who so wish may remain here in the communal sanctuary, in private contemplation or silent respect for the practices of others. The unified service is at an end. Go, or remain, in peace."

Something less than half of the congregants dispersed to passageways that led off the nave. Most headed for the exit. A few remained seated where they were. Claire cupped Planchette's face in her hand and smiled at him.

He left her, and what measure of confusion he could shed, in the church. It was growing light out. Planchette instructed Mubarak to see Claire home, and contact processing for a replace- ment to stand watch at her apartment. He sat on a bench in the asymmetrical plaza that fronted the church; in the dawn of his first morning on the planet, he dictated his first report.

He had failed to recognize that his first memory fugue occurred at the church. He was inexperienced with examining his mind, and his mind reacted: like a blow, the scene beneath the hover contorted with phantom city-scapes of other worlds. Planchette winced, sighed and surrendered to it. The crush of hallucinatory xenological architecture was too dense to sort into origins. It collided in a tangle of rude familiarity. His memories filled all the space that made it possible to move. He recognized a feature, here and there—the memorial dome of Crialba, the arboreal colonnade of Synk, just discernible amid Septurian, Fixot and Quinxian structures. But behind all that, under it, anchoring it, in a reasonless way, was the concrete reality of New York, irritating in its singular truth, objectionable in lacking the inherent force to dispel the occluding visions.

Planchette knew he could concentrate on the physical city to the exclusion of the rest. He could make that decision. He knew that everything false was in his mind, and that by choosing that perspective he could confine it. But he resented having to. This was how the minds of the beings he was designed to help worked, not his. They woke to irrelevant reflections and had to dodge preoccupation all day. The ability to sustain focus was, for them, a discipline. An art, even. How could he help them if he was afflicted with their weaknesses?

He recognized the three pyramidal spires of the city of Coleán. That was on Tehfolor, the fourteenth—or was it the fortieth?—planet that Frisa and he had visited. If he went down there, and walked the turquoise promenade, could he enter the College of Hope and Remembrance, could he translocate to that distant world? He could. Unique in the ability, possibly among all beings in the galaxy, or even the universe, Frisa and he could walk such an illusory path and follow it to reality. Except that, in so doing, he would abandon, to immediate and irremediable death, his human body. And he would not travel to the world he remembered, for he could not go backwards in time. He would arrive to a place that he would not recognize. Like Haliel, he would not even find the grave sites of his offspring.

The image of his Tehfoloran son, Rus, became startlingly clear in Planchette's mind. He saw Rus as a young boy, looking up at him with his watery, compound eyes, his gentle, sensitive snout slightly parted. He was trying to say something. ¼=ca.85 remembered thinking that Rus understood him better than any of his children. He remembered Rus as a young man, as he had appeared when ¼=ca.85, then Hirolyte, lay on his death bed. Rus bent down and whispered in his ear, "If on some distant day, Father, you feel alone, remember me."

Had Rus understood him so well? Had he perceived his father's true nature? ¼=ca.85 had never considered the possibility. But another thought came to him, one which seemed to address his condition. Children tended not to have much trouble staying in the present. It was adults, who, with the accumulation of years, and the layering on consciousness of disappointments and failures and wrongs, came more and more to look back, with frustration or regret, and thereby lose track of the moment so that it seemed to jump forward on them, with accelerating inevitability, until, in the grip of old age, the present sometimes ceased to exist as more than a clock hastening to its end, while the past arrested awareness in an aspect of futile reflection.

Planchette, Gascot, ¼=ca.85 had known no childhood. Neither adulthood nor old age. Only the steady, seamless parade of presence, of being who and what he was, one person, then another. Unless, it occurred to him—unless that had *been* his childhood. What constituted youth, for one such as he? Against what model could it be measured? Maybe the debt of age had finally caught up with him. Maybe his memory was malfunctioning because of that. Maybe, after aeons that even he could not count, he was finally growing old.

Tears sweated from his eyes. He lowered his window, leaned out and vomited. Or tried to—nothing came up.

"Detective?" Dunn gripped his shoulder.

"Take us down," Planchette croaked. He hung his head out the window and continued to wretch unproductively. The shapes were horrified.

Dunn took the hover to ground level and parked. "Detective, are you all right? Should I call for help?"

It came to Planchette that he had not been looking after his new body. He hadn't so much as given it a drink of water. "I think I need to eat."

Chapter Nine

All distinction between 'inner' and 'outer' reality collapsed; the crush of expired lives overwhelmed Planchette's perceptions. There was no room for panic. He searched for a human memory, something vivid and visceral, with which to subdue the hoard. It was like hunting through fog with a flashlight. He found his reflection, or it found him, which was confusing either way until the context clarified. He had examined himself in a mirror, at some point. Yes—in the bar by the crime scene. He remembered looking at his eyes, which thinned the mists some; but the organs of sight were too laden with alternatives. With mysteries, and he wanted fewer of those. He needed an identifying marker, a physical attribute that wouldn't exist without the fiction that required it. Which was him head to foot but he needed something distinct and durable, and at the same time ordinary. He'd rubbed his face, noticed that he needed a shave (still did), rubbed his chin—*that* was it. Never, in actuality, had he fallen down a stairway on Earth, drunk or otherwise; but his persona had, and his body bore the scar to prove it. He directed his old memories, all of his former identities, to withdraw behind the scar on his chin. Somewhat to his surprise, they complied without argument. Phantom paths and avenues peeled from the cobbled bend of road where Dunn had parked. A row of mosaic-tiled domes resolved into view, their line broken by a crooked brownstone with a hat shop on the ground floor.

Planchette detested manipulating his mind. He didn't know if his makeshift mnemonic patch would hold, or how it might affect his ability to think and react. He would have to maintain and reinforce it, a loathsome prospect. His scalp felt bruised. He was disoriented, disconnected from the moment, had to find his way back to it, recognize one thing at a time. A group of children filed past, supervised by adults. A cluster of shapes floated above them. Three of the children were giving birth.

Dunn was watching him. Her concern had a steadying effect. Planchette penetrated a veil and became himself again. His nausea subsided to a manageable level, his worries and objectives settled into place, his purpose opened before him. More keenly than ever was he aware that all of this happened by choice.

The two-story brownstone, diagonally across the street, was a mis-matched assemblage; the façade of the second floor didn't agree with the first. The lengths people took, here, to utilize anything that survived … Planchette got out and walked toward the building. His stomach lurched; he was rocked by transient vertigo and staggered, re-found balance.

"Detective?" Dunn ran to catch up.

'Basho's Bowlers' read the sign over the door, rows of hats in the windows. The cab driver had told him to get a hat. He needed to pay attention to the advice people gave him. An unimpeded brain-bath of radionuclides would not likely help his mental state. Planchette climbed the steps and entered a dimly lit shop. More bowlers lined shelves and display cases. Felt blanks of various colors hung from hooks in the far left corner. A split hat affixed to a stand on a display case exhibited the lead lining. The shapes hadn't provided him with a hat. His assistants proffered no explanation. They were hesitant to communicate with him, shaken by the magnitude of his breakdown. Planchette couldn't reassure them.

A short, dark-skinned, white-haired person emerged from a back room. "May I help you?" Over the doorway he came through hung a plaque bearing a brief verse: *'Life / a boat that sails at dawn / and leaves no trail behind.'* The clerk followed Planchette's gaze and glanced up at the plaque. "I like to think we might be related."

Planchette didn't understand.

"Frederick Bash;" the man extended his hand. "This is my shop."

Planchette shook his hand, knew the labor in crinkled skin.

"The author was a seventeenth century Japanese poet. I named the shop after him. 'Bash,' 'Basho—' My parents were both of African descent but supposedly there's Japanese in our lineage somewhere. "

Planchette re-read the quote. "The poem's survival contradicts its assertion."

The shopkeeper smiled. "Yes, it does. So far, at least. And yet it retains truth, doesn't it? Resonates with the soul."

"I need a hat," Planchette said. "I had a bowler, once." He looked around. "I didn't know there were so many styles." He wondered if he was remembered on any of the worlds he had visited. Not a question upon which to dwell. He rubbed his chin.

"Let's get your size." Frederick Bash pulled a chair over. "If you wouldn't mind—it spares me the indignity of using a stool."

Planchette sat down. The shopkeeper measured his cranium with a tape, made notes on his sheet. Dunn looked on, her expression unreadable.

"What's your color preference?" Bash directed Planchette's attention to the display of blanks.

Planchette realized the man meant to make him a hat. "No, that's not—don't you have something in stock?"

Bash did not conceal his disappointment. "What was your last one like?"

Planchette scanned the shelves. He pointed at a hard black bowler with a flat brim—"More or less."

Bash frowned. "Oh, no, no, no, that's not right for you." He studied Planchette's face. "I think I have something. Just a moment." He withdrew to the back of the shop.

Planchette grew impatient. "It isn't that important," he called after the shopkeeper. "Just something that fits!" He looked at

Dunn. "Glad you're still with me?"

She surprised him again. "I requested it."

He didn't know how he had inspired her loyalty. "You might regret that." She would feel betrayed when his deceptions were exposed. He wanted to protect her.

She raised her chin defiantly and shook her head. It stirred an ambition in Planchette, yet another unfamiliar feeling. Dunn looked boyish in a flat cap, at the same time more feminine. Yes, she was attractive—the visceral understanding registered, finally. But it wasn't that. He wanted her to trust him. He wanted to merit her trust.

The hat maker returned with a dark grey derby. The instant Planchette saw it he wanted it. It had a narrow black hatband and a rolled brim that dipped, front and back. He didn't know why it appealed to him so strongly.

He put it on. The sensation was startling. "That's comfortable!" It was like getting back a lost piece of himself. "I'll take it." He stood up and gave Bash his badge to scan for payment, went to a mirror and examined himself. It is customary to solicit an opinion of one's appearance, Spoon conveyed tentatively.

Planchette turned to Dunn. "Well?" he asked.

Her eyes widened and she blushed. "What? I don't know. It looks … all right." She turned away.

Bash gave Planchette his badge back. "You're a detective."

Planchette nodded.

"May I ask, are you investigating the death of Victor Friedman?"

Planchette frowned.

"That sort of news spreads quickly, Detective."

"Did you know him?"

"We met once. He bought a hat from me. He was an interesting man."

"How so?" Planchette sensed that Bash under-represented his familiarity with Friedman.

A look of bemused sadness came over the hat maker. "I'm not sure I can explain it. He read the poem," Bash gestured at the plaque, "and said something very curious. I remember it exactly. He said, 'Science and poetry are the same thing, and God lives in between.'" Bash smiled at Planchette. "I don't know what he meant by that. Somehow, though, it expresses something I feel about my hats. He had this quality, you see. He made you want everyone to have everything. I won't deny I get sentimental notions; I'm an old man. But I think he really was that generous."

Something about Bash made Planchette uncomfortable. He was too content, too detached, too placid. Planchette rejected everything he'd said. He was an old man who would forget his own name. He would forget his very reason for living, and go down dithering about God and science and the amnesia of the sea. Planchette wanted to get away from him.

Chapter Ten

Back in the patrol hover, they rode in silence. Dunn was agitated. She opened her mouth several times but didn't speak.

"Something on your mind, Officer Dunn?"

"No one gets a case taken from them in ten hours." She spit breath. "Unless they're dead, maybe."

"That attitude could be construed as insubordinate."

Her eyes narrowed.

Planchette watched the city slip below. "Hasker and Perls had an argument—recently, I'm guessing—and the Chief used me to get even. Sum it up?"

Dunn shot him a look. "How did you know?"

Planchette didn't answer. He was still flushing Bash out of his system. They passed beyond the edge of what had once been Manhattan, crossed over the river.

"He's pissed about your file, too. It's going to take at least three days to get it. He had to send a courier. The only way faster would be to draft someone on the other end. But that takes a court order—"

"And he'd have to let a judge know that he logged me in without confirmation."

Dunn nodded. "I wasn't supposed to tell you."

"Then you shouldn't have."

Dunn contacted Columbia College, got through to the kitchen. "What do you want?"

"Something easy to digest." Planchette sighed. Coincidences—he couldn't ignore them. Like everything had been planned in advance. The Captain has a tiff with Perls, makes an emotional decision to log Planchette in prematurely, puts him in charge of investigating the murder of a man who was probably Frisa's recipient and whose killing was witnessed by his own. On the very night he inhabits a human construct and assumes the identity of a police detective. Now he'd bought a hat from the same shop the murdered man had. Frisa and he found their recipients by a kind of instinct, a reading of signals—synaptic and etheric emanations. Maybe something similar was happening here in a way he didn't understand. Maybe, in this case, instinct and coincidence were the same thing. Planchette identified the urgency he felt: three days. If Hasker contacted The Angels Memorial Academy for his non-existent cadet records, it would complicate things sooner still. The Academy has altered its record-keeping system, Graph conveyed; they are in disarray. Planchette rolled his eyes. Another coincidence. No, we designed your profile to be difficult to confirm, Morpho conveyed. Of course, Planchette thought, so he could eliminate at least that item from his list of coincidences. Once he understood the underlying factors, he might eliminate all of them. Coincidence implied the absence of design. He had detected design in at least one of his anomalous experiences on Earth: his newfound inclination to discouragement. He could link that, by inference, to his memory problems, Frisa's disappearance, and, assuming Friedman had in fact been her recipient, the murder as well. That left un-linked, among the foremost coincidences, the disappearance of the missing shapes. But he felt certain, now, that it must be connected too. He was on the right track; Planchette felt a surge of confidence—short-lived when he realized that recognizing connections brought him no nearer to understanding them, or identifying who was behind the design they suggested. It brought him no closer to finding Frisa.

Across the river, in the rubble field northeast of the city, Columbia College came into view like a bloom in a wasteland. From a distance it resembled an artificial flower composed of a crystalline outcrop of rectangular prisms surrounded by a vast spread of corrugated white paper. "Isolated, isn't it? Like Insomnia."

Dunn laughed. "I don't think the faculty would appreciate that comparison."

The decision not to incorporate salvage principles into the architectural design was controversial, Morph conveyed. Resentment persists. The information seemed of little relevance but Planchette was glad his assistants were communicating, again. There was no longer any question that he needed them.

The outcrop of prisms proved to be a complex of multi-level glass-walled buildings, the corrugated paper sprawling ranks of greenhouses. It was the first orderly disposition of structures Planchette had encountered on post-cataclysm Earth. They landed on the roof of one of the shorter towers, near the center of the campus. Dunn led Planchette to an access door, down two flights of stairs, and into a hallway. It was odd, after being in New York, to negotiate an environment dominated by right angles.

"You know where you're going?" Planchette asked Dunn.

"I went to school here for two years, before I transferred to the Academy in New Ontario."

They arrived at Friedman's office. Planchette broke the seal that the C-techs had affixed to the door. Inside, the far wall was plate glass, overlooking the northern quadrant of greenhouses, a view lent drama framed. Planchette took in the room and thought, *No attachments to the world.* The only decoration was a small painting by the doorway. No shelves, no diplomas, no souvenirs— only white walls, a desk and three chairs.

"I'll check on your food," Dunn said behind him. "Want me to see about an interview room?"

Planchette considered. The chairs and desk had been dusted for prints. The chances that anything had been missed seemed minuscule. "This will do."

Dunn was non-plussed.

"We need to get started." He was ignoring protocol—consciously, this time—right after receiving a reprimand. It didn't matter. Once Hasker learned his identity was false, Planchette's career as a detective would be over. He had three days, if he was lucky, to find Frisa. And do everything else. After that, his odds of accomplishing any of his objectives would diminish precipitously.

It was ridiculous, two investigators canvassing a university. Somehow, somehow, somehow, he had to reconnect with Claire Fontaine.

A heavyset woman in a food-stained white uniform and chef's toque appeared at the door, bearing a tray. "Who's the police officer with the upset tummy?" Dunn and Planchette stared at her.

"Me, I guess," Planchette said.

The woman bustled in and set the tray on Friedman's desk. "Normally, I'd give you soup. My stock pots need a couple of hours yet. But eggs and toast never hurt a soul, and the steamed veggies should go down easy enough." She frowned at the fingerprint powder. "How'd it ever get so filthy in here?" She took a rag out of her apron and started dusting.

Dunn wide-eyed Planchette. He patted the air at her. "How did you know we were here?" he asked the cook.

"One of the student aides called down."

"Who? Whose student aide?"

The cook blinked at Planchette. "I don't know. Is it important?"

Planchette and Dunn exchanged looks.

The cook finished wiping off Friedman's desk chair. She pointed at the tray. "I brought you coffee but if that's too harsh there's mint tea as well."

"Thank you. And who are you?"

"Cookie Clarke. Head chef these seven years."

"Do you know why we're here?"

Cookie became uncomfortable. "You're looking into—what happened."

Planchette noted the Utilitarian pin on her lapel. "We're investigating the murder of Professor Friedman. We'd like to ask you a few questions."

"Me?" The prospect clearly terrified her.

Planchette nodded at Dunn, who conducted the cook to a chair, sat down herself and took out her sheet. Planchette sat at Friedman's desk and contemplated his prospective first meal. It was the same on every world, this learning of sustenance. Shapes did not eat, neither did they taste or smell, and were no help when it came to food. Spoon advised him to chew with his mouth closed.

"What was your impression of Professor Friedman?" Dunn asked the cook.

Cookie Clarke spoke in a quavering contralto with an English accent. "I didn't know him, did I? I only served his food."

"He taught here for five years. You've run the kitchen that entire time," Dunn persisted. "You saw him probably several times a week. You must have formed an opinion about him."

Cookie drew back as if Dunn were an unexploded bomb. Her lips fluttered but no words came out.

"These are routine questions, Cookie," Dunn said in a gentler voice. "We're talking to everyone who had contact with the professor. It's just standard procedure."

Cookie swallowed and blinked several times. "Well, I—I don't know. He kept to himself, mostly. He was polite."

"Did he have any enemies that you know of?" Dunn asked. "Anyone who might have been angry with him for some reason?"

Planchette tried the eggs, swivelled in his chair to hide his shock. The human palate was a powerful sense organ.

Cookie laughed nervously. "How would you know? They're all so formal, aren't they?" She checked herself, fearful. "I mean, that's to be expected, isn't it? All that studying." She swallowed again. "The students seemed to like him."

Planchette ventured minuscule samples of spinach and carrots, both vastly different from eggs. He had no idea if he liked either of them, decided to leave the broccoli untested. Dunn finished her questioning. She looked at Planchette to see if he had anything further to ask.

He had a thought. "What were his eating habits?"

The cook regarded Planchette like he was a new terror.

"Did he seem healthy?"

"I … suppose so."

"What did he eat? Did he have any preferences?"

After a moment's uncertainty, the cook seemed to find this line of inquiry less daunting. A note of steadiness entered her voice. "Well, now that you mention it, yes, he was very regular in his meals."

Planchette nodded for her to continue.

"Well, let me think. Breakfast was always his oatmeal, or dried cereal and yoghurt, and a bit of fruit. He never ate bananas. Lunch was a jumble salad, most days, though sometimes he'd have a sandwich if we'd got some meat in." She smiled, warming to her subject. "He liked my sandwiches. I'm always careful the bits fit properly, between the slices." Her gaze folded inward and her mirth wilted. "Poor dear. It's an awful thing." Her chin tightened. "You'd ask the night cook about his dinner."

"Thank you, Cookie," Planchette said. "You've been very helpful."

Cookie bustled out, on the verge of tears.

"That was nice, sir," Dunn said.

"She knew him better than she let on." Planchette eyed the coffee, sure to be another county, taste-wise. "Might be nervousness. Or she might be afraid of something. Or someone." Cereal, yoghurt, salad, sandwiches, nix the bananas—it was a start. Maybe he could include eggs. He twirled his hand; "It interests me, this tracking our whereabouts."

"Who's doing it?"

"No idea. We'll add it to our list of questions." His stomach seemed to be accepting his initial offerings without objection. His nerves were steadier and his mind seemed clearer. Could it be that simple? All that craziness because he'd failed to eat? The shapes, again, were skeptical.

"How are you feeling?" Dunn asked.

Coffee was a stimulant. That might be good. His body was probably more fatigued than he knew. "Better." He ventured a sip and couldn't hide his reaction this time.

"Too hot?" Dunn asked.

He shook his head, coughing. "No, just—" what was the phrase?—"went down the wrong way." He remembered the supplements, fished in his pocket, tossed them to Dunn. "Cab driver gave me those, said I should take them."

Dunn's reaction was immediate. "Oh, you have to. Every day and don't forget. Get refills at the station dispensary."

Planchette nodded, accepting them back. He pushed the tray aside, his meal mostly uneaten, and ran his hands over the glass top of Friedman's desk, scrutinizing the surface. "There's a computer in the matrix, here." Dunn touched a corner of the desk and a holoscreen came up, centered by a bar for an access code. Planchette made a face. "Contact C-tech."

"You want to know if they got the password?"

"Or why someone's not here working on it."

Dunn nodded, tapped her ear.

"And contact the Dean's office. Let them know where we are, supposing they don't already. Perls got a list of students Friedman was advising. I want them first. No, I want to see the Dean first. We need to know who Friedman's close associates were. Then the students, then faculty. The Chancellor too, at some point." Planchette tossed his hand up. "Then everybody."

Dunn spoke quietly, fulfilling his instructions. Planchette swivelled to look out the window. Beneath an azure sky, the rows of white greenhouses stretched almost as far as he could see. To the northeast stood the mammoth cycling vats where the city's waste was processed into loam and fertilizer. Much of the produce that was consumed in the city was cultivated here. The greenhouses flashed, in places, with a nacreous sheen. Some of the most potent strains of radioactivity-fighting microorganisms had been developed here, as well. The college had started as a research facility, long before re-colonization began. Was that significant? Planchette felt bogged down in minutiae. Frisa was a void that drifted side to side, circled and dove. Everything was getting away from him. His questions were unanswerable, the murder unsolvable. It was instinct that told him he'd get more out of people, questioning them in this room, from the murdered man's chair. That out-weighed the risk of compromising an overlooked crumb of evidence. He lacked confidence in his judgement. He was relying too much on Dunn. The shapes reminded him that he had been on the case less than a day. It felt like a century. There it was again: Time, trackless and malleable. His persona had been an investigator his entire adult life, which, measured by competence and physical appearance, meant decades, not hours, and yet from either perspective was accurate, one way in fact, the other in capacity. Presumed capacity.

"Processing is checking with C-tech about the code," Dunn said. "The Dean has people locating Friedman's students. He's going to have them sent over. Faculty are being informed as well. The Dean said he would see us in his office, whenever we want."

Planchette shook his head. "I don't want him that comfortable. You heard the cook—these people are hard to read. We'll see him here; go get him."

"Now?"

Planchette nodded and Dunn left. The painting caught his interest. Friedman would have seen it every time he looked up from his desk. Planchette went over for a closer look. Same subject matter as the one in the apartment, and same artist, obviously. A single grave, in this instance, situated beneath the branches of an ancient Sycamore, the headstone, name unreadable, stippled with leaf shadows. Also as in the other painting, there were birds in the sky, more in the beckground, here, visible through the branches of the tree. They didn't really look like birds, though. Everything else was rendered with such accuracy, why were the birds so abstract?

There was a knock at the door; Planchette leaned back to see. A tall, slender man in a grey suit stood in the doorway.

"Detective Chron?"

Planchette nodded.

"Mathias Willbury." They shook hands. "I have a meeting off-campus and thought you might want to see me before I leave."

"You're a professor, here?" Planchette resumed his seat at the desk, touched the corner where Dunn had, closing the holoscreen, extended his hand at a chair for his visitor.

"Thank you." Willbury shut the door and sat down. "Yes, in the Psychology Department." He nodded at Planchette's tray. "I hope our kitchen is treating you well."

Willbury was giving birth. A tiny, clear, fledgling shape protruded from the crown of his head.

Morpho and Graph supplied Planchette with some interesting specifics. "You serve on the Psychology Council, don't you? On the Neural See?"

Willbury's eyes registered surprise. "You keep yourself informed, Detective. I'm off rotation with the global synod right now. But I still chair the regional circuit. That's where I'm going, actually."

Planchette nodded. He pulled out his sheet, thumbed record mode, and set it on the desk. "Planchette Chron, interviewing Professor Mathias Willbury. Date and time, mark. How well did you know the murder victim, Professor?"

"Oh, hardly at all. We knew each other, of course. I chatted with him a few times, at College functions and the like. We never socialized outside of that."

"What was your impression of him?"

Willbury tilted his head in thought. He had dark, thinning hair, narrow features, and eyes like gun sights. Planchette doubted he ever stopped evaluating people.

"He was pleasant, polite, an engaging conversationalist," the psychologist answered. "He knew how to have fun, I think. But underneath he was a driven man. I'd say his work was his life."

"Any thoughts who killed him?"

"None. As far as I know he was well liked."

"Where were you last night between eleven and two A.M.?"

Willbury smiled indulgently. "In bed with my wife, Detective. Asleep."

Planchette wasn't meant to notice but he did. The psychologist's posture was relaxed, forearms on armrests, hands dangling loose, fingertips resting against his thighs. The forefinger of his left hand rose an inch and twitched right to left, his chin lifted an almost imperceptible increment, the two surreptitious movements followed by a barely audible foot tap. Willbury possessed formidable skills. The movements were tailored to contradict, on a subliminal level, Planchette's breathing and speech patterns, and his unconscious mannerisms. It was invisible hypnotism, designed to assert authority. It would have worked on almost anyone who lacked defensive training. There would have been a peripheral disruption of balance, and Willbury would have seemed unaccountably different, as if viewed through a stranger's eyes. But on Planchette the ploy failed entirely. The question was whether or not to let Willbury know it. He decided to find out what would happen if he did.

"All right, Professor," he said. "Thank you for stopping by."

Willbury again failed to mask his surprise. "That's all?"

Planchette held his gaze. He clicked off the sheet. "You tell me."

Willbury went blank. He was shocked and he was angry. He didn't show it but Planchette felt the rage pour off of him in waves.

Planchette sat back. "What's the P.C.'s interest in this investigation?" Willbury mastered himself. Planchette felt the anger recede. He admired the man's discipline. He was a professional.

"The Psychology Council reviews all homicide inquiries."

"You're not reviewing. I want to know who's questioning who, here."

Willbury regarded Planchette in silence, a moment. "You're a very unusual law officer, Detective Chron. I wonder, are you aware of the Council's ruling on dance?"

The shapes all settled onto Planchette's shoulders. "I'm not aware of any ruling. I know you released a memo, a few years back."

"It's called an opinion, and we don't circulate them without very extensive deliberation, I assure you."

"Okay."

"Did you read it?"

Planchette cleared his throat. "'Though it must be acknowledged that in isolated, rural communities the dynamic may vary, the character of depression prevalent in urban communities makes it likely that dancing to music, or the mere knowledge of such activity, may raise anxiety to dysfunctional levels among a significant demographic. Therefore, though the practice is not prohibited, nor definitively dissociative, the Council recommends it be discouraged among law enforcement personnel.'"

"Remarkable. I see you have an eidetic memory, as well."

Planchette was silent.

"What do you think of that opinion, Detective?"

"I think dancing is dancing. And nobody's doing it so I don't know what you're worried about."

"You don't find your attitude cavalier?"

"I find this conversation digressive. If you're not going to tell me what you're after, I guess we'll just have to watch each other."

Willbury was completely thrown, this time. He didn't even try to hide his surprise. "You consider me a *suspect?*"

"I consider you suspicious, and that's close enough."

"I've never once tested yellow!"

The fledgling shape detached from Willbury's crown. It was a partial, very small, like a shard of glass. It wouldn't achieve consciousness until it joined with another partial, or several others, or was integrated by a mature shape. Planchette watched it drift a moment, and then, with calculated timing, lowered his gaze to meet Willbury's.

A look of admiration came over the psychologist. "You are well-suited to your profession, Detective." Willbury's sheet vibrated in his pocket. He touched his ear. "All right, I'll be out." He touched it again. "I'm sorry, Detective; that was my assistant. I have to be on my way."

Planchette nodded.

Willbury stood to go. "I look forward to our next encounter."

"I'm easy to find."

As soon as Willbury opened the door, a dozen or so shapes whisked into the room and swirled around the partial. Willbury left, and the shapes guided the partial away. Planchette stared after them. If anyone could beat the DAT, it would be Willbury or one of his ilk. Planchette shook his head. He had revealed too much. The psychologist would think hard about their exchange, and want to look into Planchette's past. Well, he could queue up behind Processing and the Captain. Sooner or later, one of them would find out there was no past to look into. Not the kind they sought.

Three days.

Planchette rolled his fingers on the desk.

He looked at his hand. It came to him what bothered him about that gesture.

Fingerprints.

Chapter Eleven

"I just saw the most beautiful man in the world." Dunn came in, flopped in a chair.

Planchette was still fixated on his hand. His fingerprints were in Friedman's sealed room. "What?"

"There is a *guy* out there who causes trouble wher*ever* he goes."

He would never be able to explain it. The shapes had supplied him with dermatoglyphs, which were recorded on the chip in his badge. He would be identified as soon as C-tech downloaded the evidence to Processing. Planchette stood up. The chair wheeled out behind him and banged against the window. "I have to leave." He made for the door.

"Detective? The Dean's on his way!"

"You question him." He eyed the painting. He could use that for a reason. It had the virtue of being something he really meant to investigate.

"What? I—Where are you going?" Dunn followed him into the hall.

"Friedman's apartment. I need to check something."

"But—Sir! I'm not qualified!"

"You'll do fine."

"Detective!"

Planchette whirled. "What?"

"I haven't told you everything."

"Okay." He spread his hands.

Dunn struggled with something.

"Officer *Dunn*."

"I'm supposed to watch you. I'm supposed to report on you."

"So, do what you're supposed to do." Planchette moved on. The strategy of coincidence was acquiring definition. He was being set up to fail.

"But, sir, I have to come with you—"

"Officer Dunn!" Planchette whirled again. Impatience, *anger*—he'd never experienced the explosive potential of emotions. Not in himself. "Until I'm told otherwise, I'm still your superior officer. I need you to stay here and take statements. I'll call you from the cruiser."

"Sir—"

"If you won't follow my orders you're no use to me. Or anyone else involved in this investigation." He left her there, trapped between rationales he couldn't have reconciled himself. He'd hurt her. Maybe it was just as well.

On the way to the roof he saw something that made no sense, a row of identical, white, ovoid shapes rising up the stairwell above him. Ixilian shapes—there was no mistaking them. What were they doing here? Planchette ran up to the roof, came out just in time to see Willbury climb in the back of a government sedan. The Ixillian shapes Planchette had chased up the stairwell joined others hovering in orderly formation above the man who held the door for the psychologist. The person turned, smiled at Planchette, and got in the driver's seat. The hover lifted off and swung back toward the city. Haliel was Willbury's assistant?

A further swarm of questions that would have to wait. Planchette got in the cruiser, with Twelve's help adjusted the seat and got airborne. Tutorials only went so far with vehicles, especially ones that flew. Twelve couldn't teach him the feel of the craft. A gust of wind hit the hover and it careened out of level. Planchette's corrections were inelegant.

He put the earpiece from his sheet in his ear and contacted Dunn. "I think I've just seen the most beautiful man in the world."

"What?"

"Are you with the Dean?"

"Yes."

"Step out a minute."

"Excuse me, Dean Crawford."

Planchette heard muffled objections, footsteps, the close of a door.

"Yes, Detective Chron?" The formality in Dunn's voice stung Planchette.

"He giving you a hard time?"

"Oh, he loves being ordered around by a patrol cop. No way this is coming back on me."

"I'll take responsibility. A guy came in while you were gone. Mathias Willbury—Professor of Psychology when he's at home but he also serves on the Neural See. I'll send you the interview, which is notably brief. I want you to find out about him."

"I'll get right on that, Detective."

He didn't have to guess with Dunn; her feelings were right on top. "Make it a priority. Ask the Dean about him. I want you to check on Willbury's assistant, too."

"Assistant? What's his name?"

"I don't know. He drives for Willbury; I just saw them take off together. If Willbury has more than one assistant, you'll recognize this one from his photo. You've seen him already."

"I've seen him? When?"

"Moments ago."

Dunn was quiet. "The troublemaker?"

"That's him, if I'm any judge. See what you can find out."

"All right. Detective?"

"Yes?"

"I'm no spy."

What was this pull to depend on her, to accept and respect her trust? "I know. Sorry to put you in a spot, Dunn." Why did he want to deserve it?

"Circumstances," Dunn said, her ire diminished.

Planchette clenched his lips. "Circumstances."

He contacted Processing, told them to wake up officer Baranski and send him out to Columbia to assist Dunn. He got a flight path to Friedman's apartment, keyed it in and relinquished control to the autopilot.

The handler at Processing held the connection. "Detective Chron, my supervisor wants a word with you."

"All right."

A woman's voice came on. "Detective Chron, this is Miriam Close, Watch Supervisor."

"Yes?"

"You are aware that you are functioning in an official capacity without confirmation?"

"Captain Hasker logged me in. Talk to him."

"Yes, the Captain has that prerogative. Processing, however, does not answer only to law enforcement. We liaise with Judicial Branch and the Psychology Council. We've had a recommendation from the P.C. to suspend you pending full confirmation."

Planchette wrenched at the steering wheel. It was Willbury; it had to be. He'd been stupid to bait him. Morph was trying to get his attention. Planchette calmed himself, read his next move. "I'm sorry you're in a bind, Supervisor. Unlike you, I take my orders solely from Captain Hasker. You want to supercede him, you do what you have to do. Until I hear that from him, I'm trying to find a killer loose in this city, and assisting in a case in which I was primary on scene."

The line was silent a moment. "I acknowledge the circumstances are unique, Detective. I can delay the suspension for the time being. If I get any further objections, however, I'll be forced to take action. I can't promise my counterparts will sustain my decision."

"Understood. I appreciate your flexibility, Supervisor."

Haliel had to be involved. Slick move, getting a job with Willbury; Planchette wanted to know how he'd pulled that off. He was up to something. Planchette still couldn't fit him for murder, though. Haliel wasn't capable of killing. Which wouldn't prevent him from taking advantage of an opportunity to interfere with Planchette. Planchette had enemies he didn't know about—that was what Haliel had told him. He'd dismissed the warning too quickly. Even if he couldn't trust Haliel, it was foolish to ignore him. He'd never thought of the Ixilian as an enemy. A nuisance, yes, but not an enemy. He'd never thought of himself as having enemies at all. But if he had them he wanted to know who they were.

Flying over the city, it came to him what it was about re-colonized New York that struck him as so unusual. On every other world he had visited, ruined cities had been shunned or demolished, or in a few cases memorialized. Never had he observed this conglomerate re-habitation, the reverential reuse of all that was salvageable. It was not a city below him but a cemetery. New York's current inhabitants were the caretakers of a graveyard, one and all. Out of that shared, unacknowledged commitment, they were striving to form a society.

His mnemonic patch felt stretched in his mind, bulging under pressure. Planchette put the taste of eggs over the scar on his chin, and then his hats, both the original and its replacement. He parked in front of Friedman's building. A knot of cops loitered in the hall outside the apartment; a couple of shapes drifted nearby. Planchette went in without speaking. The office door had been cut open. It had fallen into the sealed room and smashed Friedman's desk to bits. The holoscreens were gone. Perls and the lead C-tech, a bulky person named Rouse, stood inside, surveying the mess.

Planchette stepped in. "What happened?"

Perls blinked at Planchette. "The sub-genius the City Engineer's office sent to cut through the door happened."

The coleus had fallen over. Planchette righted it, picked up a fragment of the shattered desk.

"Hey, come on," Rouse said.

Planchette feigned incomprehension.

"We haven't processed here. Restrain yourself."

Planchette put the fragment down. "Looks like there's a computer in the matrix."

"Yeah, how about that," Perls said.

"There has to be a back-up system."

"We haven't found one," Rouse said. "This was an isolated interface."

"He had a computer at the school."

Rouse shook his head. "Our guys did a download last night. It's all course related."

Twelve made a suggestion. "Did they check for a hidden partition?"

Rouse frowned.

"Well, I mean—" Planchette gestured at the door, the customized lock.

Rouse's eyebrows went up. "I'll ask."

Planchette couldn't tell them about the data he'd seen. If this was the only repository, the loss was immense. "Can it be reassembled?"

Rouse made a face. "We're good but not that good. We can scan the shards, capture data fragments. You're looking at weeks, maybe months to piece them together. The parts that are pulverized, that's gone. Irretrievable."

Perls shook his head in disgust. "'Think you ought to brace that?' I say. 'It's under control,' he says, like I'm bothering him. This is 'control.'" He looked at Planchette. "Nice hat."

Planchette blinked. "I just got it."

"Weren't you going to the school?"

"I went. Dunn's there, taking statements."

"By herself?"

"I had Processing send help. We need more people out there."

Perls nodded. "Why are you here?"

"Well, I wanted to see—" Planchette gestured at the desk. "But I wanted to check something else."

Perls lifted his chin. Planchette tilted his head toward the living room. Perls followed him. Planchette led him to the painting in the living room.

"Friedman's office at the college is like a clean room. Except for one thing." Planchette gestured at the painting. "A painting of a grave—same artist. Couldn't read the signature."

Planchette was again struck by the curious, bird-like abstractions aloft in the yellow sky. He and Perls leaned in to scrutinize the signature.

"Olive-something." Planchette couldn't make it out.

Perls' expression darkened. "Olivetta."

"You know him?"

"I was just about to have a chat with him. He's a black hole."

Chapter Twelve

"You were right about the laceration. I talked to Clarence." Perls, like Dunn, did not use the autopilot. He drove with care and steadiness, keeping his eyes on the way ahead except to check the rearview monitor.

"One cut?" Planchette asked.

Perls nodded. "With a thin blade, at least twelve inches long. Maybe a well-preserved antique, like an old sword. The attack was back-handed, facing the victim, slashing left to right. Fast and accurate. Tythe said speed was more a factor than strength; look for someone lithe and quick."

"That doesn't match up with the witness's description."

"I thought she only said the perp *might* be fat."

"It seems like a stretch from lithe, either way."

Perls shrugged. "I've known some stout guys fast with their hands."

"So, quick and skillful."

"I wouldn't rule out strong."

Planchette reflected that Frisa and he would both qualify as dangerous, even if the standard were restricted to physical prowess. Ninety-eight lives in ninety-eight bodies, one acquired a facility with musculature, balance, range of motion—that facility could be applied to violence, with or without training.

Perls cleared his throat. "So, did you take the Union Jumper or come over on a standard flyer?"

Planchette looked down through the passenger window at an intersection of globes, angles and recycled debris, mosaic color patterns puzzled amid concrete and glass. The shapes had ridden his shoulders since he'd gotten into Perls' cruiser. Planchette attended their counsel, certain that Perls had checked all the incoming flight manifests of the last several days. "I hitched a ride with an electronics shipment." He lied in the service of life, end before means, as ever.

Perls was surprised, again. "You traveled *ground?*"

Planchette nodded, "I wanted to see the country." The shapes fed Planchette images that correlated to a map, installed them as memories. By such measures did he relinquish and acquire the truth of himself. His understanding of what had befallen this world deepened, wounds adding to the catalogue.

Perls' tone became introspective. "I've thought about doing that. Never had the guts to satisfy my curiosity. Did you go through any of the scorched zones?"

Put the act on autopilot. "Some," he answered. "We kept to the northern perimeter. Oregon - Ohio throughway, then up."

"What was it like?"

"Little towns, in between a lot of much bigger ghost towns." Emotions in neutral. "Quiet. Most of it real low tech." Cold churn of enforced quiescence. "Not very different from The Angels, except there most places at least have electricity." There had never been a child more precocious than he.

"And the zones?"

"The driver kept a meter on his dash. When it got too hot he shuttered the windows, drove by holoscreen." Pure instinct, an autonomic feature of his design.

"What did you see?"

"Desert. But forests and grasslands, too. It looks normal. You get close a lot of the foliage is wrong." He detested his own verisimilitude. "We saw some giant mushrooms—five, ten meters tall. A big shelf fungus, sticking out of a hillside like a table. Maybe fifty meters, end to end." Just read your lines and believe them.

"Animals?"

"Yeah." What harm had his lies ever done, save increase his

private store of wistfulness? "Deer, wolves, antelope, coyotes, gophers—lot of gophers." Frisa had always been his refuge. Without her, persona was a cage. "We saw a cougar with no front legs. Some wolves that were hairless." Did his real feelings leak to the surface? Fiction insinuate fact?

Perls cleared his throat. "Sorry."

Planchette shook his head. "I don't mind." Truth, however oblique, a particle for his heart. "If we're going to come to terms with it we have to talk about it." His skill with deception made him dangerous, too.

"P.C. might not agree with you."

Planchette schooled his focus. "Do you care?" If he was not guided by purpose, he was lost.

"I'll be fifty next month and I was born here. My parents were among the first re-colonizers. New York's all I've known. I've got seven different kinds of cancer working on me."

"I take that as a no."

"You can take it as a hell no. P.C. can respectfully go fuck itself. Some things they've got a handle on, others not. It's been a hundred and twenty years and it's yesterday, here, every day. We're not supposed to notice."

"And to those who say 'we' didn't do it?"

"Oh," Perls grinned sourly, "we're better? We're the same. We didn't do it on our own, though. Life did it. Evolution did it. The fucking universe did it. I don't know how to deal with that, and neither does P.C. Some days …"

"When there's a killing."

Perls sucked his teeth.

They rode in silence. Planchette understood well the bitterness and disillusionment Perls exhibited. It trivialized and undermined the man's courage, and maybe he knew it. And yet, like the architecture, there was something peculiar about it. Everything was always different—Planchette did not seek to compare. But he sensed an anomaly, predictable malaise laced with a rare defiance that armored itself in cynicism.

"We're getting close," Perls said. "I should brief you about this guy."

"All right."

"Michael Olivetta. Registered sockhead, living off the reservation. Part of the latest community insertion experiment they got going a couple of years ago. See if he can be socialized; I'm guessing not. He got an indulgence because he's an artist. All the black holes we've got right now are men, which makes him first in line."

"Why?"

"Michael a.k.a. Michelle. He's a transvestite. Famous for wigs and gowns."

"Anything from forensics on that piece of fabric?"

"They haven't been able to identify it."

Planchette couldn't help being hopeful. "We have a person of interest."

"Maybe. We've got no evidence he went off his leash last night. Button logs him home, dusk to dawn."

Twelve defended hope. "Buttons have been wrong," Planchette said.

"Rarely." Perls brought the hover down toward a street that climbed a hillside. Rows of brownstones lined the lower end.

"Are those reconstructions?" Planchette asked. "They look original."

"I think they are. The hill probably sheltered them. This was the first place settlers moved in. Pretty much unoccupied now."

"Why?"

"I don't know about other people but for me it'd be like living inside a ghost." Perls parked in front of a narrow, four-story building. They got out. The irregular cobbles resembled crazing in the midday sun. The day had grown hot. Towards the top of the hill the brownstones gave way to domes and composite structures. A small cloud of shapes twisted in the sky, descended from view. Planchette felt like it ought to remind him of something.

Two chubby young women in transparent jump suits lounged in the shade of a brownstone's porch, uphill across the street. They waved.

Perls lifted his chin at them. "Snags think those show-alls protect them. You tell them, they don't listen."

"This is the sex zone?"

"The edge of it. The center's over the hill. Most sockheads wind up in this area. Feel less conspicuous, I guess."

Another hover dropped down and parked across the street. Perls and Planchette watched a middle-aged man in a black flat cap and belted grey overcoat get out and come toward them.

He flashed a badge. "Terrence Wright, C.A. Are you here to question Olivetta?"

Perls nodded.

"I came to assist you. I'm his handler."

Perls eyed Wright up and down, took his time responding. "We're conducting a homicide investigation, Terence."

"I'm aware of that—"

"How do you think a Community Analyst is going to assist us?"

An uncomfortable silence ensued. Wright looked away, inhaled through his nose. "I'm not trying to interfere, Detective. P.C. has an interest in this case—"

"What interest?"

"I haven't been briefed. My instructions are to observe and report—"

"What happened to 'assist?'"

The P.C. agent sighed. "Anyway I can."

"Okay, go on by the station and have an officer take your statement. If we have any questions we'll contact you."

"Detective, P.C. is within our purview, here. Any police interest in a Class One sociopath—"

"So they send you to keep tabs on us and don't tell you why. We look stupid?"

Wright sighed again. "No."

"You show up right when we get here, which means you guys are monitoring our movements. That is something I am now obligated to look into."

"P.C. is not sinister, Detective Perls. If there is an underlying agenda here, I'm sure your superiors and mine will work it out."

The uncomfortable silence resumed.

"How long have you been Olivetta's handler?" Planchette asked. He wanted to get out of the heat.

Wright looked at him. "You're Detective Chron?"

"I am."

Wright held his gaze. "A year, next week."

Morpho conveyed a discrepancy. "Doesn't P.C. rotate its handlers every couple of months?"

Both Wright and Perls were surprised. "Normally, yes," Wright said. "I asked for an exception."

"Why?"

"That is a complex and difficult question I have spent many hours answering to the Northeastern Regional Circuit of Counselors."

"Dumb it down for us," Perls said.

Wright regarded Perls with his lips clenched. "Anyone who thinks the DAT is ineffective, I give you Michael Olivetta. You'd never make him for a sock, and he'll have you working for him in about a minute. Spend time around him, you see it."

"That's why you stayed on?" Planchette asked.

Wright didn't answer directly. "He's an artist, no question. He's got talent and he's got ability. He could paint just fine, back on the res."

Planchette and Perls exchanged looks. Planchette lifted his chin toward the building. The three men climbed the steps. The door was scaley with peeling red paint and blackened around the edges. Maintenance was not in keeping, here, with what Planchette had observed elsewhere in the city. Inside was a narrow hallway, a flight of stairs on the left. The walls were yellowish-brown, green carpeting threadbare.

"One thing," Wright said.

Perls and Planchette turned to him.

"The art—don't let it get to you."

Perls led the way to a door at the end of the hall, knocked. "Open up, Olivetta. You've got company."

A lean person in a tight-fitting, paint-spattered black leotard opened the door. He had a pinched, triangular face, dark-rimmed eyes, black hair compressed under a nylon wig cap. He regarded his visitors neutrally and withdrew without comment, leaving the door open. Perls, Wright and Planchette crossed into the artist's domain like recipients of an unfavorable verdict. The air was dense with solvents and paints, cosmetics, perfumes, and organic decay. Stacks of canvases leaned against the walls; three stood on easels. The color drained from Perls' face.

Michael Olivetta sat on a cushioned metal stool, legs crossed, wrists crossed on his knees, gaze low, expression placid and waiting.

Chapter Thirteen

The environment inside the apartment seemed given entirely to the occupant's work, with little attention spared for organization. Worktables were cluttered with paints, palettes, jars of solvents, brushes, stacks of dishes, cups in varying states of unsavory fullness. Soiled clothes were strewn on the floor, amid a virtual carpet of sketches on paper, many bearing footprints. On the floor in the far right corner was a mattress piled with rumpled sheets, as if sleep had become an afterthought. The paintings encroached from all sides, a chorus of horrors. Most were about three by four feet, much larger than the ones in Friedman's apartment and office.

Perls squinted at the ceiling, collecting himself. Planchette's gaze settled on an unfinished piece mounted on an easel. Wright leaned in the doorway with his arms crossed, watching him. The painting was masterfully executed. It showed an old man in a tattered police uniform sitting on a curb near a broken wall. The old policeman was eating his own hand.

Perls fixed on the artist. "You're not wearing your button."

"I don't have to here." Olivetta's voice was feminine and melodious, with a petulant edge.

Planchette went closer to the painting. The artist's style seemed near photo-realistic, but on a minute scale the technique was loose, the delivery of pigment rapid.

"Is that right." The edge in Perls' voice was menacing.

The lower right corner of the canvas was blank and there were no sketch marks to indicate an underlying drawing. Planchette recognized that the person who rendered this image had been able to visualize it in vivid detail before applying a single brush stroke.

"It is," Wright said. "We've got proximity detectors on the doors and windows—"

Planchette didn't see the look Perls gave Wright but he felt it.

"It's over there." Olivetta pointed, without looking, at a shelf in the kitchen.

Perls pulled on a pair of gloves. Planchette gave him one of the evidence bags he'd gotten from a C-tech at Friedman's apartment.

Perls put the button in the bag and sealed it. "This will be checked for malfunction or tampering. Until you get it back, you're restricted to the premises."

"That won't be necessary," Wright said. "I've brought a replacement." That earned him a sustained look from Perls. "It's—It's logged and verified. Scan it yourself."

"I will." Perls snatched the button from Wright and ran his sheet over it. A hint of a smile crept across Olivetta's lips. Perls gave him the new button; "Put it on." Olivetta complied, resumed his pose. Perls placed the sheet on the corner of a workbench near him. "Interview of Michael Olivetta—"

"Michelle."

Perls clicked off the sheet and loomed over Olivetta. "Save it." He clicked the sheet back on. "Michael Olivetta is a registered Class One sociopath. Detective Planchette Chron and C.A. Terrence Wright are in attendance. Date and time mark. Where were you between eleven P.M. and three A.M. last night, Mr. Olivetta?"

Olivetta didn't look at Perls but irritation showed in his expression. "Here. Working."

"Are you familiar with a man named Victor Friedman?"

"I'm not familiar with him; I know who he is. He bought a couple of paintings from me."

"When did you last see him?"

"I don't know. A couple of months ago. He came here to my studio. Check your log."

"Are you aware that he was murdered last night?"

Olivetta frowned. "No."

"What can you tell us about his killing?"

"Nothing. Obviously."

Perls questioned Olivetta in a methodical and exhaustive manner, rephrasing questions, trying to trip him up. Planchette took in the paintings. The innocuous physicality of the artist met fearsome contradiction in his work. The heaps of carnage, amid which the corpses of infants figured prominently, were almost predictable—adolescent and insipid. But other images made it impossible to dismiss Olivetta as naive or self-deluding. A pile of bones, supplanted by the exposed fins of an unexploded bomb, crawled with vermin, which on close examination proved to be tiny, malformed people. A torn and yellowed calendar with a date circled in red hung pinned to a wall above robed and hooded figures who knelt before it in postures of supplication, their garments seeping blood from hidden wounds. The work was devoid of compassion for the viewer but there was truth in it. Naked children, bruised and sickly, planted rusty, metal flowers in a denuded field. A vacuous old woman in rags, her throat slit and bleeding, poured fire from a watering can onto an empty baby carriage, numb to the burning of her blackened hand. Twelve noted that the dimensions of the canvases all conformed to the 'golden ratio,' a proportion Planchette had seen applied in the art and architecture of many worlds. He resisted recalling specific examples.

The cemetery paintings interested him most. The arrangement of headstones in many of them also conformed, in various subliminal ways, to golden ratio composition. It was an intentional perversion of mathematical idealism. And in all of them were the curious abstract birds. Again, the paintings were rendered, overall, with realism, except that the birds were always rough and distorted. It might have been an elegiac gesture; but it seemed to bear a more elusive intention.

"Excuse me," Planchette interrupted Perls, "what are these?" Perls frowned. Planchette lifted his hand at him.

Olivetta looked up at Planchette, seeming surprised by the question. There was something ethereal about his face. It was in the eyes—the distance from which the person behind them regarded the world. "They're demons," he said.

"Demons? They're not birds?"

"Do they look like birds?"

Planchette reconsidered the painting in question. A pyramidal mausoleum occupied the eye of a spiraling array of headstones. The flight paths of the 'demons' contradicted the spiral. "So, they're conceptual."

"Maybe you'd like to think so."

Planchette frowned at the artist.

"I paint what I see, Detective. I'm crazy."

"Sociopathic," Wright corrected.

Olivetta shrugged.

Planchette stared at the painting. An impossible notion came to him. "You're saying you see things that look like this."

Olivetta checked Wright. "Does that make me delusional?"

Wright shook his head. "Just a liar."

Olivetta smiled. "You're sweet, Terry."

Perls busied himself scrutinizing Olivetta's art supplies and other belongings, letting Planchette take the lead.

"Have you always been able to see them?" Planchette asked. "Do you see them now?"

Olivetta regarded Planchette with curiosity. "A woman showed them to me, about a year ago. And no, I don't see them now."

"She showed them to you? How do you mean?"

"I don't know how she did it. She asked me if I wanted to see something that might clarify my work. People are always saying things like that to me. They want me to be a good girl and paint pretty. They want to cure me, like Terry."

"I don't want things that are impossible, Michelle," Wright said.

Olivetta gave Wright a coy look. "You don't have to hide your feelings, Terry. I know you love me."

"You were saying?" Planchette asked.

Olivetta shrugged again. "I played along. I said, 'Sure, show me.' She touched me here," Olivetta touched his knee, "and here," he touched his forehead, "and then I saw them. They were all over the place, swarming through the studio like angry wasps."

Planchette swallowed. His mouth was dry. "You must have found that unsettling."

"Do you think so?"

Planchette drifted to another painting, one in which the 'demons' seemed to be the subject. In a triangular arrangement, three, indecipherable, fleshy figures occupied the upper, middle and lower thirds of the canvas, against a black background. All three were mottled and pale, as if diseased. "Tell me about her, the woman."

"She just showed up, one day, and said she was interested in my work. Which was strange. She didn't seem the type."

"Why not?"

"She was too pretty, like she'd grown up protected from everything. Too nice. But that was an act."

"How so?"

"She showed me the demons."

"I don't follow you."

"I knew that she was one, too, then. They can look like people."

"The woman was a demon?"

"I don't expect you to believe me."

"I don't have an opinion one way or the other. Can you describe her?"

"Mid thirties, about five-five, dark hair. Really pale. She had the whitest skin I've ever seen."

Planchette and Perls glanced at each other.

"There was something wrong with her vocal chords." Olivetta said.

"What do you mean?"

"When she spoke her lips and her throat didn't move. I think she had some kind of vocal projector on her somewhere. Or maybe that's how demons talk."

"What was she wearing?"

Olivetta giggled. "Like she came from another *planet*. She had on this one-of-a-kind gown that came alive when she moved. Like hundreds of scarves blowing in different winds. Michelle *liked* that gown. That's why I painted her."

Planchette and Perls looked at each other again. "You painted her portrait?" Planchette asked.

Olivetta nodded, becoming excited. "You want to see it?"

Planchette cleared his throat. "I do."

Olivetta sprang from his stool and pranced to a stack of canvases. His movements were airy and graceful. Planchette perceived that he possessed a muscular strength not readily apparent. He pulled out a canvas, moved a work in progress from an easel, and replaced it with the portrait.

The woman in the picture bore little resemblance to the one Olivetta had described. She was morbidly obese, much older than thirty-anything. Her face was deeply lined, a light of insanity in her eyes. Her gown was the real subject of the painting. It was composed of innumerable multi-colored pieces of fabric that indeed resembled living scarves. Planchette experienced a keen discomfort, viewing the image.

"We want a photo of this," Perls said.

"I can give you that." Olivetta opened a holoscreen on a workbench. "I document all of my work. Where do I send it?"

Perls contacted Processing, coordinated the transfer.

"This person is young and pretty?" Planchette asked, staring at the portrait. A horrible apprehension rose in him.

"That's what she *really* looks like. That's her demon nature. You wouldn't see her like that."

Perls cast an exasperated look ceiling-ward. "Oh, good."

"You two realize you're being played with, don't you?" Wright said.

Olivetta's expression darkened. "I've never done anything wrong," he told Planchette. "I have to wear their pin because I couldn't pass their fucking test."

Planchette didn't have any room left in him for being shocked by unexpected discoveries. If the things he was seeing in this room proved to be what he suspected, it would throw into question everything he thought he understood.

"You couldn't pass it twenty-seven times, Michelle, starting at age twelve."

"Ever think someone might fulfill your expectations when you stigmatize them at puberty?"

The only thing Planchette had to rely on was his immediate reality, which was the realm of his persona. He had embraced it once and faltered. He embraced it again.

"You want a review? I can arrange it anytime. All you have to do is ask."

Olivetta glared at Wright. "What's the point?"

Perls drifted away again.

"The point is you're a clever girl," Wright said, "and you're well on your way to becoming the prime suspect in a murder inquiry."

"I have absolutely *no* history of violence."

"We're going to figure out what you did, Michelle. You might as well tell us. We know you tricked the button."

"With *what?* You see that kind of tech in here? Go ahead, tear up the floorboards. It won't be the first time."

Planchette spotted a mannequin on a rolling platform. In all the clutter he hadn't noticed it before. "What's that?" The mannequin was draped in a fine wire mesh studded with holo-projection nodules.

"What?" Olivetta followed Planchette's gaze. "It's a holo-suit. I use it for portraits. I'm not allowed to paint from live subjects."

"So, you can put it on and look like someone else."

Olivetta made a face. "It can't be *worn*. It doesn't work if you take it off the mannequin."

"This is how you painted the woman?"

"I—Yes."

"You holo-graphed her?"

"Of course. With her permission."

"So you have an image of her on file, the way that *we* would see her."

Olivetta became flustered. "I—maybe. I don't know. They don't let me have much data space. I have to purge files, every few weeks."

"Would you check, please?"

Olivetta went back to his computer. Wright leaned against a wall, watching him with undisguised skepticism. Perls opened a door by the mattress and whistled. Planchette looked at him.

"Wardrobe," Perls said.

Olivetta glared at Perls, continued checking through his computer files. He nodded. "I have it."

The picture was of a young woman who this time did match Olivetta's description. Her skin was unusually pale, and she was wearing a less dramatized version of the gown depicted in the portrait. Perls had moved to a chest of drawers. He looked at Planchette. Planchette mugged mystification and nodded. "Use the same routing for that image," he told Olivetta.

Olivetta complied.

"Oh, Mikey—" Perls gazed into an open drawer—"what have we here?"

Planchette went over and looked. Perls had discovered a flat, rectangular, leather case, heavily worn around the edges. He opened it for Planchette, exposing an assortment of antique surgical tools, fitted in red velvet: retractors, forceps, tweezers, a small bone saw, three scalpels—there were spaces for two longer knives with slender blades, the longest about sixteen inches. The latter was missing.

"I have permission for those," Olivetta said. "I need to study cuts and wounds."

Perls gave Wright another look. "How do you go about that, creep around slitting throats and taking pictures?"

"I encase partially desiccated gelatin, rutilated with animal blood, in synthetic skin. There's maquettes in the refrigerator. You can go look."

"What's that?" Planchette pointed at the long knife.

"It's a Liston knife. They used to use it for amputations."

"Where's the other one?"

"I don't know. It was an incomplete set. I got it that way."

Perls sniffed. "I think it's about time we had C-tech in here, don't you Chron?"

"No!" Olivetta whined, "I've cooperated! Damn you, you fucking bastards! The last time you were in here it took me *weeks* to repair the damage!"

"I've never been in here, Mikey," Perls said.

"Not you, *him!*" Olivetta pointed at Wright. "Him and his fucking brain-rapers!"

Wright said nothing.

"So, we should get a warrant?" Perls said.

"No!" Olivetta was fuming. "All right, yes. Fuck it, yes, get a warrant. We never insist because it makes us look guilty. But this time I'm fucking insisting."

Perls shrugged. "Have it your way."

"And you can stop snooping through my stuff, too, until then. In fact I want all of you out of here. I'm not answering any more questions until you assign me an advocate."

"You can't order *me* out, Michelle," Wright said.

"You want to stick around and fuck me, Terry? Might be your last chance."

Perls and Wright ambled to the door. Planchette drifted behind, looking at paintings. He was at the threshold when Olivetta stopped him.

"Thank you for viewing my work so thoughtfully, Detective." Planchette nodded.

"You should watch yourself. I lied to you, earlier. I have seen demons in the room, while you've been here."

Planchette knew what was coming.

"Five of them," Olivetta said. "They're sitting on your shoulders."

Chapter Fourteen

Wright stopped by the stairs. "I'll wait til C-tech gets here. Keep an ear on him."

"Appreciate it," Perls said, with mock sincerity.

"Just so you know who you're dealing with, Michelle—*Michael*—is heterosexual."

The information did not startle Planchette. Seeing how incredulous Perls was, he supposed he didn't appreciate why it should. He had more confounding matters to digest.

"Every few days he dresses up, goes over the hill and rents a snag. Not many will bed with him."

Perls patted the air at Wright. "Okay, Terrence. Detective Chron and I have police business to discuss, if you'll excuse us."

Wright grunted and sat on the steps. "You should come work for us, Chron. You'd be good at it."

It was hotter outside. The buildings across the street cast short shadows. Planchette's greatcoat felt like a sauna. "I thought he did all right," he said.

"You go on thinking that," Perls said. "I'll stay with not trusting him. What'd you make of it in there?"

Planchette toed a cobble. "Olivetta's involved. If he did kill Friedman, I don't think it's that simple."

Perls shook his head. "We've passed simple. I don't know what's going on. This thing started weird and went pell-mell towards crazy." He looked around, getting ready to say something else. "Good work, in there."

"Thanks."

"I wouldn't have gotten where you did. I couldn't look at that stuff."

"It's not pleasant."

"No."

Planchette decided to take a chance. "Listen, Perls, you might not have me much longer."

"Why not?"

Planchette told him about his meeting with Willbury, both on and off the record, and his exchange with the watch supervisor from Processing.

"So, that's why we've got Wright up our ass," Perls said.

"Probably."

"Turning tables on that stick—I'd like to have seen that. Last time I dealt with one of those high-balls I wanted to scrub my skull out with rocks."

"I'm not sure it was smart."

"I'll talk to Hasker."

Planchette shook his head. "It won't do any good. I tell you, though, if they're going to suspend me, I feel kind of wasted interviewing all and sundry at the College until they do."

"What do you want?"

"I'd like to see the witness again. On my own; I think she trusts me. I want to show her what we got from Olivetta."

"I haven't ruled her out as a suspect, you know."

"Neither have I," Planchette lied. "Has forensics processed her clothes?"

"They've given 'em a once over. Didn't find anything. Yet." Perls made a face. "You gonna dance with her?"

Planchette didn't answer.

"What else?"

"I'd like to have another look at the crime scene. In daylight. Take it from there."

Perls put his hands on his hips, studied the ground. "Record the interview, this time."

"Sure."

"You fuck up, it comes to me. With teeth, at this point."

Planchette nodded.

"You want Dunn?"

"I do."

"Okay, I'll take some people off door to door, send them out to relieve her, have someone bring her to you. Come on, let's head back."

They got in the cruiser. "What are you going to do?" Planchette asked.

Perls took them airborne. "See what they've come up with at Friedman's, canvas the rest of the sockheads, go over what we have. Think."

"Let's stay in touch."

"I want to have another briefing at four."

They drove back to Friedman's apartment. Planchette waited until Perls was inside the building before putting Dunn's cruiser in drive. He knew the latitude Perls had extended him was heavy with reservations. Which would be validated when the truth came out. Ironies were piling up on top of the coincidences and mysteries. His form was better, handling the hover. He keyed Claire's address into the autopilot.

The shapes had been non-communicative since they'd left Olivetta's studio. It was time to examine matters both they and Planchette found disturbing. None of the shapes doubted that Olivetta had seen them. Perhaps not as Planchette did, but it was certain he'd had a visual impression of them. Either something impossible had occurred or someone had intruded quite severely upon his neurology. Planchette knew of only one person, other than himself, who could do that.

Frisa.

It should have been reassuring to find evidence that she was indeed on Earth and in this city, but the nature of the evidence increased his anxiety. The implication was inescapable, that the person Olivetta had shown them on his holo-monitor was his

partner. If she had visited him, and, for some unfathomable reason, induced in him a rudimentary ability to see shapes, it followed that, while she was there, Olivetta had seen a number of shapes in his studio sufficient to be characterized as a 'swarm.' Which meant that those shapes, somewhere in New York, had been aware of her presence long before he arrived. We have queried the Cloud, Morpho conveyed. The question flows outward. None are aware of such an event.

Planchette had been preoccupied with the paintings. It was possible he had missed a deception. Either Olivetta lied, he reasoned, or the shapes that he saw are the ones that are missing. That would seem a logical deduction, Morph concurred. There is another possibility, Spoon conveyed, that a group within our collective withholds information, just as we withhold knowledge of your thoughts.

Planchette had set a precedent, the ramifications of which he had not considered, when he asked his assistants to keep a secret for him. Shapes did not keep secrets. In all of his experience, he had never known shapes to withhold anything, nor had he ever withheld anything from them. But Spoon could be right, and someone had set the precedent before him. Maybe Frisa had done so. If Olivetta was to be believed, she had entered the collective time stream at least a year ago, possibly longer. Maybe Planchette had compounded a schism in the Cloud that already existed. There was no knowing how that would affect its culture, nor the relationship between the shapes and their parents. We sustain discontinuity only to realize greater continuity, Morpho conveyed. No doubt, Planchette acknowledged. But he felt the quaver of uncertainty in his companions, and they could not deny it. Neither he nor they could dismiss the possibility that the instability afflicting him had begun to affect them. The infection could spread outward into the Cloud, if it hadn't already.

Disconnecting from each other now would solve nothing, and they all knew it.

A year apart in time—how had it happened? And what was that gown? Frisa and he had always striven to blend in. Again Planchette sensed design at work, and the shapes sensed it, too. Considering who might be its architect led them all to the same suspect.

Planchette contacted Dunn.

"Yes, Detective?"

"How's it coming?"

"I've questioned the students Friedman was advising. Making my way through the faculty. Thanks for Baranski, by the way, he's good. The students liked Friedman. They think his research was important—a lot about that was over my head—and it's a great loss, et cetera. Nobody, so far, seems to have any idea who might have killed him. One student overheard him having an argument with the head of the City Engineer's Office, a few weeks back. She didn't hear enough to know what it was about, maybe something to do with the transit system. She was in the hall, waiting to see Friedman, saw the Chief Engineer leave in a huff. She'd attended a talk he'd given, so she recognized him."

"Have you found out anything about Willbury or his assistant?"

"Willbury's file is sealed. I don't have the clearance to access it."

Graph objected. "A murder inquiry trumps any seal," Planchette said.

"Not coming from me, apparently. Processing was adamant. You might have to go through Hasker."

Planchette sighed. If he did that, Willbury would be alerted, and make sure Processing suspended him in a blink. It was a deft move, if not comprehensively effective—it confirmed to Planchette that Willbury had something to hide, and was vulnerable. "What about the assistant?"

"Willbury has a lot of staff but only one personal assistant. His name is Halbert Leal. I've seen his ID picture; he's the one. That's about all I could get. His file is attached to Willbury's. One interesting thing, the security blocks on both files were logged this morning."

"What time?"

"About fifteen minutes after you talked to Willbury."

Willbury was closing doors as fast as he could. Haliel had to be manipulating him. He'd insinuated himself into the system with bewildering speed. Then again, he hadn't done it any quicker than Planchette had himself. Unless—

"Do you know where they are?"

"Willbury's in a meeting with the Northeastern Regional Circuit of Counselors. I would guess that Leal is with him, or nearby."

"Where are they meeting?"

"That information is—"

"Sealed."

"Sorry, Sir."

Another closed door. Planchette would have to find a way around Willbury. He gave Dunn a brief summary of developments at Friedman's apartment and Olivetta's studio. "I'll forward the interview. Perl's is sending some more people out to the College. He'll have one of them bring you to me."

Dunn was quiet a moment. "Thank you, sir."

"Let me know when they get there. I'll tell you where to meet me."

Like Friedman, Claire Fontaine lived in a tower, one of three that were joined, each architecturally different from the others, glass, brick, and concrete, respectively. They were a few stories shorter than the one Friedman had lived in, skirted by a spacious plaza, situated on a broad boulevard that went straight for a distance uncommon in present day New York—about the erstwhile length of two city blocks. Construction flanked the rest of the straight stretch, crews at work on several new buildings. Scaffolding rose almost as high as the towers across the street from them.

A uniformed cop sat on a bench near the entrance. He stood up as Planchette approached. Planchette showed his badge. "Where am I headed?"

"Tower two, Detective. Fourteen-o-seven. My partner's by the door."

The towers shared a vast lobby punctuated by stout columns and elevator bays. The floor, walls and ceiling were tiled in a mosaic of stone and colored and mirrored glass, that formed flowing geometric patterns. On the right, a sunken communal area, furnished with mismatched sofas, easy chairs, lamps and tables, faced a wall window that looked onto a garden atrium. The plants were surviving, not thriving. The lobby was vacant.

He found the elevators for tower two, was about to push the up button when his sheet vibrated. He put the ear piece in his ear.

"Eighty-five?" It was Haliel.

Planchette clicked open the holoscreen. Haliel stood by a wood-paneled wall, somewhere indoors.

"Where are you?" Planchette said. "I want to see you."

"That's a switch." Haliel smiled. "I want to see you, too. We need to talk."

"When? Where?"

"By the bar where that man was killed." Haliel drew his chin in. "The one you're investigating, *Detective.*"

"You want to meet me at the crime scene?"

"Crime scene? You do get into your roles, don't you? Yes, the 'crime scene.'"

"When?"

"One hour."

Haliel cut the connection. The routing was blocked, too. Planchette resisted the urge to break the sheet into pieces. There it was again, the roar of emotions. He jabbed the button for the elevator.

The carpet in the fourteenth floor hallway was yellow ochre, trimmed in burgundy, the walls forest green, the ceiling light tan.

A cop stood post near the end to the left. Planchette hung his badge on his breast pocket. The air smelled of fresh paint. He nodded at the cop, a plump, middle-aged woman with a round face, and rang the bell.

"Has she been out?"

"I haven't heard any movement in there at all, Detective, since I got here."

Planchette tried the door, rang the bell insistently, heard something fall, a muffled, "I'm coming!"

Still in C-tech's coveralls, Claire Fontaine opened the door scowling. She recognized Planchette and her anger evaporated. She smiled, and Planchette's doubts fled to the shadows. Reassurance washed over him like a warm wave of grace.

Chapter Fifteen

She still couldn't connect with him. He saw it in her eyes, a peripheral uneasiness that he wanted more than she felt.

He masked his yearning with professionalism. "I have some pictures I want you to look at."

"Come in."

The air was clean and fresh and the light inviting. Paintings and photographs hung on pale brown walls. The carpeting was gold-colored with green flecks. To the left opened a sunken living room furnished with sofas and easy chairs, pole lamps and a low, glass, trapezoidal table. A wall of photo-reactive plasti-glass looked onto the scaffolding across the way. The kitchen and a small dining area were on the right, ahead a hallway to the apartment's inner rooms.

"How are you feeling?" Planchette asked.

Claire took her time responding. "I do not have words to describe it."

Planchette nodded. He started to ask another question but she stopped him.

"I'm sure you're in a hurry but could you give me a minute? I want to get out of this thing and eat about twenty aspirin."

"Sure."

"Take your coat off. You'll earn my eternal gratitude if you make coffee. I like it strong." She went down the hall and started into a room on the left, leaned back and smiled. "Great hat, by the way." She went in and closed the door.

Planchette draped his coat over the back of a chair by the dining table, happy to be out of it, set his hat on the table.

Uncertainly, he ventured into the kitchen. Twelve helped him identify the coffee maker and divine its workings. He found filters and a sack of coffee in a cupboard, filled the machine's reservoir with water from the tap. He was confronted, then, with the question of measure. The shapes all seemed to have different opinions, which was not helpful. Claire had said she liked it strong. Planchette decided to err towards excess and filled the hopper.

He turned on the coffee maker and looked around. Everything interested him; the recipient lived here. If ever he did convey the message to her, it would happen in this place, among the things that she valued. It was clear that she valued her art collection most.

The majority of it was by two artists, a painter and a photographer. The paintings were mostly sentimental still lifes of minutia from the veldt: a coin and a burned book resting on a broken cinder block, a thistle growing from a decaying wall, a row of broken plates. The photographs, black and white, showed people, mostly unsmiling, contending with life against the dramatic backdrop of the reconstituted city. The one he liked best showed two young people kissing on a sidewalk amid a confusion of taut, crossing cables. It was another that stopped him, though. It had been shot from an elevated angle, the subject a towering mound of wreckage that billowed smoke and flames. Firemen and emergency personnel were captured in urgent activity, while a crowd looked on from the lower left periphery of the image. A young boy stood near the foot of the mound, staring up at it. Planchette recognized him as the boy he had seen sitting in the old tree in the park.

Claire emerged wearing a white robe. She'd brushed her hair and cleaned her face. "I smell coffee." She grinned, going past him into the kitchen, poured cups for both of them. "Soy milk? Sugar?"

Planchette had no idea. "No," he said.

"Good answer." She handed him a cup, playfully stroked his O-bow. "Never dilute the water of life."

He followed her into the living room, vulnerable in her

presence. He had moments like this with every recipient, when he feared them as one fears God. He dared not let her see it.

They sat on the two sofas, catty-corner to each other. Claire sipped her coffee. Her eyes widened. "You took me seriously!"

"Sorry." Planchette flushed. He made himself take a sip. It was somewhat more shocking than it had been the first time. He managed to swallow. "I'm not good with … coffee."

"No, no, it's all right." Her grin broadened. "I need a kick in the face. What did you want to show me?"

Planchette took out his sheet, forced his attention to immediate concerns. Twelve instructed him how to hold the shaft of the sheet with both hands to form an interface. Two, small nodules unfolded and affixed themselves to his thumbnails. He was clumsy using the holoscreen keypad, but managed to retrieve the image of the portrait Olivetta had painted. He showed it to Claire.

Her expression became complex, sadness mixed with admiration. "Oh, Michael."

"You know him?"

She nodded. "I've reviewed his shows. He's brilliant. And a mess."

"You don't think he's a sock—sociopath?"

"It's not up to me to know that. If he is, it's not all he is."

"Does the woman in the picture resemble the one you saw in the alley?"

Claire frowned. "*No.* She was nowhere *near* that old." She hesitated.

"What is it?"

"Looking at the gown."

"Is that what she was wearing?"

"A lot like it. Well as I can remember. The alley wasn't well lit."

"But it could be it."

"Could be, yes. But—"

"What?"

"Well, you're making me think. Michael exaggerates the grotesque in almost everything he paints." She gave the sheet back to Planchette, grimacing. "You think he painted the murderer's portrait?"

"It's possible." Planchette retrieved the other image. "How about her?"

Claire leaned back in surprise. "Wow, this was his subject?"

"According to him."

She peered at the holo-graph, shook her head. "No, this doesn't look like her either."

"You're sure?"

Claire nodded. "She's too pretty. Woman I saw, her face was scrunched, kind of like a frog."

Planchette couldn't hide his disappointment.

"You look tired," Claire said. "And, wow, do you need a shave." She stood up and extended her hand. "Trust me?"

With my very life, he thought. He let her lead him to the bathroom, grateful for any intimacy, however oblique. Just the touch of her fingers against his was a balm that suffused his whole being with relief. He sat on the edge of the tub. She draped towels over his shoulders, front and back, lathered his face.

"How'd you get the scar?"

"Do I have to tell you?"

She laughed. "No, keep your secrets. Can you tell me how you learned to dance? Or is that embarrassing, too?"

"I just—felt it."

She squatted down so that she was looking up at him, forearm and elbow on knees, razor held upright at a lax tilt. "Listen to me, Detective Planchette. That was very probably the most profound experience of my life. You turned a horrific night into a magical mystery tour, and I bless you for it."

Planchette swallowed. "You're welcome."

She went to work on his beard. It was a startling and yet

pleasant sensation, soon lost in the closeness of her, the caring with which she ministered to his need. He surrendered, let his aura become immersed in hers. It was like coming home. He always wanted to believe that it was not just the way he was made, that he chose to love, each time. He remembered that he did, and made the choice again.

Now he could go looking for her, and now she might find him. He remembered that the art of the hunt was playful. "What's the story with the tattoo?" he asked. It was a curious expression to employ by reflex. Everything was a story. He felt her withdraw a little, feared he'd made a mistake.

"I was in a mood, pissed about something. It's kind of a pain. I have to keep shaving it."

"It suits you."

"You are a peculiar cop, Detective Planchette."

"Thank you."

She finished shaving him, toweled his face. "Take a look."

The person in the mirror seemed younger. Also fatigued, and not a little haunted. He had never looked like this, fourteen hours after being born. Then again, he had never looked like this.

They returned to the living room.

"Can you stay awhile?"

Planchette realized he'd forgotten to record her reactions to Olivetta's pictures. "Actually, I need to question you again about last night, and record it. I'd also like you to take another look at those pictures."

"All right."

Her recollections were much the same as they had been the night before, if a little hazier. Her responses to the pictures were the same. Planchette clicked off the sheet.

He didn't want to leave. He felt safe with her. She was an oasis of calm, whether or not she recognized him.

"Tell me about Olivetta," he asked, resorting to conversation where silence seemed destined to fail. He was interested in her thoughts, how she expressed herself. Or perhaps it was fear of rejection.

She sat back, became reflective. "I know he was abandoned, grew up in a foster home. Doesn't talk about it. He had to have natural ability, to paint like he does. Showed up early, I'm sure. He was classified as a black hole very young."

"At twelve, according to his handler."

Claire nodded and shook her head. "So, he was bounced from one reservation to another for about thirty years, until eighteen months ago he was granted an indulgence to move here. He's put on three exhibits since then, all new work. Doesn't have many collectors, which isn't difficult to understand. Continental Archive keeps him alive. Takes whatever he sells them, which he keeps to a minimum. With them it winds up in a vault and no one sees it. Together with everything he painted on the reservations." Claire looked at Planchette. "How would that make you feel, painting for storage?"

"I don't know."

"You've been to his studio?"

Planchette nodded.

"Crammed with work, right? All of that he produced since moving here. The man eats, drinks and breathes paint. Output unprecedented. I mean, we lost so much in the cataclysm, I don't know; but there can't have been more than a few artists in history who could pump out work at that level. I know artists who take a year to produce just one piece with that degree of detail. He pulls it off in days. Not just little pieces—five, six feet tall. If they'd let him have a bigger studio he'd paint bigger."

"You respect him."

"Of course I respect him. Don't get me wrong, his work isn't easy. Some of it is self-indulgent as hell. That doesn't invalidate it. Doesn't mean there's nothing there to value."

"What do you value in it?"

"Honesty. Painful honesty."

"Brutal honesty."

Claire clasped her hands and looked out the window. Planchette wanted to sit next to her, draw her close, let silence speak between them. This theoretical discussion required concrete distance.

"So little personal art is produced. You can't write that all off to cultural dynamics. Just having a personal vision that you're not willing to subordinate to public service will garner you some level of sociopathic classification, guaranteed. I got a blister just for writing about it. P.C. won't admit it but it's true." She looked at Planchette with her chin tucked, pointed at her tattooed eyebrow.

"That's what you were pissed about?"

She nodded. "What they really don't like is I'm not critical. Just try to help people understand what the artist is after. Let them decide for themselves." She waved it away. "Michael tried the community thing. That mural in the alley, where we were last night? That's his. He made the proposal, they brought him down from the reservation, pretty much kept him under lock and key when he wasn't working. Did that whole thing, every brush stroke."

"Olivetta painted that mural."

Claire nodded. "That's how he earned his indulgence." She caught his look. "Is it significant?"

An instinct sparked in Planchette that the answers to his questions lay in what he already knew. Too many factors were clustering too closely together. Correlations, not coincidences. He needed to review very carefully everything he had heard and witnessed.

"Detective?"

A construction worker scaled the scaffolding across the boulevard with acrobatic grace. Planchette looked at Claire. She searched his eyes, and for an instant the connection was made.

"Oh!" Her eyes widened. "If Michael painted her portrait, and she killed that man right in front of his mural—why didn't I see that? But no, that has to be a coincidence."

"Probably." He didn't want to frighten her again.

She swallowed, and the distance grew between them. But then she reached out.

"I—I don't know what Michael's done or hasn't done. But there's something I want you to see."

Claire led him back down the hall to a room on the right. Inside was a private gallery, with a cushioned, backless bench in the middle. The paintings here were of a different character—cityscapes of New York and the veldt, and a few portraits. There was no sentimentality in this room, but there was heart. An aged construction worker sat on mis-matched stone steps beneath scaffolding, peering hard into the far distance. A waiter shook out a table cloth across the street from a line of grazers. A hawk perched in a nook between contrasting architecture that joined at asymmetric angles.

"I only collect from artists I've met," Claire said. "The best is in here. Most of it isn't great, maybe, but it comforts me. It reassures me that the human spirit hasn't gone grey."

"I'd think the efforts to re-colonize this city would satisfy you of that."

"Maybe, but that's mass mind. The individual carries the flame."

"Isn't that an over-simplification?"

"Anything we say is an over-simplification. But *that* is *not.*"

Claire pointed at a painting that Planchette immediately recognized as Olivetta's. It was a self-portrait of a fantastic kind. Olivetta lay sprawled in his studio on his afterthought mattress, naked except for torn strips of linen wrapped around different parts of his body like bandages—an ankle, both thighs, his groin, chest, fingers, left arm and head. He gazed hollowly at the viewer, as might one exhausted from battle. All around him, among his paintings, easels and worktables, stood his guardians, children defiant in postures and attitudes. In the extreme foreground were two naked infants, one cowering in fear, the other with his arm over the frightened one, protecting him. The latter stared down the viewer with a ferocious glare beyond the capacity of one so young.

"You tell me," Claire said. "Does the person who painted that feel nothing for others?"

"It's hard to believe so. The rage—"

"You can be distracted by all kinds of things."

Planchette nodded. He recognized one of the children. It was the boy from the park.

Chapter Sixteen

Planchette's sheet vibrated.

It was Dunn. "They've arrived, Sir. I've got my driver."

Planchette checked the time. He had to meet Haliel in fifteen minutes. "How long would it take you to get back to the crime scene?"

"I should go over a couple of things with Baranski, brief the new people. Say half an hour, forty-five minutes?"

"Okay, I'll meet you there. Perls wants a briefing at the station at four." Planchette clicked off and pointed at the painting. "I've seen this boy," he told Claire.

She looked.

"He's in a photo in your hallway, too. I saw him in the park last night."

"That's Thaddy Myers," she said, like he would recognize the name.

"Who's that?"

"How can you live in New York and not know Thaddy Myers?"

"I just got here last night."

She blinked at him. "You hit the ground running."

Planchette grimaced. "That's what my Captain said."

"You mean Old Pine Park? By where we were?"

"Yes."

"He sleeps there sometimes."

"He *sleeps* there?"

Claire beckoned Planchette back into the hallway. She opened her hand at the photograph of burning wreckage. "This was one of the worst disasters New York's had since re-colonization began.

It's why the ban on hovers was put in effect. Freak accident—young couple, Ellen and Laurence Myers, drove their hover into a temporary stabilizing cable by a construction site. Happened early in the morning when it was foggy out—probably didn't see it. Cable wasn't anchored securely and broke loose, started a chain reaction that took down this building—this burning pile of rubble—and two behind it you can't see because of the smoke. The other two were in use; eighty-five people died. The Myers were killed instantly, along with their daughter, Thaddeus' twin sister. Thaddy was spending the night at a friend's house and wasn't with them."

"When did it happen?"

"About a year and a half ago."

The boy's upturned face showed in profile, less pain in his expression than incomprehension. "He's in front of the barricade. They let him do that?"

"Sometimes I think I have this picture just so I can look for an answer to that question. Closest I've come is maybe shock can be so powerful it pushes people away. See someone suffering, you mean to go to them but, without knowing why, focus elsewhere. Maybe don't want to get involved. This fireman, running here? He's just a few feet from Thaddy but looking the other way, like he's avoiding him. What I don't like to think is that they're punishing him. Unconsciously, maybe. Letting him suffer for his parents' mistake. There was a lot of anger towards the Myers."

"So people shun him. That's why he sleeps in the park."

"No, a lot of people would take him in. I've told him he can stay here." Pain constricted Claire's eyes. "People are kind to him. Feed him, give him clean clothes to wear. He knows where he can go. No one's heard him speak since it happened. C.A. advised me to let him be."

Planchette saw, then, what the photographer had seen. Claire had misinterpreted the gestalt of the image. The child had found the center of the chaos. He was in the eye of the storm, invisible.

Planchette didn't think Claire should keep the picture in her home. She should take it down and never look at it again.

"I have to go," he said.

He put on his coat and hat. Claire stayed with him to the door. He started to say goodbye and found himself in her embrace. An accumulation of ache broke loose and crumbled away.

Ten steps down the hall the urgency of everything descended again. The shapes had seen it coming and held their counsel. Planchette had no certainty of Claire. The best he could muster was frail hope. The person he needed most was beyond reach, entangled, somewhere, in circumstances he could not imagine. He ran to the elevator, pushed the down button repeatedly.

Driving to the crime scene, he tried to reclaim the calm he had felt in Claire's presence. It was impossible. Mere moments apart from her and his emotions were a shambles. He had indulged himself, going to see her. You did make a connection, Morph reminded him. Yes, for an instant she had seen him. And immediately deflected what she'd seen with a facile assumption. It happened, Morph insisted. Remember your decision to fulfill your mission, conveyed Spoon.

His assistants were right. He needed to focus on what was available to him, not on wishing things were different. Ninety-eight lives he had lived; he had resources. One in particular that he'd always understood in others, but never so well as he now did in himself: Defiance was his surest ally.

From inside a cruiser, two uniformed cops kept watch over the crime scene. Planchette scraped the side of his cruiser, bringing it down, and saw the patrol cops rock with laughter. He parked on the side of the taped-off area facing them, with his back to Olivetta's mural. No third hover in the alley—Planchette checked the time. He was six minutes late. Haliel had come and gone or not arrived yet. He got out and went to the other cruiser. The alley lay in shadow but the afternoon was still hot. A faint odor of organic rot inhabited the air. The driver rolled down his window.

"Has anyone else been here, recently?" Planchette asked.

The patrol cops, struggling with their amusement, shook their heads.

"I asked a question."

Their mirth evaporated.

"No, sir, no one's been through this alley for several hours," the driver answered.

Planchette recognized him from the night before—Dunn's regular partner. He was handsome and muscular, younger than Dunn. Not as bright as her. "What's your name?"

"Hockurt, Detective. Raymond Hockurt."

"Have you been here since last night?"

Hockurt nodded. "Yes, sir."

"I'll have someone relieve you."

"Detective Perls took care of that, Detective. Our relief should be here in an hour."

Planchette moved away, took in the scene. The brickwork and architecture in this stretch of the alley matched their counterparts in the mural. It was all reconstruction, bricks mis-matched, whole ones interspersed with fragments. Planchette wondered if the mural had been made to agree with the alley, or the alley to accommodate the mural.

Another question came to him. He called Claire.

"Hi!" She smiled. "You were just here!"

"I was." He couldn't connect with her through a holoscreen. She was a universe away. "I have a question."

"All right."

"Olivetta told me he's not allowed to paint from live subjects. Those kids in his self portrait, he holo-graphed them, right?"

"Actually, I don't think he did. I think he just painted them from memory."

"That's what I was wondering—his memory is that good."

"Photographic. Better than photographic—holo-graphic."

"I saw a holo-suit on a mannequin in his studio. He gave me to believe he uses it like an artificial model."

"Why would he need that?"

"Right."

"All sorts of reasons. Help him visualize a figure in different poses, examine the effects of light, manipulate expressions."

Planchette mulled her answer.

"Does that help?"

"I don't know. I'm trying to rule things out."

"Can you come by later?"

"If I can, I will."

"Call me."

Planchette clicked off. At least she was interested in him, if she didn't know why. He looked up, saw no hover above the alley. Maybe Haliel hadn't wanted to be seen. Maybe he'd flown over when Planchette wasn't looking, spotted two cruisers and driven on. Planchette put his hands on his hips and sighed in frustration. If Haliel hadn't cut him off they could have arranged an alternate rendezvous.

Well, he was here, and he'd come for a reason. *Review everything you've heard and seen, everything you know.* He went inside the bar. The coat check station was closed. He walked into the bar area. The place was deserted except for a worker mopping the bartender's dog run.

"They're not open yet."

"When?"

"Five."

Planchette showed his badge and the man went back to his job. There had been unfinished drinks on tables, the bartender in his pit, Claire at the bar. Two women in the corner to the left, who hadn't gone outside with the others. Planchette went over to the table he'd seen them at, lifted cushions, searched around. Nothing.

"Have you vacuumed here?" he asked the workman.

The man looked up. "Yeah."

Planchette checked the bathroom. It had been cleaned, trash removed. He remembered looking at himself in the mirror, became conscious of the bulge in his mind.

He didn't know what he was looking for, went back outside.

Dunn had arrived. She was leaning on Hockurt's cruiser, chatting with him through the window. Planchette waved to her. She crossed the alley with a jauntiness he sensed was not for his benefit.

"Good to see you, sir."

Planchette didn't know what to do with how glad he was to see her. "Hockurt still jealous?"

"Ray doesn't like you. *I* do not care."

Planchette smiled, surprising himself. "We need to find something here, Dunn." He looked both ways down the alley. "We've overlooked something. I don't know what it is but I know we missed it."

"You want me to call forensics, see what they've found?"

Planchette shook his head. "I don't think it's in the physical evidence. It's in the logic of this thing, something basic that doesn't add up." He didn't know if he could rely on his mind. "Read back the witness's statement to me, the one I transcribed." How impaired he had become. Or was it excess of doubt? The shapes ventured no opinion.

Dunn retrieved the transcript, read aloud. Her voice was comforting. Planchette tried again to visualize what had happened. Claire took a pod from her apartment to the transit platform on the far side of Old Pine Park, and from there walked here. She reached the entrance of the bar, where Planchette stood now, and saw Friedman come up the alley from the opposite direction—

"Stop," he told Dunn. "That's it." He pointed toward Olivetta's mural. "Is there a transit platform that way?"

Dunn stared. "I … wait a minute." She searched on her sheet, nodded. "There is but it's kind of far. Over a quarter of a mile."

"Which is the easiest one to get to from Friedman's place?"

"Well, they're on the same line—"

"Which would he reach first?"

Dunn consulted her sheet. "The park."

"All right, I walked in here from the park, last night. The alley in that direction wasn't brightly lit but there was more than enough light to see by. What, forty, fifty feet past the mural, it was pitch black going the other way. So why does Friedman pass up the park platform, go to one farther away, and come up an unlighted alley to get here?"

The mural was no deception in daytime. The night sky gave it away at a glance. The alley wound beyond, irregular in width, between jigsaw tenements, domes, open lots piled with debris where nothing had yet been built. Garbage collectors had a tough time in this city.

"I gave C-tech your instructions, Detective. I'm sure they've been through here."

"*We* haven't."

They walked it to the end, where it met a street lined with taller buildings.

"Where's the platform?" Planchette asked.

"Down there." Dunn pointed left.

Planchette saw it, about three hundred feet away, where the street curved from view, anchored to the rounded face of a brick and concrete high-rise set with mismatched windows. Several people waited there for pods.

Planchette turned back to the alley. "Let's do it again."

"What are we looking for?"

"I don't know."

They went slower, this time. The use of recycled materials was obvious in most of the buildings. The effort to achieve an integrated result varied from one to the next. The back walls of many were slab concrete.

"Everyone who lives or works along this alley has been questioned?"

"I'll check." Dunn contacted Processing.

Planchette drifted aside to look at a three-tiered pyramid of domes. The overall impression was hive-like; but there was a homeliness, too, that spoke of warmth and fellowship. And shared suffering. Exterior staircases accessed the higher doorways. Windows were placed irregularly and, as ever, mismatched. The mosaic surface was composed of random materials, cemented in place with care. Those most vulnerable to the elements, wood and metal, had been coated with a transparent, protective agent. Thistles, dandelions and bunch grass grew around the base of the pyramid. It must have been awhile since grazers had been through here. Maybe they were programmed to leave volunteer flora unmolested. In the center of the alley a spot missing cobbles had filled in with soil. The dirt had wavy lines in it, like something had been dragged through it when it was wet. Sack full of trash, probably.

"A few people weren't home," Dunn said. "They'd already left for work by the time door-to-door got to them, apparently."

"Has anyone gone to their workplaces to question them?"

"It seems not."

Planchette made a face. He couldn't re-allocate personnel without clearance from Perls. He'd leave it for the briefing.

"There are quite a few vacant units along here, too, Detective."

"Requisition a list, Dunn. They all need to be checked out." This creeping investigative process was maddening. Planchette tracked the flight of a flurry of shapes, a few blackbirds among them.

Dunn finished submitting his applications. "Isn't there another possibility?" she asked.

They resumed walking. "Go ahead."

"What if Friedman did get off at the park platform, came down here to meet somebody or do something, and was returning when the witness saw him?"

"That's good. The question remains the same, though. What are the specifics?"

"Maybe he met the killer, and they had an argument. Maybe the woman was his lover, and he ended it. They could have had a place they met, here, maybe one of the vacant units."

"Why would Friedman hide an affair? He wasn't bonded."

"Maybe she was. Maybe that's why they fought. He was tired of secrecy. He could have been dumping her for the witness. We only have her word that they'd never met."

Right or wrong, Planchette liked the way Dunn was thinking. It stimulated him to re-evaluate what he knew, turn it over, assault it with theories. It occurred to him that there was something significant missing besides Frisa and an unknown number of shapes. He contacted Processing and asked the handler to have the tech who had examined Friedman's computer at Columbia College call him.

"Why else would he come down here?" Planchette asked Dunn. "Keep thinking out loud."

Dunn was quiet for a moment. "I don't know. Maybe he just felt like a walk. Maybe he liked dark alleys. Maybe he dozed off and missed his stop. Or—something else. Maybe something down here interested him."

"What?"

Dunn looked around. "I have no idea. Maybe he just came down here to pee."

Planchette's sheet vibrated.

"Detective Chron? Jesús Amado."

"You're the tech who went over Friedman's computer at Columbia?"

"I am."

"How thorough were you, looking for a hidden partition?"

Amado sounded irritated. "Very thorough. I did a cross-section scan of that table in three directions. I always do a third scan with homicides."

"You know what was found at his apartment?"

Amado laughed. "I'm working on it now."

"You're at the apartment?"

"Yes, sir."

"Have you found a back-up system?"

Amado's irritation acquired a patronizing edge. "No, Detective, but we will. Clips are easy to hide."

"But you haven't found any in the room that was sealed?"

"Not yet."

"If they exist I think that's where you'll find them, Technician. I doubt Friedman went to the trouble to secure that room and then hid his back-ups under the sofa." Planchette clicked off.

"Looking for data clips?" Dunn asked.

Planchette nodded.

"Friedman might have given them to someone for safe keeping."

"In which case it won't be C-tech that finds them, will it?" Planchette snapped. The stress was gnawing at him, eroding his restraint. He scratched his eyebrow. "Sorry."

They returned to the crime scene, strolled to Dunn's cruiser. Dunn opened the driver's door; Planchette leaned on the roof from the passenger side with his hands clasped.

"No," he said, straightening. "It's here." He went to the center of the alley and faced Olivetta's mural. Dunn shut the hover door. "What's the one thing we know that connects Friedman to this place?" Planchette asked. "Olivetta. Friedman has Olivetta's paintings hanging in his office and home. He's been to Olivetta's studio and met him. Olivetta painted a portrait of a woman who, at least in the way she was dressed, bears a resemblance to the murderer described by Claire Fontaine. And Friedman was killed here, not a hundred feet from a mural painted by Olivetta. It's here, Dunn. We're just not seeing it."

In the painting it was a cloudless night. The alley was illumined by windows and unevenly placed streetlights. It could be inferred that it was vacant because everyone was indoors. Perhaps it was a cold night, and people were disinclined to go out. There are likely historical inaccuracies in this depiction, Graph conveyed. What did he have to go on? Planchette responded.

He went close to the painting, touched it. The surface was smooth. Olivetta had prepared it carefully. The brush strokes were tighter and more blended than in his other paintings, no doubt to heighten the illusion of reality. Planchette took off his hat and scanned the surface of the mural with his face against the wall, detected a couple of shallow, rectangular indentations, up high among the false stars, where windows had been sealed off. He squatted and looked for Olivetta's signature. It wasn't in the traditional place, in the lower, right-hand corner. He searched the bottom perimeter of the mural and didn't find it. Planchette doubted Olivetta left the work unsigned. He stood up and scrutinized the façades of the tenements.

A few shops opened onto the alley, in the painting. A sign over one on the right read, "NOTIONS." There was lettering underneath that was hard to decipher. The sign was depicted in deep shadow. Planchette squinted and made out: "M. O. Proprietor." A round medallion hung from the sign. Almost indiscernible on it was the square-and-compass symbol of the Utilitarians. Planchette traced the perimeter of the medallion with his fingertips and detected an incision in the painted surface. An instinct possessed him and he pressed in on the center of the medallion. It gave slightly and he pressed harder. The medallion sank into the wall about a quarter of an inch.

Dunn gasped. A waft of cool air brushed Planchette's face.

Chapter Seventeen

Anger is a product of frustration. Infant reality is unavoidably frustrating.

—Rationale 1A
Psychology Council Codex and Principles

In the art find the man, Graph quoted. From source unknown—void of the cataclysm. Was it there, in the maze of brush strokes, the argument that explained the artist? In the decision to depict an infinite, un-peopled passageway into the past? (Or had that decision been made for him?) The salient finding, in any case, was that Olivetta knew about the disguised door. He had to, for it was plain that he had collaborated in its making.

The right side lined up with the edge of the mural. The top and left sides—the latter the hinged side—cut a puzzle piece out of the painting, following crenelations of brickwork, a line where two buildings met, and the diagonal margin of the false alley. Closed, the door was invisible; when the medallion was depressed, it popped open to expose a recessed hand grip. The door was about eight inches thick, fashioned from a composite material, steeply beveled so that it fit in its frame like a form in a mold. Inside, past a short landing, metal stairs led down.

Hockurt and his partner of the day were out of their cruiser, gaping at Planchette and Dunn. Planchette waved them over and they came running. "If this thing shuts on us and we can't get it open," he told them, "push here." He indicated the medallion. Dunn followed him inside. The landing was narrow and cramped. It was about ten steps to the bottom of the stairs. Planchette stayed in the lead. When Dunn stepped off the landing the door closed. They looked back.

"Must be a pressure plate," Planchette said.

A holoscreen monitor appeared on the inside surface of the door, showing a split view both ways down the alley. Hockurt and his partner shouted inaudibly in the right half of the screen.

"See if you can reach them," Planchette told Dunn.

She called Hockurt. They watched him fumble with his sheet.

"If they're desperate to see us, tell them do what I showed them."

Dunn relayed an unsarcastic rendering of the message. Hockurt reached off screen and the door opened. He leaned in. "Are you all right?"

"We'll call if we need you. I want to close it." Planchette waved him out. Hockurt's expression flattened and he withdrew. Planchette gestured at Dunn. She stepped onto the landing and back down. The door closed.

"I didn't hear it," she said. "It didn't make a sound."

"Just a whisper." Planchette pointed at the monitor. In the right half, Hockurt was flipping them off. "Friedman waits until it's clear, then he goes out. He must have done that just before Claire came around the bend, up there past the bar."

"Was the killer with him?"

"I don't know."

Planchette continued down the stairs, Dunn close behind. From the bottom, a passage led to the left about fifty feet.

"Ray's a good guy," Dunn said.

The passage ended at another flight of stairs that led up to the right. At the top was a hallway, with a plank floor and unfinished fiberboard walls, lit by two globe fixtures in the ceiling.

"Is it all right if I think this is creepy?" Dunn said.

"This took organization, Dunn. Planning. It extends beyond Olivetta."

"I think something like that is what I meant, sir."

About a hundred feet on, the left wall became concrete, and a short distance farther was inset with a metal door. The lock on the door looked identical to the customized one in Friedman's apartment.

"I'd say we've found where he went," Planchette said.

Dunn didn't respond. She'd stopped about ten paces back.

Planchette went to her. "Dunn?" She was arrested in mid-stride, didn't even appear to be breathing. Planchette waved his hand in front of her eyes. Her gaze was fixed.

"She's all right." Haliel appeared from nowhere, behind her. "Were you *looking* for me out there?" He sidled around Dunn and brushed past Planchette, stopped at the locked door. "I thought you can tell when I'm around."

Planchette hid his shock. He'd always been able to detect Haliel's presence, but this time hadn't had the slightest sense of him. He still didn't. "What did you do to her?" he asked. What was happening to his perceptions? The shapes had no answer for him. Or did, rather, but didn't want to convey it right then. Planchette didn't want them to, either.

"What?" Haliel glanced at Dunn. His retinue of shapes stacked up down the hallway behind him. "She's fine. She's just … on pause."

"Well, take her the hell *off* pause."

"Eighty-five," Haliel said, exasperated, "let's see what's in here first, shall we?" He examined the lock with his head tilted, smiled faintly. "Clever." He took a small black cube, about half an inch square, out of his pocket.

"What's that?" Planchette asked.

"What?" Haliel stared at him. "The things you don't know amaze me. It's my ship. I *need* one, remember? Unlike you." He placed the cube against the lock. It adhered when he took his hand away. There was a click, and sounds of bolts retracting around the door's edge. Haliel smiled.

He opened the door, found a switch and turned on the lights.

The result was disorienting. The walls and ceiling were irregularly faceted, paneled in non-equilateral metal triangles with nacreous surfaces etched with asymmetric patterns. In every other respect, the room was as austere in its appointments as had been Friedman's office at Columbia College. More so—the only furnishings were a rolling chair and a glass-top desk, the latter strewn with wands and an interface gauntlet.

A bemused expression crossed Haliel's face, as if a question had been answered. Planchette reached out with his senses, trying to detect Haliel's signature. The effort brought him into blunt confrontation with his mnemonic patch. The metaphorical impression—the interpretive image his imagination presented— was of a fogged window, a kind of waxen hatch with a gelatinous border. His elder memories were shadowy fish on the other side. Planchette had never been so divided from his core self. Haliel sat at the desk and touched its corner. Nothing happened. He touched it again with the same result. Distractedly, Planchette watched him. An imaginary construct in his mind was having an organic impact—that was the only explanation. He concentrated, drawing connection with his core through the patch, careful not to dislodge it. The milky pattern that distinguished the Ixilian registered—faintly, but Planchette held focus and it clarified. Haliel's retinue filed in and crowded the far end of the room. Planchette noticed again how few they were. Twelve scrutinized the metal walls. Haliel took his cube out again and started to place it on the desk.

"Don't," Planchette said.

"It's not working," Haliel objected.

"It isn't connected to the power grid." Planchette went behind the desk. The Ixilian shapes jostled each other to make way for him. Planchette pulled down his sleeve to pick up the plug and inserted it into a wall outlet.

"Oh." Haliel pocketed his ship. He touched the corner of the desk again, and an array of holoscreens leapt to life, encircling the desk. He swivelled in the chair, taking in the spectacle. "Friedman was a busy fellow."

"Why are you here, Haliel?"

"What? To find out what's going on. Aren't you?"

"I'm looking for Frisa."

"Yes, I know that. It's been on my mind since you told me she was missing."

"I have questions."

"Starting with why she left you, I imagine."

"She didn't leave me."

"Then she's been interfered with, and we have to find out who's responsible." Haliel gestured at the holoscreens. "I'm guessing it has something to do with this. I'll have to run a translation—"

"Don't even think about it."

Haliel made a face. "In *here.*" He patted his shirt pocket, where he had deposited his ship. He scanned the ranks of equations. Planchette turned his attention to them too. He recognized permutations of a few strands he'd seen in Friedman's apartment. But it was hopeless. Even with Twelve's and Graph's assistance, he could only comprehend a small fraction of the displayed data.

"Have you ever seen anything like this, Eighty-five? I mean, here—" Haliel stood up and went to a large holoscreen, opened his palm at a region of figures—"He's very close to establishing a theoretical basis for parting space. He's figured out that what they've been referring to as dark energy is made up of discrete elements, what we call the 'hidden streams' on Ixil. He's even identified a few of them, though I'm sure he has no idea how many more there are. But here—" Haliel went around the desk to another screen—"this is remarkable. This—*this*—is genius. It constitutes a leap in reasoning for which he had no perceptual rationale. He's actually trying to demonstrate that the quanta he's working to differentiate could form a basis for life." Haliel looked at Planchette.

"Shapes," Planchette said.

Haliel nodded. "He doesn't know it but he's trying to prove

that shapes exist." Haliel gazed at the holoscreen in admiration. "If he'd lived, he might have succeeded."

Planchette swiped the corner of the desk and the holoscreens vanished. He wiped the corner with his sleeve.

Haliel frowned at Planchette's sleeve, frowned at Planchette, smiled. "Fingerprints?" He twiddled his fingers at Planchette. "Self-erasing. Something you can accomplish with technology."

"Questions," Planchette said.

"All right." Haliel sighed. Planchette opened his mouth to speak again, but Haliel anticipated him. "When did you become separated from One-ten?"

"She was gone when I came out of hibernation."

"Really." Haliel's eyes tracked in thought. "That explains it."

"Explains what?"

"What? Well, for one thing, why you took so long to find me. I have to ask, Eighty-five, would it be that surprising? If she did leave you? Wasn't one of you *bound* to weary of this ordeal of yours, sooner or later? If you didn't weary together?"

Planchette said nothing.

"You think not. Well, it's to us, then, to figure this out. The humans can't help. They'll get in the way."

"How long have you been here, Haliel?"

"I was here when you got here. I didn't know I'd be undetectable to *you*. Forgive me if I'm a little pleased about that."

"Not *today*. On *Earth*—how long have you been on *Earth?*"

"Oh. I don't know, about five of their years, here. Same as you, minus the leap. Why are you shaking your head?"

"I got here last night."

Haliel's head came forward. "Last *night?*" He stared at Planchette. "That's not possible. Is it? How is that possible?"

Planchette closed his eyes in frustration. "No—I got to Earth I think about a hundred and twenty years ago. But I only entered the temporal continuum, here, in New York, last night. Shortly before we talked."

Haliel continued to stare. "Oh, this is a mess. You're sure One-ten didn't leave on purpose?"

Planchette wasn't sure of anything.

"It's all right, Eighty-five. She's here. We'll find her and you'll work things out. The universe will forgive you for leaving one species to its own devices—"

Planchette seized Haliel by the throat and flung him against the wall.

Chapter Eighteen

Planchette stepped back, appalled by his own violence. Something else shocked him more:

Fear.

He had been designed to read emotions, and the emotion that always shone brightest was fear. He might not be able to tell when Haliel was lying, but the fear emanating from him was real, and it didn't make sense. The figure sprawled on the floor, the thing Haliel dignified as a construct, was not even a living organism. It was an automaton. Haliel did not inhabit it as Planchette did his human body. He operated it from a neural hammock, somewhere in the compressed space of his ship.

A skilled artist might come to regard a brush as an extension of his hand. If the only means one had to interact with others was through a projected self, sooner or later one would come to identify with that projection. For millennia, Haliel had had limited contact with his own kind. He'd spent protracted periods alternating between stasis and a state similar to suspended animation, in which he functioned through an automated surrogate. He'd spent more time doing that, now, than he had being himself. Frisa and Planchette had avoided him, so the only beings he'd had to interact with, most of the time, had been ones among whom he could not reveal himself. His existence had come to resemble ¼=ca.85's in ways that ¼=ca.85 had never considered.

Haliel's fear diminished as Planchette's ire subsided. His automaton leaned back, winced, glared at a protrusion in the faceted wall that had jabbed it, peered up at Planchette. "I know what you're worried about."

Planchette sought high for patience.

Haliel hardened his gaze. "I have *watched* you two for a *very* long time." He held out his hand and Planchette pulled him to his feet. "She didn't do what you're afraid of. She's not capable of it." He rubbed the back of his head, looked where he'd fallen. "I didn't deserve that."

"Maybe not."

"You nearly damaged my construct. They're hard to make."

"Sorry."

"You would have had an interesting job explaining my body. I'd like to have attended the autopsy."

"Can we move on?"

"To what, specifically?"

Planchette opened his mouth, closed it. He needed solitude to sort out his mind.

Haliel smirked. "You don't know what to ask, do you?"

"How did you come to be Willbury's assistant?"

"I falsified records and applied for the job."

"Why?"

"I have to amuse myself."

"That's no answer."

"What am I supposed to do, wake up for a few days and go back into stasis? Leave it to my ship's instruments to monitor your doings? I have to have some experience of life, Eighty-five, some sense of continuity."

Planchette shook his head. "The first human who interferes with me is your *employer*? I'm supposed to believe that's a coincidence."

"I didn't create that situation, you did."

Planchette shook his head. "You're manipulating him."

Haliel stretched his neck. "Let me show you something." He held his hands apart at breast level, palms facing each other. A holoscreen-like image appeared, between them, of a large, interstellar vessel, somewhere in space. Haliel lowered his hands and the image remained suspended. "My instruments picked them up about three months ago. They're parked in orbit around the planet next farthest from this system's Sun. They're from Kulqa, a world you visited a long time ago." Haliel moved next to Planchette. He touched the image and several parts of the ship were highlighted. "Those are armament batteries."

"Why are they here?"

"I'd think it unwise to assume their intentions friendly."

Planchette frowned at the image. Here was another player on the stage. Clearly Haliel was right—he had never given adequate thought to the repercussions of his actions. "'At least that used to be the case.'"

"What?"

"Last night, when you were elucidating how removed I am from the common experience of time, you said you've always had to explain yourself when you've been resuscitated from stasis. Then you said, 'At least that used to be the case.' Is this what you meant?"

"All I know is they were ready for me. They knew about me and they knew about you. I didn't have to explain anything. There was considerable disparity among the Council in their attitudes toward you."

"Disparity?"

"Before you came along, Eighty-five, the policy of the Council was simple. If a species survived its violent tendencies it was accepted to the interstellar community. If it didn't it was allowed to fail. There are a lot of dead worlds that didn't make it."

"Which is your argument for opposing us. Not 'saves intelligent species from extinction,' just percentages."

"Percentages, yes. As in being outnumbered."

"How you go along, all of you, knowing you can help, and do nothing, with no better rationale than that, I'll never understand."

"The rationale you're disparaging, just so we're clear, is survival. But setting that aside, what help do you think we could give?"

"You have maps! You know which species are at risk. At least some of them. We could anticipate crises. Hundreds of billions, trillions could be spared horrible suffering and death. To say nothing of the loss of creative potential."

"You don't know that. For you to know that you'd have to know how you do what you do. You don't understand that any better than we do."

Planchette had no reply.

"What happens when you come out of hibernation?"

Planchette took an unconscious step back from Haliel.

"See, I wonder if you know *that* much."

"I know what happens."

"Okay, tell me if I go wrong. First, you get to a planet like this, you go where something really bad is about to happen."

Planchette kept silent.

"The next part is a little disconcerting, isn't it? Because you don't prevent anything, not that I've seen. Everything goes to hell and you just watch. Or have I missed something?"

"We imprint defining events—"

Haliel laughed. "'Defining events?' Wow, talk about understatement. That's a telling choice of words, though. What do they define, Eighty-five? The future? The past? *You?* Sounds to me like you've developed an insulating perspective. Not that I blame you. How *does* one reconcile needing billions of people to die in order to do his job?"

Planchette let his gaze drift tiredly, at a loss to answer Haliel's scorn. He knew his place in the scheme of things. There were matters he'd learned not to dwell on, that Frisa and he didn't discuss. Bombs, plagues, battles that drenched whole continents in blood—what point perseverating over tragedies they could neither limit nor prevent? There were dark moments, though, when $\frac{1}{4}$=ca.85 cursed their creators for not making them better. The only thing that dispelled such moods was Frisa at his side.

According to Haliel, she'd been alone on this world not one

but *five* years. Planchette could not imagine what she'd gone through. He shook his head. He'd had enough of examining the phenomenology of his existence. He needed to do something.

His attention snagged, again, on Haliel's shapes. "Didn't your retinue used to be bigger?"

"What?" Haliel looked at his shapes, threw his hands up in frustration. "Why am I trying to help you?"

Planchette didn't know what to say. He didn't know what to think. The whole exchange felt like a digression. He studied the image on Haliel's screen. He had no experience with star ships. Haliel said this one was dangerous. Planchette could only take his word for it. Kulqa—Planchette knew he'd visited the place but could not, in that moment, remember it. Why would a species he had helped want to prevent him from helping others? Haliel kept pressing him about time—through the passage of which continents shifted, stars died, and, among the conscious, attitudes changed and memories dimmed. Planchette had never sought to be remembered—didn't think he had. It seemed to him, in his fractured state, that he had always concealed his efforts. It was better for people to believe themselves masters of their own destinies. "If outsiders are interfering with me, I need to know why, and what they're doing."

"Let's go ask them."

Planchette shook his head. "I would have to relinquish this body to do that, Haliel. I doubt the shapes of this world would help me construct another one."

"I said us. I'll take you to them."

Planchette smirked. He was not about to trust his human construct to Haliel.

"Has it never occurred to you that I might want to be your friend?" Haliel said. "That I might need a friend myself, out here in the primordial hinterlands?"

"That does not mean I need you." Planchette hadn't meant to be dismissive but the reply felt facile. Mistrustful as he was of the

Ixilian, he couldn't deny that he'd found comfort in his company, this day. "I've lived all of my lives without friends, Haliel."

"How can you say that? You've had One-ten!"

"That's different; we were made for each other." Planchette recognized the pain in those words even as he spoke them.

Haliel saw it and looked away, with false flippancy said, "No wonder she left you."

What was this awkwardness? Like a shyness between old fools. "You said it yourself, I can't explain myself to you." It was not lost on Planchette that Haliel had let him keep his dignity. "If you really want to help, maybe *you* can find out about that ship."

Haliel nodded. "I'd think carefully before letting your human colleagues access this computer. This room was designed to deflect scans."

Twelve confirmed Haliel's assertion. Disconnecting the desk from the power grid had further obscured its location, the shape of measures conveyed.

"Which means Friedman knew others were looking for it," Planchette said.

"And may have been killed because of his research, yes," Haliel said. "If our friends out there are responsible," he inclined his head toward space, "anyone with knowledge of this computer will be in danger."

Planchette's skepticism returned. He did not believe Haliel cared about the inhabitants of Earth. Another incongruity occurred to him. "Why did you follow _=ca.110 to this planet and not monitor me as well?"

"I didn't know I hadn't."

Planchette squinted at Haliel.

"The beacon tracked your movement," Haliel explained, "or I suppose One-ten's, when she abandoned—became separated from you. That's all it can do, really. The log did show a temporary bi-location at a point in space where I presume you hibernated. I just figured it was a false reading or a malfunction of some kind.

We've never been able to design a system that can differentiate between you and One-ten, Eighty-five. When you separate, and you might be surprised how infrequently that is, our scans only describe a field in which the two of you could be anywhere."

"I don't understand."

"Our scans don't show you as separate entities, Eighty-five. They show you to be a single organism."

Chapter Nineteen

Hasker, picture of consternation, sat at Friedman's formerly secret desk. Perls stood behind him. Equations crawled incomprehensibly across holoscreens. Dunn paced in the hall, checked and rechecked her sheet, frowned and frowned, shook her head, shook her head.

"Are we sure this is a duplicate of the busted one in his apartment?" Hasker asked.

Perls looked to Planchette.

"We're not sure of anything, Chief." Planchette wondered if he had condemned these people to death by summoning them here. Maybe their entire world. If he had he would never forgive himself. He wanted to believe he'd done it because he hadn't been designed to interfere. But he had been designed precisely to interfere. It just went against his grain, to withhold something so significant from the species to whom it belonged, not even for their own safety, not for one day. However unsound his own reasoning, he knew for certain that he didn't trust Haliel's. Not for one minute. He watched Dunn pace, wanted to tell her she never would account for the seventeen minutes she'd lost. Haliel had offered to alter her memory—hers, Hockurt's and his back-up's. Planchette sent him and his curiously diminished retinue packing.

"So, who tells us what's going on here?" Hasker asked.

"Friedman corresponded with a Professor Yu Li in New Beijing," Perls said, "and a Professor Oxgarten in Sweden. They've been contacted. Oxgarten'll be on his way by ship in the morning, Li will fly over as soon as a seat comes available, hopefully by next week. We've apprised Air Authority of the urgency. Probably they'll arrive about the same time."

The Captain sighed. "Okay, no one touches anything until they're here." He glanced at Planchette in chagrin.

Outside, Perls and Planchette watched the Captain's hover rise out of the alley.

"The door was open," Perls said. "Friedman meant to go back."

"Or someone there with him stayed behind. Or came after he left."

"Someone else who could work that lock?"

"Maybe." The shock it would give Haliel if C-tech found evidence of his tampering was entertaining to imagine. It would never happen.

Perls put his hands on his hips, inhaled looking up, blew looking down. "Olivetta's gone runner."

Planchette groaned.

"He invited our man Wright back into his apartment, clobbered him with something, tied him up with bras and panties. The proximity alarms went off but he was long gone by the time anyone got there."

"I think we want to talk to him."

"Him and a few others." Perls looked back at the mural, eyed it up and down. "I'll find him. I moved the briefing to nine."

Planchette nodded. "I want to nose around here a little more." He wanted time by himself. A couple of uniforms he didn't recognize stood by the disguised door. Something about their attitudes irritated Planchette. "You two replace Hockurt and his partner?"

They nodded.

Perls loomed over them. "Take those off."

The patrol cops stared up in shock.

"You know what I'm talking about."

They removed Utilitarian pins from their lapels.

"I see that again, I'll suspend you. On duty you're cops, got it?"

They nodded. Planchette made note of their names: Delgado and Smith.

"No one goes through that door without direct clearance from me, Captain Hasker, or Detective Chron, here."

Perls left. Planchette went to Dunn, who was sitting in their cruiser. "I'm going to walk the alley again by myself," he told her. "Why don't you take another look around here, see if anything catches your eye."

She nodded.

"Meet me down by that transit platform in about twenty minutes or so."

Once he rounded the bend past the mural and was out of sight of human eyes, Planchette staggered and groaned, awash in a terrible broth of emotions. His skin crawled with phantom burn. He trudged along blindly, trying to think, trying not to think, made it to the pyramid of domes and slumped against it, holding his head. To be human seemed impossible. He did not know what he had lost. He could not be who he was, who he *meant* to be, without command of his memories and the faculties that sustained them. His history—call it fiction—was the same. The one reality did not exist without the other. If Haliel was right—if whatever instruments he used to track Frisa and him were accurate—then he was not only halved but quartered, cut off from both his elder memories and half of his very being.

More and more he was experiencing consciousness the way the species he was designed to help did. Not knowing beginnings or ends, uncertain of purpose, enduring existence as a series of guesses, hoping, groping, praying for fulfillment, that the end be not too dreadful, too heavy with failure and pain and regret. Meanwhile searching for someone to keep company. And if you found her, or thought you had, and lost her, oh! the bitter self-appraisal, the disenchantment with color and form and all the charms that lent life savor.

In his inward vision, the patch in his mind was thicker, more opaque. How or why it had thickened was beyond him. He had not meant to impair himself. The patch seemed more like a scab, something itching, hardening, nagging to be removed so the tissue underneath could breathe. He pulled at it, fashioned mental claws to pry at its perimeter. It hurt, like sticking skewers through his head, which made him more determined, more brutal in his efforts. If he bled so be it; he could not go on like this.

Soothing voices entered his mind, voices he had forgotten or ignored; the shapes strove to calm him. Spoon rapped his knuckles. Gently, the shape of etiquette conveyed. Let us help you, Morph and Morpho offered. We see how the partition is secured, its composition and design. Planchette surrendered to their ministrations. Gradually he understood what had happened. He had placed one human memory, then another, over his elder memories of other lives, and his human mind had continued, autonomically, to lay further memories over those. Each memory had to be identified and peeled away: his search of the alley with Dunn, drinking coffee with Claire, discussing art with Claire, being shaved by Claire, exchanges with Perls, Hasker, Olivetta, dawn in the plaza outside the Church of Unification, on and on—it was surprising how many involved Dunn.

The shapes peeled the patch down to a workable thinness. The link was not spontaneous, but Planchette could access his elder memories again. He had his reference library back. He breathed deep and leaned on his knees, sitting against the dome pyramid. He opened his eyes and found himself looking at the spot in the pavement missing cobbles he had noticed earlier. The wavy lines in the soil that had filled the void—he had assumed they were caused by a bag being dragged through the spot when it was wet. He saw that he was wrong, although he could hardly credit the nature of his error.

He squatted to examine the impressions. He recognized what had made them, or, at least, the species of phenomenon required to do so. He reached into the deepest, oldest part of his memory for confirmation, found it. The tiny swirls that overlapped and curled back and forth were unmistakable. But it couldn't be. It meant that these tracks had been made by a creature that had been extinct for at least a hundred thousand kerns.

Another possibility occurred to him, one that made less sense than anything.

The direction of the tracks indicated that their maker had gone toward the crime scene. Planchette touched the soil. It was damp; the impressions could have been made last night. So where had their maker come from? Planchette continued down the alley. In dirt and dust accumulated here and there between cobbles he spied more of the tracks, further evidence of the impossible. He supposed they could have been faked, but couldn't imagine how anyone would have acquired the knowledge and ability to do so.

He reached the end of the alley. The way left split past the transit platform. A big, street-level grazer was rounding the farthest visible bend in the left fork. Pedestrians scattered homeward from their work days, up and down the streets. Planchette couldn't see any more tracks. He went toward the platform.

The air was cooler, the street in full shadow. Planchette caught a faint whiff of the sea. Pods were stacked up twenty deep, past the lower platform. The tracks split with the street, and more pods approached on both lower courses, a crush of passengers stalled on the platform. Planchette couldn't see what was holding things up. He hung his badge from his breast pocket, forced his way up the stairs. Posters in flanking shop windows advertized fertility drugs, extolled the virtues of parenthood. At the top, would-be travelers jammed against the cage. "Police officer! Let me through!" Through the slats, Planchette saw passengers in the stacked up pods craning to see what was going on. He held his badge high, struggled forward to the source of disturbance. A man and a boy sat inside a pod, apparently unwilling to either disembark or let the pod move on. Several men stood around the pod door, arguing with the man inside. The boy was Thaddy Myers.

"He won't get off," said one of the arguers, when he saw Planchette's badge. "He's being threatening with that thing. He won't let the boy off either."

"Okay, give me room." Planchette felt a tap on his shoulder.

A man leaned close and in a low voice asked, "You know who that is?"

Planchette responded quietly in kind—"The Myers boy?"

"No, Seven Days."

"What?"

"Seven Days. That's what everyone calls him. He's always been wound tight, kind of tilted, you know—worse since his Dad got killed in that Myers thing." The speaker emphasized the end of his statement.

"His last name is Grace," another voice supplied.

Seven Days Grace? Planchette crouched by the pod doorway. Thaddy sat rigid against the far window, gripping the edge of his seat, fixed on the pod's other occupant. The latter person regarded Planchette with fear, defensively pointed a sheet at him. It wasn't much of a weapon but in a frenzy he might hurt someone with it. He hadn't shaved in days and reeked of sweat and alcohol. Morph reported an elevated heart rate and incipient hyper-ventilation. The man wasn't wearing a hat; his hair was a black, greasy tangle. Planchette could tell he was delusional.

"People call you Seven Days?" Peripherally, Planchette caught Thaddy's glance. The sense of connection with the boy returned.

The wild-eyed man stiffened. "Street fish call me Mr. Grace."

"All right, Mr. Grace, what's the trouble?"

"This boy. He shouldn't be riding these lines. Nobody should be riding with him, neither."

"I see."

"He got the Death on him."

"The Death."

Seven Days nodded. "The old mark from beginning times. What brought the ruin, and everything that's followed. Pops told me about the Death—" he inclined his head toward Thaddy—"and there it sits."

Planchette modulated his tone to be both accommodating and more authoritative. "That's a serious matter, Mr. Grace. You were right to bring it to our attention. You'll agree the best thing now is to get the boy off of the pod and away, so everyone's safe."

Seven Days drew his head back. It seemed he might cooperate, but then, in the slow, deliberate manner of the deranged, he shook his head. "I know what you're trying to do. You'll treat me up and set him loose. You don't believe me."

"I'm only interested in everyone's safety, Mr. Grace. Yours included."

"I'm not letting him go 'lest you take it properly."

"Help me understand, Mr. Grace."

"What you need help? You got to *kill* it, Fish! Or you got to b-bind him, gag him, and blind-blindfolded him. Leave it to the wasteland."

"Detective?" said a voice behind Planchette. Seven Days looked up and his fear melted into dread. Planchette noticed the boy react similarly.

He straightened to face a man in a flowing black greatcoat and black-enameled pillbox hat. The latter, Spoon informed him, was the identifying dress of a high-ranking Psycho-technician, an officer of P.C.'s enforcement branch. His eyes were deep set, his round, chinless face devoid of expression. He smelled of some sickly sweet scent. Planchette read meanness beneath a veneer of composure. The crowd on the platform had thinned with his arrival. Those who remained drew back the way people do around bullies with authority.

The P.A. was clearly accustomed to his presence instilling fear. When Planchette did not react as expected, he became curious. "I'm noting your name and badge number, Detective." The man had good voice control. Nowhere near as good as Willbury's but the training was plain.

Planchette drew his chin in. "And you are?"

The P.A. became irritated. "Myron Birns, Psycho-technical Agent Major. This is a behavioral disturbance, Detective. P.C. has providence."

Graph conveyed that Agent Major was a rank roughly equal to Planchette's. "How'd you find out about it?" Planchette asked.

P.A. Birns gave Planchette a re-appraising look. "I received a go-to-scene from Processing. I am here to take the perpetrators into custody for treatment and counseling."

"Perpetrators? The boy hasn't done anything."

"That will be determined pending evaluation."

"I've made the determination."

"You have no authority. No crime has been committed here."

"Really? How about reckless endangerment, unlawful restraint, endangering a minor, interference with public transportation, kidnaping—shall I go on?"

"Those are exaggerated interpretations of circumstance—"

"They're the interpretations I'm going with unless you leave the boy out of it."

Birns held Planchette's gaze, clenched his lips and gave a minuscule nod. Planchette stepped aside.

Birns crouched by the pod door, placing his left hand on the roof. "Not taking our court-prescribed medication, Mr. Grace? A little confused, are we?"

"I—no! I'm not con—"

Birns rapped on the roof of the pod. Seven Days looked up, startled.

"Do you want me to stick a candlestick or a green banana up your ass?"

Planchette rolled his eyes. Birns had the delicacy of a drunk in a daisy field.

Seven Days' head nearly vibrated with fright and bewilderment. "I don't—what? No! I don't want no—"

Through the grate of the platform floor, Planchette spotted something on the ground below.

"Seventeen, forty-eight—" Birns counted aloud randomly, tapping counter-rhythm on the pod roof, beckoning Thaddy with his right hand.

Set in the sidewalk directly under the transit platform was a broad pair of iron maintenance doors. A fragment of multi-colored cloth fluttered, caught between them. The grazer had advanced past the Y intersection and was mere yards from sucking it to oblivion.

"Sixty-five, eighty-seven, three—"

Seven Days, in an immobilized state of disorientation, looked back and forth between Birns and the boy. Birns kept counting, pulled Thaddy from the pod and handed him off, behind his back, to Planchette, then boarded the pod and closed the door. The pod departed the platform. A few people clapped.

The boy looked up at Planchette with a mien beyond his years—clear as purest water the readiness to receive, the recognition that Planchette had something to give. Planchette looked down at the cloth fragment. The grazer was only a few meters from it. He noticed Dunn bringing the cruiser down on the side street, called her.

"Stop the grazer!"

"What?"

"The grazer! Right below me! It's about to destroy—" The grazer lurched forward over the cloth fragment. Planchette sucked his teeth. "Never mind." He clicked off.

Thaddy was gone. Planchette whirled, found the boy looking back at him through the window of a departing pod.

Chapter Twenty

Sunset tinted the city red. The immobilized grazer hunkered with its back open about sixty meters past the transit platform. Sealed in a protective suit, a roustabout from the Department of Surfaces rummaged through its traps. Two co-workers leaned against a maintenance vehicle nearby, talking. In the passenger seat of a forensic van parked in front of them, an idle young technician sat sideways with the door open, gazing at nothing. His partner, a brusque, stout, middle-aged woman, knelt on the iron utility doors, examining with a magnifying scanner the place where Planchette had seen the cloth fragment. On-lookers had gathered, here and there.

Dunn walked over from their cruiser.

"Get a back-up unit out here," Planchette told her.

She handed him something tube-shaped, wrapped in paper. "It's a food roll," she answered his look. "Grilled vegetables, rice, soy protein, wrapped in flatbread. It's got a little sauce that I like. It's good."

The roll was warm and soft. Planchette peeled back the paper and bit into it. The mixed flavors were another shock but he was too beset to care. "Thaddy Myers," he said, chewing.

"Thaddy Myers?"

"He was in the park, last night. I want to talk to him."

"I ... don't think he talks, sir."

"Then I want him to not talk to *me*. He's a possible witness and we need to find him." He took a couple of more bites, wadded up the remains of the roll, gave it back to her.

She held out a plastic vial with an attached straw. "It's time to take the supplements, again."

Planchette eyed the vial, unsure the fluid it contained was a color he wanted to associate with sustenance.

"It's citrus," she said.

He popped two capsules in his mouth, sucked on the straw. He thought his face would explode. He swallowed the pills, coughed convulsively. "I think—water?" he wheezed.

She hurried back to the cruiser and brought him some. He loved water. He loved water. He drained the vial.

"I can't find anything," the C-tech told him. "Those grazers are thorough."

Planchette gave his head a clearing shake. "You might get something when we open it." He wiped his eyes, found Dunn beholding the wonder of him. "What are we doing?" he asked her.

"Uh, waiting. It's a pod service bay. For some reason we need clearance to open it. They're getting somebody. Supposedly. It's like right doesn't know left."

Planchette called Processing.

"Handler 42, Ganeel. Yes, Detective?"

"Officer Natalie Dunn," he told the handler, "is my personal assistant. Any application she makes regarding the current enquiry is to be treated as if I'd made it myself. Is that clear?"

"I ... yes, Detective. Is there—"

Planchette clicked off. He went to the middle of the street, looked back and forth between the alley entrance and the maintenance doors. The killer could have come from the service bay. It would explain how the cloth fragment caught where it had. But the doors could only be opened remotely from the Transit Authority's control center, or by someone already down in the bay.

Or by someone extraordinarily strong. Planchette rubbed his lips. *He* could do it, probably. He didn't like where the thought took him.

He went to a group of onlookers. "You people live around here?"

They all nodded.

"Have any of you noticed anything unusual happening around

this transit stop in the last few days? Last night in particular."

They looked at each other, shook their heads. A tall man in a grey flat cap drifted over. "Do you mean the explosion?"

"That wasn't last night," said a woman in blue overalls.

"You said the last few days," the tall man said.

"It wasn't an explosion," said an elderly man.

"What are you talking about?" Planchette asked him.

"Underground," the old man said. "There's a transit bay down there. Something collapsed."

"It sounded like an explosion," said the man in the flat cap.

"Were you questioned about it?"

The old man nodded.

Planchette looked at the others and they nodded too. He asked if they had been questioned about the homicide and they all nodded again, except for the tall man.

Planchette went back to Dunn. "That thing Schnitke's investigating—something about sabotage at a transit facility—find out where that is."

The roustabouts came over. The one in the suit took his hood off. "Everything in the traps is pretty much atomized, Detective," he told Planchette. "I didn't find anything like what you described. You want me to give the catch to your guys?"

"Ask them." Planchette pointed at the C-techs lingering by their van.

Dunn nodded; "It's here." She handed her sheet to Planchette.

Planchette scanned his badge with it.

"Detective Chron?" the handler asked.

"Speaking." The streetlights came on.

"Okay, yeah, you're there, Detective."

"This is the station?"

"You're standing right on top of it."

Planchette clicked off, called Perls on his own sheet. "Door-to-door missed some people this morning. We need uniforms back here to clean up."

"Already happening," Perls said. "I'm tracking down that mural project. Sponsored by a philanthropic organization called the Temple Trust. Membership anonymous, big shock. They didn't know they'd try that on me."

"Someone from P.C. had to grant Olivetta an indulgence," Planchette said.

"Yeah, give me a minute, I just started."

Planchette filled him in on his situation.

"You think the two cases are related?" Perls asked.

"It's looking like they might be. Can you get hold of Schnitke, have him cut the damn tape? I want to get down there."

"I'll cut it myself."

Ten minutes later the maintenance doors butterflied open. A transit engineer rode a platform that rose between them. The C-techs spotted a brightly colored something on the inside edge of the left door, scrambled to collect it. Planchette followed. It looked like a piece of the same fabric. He waited for the backup unit to arrive, gave them instructions to secure a perimeter around the maintenance doors, then boarded the platform with Dunn. The engineer introduced himself as Martin, took them down; the retracted halves of the magnetic chute and lifters that transferred pods to and from the tracks came into view, right and left. Stars shone in the receding rectangle of sky. The service bay was cavernous and dimly lit. Machine noise clattered and crackled from the depths.

The platform locked into alignment with a metal catwalk. "The elevator's gone," Martin told them, his large face indistinct in the dimness. He had shoulders like matched rocks. "We have to walk down."

He led them to a vertiginous zig-zag of stairs. They descended through shadowy ranks of pods that hung from rails in tiers. A smell of ozone drifted on the stale air. There are forty-two pod service and transfer facilities like this situated about the city, Twelve conveyed. The cant of the space curved right; the site of damage came into view. Several tiers of suspension rails were broken, torn down, bent apart. At the bottom, transit engineers and C-techs cut with torches into a giant tangle of wreckage. Schnitke stood on a landing, overseeing the effort. He did not turn when Planchette and Dunn reached him.

"Word came down the hard line to let you in. How come?"

"You haven't talked to Perls?"

Schnitke didn't respond.

Planchette gave himself a breath. "Because your case and ours might be related, and it's gotten too complicated to worry about who's pissing downhill."

Schnitke nodded; "Go on."

"Trail from our crime scene leads here. Seems to. It's possible the perp may have been down here last night, sometime before committing the murder."

Schnitke looked at him. His eyes tracked in thought. "See what we got;" he beckoned them to follow him. "This wasn't a bomb," he said, leading them farther downstairs. "You can tell just looking, and there's no explosives residue." He twirled his hand overhead, indicating the city above. "The system's maxed out. Big push to get expansions online but they ran out of rail. Foundries up north are backed up. Most of what's damaged was temporary, gurney-rigged to keep things moving." He pointed straight up. "The hit was perfect, probably an inside job. Something pulled down hard on the guy rods holding up the cobbled-together stuff. Mooring pins came loose—" he pointed side to side at spots high on the walls—"the rest fell like it was dumped—everything attached or in the way."

The tangle of cage rail, angle iron, rubble, mashed pods, cable and conduit occupied the floor of the bay in a giant heap. Wrecked pods that had been separated from the pile were stacked against a wall. Behind and in front of the mess, a pre-cataclysm subway tunnel had been reclaimed and transfer rails installed in the ceiling. Planchette noticed that a cross-tunnel had once existed on a higher level. To the left the opening was walled off; to the right, directly above them, it appeared open but was barricaded and there was no access stairway or ladder.

Planchette summarized events that had led him here.

"I love it when everything makes sense," Schnitke said. "I'm sitting on my thumbs down here 'cause I'm sick of chasing buttons." He gestured at the cutting crew. "Took 'em four days to get to that. Had to clear all the hanging shit. I got no leads. I'm trying not to hope whoever did this is mashed under there, somewhere."

Dunn pointed at gashes in the side of one of the wrecked pods. "That looks like claw marks."

Schnitke chuckled. "Ever see claw marks?"

Dunn opened her mouth, closed it. "I don't know."

"Yeah, well I thought the same thing, and then we found tracks."

"Tracks?" Planchette said.

Schnitke chuckled again. "Yeah, like a bear or something. I got this zoologist, or whatever, down from the college. He says they're fake. Somebody's fuckin' with us, trying to make it look like a giant lizard did this."

"A bear isn't a lizard," Dunn said.

"I've never seen one and they're probably extinct; what do I know? They're not hanging out in the tombs under New York City."

Martin, who was swapping out acetylene tanks for a cutting crew, overheard. "It's an old myth," he interjected.

"What is?" Planchette asked.

"Goes back Pre-C," the engineer said. "Like five hundred years. Alligators under New York."

"Alligators?"

"You ain't heard the story? These nackered storks bring baby alligators to a bunch of mothers by mistake. The mothers flush 'em down the toilet but they live. Alligators under New York."

"What's a stork?" Dunn asked.

Graph conveyed that there was indeed such a legend, though versions differed wildly. Twelve, who had been measuring and calculating the logistics of the damage, conveyed to Planchette that the initiating force might have come from above.

"What's up there?" Planchette pointed at the barricaded tunnel.

"Ghost tunnel," Schnitke said. "It's been stabilized but it's abandoned. Grazers don't go down there."

"Well—" Planchette let the word hang.

"I checked it out," Schnitke said.

"How far?"

"Long ways." Schnitke grinned sourly. "Didn't see anything."

"What were you looking for?"

Schnitke peered aside. "Be my guest." He gestured at Martin, who brought around a wheel loader with a boom and bucket.

"We got no reception down here;" Schnitke tapped Planchette's sheet. "Pay attention to the time. I don't hear from you more than an hour I gotta send somebody."

Planchette nodded. Dunn and he boarded the bucket with Martin, who took them up. Schnitke watched with his hands on his hips, shrank below. Planchette and Dunn climbed over the concrete barricade, turned on their flashlights.

The engineer handed Planchette a coil of fingernail-sized transmitters. "These are stringers," he said. "Line-of-sight they got a range of maybe a thousand feet. You know, don't stretch that. But you turn a corner, go up or down, play it safe and use three—one before, one after, and one dead center. You snap them off—" Martin broke a transmitter off of the end of the coil— "squeeze it—" he pinched the unit between his thumb and forefinger and a blinking green light came on—"see that?—then hold it to the wall until you feel it grab." The engineer demonstrated. "You get into trouble, enter one-one-nine-dash on your sheet. That links your signal. Got it?"

"One-one-nine-dash." Planchette pocketed the coil.

This tunnel was smaller than the restored one. The old rails were gone—probably pulled for salvage. The bed was littered with dust and debris.

Planchette felt Dunn stop behind him. "What's the matter?" He shined his light at her.

She shielded her eyes. "Nothing."

How many uncertain passageways would she follow him down before this was over? Only to learn she'd been deceived. Do not take her for granted, he told himself. "Do you want me to get someone else—"

"No," she said firmly.

They moved on. There were smear and drag marks in the dust on the rail bed. Not like the wavy impressions that had led him here. A couple of hundred feet in he spotted marks that *were* like those he'd found in the alley. He shined his flashlight up the walls, along the ceiling.

Dunn studied something else. In a thick accumulation of dust was an impression that could have been the footprint of a large animal.

"Does that look fake to you?" she asked.

Planchette squatted to examine the impression. It was more than twice as large as his hand. If it was a footprint, the creature that had made it was huge. But it was indistinct, could have been anything. "I'm not sure what it is." He looked up at Dunn. "It doesn't worry me."

She held his gaze, nodded.

Planchette angled his light back down the tunnel, moved on. The air was dank and musty. They reached a place where reinforcement struts had been installed. Faint mechanical rumbles reverberated through the walls. Beyond the struts the floor was cracked and uneven. Planchette spotted the wavy tracks again. Near them, a streak of light-colored fluff had adhered to an upthrust edge of broken concrete.

Planchette beckoned Dunn. She crouched beside him, joined her light with his.

"That looks like—"

"The stuff we found by the crime scene. I've got bags. You bring gloves?"

She sighed. "Of course not. Why would I do that?"

"I didn't either. Go back and get some. Gloves, markers, the lot."

Dunn hurried off.

Planchette welcomed the return to solitude. He could feel the mnemonic patch thickening again. It will continue, Morph conveyed. We will help you reduce it as we can. At least Planchette knew he still had his memories, whether or not he could access them. He'd lost all sense of what trail he was following, what line of reasoning. You are following evidence, Morpho conveyed. Evidence, yes. Was there ever a less assuring guide? *Look here, look here, be true to what you find, though the unknown close about you from all sides*—More anonymous verse from Graph. Again unhelpful.

Like a neglected rest note, an embarrassment, a pause between thoughts in which the thread of volitional consciousness escapes grasp, a presence that he should have noticed sooner caught his attention. Planchette looked both ways down the tunnel, saw no one.

"*Gascot!*" a voice called faintly. An auditory phantom this time, he thought, echoing from a misfiled life. The shapes were mute, hesitant. He played the light along the walls, every bump, crack, stain, shift in coloration acutely distinct, the motes within the beam as well, the nimbus bordering its circle, the gradations of darkness to the back of his mind. "*Gascot!*" the voice called again. The shapes reacted, this time. It was no hallucination. Planchette lurched forward; it seemed to come from ahead. He stumbled on the broken pavement, ran. "Gascot!" the voice called a third time.

He stopped and looked up at a ventilation grill in the ceiling. "Frisa?" Why was he afraid?

"Gascot!"

He recognized her! Not the voice, which must be new, but the texture of her inner self. "I'm here, Frisa! Where are you? I'll come to you!" Within recognition was a distortion he did not know.

"Gascot! Why did you leave me?"

Leave her. Planchette stared at the grate. Leave *her?* "Frisa, tell me where you are!"

"Why did you abandon me, Gascot?" Her voice was fainter. She was moving away!

"Frisa! Help me find you!" He ran down the tunnel, strained his senses. "I never left you! I woke up and you were gone! Frisa!" The patch was in the way. The patch, *again!* Help me! he pleaded with the shapes. You must calm yourself, they conveyed. "Frisa! Don't go!" He rounded a curve and met a wall of rubble, fell against it. *"NO!"*

She was gone—warmth, purpose, fellowship, all. Gascot slumped to his knees in shock. She'd been there. She'd been right there, somewhere through the walls, through the wretched density of matter that had cooled to form this world. And then it came upon him—horror—the knowledge that he had made a choice. In some infinitesimally minuscule moment he'd made a choice to remain human, to not abandon his life, this life, and pursue her. He did not know how to live with that choice.

She had run from him. He pulled off his hat and rested his forehead against ruin. "Come back." He had no defenses left. "Please." He groaned for the ending of worlds.

Chapter Twenty-one

¼=ca.85 had often thought, in the course of his prior existences, that people would do better to approach life as an experiment than to invest it, as was the common wont, with hopes and desires and aspirations. He knew that, for many, the unknown was the biggest obstacle they faced. It was an invisible monster that turned the gregarious reclusive, the bold meek, and supplied repressive ideologies and beliefs with unassailable rationales. He had viewed their circumstances with tolerance and bemusement, and saw now that he had been arrogant, or perhaps disingenuous. For him, the unknown had always brimmed with purpose. Now, as it clouded with futility, he saw how an attitude of experimentation could be taken too far, ever venturing the toe, never risking the foot, let alone the whole being, like someone too skittish or timid to love. He had not lived like that, he told himself. He had not been aloof, had brought the whole of himself to his relations with others.

Always knowing, with perfect certainty, that his life had meaning, that its purpose was pre-ordained, and that the one he was living would not be his last.

Schnitke crouched behind the C-tech he had brought with him, peered at the fibrous fluff Dunn and Planchette had found. Dunn held a light while the C-tech bagged samples.

Schnitke looked up at Planchette. "Someone shit in your soup?"

Planchette raised his eyebrows an implacable increment.

Schnitke returned to the fluff. "Tough guys," he muttered.

Dunn said something under her breath that made both Schnitke and the C-Tech draw back.

"How far?" Planchette asked.

Schnitke frowned at Dunn, looked at Planchette. "What?"

"You said you checked this tunnel. How far did you go?"

"What are you asking?" Schnitke stood up.

"Those fibers kind of stick out. Did you make it here?"

Schnitke grimaced and sniffed. "One day in this town, you're calling me lazy or incompetent, which is it?"

"How about both?"

"You shouldn't be too sure where everybody's lines are."

Planchette would have welcomed a punch in the face. "You said you went down this tunnel a long ways. How far?"

"At least half a mile past here."

"Three hundred feet it's completely blocked."

Schnitke stared at Planchette. He pushed by and strode down the tunnel. Planchette followed, surrendering to motion, the next immediate thing, better than keeping still, though either way his mind was a burden. The tunnel, grey and impenetrable, was a dreary echo of something he'd never understood, still didn't, couldn't any longer avoid. Past the bend he found Schnitke incredulous.

"It was open—" Schnitke glared at Planchette—"this was *not* here."

Planchette played his light over the rubble. The collapse could have been recent.

"Wait a minute—" Schnitke hurried back down the tunnel.

Planchette followed again, at a leaden gait. The shapes flanked him with the solemnity of pallbearers.

Schnitke passed Dunn and the C-tech, continued to a maintenance door in the shorn-up section of the tunnel. The door was hidden by reinforcement struts and a chest-high square of sheet metal someone had leaned in front of it. "You should've checked this," Schnitke muttered at himself. Planchette helped him move the metal square aside. Schnitke tried the handle, kicked the door and fell down. Planchette helped him to his feet, for which he received a scowling brush-off.

The next hour was interminable. Schnitke brought tunnel-workers and another C-tech up to look at the cave-in, told them he wanted to know how and when it happened. Another team went to work on the locked door with a couple of spreaders and a breaker hammer. Planchette's ruminations were recursively elliptical. What Frisa had said was poison, what she hadn't said bottomless. He imagined interactions in which he might justify himself, or she explain—empty fantasies that worsened the hurt. He had never felt resentment towards Frisa. It was an ailment, like his blood had become acid, and the only cure was to tear himself apart. This was no time for riddles and ambiguities. Guessing games!

The door was stubborn but they split the hinges and moved it out of the way. "I want to know if it's been opened recently," Schnitke told the C-tech.

Planchette slipped by them into a defunct maintenance hallway on the other side. The air was redolent of old concrete. He could feel Frisa's trace. She had spoken to him from here, somewhere. He headed down the passage.

"Sir?" Dunn hurried to catch up.

"Hey!" Schnitke called from the doorway, "where do you think you're going?"

Planchette kept going. Schnitke jogged after him, grabbed Planchette by the shoulder. Planchette squared to face him.

"What the fuck is *with* you?" Schnitke demanded. "This is *not* your case!"

"Which one?"

Schnitke was a beat late answering. "Down here *I'm* lead."

"So lead," Planchette said.

"Oh, man." Schnitke leaned back in restraint. "Let me have those stringers Martin gave you." Planchette handed them over. Schnitke went back to the doorway, wagging his finger.

"Sir, are you all right?" Dunn asked.

"I'm fine."

Schnitke returned, without speaking passed Planchette and Dunn and proceeded down the passage. Their footfalls rippled into darkness. It was too narrow to walk three abreast. Dunn shone her flashlight over Schnitke's left shoulder, Planchette his right. Reflections on cement joints made glowing concentric rectangles into the distance.

They went a couple of thousand feet before Schnitke stopped. "This isn't following the train tunnel. It should have curved way back there."

Planchette moved in front.

"What are you doing?" Schnitke asked.

"Investigating," Planchette answered.

"Yeah? For instance?"

"Give me back the stringers you don't want to come."

"I'll go with you," Dunn volunteered.

Schnitke squinted at Planchette. "Okay, setting aside you don't know this city at *all*—"

"You know these tunnels?" Planchette asked.

"I know there's hundreds of miles of them, about two percent of which have been checked out. And those had very serious problems—"

"We should only go where it's safe, that's what you're saying?"

"This isn't about testicle size, boyo. We get into trouble down here, people have to come *get* us. This is a job for the tomb rats. Let 'em put a crew together, give 'em a couple of uniforms, see if the City Engineer's office maybe has *maps*—"

Planchette groaned. He wanted to mangle Schnitke. Sketchy counsel Graph gleaned from the Cloud indicated that this passageway led to regions as yet unexplored by re-colonizers. Frisa's trace was coming apart like decomposing gauze; Planchette was desperate to keep moving. If he took off on his own it could compromise him in ways he might rue later. "The evidence led us here—"

"*I* led us here."

"After Dunn and I *found* evidence—"

"In the *other* tunnel—"

"You weren't looking for a killer until we showed up. You think I'm off my leash down here because your buddy Perls likes me? He respects my instincts."

"With good reason," Dunn slipped in.

"I've had all I want from you tonight, Dunn." Schnitke rubbed the back of his neck. "We give this another half an hour, come up blank, we head back, right?"

Planchette privately reserved his options, but nodded to get them moving. He noticed an access panel overhead. They must have passed others. He hadn't paid attention.

Frisa's trace continued to fade. If it got much thinner Planchette would have to run to keep track of it, giving rise to questions he couldn't answer. An old memory peaked, like a point at the center of everything. Oldest of the old—the first time he'd seen Frisa. The memory was hazy; Planchette strained against the re-thickening mnemonic patch. Her birth, it was, moments after his own, like an answer to the bewilderment with which he had awakened. He'd had no depth perception, then somehow understood that he was in a vast space, with thousands of eyes upon him. The eyes of elder beings, all of whom expected something from him. It was terrifying. But then, close by, two more eyes, on sleek, white stalks, rose from the amniotic bath to meet his. Very close, hardly a pseudopod-length's distant. Thus had _=ca.110 arrived to ¼=ca.85's inimitably nascent existence and rendered calm. Planchette had no idea how long ago that had been.

The trio came to another door, set in the right-hand wall. It, too, was locked, but had not weathered the years so well as had the one through which they'd entered the passageway. It was pitted with rust along its right and bottom edges. Planchette put his foot on the jamb and yanked on the handle, letting his core contribute force. The handle ripped loose. Dunn and Schnitke cried out in surprise. Planchette worked his fingers in the hole, pried and prodded the latch mechanism, got the door open. A long stairway led down. Frisa's trace was stronger.

Planchette didn't wait for consensus, started down, heard Dunn follow.

"Oh, we're going here, now—" Schnitke hurriedly placed stringers, grousing.

The stairway went straight down a hundred steps or more. About halfway a scattering of human bones lay strewn, in a loose, disconnected suggestion of recline. The door at the bottom had a bar latch. Planchette kicked it open, sent a spray of water and a low wave arcing off, pursued by ripples.

He stepped into a high chamber—what appeared to be an old subway station. His feet were immediately soaked; the platform was submerged in about four inches of icy water. The air smelled of dank, mineral wetness, and a phantom animal rot. The platform's edge was described overhead by a stained glass valence, about half the panes of which were chipped or missing. Beyond stretched a cavernous space, result of a massive cave-in of indeterminate scope and origin. The void had flooded, creating a subterranean lake. Planchette shone his flashlight across the water. The beam cast a pale round on a rough wall several hundred feet distant. Fallen concrete forms or masonry—culverts or pillars, maybe—made a clot of white, oblong islands over there.

Dunn sloshed onto the platform, caught her breath. Schnitke followed, cursed, kept cursing. "Somebody tell me what I'm doing down here wrecking my shoes?" He shone his light into the cavern alongside Planchette's. "Oh, my life, what are we building on up there?"

Morph and Twelve flew off to reconnoiter the cavern's inner reaches. Frisa's trace was everywhere and nowhere. By the near end of the platform, where the opening of a train tunnel once existed, was a slope of rubble. At the other end the tunnel appeared intact. Flooded but passable, maybe. The platform was about three hundred feet long. Stairs led up through archways from both ends.

Planchette moved slowly across the platform. The submerged surface was uneven, strewn with a brittle material.

"What the hell are we walking on?" Schnitke said.

They'd stirred up silt, moving through the water, making it murky. Planchette caught glimpses of pale grey debris, here and there, couldn't tell what it was. Plaster or decomposed concrete, possibly, though it didn't have that texture. Frisa's trace was fading, dissipating, seeping into the ineffable firmament that the shapes inhabited. Its lack of directionality was disheartening. She had confused her trail on purpose. They passed concrete benches, trash receptacles, the tatters of moldered advertisements. Centered in the tile work on the long wall was a mosaic that once bore the station's name. 'East' something—most of the tiles had fallen.

Heaped against the far wall was an irregular line of low mounds. They got close enough to see what they were and Dunn inhaled sharply.

Piles of bones, among which several human skulls lay sightless. The material underfoot was revealed. Planchette caught Dunn looking down with distaste. As if compelled by unwitting desecration to bear witness, they continued to the bone piles.

"What happened here?" Schnitke more breathed than voiced. "Where the hell have you led us, Chron?"

"Is this Pre-C?" Dunn asked.

Planchette shook his head. "I don't know."

"This isn't skeletons lying around," Schnitke said. He picked up a broken skull. "They're all mixed up. It's like a dump site."

"They're not just human." Planchette shined his light on a small skull.

"What is that?" Schnitke bent to look.

Morpho conveyed identification. "Rodent, I think," Planchette said. Human remains were a small percentage of the mix. Watermarks striated the piles. "Looks like they were pushed together by the water, at some point." They had been here a long while. Very few of the bones, including the skulls, were intact. Most were broken and deeply scored, like they'd been crushed or mangled. Or chewed.

Morph and Twelve conveyed alarm from across the dark lake. Too late Planchette guessed what they'd found. The other shapes were incredulous. Schnitke met his gaze. He'd had the same thought.

"Detectives?" Dunn trained her flashlight on something halfway back across the platform that hadn't been there before. Something huge and white and spoiling with chaos.

Chapter Twenty-two

Planchette fired his O-bow before he knew he'd drawn it. A round of water by the alligator's head sank and plumed. The discharge's reverberations loosed tiles from the ceiling. The reptile flinched but kept coming. It was a monster, twenty feet long at least. Dunn and Schnitke fired and it reared up, stunned, one webbed foot raised, chest and under-jaw exposed.

"Reset," Planchette said. They flicked their safeties and fired again. The alligator flopped on its back, a rupture in its chest oozing black fluid.

"We need to get the fuck out of here." Schnitke started back across the platform.

"Not that way!" Planchette grabbed Schnitke by his arm and yanked his attention to the lake. The oblong islands Planchette had taken for pipes or pillars were on the move, now a deadly flotilla.

"Oh, my fucking mother," Schnitke moaned.

They would never make it to the maintenance stairway before the beasts in the water reached the platform. Planchette shined his light up the old commuter stairs to their right. Schnitke tried to place a stringer but Planchette pulled him on. "No time!" He checked his O-bow as they ran up. "Resets automatic." Schnitke and Dunn disengaged the safeties on their weapons.

They emerged onto a vast landing, the dimensions of which were not readily clear, shone lights on a domed ceiling, portals of passenger tunnels—three, four maybe—a hub of some kind. Abandoned—the portals were bricked up. The wall sealing the one diagonally across from them had been breached, the jagged gap big enough for both humans and alligators. Morph shot ahead and confirmed that the way was passable, at least initially. It was the only way to go.

They ran. Bones littered the floor everywhere. Wet slaps and hisses sounded from the other stairway. Their pursuers emerged, flesh translucent, eyes milked over, sightless, teeth bright as wire—

"Hold!" Planchette shouted. They fired until stunned alligators blocked the stairwell—not a barricade that would last long.

The old pedestrian tunnel was vaulted and brick-walled, sagging in places. Twelve, Spoon and Morph scouted ahead; Graph and Morpho hung back. Graph conveyed that the alligators had broken past the stairs and entered the tunnel. Planchette could hear them—claws on concrete, growing louder. Hatefully fast.

He checked his O-bow. "What's your charge?" he asked Dunn.

"Less than half."

"Schnitke?"

"Same."

They could fight the beasts off maybe twice more. Dunn was panting, hyperventilating. "Slow your breathing, Natalie."

Morpho cued Planchette. He told the others to turn. A riot of menace boiled up the passage at them, no telling how many there were. It was like shooting inside a bell. Mortar sifted from masonry; bricks fell. Planchette's ears throbbed with the reverberations. They kept firing until, again, the passage was blocked. One alligator slipped through, snapped at Dunn, missed, knocked her against the wall. She collapsed like a bird. Schnitke fired straight down on its head, point blank, cracked its skull. The burst echoed from the ceiling like a pile driver, knocked Planchette and Schnitke off their feet. They helped each other up. Planchette was completely deaf. They got Dunn upright, put their arms under her shoulders, ran on, carrying her between them.

Planchette knew he'd wanted this, something mindless to defy. He didn't like violence but he liked the clarity of peril—the defense of family—be the adversary storm or aggressor. He didn't have family, here. He had a partner, and he'd led her to hell.

They came to a T-intersection, where the portal had again been sealed and the wall broken through. The crossing tunnel had a flat ceiling and white-tiled walls.

Schnitke was breathing hard. "Which way?"

Planchette read his lips, had no idea. He thought maybe he sensed a hint of Frisa's trace. "Here;" he pointed his O-bow. They went right. The tunnel sloped upward. Graph conveyed that the alligators were coming again.

Save one, save them all. Frisa and he had defended offspring and mates on scores of worlds, always with that grand rationale vindicating them. The shapes were appalled at the turn of his thoughts: If he could not save the lives he should, he would save those he could. In some way that he had never been sure of anything before, Planchette knew he could not let Dunn die without losing a vital part of himself. *Save one, save myself.* Never had he served so narrowly his own need. Or maybe he had and not seen it.

The passage forked. The right tunnel was blocked, or nearly so. An accordion gate, drawn across the entry, bulged with debris from a cave-in on the other side. The left end of the gate was open a crack, and beyond a narrow defile. There was just enough room for a person, and not an alligator, to get through. Morph went in, didn't know what to advise.

Planchette left Schnitke with Dunn, edged through the opening. A terrible stench assailed his nostrils. He clung to the wall, climbed over cement scree. Not far in was a void in the rubble, about ten or twelve feet in diameter, beyond which the passage was entirely blocked. The floor of the open space was caked with a horrid accumulation of filth cris-crossed by the impossible wavy tracks he had encountered in the alley near Olivetta's mural. Frisa's trace was thick as fog, like it had soaked into the walls. There were bones, too. Not rat or human—reptile. Bones of baby alligators, some with flesh clinging to them. Planchette scrambled back out, repelled.

"It's a dead end," he told Schnitke.

"We can't hide in there?"

Schnitke's voice was muffled in mud; Planchette missed reading his lips. He guessed from his expression what he'd asked. "It's not stable," he lied. He was not going to linger in that wretched place.

He got Dunn's right arm back on his shoulders and Schnitke and he resumed their flight down the adjoining tunnel, which curved to the left. The ceiling was compromised all along, the floor strewn with fallen tiles, conduit, fluorescent light fixtures, mangled cosmetic panels, chunks of cement. Planchette doubted the debris would hinder the alligators as much as it was hindering them. He spied a rupture in the ceiling where a rough-edged rectangle of concrete was a nudge from breaking loose at one end. Not far beyond, lengths of pipe and conduit hung down. With reluctance Twelve made calculations.

The alligators were coming, Morpho conveyed. "Give me your shouter," Planchette told Schnitke.

"Why?"

Planchette heard the question faintly. "I've got an idea how to block the tunnel. You get her out of here."

"Bullshit."

"There's no time to argue. Give me your O-bow. Hers too."

Schnitke held his light on Planchette's face. He grimaced and handed over his O-bow, searched for Dunn's, muttered something.

Dunn's holster was empty; her O-bow was probably back where she'd fallen. Planchette gestured down the tunnel—"Get going—" returned to the hanging pipes, seized one, let his core connect and wrenched the segment free, advanced, aimed Schnitke's O-bow up and fired at the spot Twelve indicated. The hanging slab came loose from that end, amid much downfall of debris. A big chunk struck Planchette and he went down. He forced himself to his feet, dazed, wiped blood from his eyes. Schnitke tried to help but Planchette pushed him away. "Get going! Get out of here!" The loosened slab hung at a high angle from the re-bar in its other end. Planchette reached up and pulled, overrode the strain to his muscles and brought the slab low enough that he could lean against it, with an animal roar forced the re-bar to bend until the slab formed something of a wall. He wedged the pipe under it, put his shoulder under the pipe, just managing to set the barrier before alligators slammed into it from the other side. Planchette leaned hard into the pipe, felt his collar bone snap.

On the right an alligator forced its snout through. Planchette fired directly into its mouth with Schnitke's O-bow. The monster was blown back but its jaw clamped shut, taking the O-bow, and nearly Planchette's hand, with it.

Schnitke's muffled exclamation emanated from the bottom of a well. He was still there, gaping at Planchette.

"*GO!*" Planchette yelled. Schnitke scooped Dunn in his arms and took off. The alligators kept slamming into the slab from the other side, like they knew he couldn't stop them forever. The slab cracked, crumbled on its edges. *Save one, save them all.* She's not the one! the shapes wailed. She's the one I can save. You don't know that! You're giving up! Planchette promised to hold on as long as he could. It was all he could give them.

He felt a presence behind him, looked back and saw a figure, much taller than Schnitke. The figure looked human but Planchette could tell it wasn't. It hurried forward and put its weight against the slab, next to him, made strange noises, muffled in Planchette's still-impaired hearing. The noises were vaguely familiar but the patch was so thick Planchette had no hope of understanding any language he had learned in another life. The only thing comprehensible was that this creature regarded its communications as urgent.

Which was almost laughable, in the circumstances. The slab was coming apart; in moments the beasts would break through. Planchette reached into his mind and ripped the patch off. The milk of memory flooded about him, hallways and tunnels from scores of worlds. He searched through the accompanying auditory morass for the voice of the being next to him, found it, searched his elder memories for the linguistic source. It was Tehfoloran—not any dialect Planchette understood. Some variant, maybe, that had evolved in the millennia since his time on that world.

The Tehfoloran kept repeating something that Planchette began to think he should understand. In some way that he didn't, it didn't make sense. It was plain the alien wanted Planchette to save himself. With insistent gestures it signed that it would preserve the barrier until Planchette reached safety. How the Tehfoloran would survive itself was not apparent.

It went against Planchette's nature to let anyone sacrifice themselves for him. The shapes pleaded with him. Their world's fate was in his hands. Whatever had happened to Frisa, whatever else was going on, none of it could be solved without him.

Somewhere through the roaring maul of memories, the Tehfoloran did something to its face. It tore a mask aside, locked on Planchette with its compound eyes, and, for an instant, Planchette saw the person—male, he was, tough and seasoned—the way strangers can sometimes know each other without speaking. He perceived the profound sincerity with which the Tehfoloran was desperate for him to survive.

Planchette let the Tehfoloran take the pipe. With the release of pressure his pains assailed him. He had overridden stress with will and the exertion of his core. Now body consciousness returned. He went a few steps and dropped to hands and knees, crawled until his hand touched something soft that seemed unaccountably important. Even with the flashlight he couldn't see what it was. In a bubble of delirium, he ran his hands over the torn and dented ruin of his hat, forced it onto his head. The Tehfoloran was screaming at him. Planchette couldn't understand but made out alligator snouts around the edges of the concrete slab. He got up and stumbled down the tunnel, careened from wall to wall, near blind, the pain in his shoulder excruciating. He thrashed at hallucinations in search of the legitimate world. The light of his flashlight had a distinguishable character. He focused on that, went faster.

An explosive roar burst behind him, and the tunnel filled with dust, blinding him further, making him choke and cough. He ripped a piece from his shirt and held it over his mouth, stumbled, fell, stumbled, and on. He did not know how long he went before he sensed movement ahead. Other lights shone toward him, police officers, Schnitke among them. Arms supported him, bore him onward. Faster, now, they went a long ways, came at last to stairs that led above ground. The fresh, night air was a bath of grace. Planchette had an impression of a vacant lot, emergency vehicles, personnel milling about. He was drowning in ghosts. He fought them, searched for Dunn. She sat in the back end of an ambulance, conscious, a blanket over her shoulders. She saw him, tried to get up. A med tech pressed her down.

Planchette was helped to a gurney, coaxed to lie down. He made out Schnitke pacing nearby, talking on his sheet. "Yeah, I want to talk to that clown we had down here from the college. Professor Dickhead, whatever his name was. Yeah, find him, have him call me." To the paramedics tending Planchette he said, "You take care of him, right? Crazy son-of-a-bitch saved my life. And hers." He pointed at Dunn. "We should be dead. We should be dead, we should be dead." He leaned over Planchette. "Pull it together, Pal. I need you to come tell me I'm an asshole. Got my chin ready for you."

Planchette couldn't speak. He couldn't fight the ghosts any-more. His memories took him like a sea, an ocean risen from his very self. Somewhere there, in a trench of insanity, Frisa fed on baby alligators.

Chapter Twenty-three

Frisa watched Gascot's fellow officers bear him down the tunnel to safety. The lights of their flashlights shrank to a wavering mote and were swallowed by darkness. She ached to go after him, to comfort and be comforted. Even in her incomplete body the yearning was physical. She needed him.

She was so deeply tired of needing him.

She lowered herself to the floor, stayed a moment catching her breath. She was hungry and thirsty. The way back to the alligators' cave was blocked, she was sure. How Gascot had accomplished that she did not know. Explosives were not likely standard issue to law enforcement in present day New York. He had always been resourceful.

With her new-old eyes she could see in infra red. A rat dashed across the passage into a narrow side tunnel. Rodents were even less savory fare than reptiles, but it would have to do. Her sense of taste, mercifully, was rudimentary. It was the texture she found repellant.

She drew Olivetta's long knife and hurried after the creature. In the side tunnel she took to the left wall, spotted the rat rummaging in a mound of rubbish, got ahead of it, swooped down and ended its life with a swift, clean stroke.

After feeding she was thirstier. She searched for a pipe she could access. The first she found was a sewage line, no parallel water line anywhere. The infrastructure of this city was exasperatingly random.

She kept searching, found a water pipe and followed it down two maintenance tunnels without encountering a valve. Above a pile of rubble a breach in the ceiling revealed stars and a crooked surround of tenements. The last time she had ventured above ground some shapes had spotted her and she'd had an awful time getting away from them.

Thirst drove her to take the risk. Climbing the jagged rubble hurt. The cool, fresh air, though, felt good on her malformed flesh. She scanned the sky for shapes, saw none and ventured out, found herself in a vacant lot between multi-storied buildings composed of disparate materials. The one on the right seemed held upright entirely by a web of cables. Lights were on in both.

She found a stand pipe, with much wrestling managed to unscrew the plug. The water was brackish but drinkable. She slaked her thirst and did not tarry before returning below ground. She went deep in the tunnel and collapsed against a wall.

She strove to focus her thoughts. She had assumed Gascot was avoiding her. She'd felt his presence on the other side of the hill before the bombing of London, but he'd kept his distance and then time-jumped, leaving her behind. She'd thought he had tired of her complaints, little though she had voiced them. But like her he'd been interfered with, only differently. His body was intact but his mind and senses were occluded. Her fears had been foolish. Their partnership was anchored by an organic accord inherent in their conception that rendered discord immaterial.

Really, though, she never had complained, only asked difficult questions. Her understanding of their composition was greater than his. He took his identity for granted, and she let him. It was not in his nature to need to understand, and understanding might dishearten him. She'd kept terrible knowledge to herself to preserve his naivete. She needed him to be naive, to be true and effective and selfless without knowing how barren of self he was.

They were not like the beings they helped. They did not possess psyches. A conspiracy of voices—a guided cacophony—supplied the fiction of their identities. That knowledge would have long since turned her cynical had it not been for Gascot. His fiction was so kind and unyielding, child-like, really, that it steadied her.

Undoubtedly its intended design.

Gascot believed in love and she let him. Knowing love to be a product of complex electro-chemical processes, in their case rendered inviolate by their creators, hence autonomic and beyond volitional influence, believe she did not. All that mattered was that he fathered offspring and she bore offspring. If love were required, perforce she loved. She squandered neither time nor energy on inconsequential emotions. The intellectual component of the message did not depend on them. Most of her recipients had been emotionally limited. For fellowship she relied on Gascot, never free of the irony in that dependency.

But they were separated, now, damaged and threatened, and his steadying warmth was unavailable. Denied even the fiction of love, Frisa could not deny its merits. Gascot's mind was compromised and could not be trusted to answer the dangers they faced. She was not sure that her own impairments were exclusively physical. As near as she could tell her mind was intact but uncertainty remained because her mind was not really hers, and her investigative efforts had thusfar been ineffectual.

She tried to think of Friedman's death as an accident. She wanted it to count for something, but desire summoned existential quandary. She had to accept the fiction of being someone to want anything, and without the stabilizing context of either a partner or a recipient, the fiction was insupportable. In her current state she was, if anything, more monster than person, and it was not a monster's place to exact retribution.

Or perhaps that was exactly a monster's place. Or maybe she had always been a monster. She was too aware that these were not her thoughts; they were the thoughts of half of an artificial mind trying to function as a whole. 'Her' 'mind' did not function well, focused inward. She strove to train it outward on objective predicaments.

Haliel's behavior was bewildering. Without question he was being manipulated. Other off-world agencies were surely involved, and it seemed humans must be too, maybe even their shapes. A bizarre conspiracy had coalesced around Gascot and her.

The shapes accompanying Gascot seemed to be functioning as his aides, which was also bewildering. Shapes had to have been responsible for the impairment of his mind. It would have made sense, thereafter, for them to pretend to help him, but these shapes weren't pretending. She'd confused her trace to throw them off but they hadn't recognized her pattern at all. Which meant that shapes were keeping things from each other, here—that factions had formed among them, which was inimical to their nature.

Gascot was in worse danger than he could possibly know.

Children, too, muted her cynicism, though viewed solipsistically that was also per design, hence illusory. Nevertheless, she longed to give birth, and resume the anchoring role of motherhood. She could not help it. And each time she learned more. If she could unravel how her creators had secured their own extinction, the genetics and chemistry of it, maybe she could make a child in their image, or render her own illusory personhood real—create a being who was its authentic progeny.

She needed Gascot for that, and he was unstable. She had to get to him before he came so much apart that he saw what he truly was.

Chapter Twenty-four

From a mechanistic standpoint, the perceptual schism between mind and body seems readily attributable to the relationship between different parts of the brain, adherence to belief in a spiritual self to fear of death. This characterization is neither satisfying (particularly not in rendering the impression of selfhood illusory) nor incontestably certain, a circumstance which confounds definitions of "proof."

—Rationale 12 E
Psychology Council Codex and Principles

Planchette could only surrender. He was aware of being injected with a pain suppressant, which his core neutralized autonomically. He was aware of being transported, of surgery performed on his shoulder, of the wound on his head being closed and bandaged. He saw none of it, heard none of it, surrendered, scrap at the mercy of storms. Eyes open or shut, scenes from his lives, layered indeterminately, swamped and thrashed his visual world, a mnemonic cacophony of sounds and voices attendant tidal roar. The disruption of his memory had impacted two of his senses, now. He was being forced, more and more, to regard his core as distinct from his humanity, his mind distinct from his body.

While medical personnel treated the latter, the shapes labored to mend his mind. Spoon stayed nearest the wound, smoothing human memories into place as the others identified and isolated them. This medicine the shapes invented in practice. Planchette had inflicted upon himself a psychic hemorrhage with no antecedent. It had precipitated a dispersion of micro-strokes in his human brain.

The din quieted, his vision cleared, the space for thought relaxed. The ghosts of his mates and children withdrew, taking with them a noisome hoard of acquaintances, and the indecipherable crush of over-lapping environments they inhabited. Planchette found himself in a hospital room, with wireless electrodes attached to his chest, wrist and head. His left arm was immobilized in a sling.

The lights were off, the only sources of illumination holo monitors and a dim fixture in the restroom. Walls and ceiling merged in womb-like contours. The room had no corners or hard angles—except for a trapezoidal plate-glass window to his right. The shutters were open; it was dark out. Twelve conveyed that it had been about three hours since they had returned above ground. Planchette's clothes hung on a rack opposite the foot of the bed.

He sat up, a complement of pains and stiffnesses making themselves known. He closed his eyes and breathed. Never had any construct he'd adopted been so tested this soon after its creation. He swung himself to face the window; in the dark menagerie of buildings visible, lights shone in few. The people who could not sleep, or were awake with purpose, their thoughts differed from those of their ancestors. Darkness weighed on the descendants of apocalypse like a caustic shroud, imbrued with the spectral ichors of mayhem. They brooded upon what had happened, could happen, still happened, and the existence of those, like Planchette and his colleagues, who served as deterrents. Before the cataclysm it had been different. One might hate or disregard the police, depending upon one's circumstances. Now it preyed on everyone—most, at least—that after all humanity had endured, and even though most dangerous sociopaths were identified before they could do harm, murder, rape and violence still happened, and police were still needed. It preyed on the police, as well.

He had been complacent without knowing it, for uncounted millennia. Everything had been so predictable, never deviating from the course he understood. So much that he had never considered had been thrust at him in the last twenty-four hours that just absorbing it, let alone answering it, seemed insurmountable. It was like starting over, trying to firm up, in a flash, a body grown flaccid through decades of neglect. In some fundamental way, he had failed Frisa. It seemed that, in order to reach her, to reclaim her esteem and deserve her renewal of faith in him, he would have to revisit every comfortable, familiar assumption, tear it down and rebuild himself.

His shoulder, surgery notwithstanding, was nearly healed. The gash in his scalp as well. His mind, with all its newfound vulnerabilities, seemed sound enough to function. The shapes gathered before him and weariness descended on Planchette as he felt their reproach. He had never developed relationships with shapes before. These had formed an attachment to him. He had no energy to contend with their criticism, justified or not. He had to stop thinking about Frisa, too. It invited despair. He needed to focus on solving mysteries, on healing and clearing his mind.

And yet he could not help thinking about her. Averse as he was to venturing below ground again, he yearned to resume his search for her. He knew, though, that even with the help of the shapes, it would be futile. If she did not want to be found he would not find her. His only hope of coaxing her into the light was to eliminate her reason for clinging to shadows.

He stretched his neck, fought off fatigue. Lying still in the throes of mnemonic fugue had not been restful. He wanted to fall back now and sleep in earnest. But there was something he needed to check before he could do that. He had to go back to the beginning.

He got out of the sling, gently worked his shoulder. Twelve cautioned him that removing the electrodes—'scarabs,' they were called, or more often 'scabs'—would draw the notice of medical staff. Planchette left them attached and pulled on his clothes. His badge, sheet and O-bow were missing, as was his hat. Someone had brushed his coat, and provided him with a clean, grey shirt.

He opened the door a crack and peeked out. To the right was a nurse's station—vacant, at present. Planchette poked his head around the jamb. The hall was empty, too. The hospital entrance was three floors down, Morph conveyed, elevators and stairs to the left. Planchette went in that direction, moving slower than he wanted to. This hospital was a plastic realm, the halls as undulant as his room. Twelve conveyed that the staff would also be alerted if the scarabs were borne beyond their transmission range, which was quite limited. As if on cue, an alarm sounded at the nurse's station. Planchette was far from steady on his feet but he picked up his pace. He rounded a bend, saw the elevators, one in use. A bell pinged and the up arrow lit. He lurched past to the door to the stairs, slipped through just as the elevator opened.

He stumbled against the railing and clung to it, the stairwell spinning and swaying below. He closed his eyes, slowed his breathing. The vertigo passed. He went down quickly as he could, holding onto the railing. The hall on the first floor was empty. Planchette heard low voices to the right, where he needed to go. He tucked in his shirt, smoothed his hair, mustered what composure he could. A short way along, the hall opened onto a reception area arranged with mismatched chairs and tables. A few weary-looking persons lingered there, none talking. To the right, facing the entrance, was a reception desk. A middle-aged woman behind it conversed quietly with a uniformed cop and an orderly. Planchette gave them a nod as he passed, did his best to walk a straight line. Their conversation stopped but he made it to the exit without incident. Sliding doors opened onto a broad avenue sparsely lit by ovoid lamps. An enclosed pedestrian bridge extended from above the hospital's porte-cochére to a four story annex across the street. The bridge met with a transit line and an enclosed platform on the other side.

Planchette, staggering like a drunkard, headed toward the platform. The medications he'd been given were affecting him more than he'd thought. Or maybe his body was just beat to crap.

He kept expecting ghosts to leak into his field of vision. When he neared the other side of the street, a small person emerged from the shadows beneath the stairs to the platform. Planchette found himself again in the presence Thaddy Myers, which was one thing too many to deal with. He wanted to question the boy but this was not the time.

Morpho conveyed that hospital staff were looking for him. Thaddy looked behind Planchette and frowned. The cop and the orderly who had been talking with the receptionist came out of the hospital. Thaddy gave Planchette a studying look and seemed to come to a decision. He bolted up the stairs. Planchette had no better option than to follow. The cop shouted, coming after him. Halfway up, Planchette got dizzy and had to stop. The cop's footsteps drew near. Planchette made himself climb the remaining stairs, went through the sliding door to the platform. An open pod waited, Thaddy on board. Planchette collapsed onto the opposite bench. Thaddy pointed to a stop on the route map posted above the door. Planchette wasn't sure what to do. He shook his head and focused on the map. This transit line connected with one that went where he needed to go, but the stop Thaddy pointed at was not a junction. The cop was almost up the stairs. Thaddy pointed insistently at the map. "Seventeen C," Planchette read in a croaking voice; "Bleaker and Vine." The door closed and the pod departed. The cop reached the platform, waved urgently at Planchette, talked on his sheet, receded in distance. This effort to evade interference was apt to be short-lived. A cruiser would find them with ease. Planchette's colleagues would not understand what he was doing, now. He had understood his circumstances too slowly, failed to recognize that he had been under attack from the start. He needed to know if the attack had one source or many.

At the next platform—not the one he'd indicated to Planchette—Thaddy pulled a cord by the door. The pod stopped and he got off, beckoned Planchette to follow. Apparently he had never meant them to go to Bleaker and Vine. Planchette half stumbled to street level, where Thaddy led him to a door that accessed an underground passage. Down more stairs they entered a narrow tunnel. The shapes made no objection but Planchette was less than thrilled to be subterranean again.

He followed the boy through the tunnel, then up to cross a bridge four stories above ground, and down through two more tunnels before they emerged near a platform Thaddy evidently found agreeable. Planchette had to rest several times along the way but his balance returned, and, more gradually, his strength. The platform was located on a narrow street beneath an indecipherable confusion of intersecting architecture. They hurried up and boarded a pod. With Graph's help, Planchette identified a stop on the map near the destination he sought. He spoke the stop's name and location. The pod got underway and Thaddy turned off the light. Planchette slumped back and sighed. The boy was smart, making them look like a vacant pod redistributing through the system.

Planchette and Thaddy watched each other in darkness. It was bewildering to Planchette, the relationships he was forming on this world. Except for Claire, they were all tangential or unrelated to his purpose. And then, perhaps not. Thaddy could serve as an alternate recipient for Frisa; Planchette was sure of it, now. Not for years, yet, but the potential was there. Frisa and he had always known that an indeterminate number of potential recipients existed on every world they visited. They just never sought beyond the first ones they encountered, nor questioned their fittingness or compared them with others. They never needed to.

"They say you don't talk. You can if you want."

The boy looked out the window. In profile and beshadowed, he gave the impression of someone decades older regarding the world with philosophical detachment. It was a defining aspect of being, the capacity to bear witness, to take in one's surroundings. The lay of the land, the changing horizon, mountains, moons, canyons and coliseums, distances born of mindless forces or wrought through the deliberate sculpting of space. Defined by individual perspective—I see thus, respond thus, want thus, fear thus. This vastness draws me, fills me with hope, humbles me, renders me insignificant. And in the dark goes deeper, for I perceive what is not there. Even ¼=ca.85 could not see as another, many as he had been.

They arrived at the chosen stop and disembarked. A few hundred feet to the left, from the bottom of the stairs, was the broad, triangular intersection where ¼=ca.85 had entered the collective time stream of this world and adopted a human construct. It was hard to believe that had been little more than a day ago. *Back where I started.* They reached the corner where the high rise with the bird-like profile stood. The windows in the beak-shaped addition at the top were dark, as was the entire building, and those nearby. The front entrance was not locked. Planchette looked at Thaddy. The boy seemed to understand what they were doing better than he did, which was impossible. But they had become a team, this night. Again Planchette felt an urge to bond with a human who was not his recipient.

"We need to talk, at some point."

Thaddy shrugged.

"I need you to answer some questions."

The boy regarded Planchette as if he were being tiresome, overstating the obvious. Planchette went inside the building, and now Thaddy followed.

The entry vestibule was small, passageways extending ahead and right. Dim light filtered in from the street. The elevator across a narrow hall was inoperable. A door to its right accessed a stairwell, pitch black inside. Planchette couldn't lead Thaddy up however many flights in total darkness, and didn't want to leave him. He understood his impulses less and less. He felt his coat pockets absently, discovered gloves, evidence bags, and his flashlight.

They climbed six stories to the top landing, entered a hallway. The hall was too long to be the floor Planchette sought. The shapes fanned out, located, at the near end of an adjoining hallway, another non-operative elevator that accessed a penthouse, but no stairs. Planchette went to the elevator and hunted around. He found a column of metal rungs on a wall. In the ceiling above was an access panel. He climbed, pushed open the panel, pulled himself through, lifted Thaddy. They were in a short passage with tall, double doors at one end.

Planchette hesitated, unsure what he would find here, or what he wanted to find. From his first moments in common time on this world, he had misinterpreted the importance of everything he had witnessed and felt. Horrible as his suspicions were, they would be worse confirmed.

The doors opened onto a large triangular space, still under construction, the floor bare fiberboard, metal studs of the walls exposed. Planchette recognized the row of windows where the woman had stood. He searched for a light switch, found only boxes with capped wires. No fixtures had yet been installed. He remembered clearly the windows coming alight, the female silhouette.

The shapes went shrill with distress. It took Planchette a moment to understand what had upset them. He did not need light to see what they had found. It was not a photo-reactive sense that revealed it. Planchette shined his flashlight at Thaddy, who was watching him intently.

Strewn on the floor, to the right of the doorway, were the remains of hundreds of shapes. They had been killed, and it was clear who had done it.

Chapter Twenty-five

There was no name for what he felt. If he searched the thousands of languages he had assimilated he doubted he would find one fitting. The remains of the murdered shapes were steeped in Frisa's trace. The only explanation was that she had killed them. She must have gone mad, which was reason as formless and fathomless as space. Planchette began to think he would never understand.

He drifted to the penthouse's narrowest corner, tip of the beak, gazed out, like one seeking anchorage, at the dormant city. Northward, the perimeter of ruin was maybe half a kilometer distant, to the south the re-made city filled the view. The shapes gathered before him. He released them from their vow. He would not ask them to hide this atrocity. They were as uncertain as he what to do.

He noticed that they had changed. He hadn't much looked at them in their time together. They had become more individuated than they had been when they first undertook to assist him. If the events of the day had not left him benumbed Planchette would have been shocked. Shapes did not easily develop identities. They were ego-less, or nearly so—conscious repositories of information. It took a long time—decades, centuries—for them to become so trained in character as these had in a single day. Their colors were more subtle, their features defined. Spoon's handle had taken a swirling pattern, Twelve's edges a traveling gleam, Graph's ambiguous ideography an elusive third dimension. Morph and Morpho were easier to tell apart: Morpho oscillated, Morph unfolded; Planchette realized that they had striven to distinguish themselves from the moment he'd thought he might confuse them with one another. The most striking thing was the clarity of all of their emotions. They empathized with Planchette to a depth he found humbling.

The reason for their profound and rapid transformation became apparent to him, startling as the change itself. It was embodied in the phrase "I am," to which these few, among their kind, could append names. Names Planchette had given them as lightly as one might pass the salt. But to them it had been a baptism in the mystical ethers of identity.

Planchette could not absorb it. He was shaken and disoriented. He looked for Thaddy. The boy had curled up against the wall under the north-facing windows. With the enviable facility of youth, he'd gone to sleep. Planchette took off his coat and draped it over him.

Fatigue ploughed into him, like converging waves. Even his core craved rest. But a fear seized him: When Frisa and he went into hibernation, they never knew how long it would be before they awakened, nor indeed if they ever would. Given the troubles he'd had with his mind, he did not know what might happen when he relinquished volitional consciousness. It seemed an unconscionable risk, with Frisa out there alone, believing he had abandoned her. She had sounded so forlorn.

He didn't know what to trust. He lay down on his side, in the middle of the floor, curled into a foetal position. The bare fiberboard was hard and chill; he missed the soft hospital bed and its blankets. But he was too tired to be kept awake by discomforts, or doubts, either one, and soon descended, like a withering stone, into the vastness of his peculiar sleep. His mnemonic patch melted away, and his core and human psyches merged.

¼=ca.85 had dreamed little in his long existence. Most of his dreams had been amorphous in nature, the only objects to inhabit them nameless symbols, or curious, asymmetrically rounded stones that drifted in gaseous fields of color. Sometimes waves passed through the color fields.

This night his dream was different, one of a handful he'd had that involved recognizable places and unfolded in manners linear and story-like. He was back by the bar, where Friedman's body was found, with Olivetta's mural before him. It was night, again, but the body was gone, and ¼=ca.85 was alone. He looked at his hands, saw that he was human, and thought, *I am Planchette Chron.* He stood for some time marveling at this truth, scrutinizing his hands and arms in wonder, touching his face …

He went to the mural and found that it had become real. The alley extended, empty of souls, straight as a representation of infinity into the firmament, without adhering to the curvature of the world. Planchette strode its course out among the stars. The canal of sky above the rooftops spread to encompass him as buildings faded from view. He crossed light years heavy with darkness. Never had Frisa and he encountered others who could negotiate the reaches of space in this manner, though he was not so arrogant as to suppose none existed. If any did, he would like to meet them. At some point, his work in this galaxy would be done, and he would be confronted with the interminable journey to another, with nothing more than a guess to guide him. The thought of making such a journey alone burdened him with dread.

He fixed his concentration on his course. He knew where he was going. It was a long way to the far side of the galaxy. But distance, as was periodically the case in his waking life, was an abstract in his dream. His strides covered greater and greater measures of space, and in moments he was gazing upon the pale, dusty globe of his home world.

He descended to the place of his birth, the long-dead city of Parxa. It had been many millennia since he had returned. The once great city was a broken remnant of itself. The regal avenues were shattered and choked with vegetation. A few aerial creatures tossed through the sky but not a single shape. Planchette went to the Center for Salvation, where he had first breathed life. The domes had cratered and the floors collapsed on one another, leaving ragged octagonal shells perforated with rows of paneless oval windows. The particle accelerators and spatial condensers were a litter of rust and metallic flake; the amniotic pools had filled with sand. In the distance, the soaring buttresses that once supported the sky-ways resembled a skeletal giant's broken rib cage. Only the Summoning Tower at the city's southern gate remained un-abbreviated by the ravages of time. Planchette went that way, winding sadly amid the sundered domes and terraced communes that were now little more than overgrown mounds. Eventually all trace of Parxa would be gone, the history of a noble species erased.

The Summoning Tower was approaching its denouement as well. Its once sleek, elliptical sides were pitted and cracked. Even its adamant structure could not withstand eternity. Cyphons had nested in the cryer's cell. Their dart-like red bodies dove in search of zeel and muerrz. Still, it was a testament to the arts of his progenitors. Over a hundred thousand kerns, and still the city stood, however diminished its state. But then Planchette realized he was witness to fantasy, and saw things as they were. Parxa, once home to millions, was now hardly a ruffle in the sand. The once rich green-lands that encompassed it had turned to desert. The Summoning Tower had fallen long ago, leaving no trace. He had been gone much longer than he supposed.

This was not where he had needed to come. He looked south, where the Silver River once flowed, out across the now-dry marsh plains, still rimmed by mountains at the horizon. Something there he needed to see.

Deep in that direction he traveled, until the mountains loomed up; then he turned east, surrendering to instinct, uncertain of the call. Small creatures flourished here, those with many legs and those with few, what seemed a descendent of the purple tulak, with its clustered eyes, most prolific. Planchette noticed a creature he did not recognize.

It had a round body and a trumpet-like snout, bluish-pink skin, a fat, stubby tail with a pointed end, four, short, slender arms with tentacular fingers and, like Planchette's forebears, a single undulant foot. The eyes, which rested on either side of its snout beneath leaf-like ears, were large, oval, liquid and pupil-less. Planchette did not know why this small, gentle creature touched him with such poignancy. Then he noticed the shape that trailed it, and with shock understood.

The shape lacked definition; it was little more than a minuscule haze. It was not well-formed enough to fly or hold an idea or any element of consciousness. It was a mere potential, hardly alive.

Planchette spotted several more of the creatures in the surrounding area. Not far east was a cluster of mounds with low, arched entrances that he had mistaken for a geological formation. The red cast of light illuminating the desert registered and Planchette looked at the sun, taken by a dread realization. The star that warmed this world was dying. This new species would not have time to reach its potential.

The ghosts of Planchette's ancestors rose from the soil, their multitude stretching into the far distance. Their feet, pooled like fat, did not undulate; their pseudopods hung limp and impotent at their sides. They had no comfort for him, only regret. With their eye stalks retracted, their bulbous eyes regarded him hollowly, beseeched him to carry on, no matter how lonely or discouraged he became.

Planchette looked again at the small blue creature whose prospects would be too brief. He bowed to his ancestors and renewed his vow. Never again would he think it a burden.

His ancestors' feet undulated and they drew close about him. Their eye stalks extended, batting rhythmically against the residual shells on the backs of their heads, their pseudopods joined and snapped in applause, and they opened their spectral throats in a deep, ululating cheer.

Chapter Twenty-six

So it was in the beginning, as it is, so it shall be—

Planchette opened his eyes and blinked. Something had awakened him. He saw the message on the floor, written in dust, experienced transient embarrassment, absurd, like he'd ejaculated too soon. Particulate matter had gathered while he slept and formed the message around him in a radiating spiral. Sometimes this happened; he had no control over it. The remains of dead shapes had mixed with the dust.

A conviction that Frisa was innocent spilled through him. His assistants jostled to concur, or at least allow it might be possible. Astonished, Planchette sat up. They had watched over him while he slept, conveyed nothing to the Cloud. Twelve was less confident of this course than the others but reserved judgement. However much Frisa had been involved with the killings in this place, they were agreed it was not that simple. No, Planchette thought, we've passed simple. Someone else had said that recently, he couldn't think who.

He felt like he'd been given his life back.

He became aware of Thaddy watching him. The boy was sitting up with Planchette's coat sloughed about him. Thaddy inclined his head toward the far end of the room and Planchette saw what had awakened him. Dunn stood there, arrested in mystification. She was fixed not on Planchette but the message, which extended about five feet out from him in all directions. It was rendered in the symbol system of his ancestors, in a compact script of such elegance it wrung Planchette's heart to see it, even in dust. It was not beauty, though, that held Dunn's attention, but incomprehensible phenomenology.

"Good morning," Planchette ventured.

She looked at him like a worried child.

"How did you find me?"

Her gaze returned to the message. "I … didn't. I found him."

She meant Thaddy, which confused Planchette. The boy is an unsupervised minor, Morpho explained. As if he'd heard, Thaddy raised his left hand, exposing a bracelet on his wrist. A tracking device, Twelve conveyed, equipped with a panic button—P.C. monitors his whereabouts. Planchette nodded; the cop at the hospital must have recognized Thaddy. "Are you the only one who thought of that or just the only one looking for me?" he asked Dunn.

She stared at him again. "What do you mean? Everyone … Everyone's looking for you."

Planchette assessed her breathing, heart rate, synaptic response patterns. She needed reassurance. He got up and went to her, scuffed the message in crossing.

It startled her. "Wait—"

He stepped close, wrapped his aura around her. He would not allow Haliel to intrude on her mind, and was not about to himself. At the same time, it would do neither of them any good for her to fixate on an aberration that she could not understand and he could not explain. A sparing deflection would do no harm. She stared up at him, her lips parted around an unformed question. He gently removed her flat cap, examined the bandage on her head. "Are you all right?"

"I …" She frowned. "Am *I* all right? You should be in the hospital!"

For a change truth seemed fitting. "I don't like hospitals." She carried on frowning. "I'm fine, Officer Dunn." He snugged her flat cap back onto her head, glanced around the triangular penthouse. "I was thinking of homesteading this place. What do you think?"

Her attention went back to the message. "What is that?"

Planchette glanced back with studied disinterest. "Weird, isn't it."

"*Weird?* It's—"

Thaddy tugged on her coat sleeve. "You should trust him," he told her. Dunn's confusion found a new object. "He needs someone to trust him. You should trust him." The boy nodded at Planchette and left.

Dunn stared after him. "Did he . . ?"

Planchette put his coat on, steered Dunn toward the doorway. "I don't suppose you brought anything to eat, did you?"

She shook her head.

"I'm hungry. I think I want coffee."

Dunn looked back at the message. "What is that?"

"I don't know," Planchette lied. "Must come with the place."

Climbing down the access ladder was the trickiest part. She was in a state like mild shock, recurrent disorientation bedeviling her focus. The stairwell was as dark in daytime as night, and Planchette became concerned for Thaddy. But the boy was waiting on the street when they came out of the building.

"Where can I find you?" Planchette asked him, after he had Dunn in the cruiser.

"The tree," Thaddy said.

Planchette nodded and got in the hover himself. Dunn sat behind the wheel, staring out the window. "Are we waiting for a reason?" he asked.

She blinked at him.

"You have my sheet and my shield?"

"The ... watch sergeant has them." She berated herself for something. "Hasker wants you." She made a call, passed her sheet to Planchette, wiped off her ear bud and gave it to him, too.

Hasker's mood was predictably cloudy. "Where the hell have you been?"

"I don't like hospitals."

"They big on you, as a rule? Your doctors think you're dead or a medical miracle. We're stuck with miracle, I guess, plus the pain in my back side."

"Sorry, Chief."

Hasker looked aside and chewed his lip. "You fit for duty?"

"Absolutely."

"Let Perls know. We got a briefing in 'bout hour and a half."

"I'll be there." Planchette started to click off.

"Chron ..."

"Yes, Chief?"

Hasker looked at him for a moment. "See you at the briefing." He cut the connection.

Planchette stared at the blank holoscreen. He gave the sheet and ear bud back to Dunn. She put the bud in her ear, the sheet in her pocket, went back to being disoriented.

"Food? Coffee?" Planchette re-suggested.

She took him to a café where the walls were covered with a mural of rolling farmlands and billowing skies rendered in pottery shards. The place smelled of grilling meat, coffee, fresh bread and sweat. It was crowded, tables close together, a jig-saw counter at the kitchen's perimeter. A few shapes lingered about, probably waiting to escort away any newborns released from the heads of pregnant customers. A ring-shaped one passed near and Twelve flew off to mingle. Planchette ordered scrambled eggs and toast, Dunn nothing. He ate his food sans condiments. The process of nourishing his body was acquiring nascent familiarity.

"You really like things plain, don't you?" Dunn asked.

Planchette shrugged, not knowing how to answer. He picked up his coffee cup and glanced around at the other people eating and talking, forging into their days, took a sip and found it pleasurable. "Coffee's growing on me." Life was still good, still worth living. That alone was reason for hope. He would persevere, find Frisa, defeat his adversaries, convey the message, save humanity—

Dunn was peering at him with her head tilted.

"What?"

Chapter Twenty-seven

"Blind, albino alligators." Gable MacGrory, Chief Engineer of re-colonized New York, preceded Dunn and Planchette through the layout bullpen of the Planning and Assessment Department, moving quickly toward his office. "Gotta thank you for that one."

"We didn't *put* them there," Dunn objected.

"Whizbang from the College says they sound more like crocodiles, the way they chased you. Pain in my butt, by any other name."

Planchette's mood had lost the ebullient shine with which he had greeted the day. He was ill-disposed to countenance sarcasm, still disturbed by what had transpired at the briefing, everyone cheering as he came through the door. Two colleagues nearly killed and they applaud him. He took in his surroundings, trailing Dunn. Except for glass-fronted offices at either end, the bullpen took up the entire floor, beige-carpeted, white-ceilinged, framed in dark metal molding. Undulating, floor-to-ceiling plasti-glass ran the perimeter, affording a nearly uninterrupted three-hundred-sixty-degree view of the city. They were on the top floor of the District Administration building, nine stories up from street level. At drafting tables with digital imaging boards, draftsmen examined and amended technical drawings of the city's eccentric construction projects. A couple of the workers were giving birth. Escort shapes hovered in waiting.

MacGrory flashed Planchette a look. "Environmental Oversight wants us to trap them out and relocate them." He paused in his office doorway to present Dunn and Planchette with a sardonic grin. He was a little shorter than Planchette, bulkier, pie-faced, with dark hair and a ruddy complexion. "'Trap and relocate,'" he repeated, "that's a quote. Meanwhile I'm down for an unscheduled DAT. Why? Because I hold a position of 'unusual authority.' Means I'm automatically required to submit to testing three times a year, on top of whenever something untoward comes up that P.C. thinks merits a review. Like murder, because obviously anyone with my unusual authority is a prime suspect for shit like that. So off I go, again, to have my head peeled and sliced at the behest of a bunch of high-balls who might reasonably be said, I think, to possess unusual authority." He squinted at Planchette. "Got a blister in your pocket, Detective?" MacGrory winked.

"Tell us about your relationship with Victor Friedman," Planchette said.

MacGrory sneered. "I didn't *have* a relationship with Victor Friedman."

"A student heard you arguing with him in his office at Columbia."

The Chief Engineer's gaze traveled high and low in weariness. He went to his desk, sat down, extended his hand at chairs opposite. Dunn closed the door, logged her sheet and placed it on MacGrory's desk in record mode, sat to Planchette's right.

"You had an argument," Planchette said.

MacGrory nodded. "More than one. Many."

"About what?"

"Stupidity versus getting shit done."

"Elaborate."

"How long you got?"

"The overview."

The Chief Engineer blew out a breath. "Where do I work?" He gestured at the bullpen. "Planning Office, it's called. You find any planning going on out there, let us know. We'll buy you a prize."

Planchette let his impatience show.

MacGrory clenched his lips. "I've got forty-two building sites, right now, not including bumps, with adequate oversight on maybe a third of 'em, being optimistic. There's supposed to be an overseer from this office on every project that goes up. Sixty to eighty percent volunteer workforce, varying day to day, which is great for doing things cheap and 'we're in this together,' except it's a minuscule fraction of those people have any fucking idea what they're doing. So I've got twelve multi-levels, quote-unquote 'complete,' that have to be retro-fitted because they installed plumbing, conduit, insulation, every damn thing, sealed and painted the walls without installing the lead shielding. Which to me seems kinda basic in a hot zone. 'Bout half those places got people living in them."

"What's this have to do with Friedman?"

"He was in his third rotation on the Planning Commission. As a volunteer. They loved him down there, kept re-recruiting him. He drove me nuts."

"Why?"

"You can't just throw crap together and expect it to work because you want it to. It's called infrastructure—how things run, get from here to there. This city's held together with a wish and a prayer. The word from the Mayor's office and P.C. is build, build, never mind can we maintain what we've got. I talk about toughening restrictions or oversight regulations, or standardizing a street plan, or restoring part of the subway system, or pretty much anything that makes any fucking sense—no, say the nitwits, it contradicts the principles of re-colonization. Last couple of years the chief nitwit's been Friedman. So, yeah, we had words."

"What specifically did you argue about?" Dunn asked.

"All of it. Me on the side of reality, Friedman leading the charge for hey, watch this."

"Can you give us an example?" Dunn asked. "The most recent thing you argued about?"

MacGrory shrugged. "Transportation. Top of everyone's list."

Dunn looked at Planchette. He was stuck on pause, didn't know what he wanted to know. MacGrory irritated him. He nodded at her to continue.

"Can you be more specific?" Dunn ventured.

The Chief Engineer looked out the window with frustration, shook his head. "Used to be, in the old Pre C days, you got consideration for holding high office. Question one on my personalized DAT is, 'Do you feel indispensable?' Which ain't exactly a yes or no issue in my case, is it? This?" MacGrory pointed at his head—"the knowledge and instincts I've acquired? Indispensable? Realistically? Yeah, maybe. Not because no one else can do the job but show me who's lined up to replace me. Nobody wants the headache." MacGrory reached in his pocket and tossed a yellow button on the table.

Dunn started to respond but Planchette lifted his hand. "Friedman," he said. A thought had finally come to him.

MacGrory blew his breath out again. "He had all these theories about randomized order. I'm begging for a little pragmatism. Let me bring some of the old underground system back online. I know everyone likes the pods 'cause they're cute and cozy. They're also potentially dangerous, get in with the wrong person at night. But look at the numbers. We *need* larger transport options. Friedman comes with, 'Let the chaos evolve. It'll reveal its own system.' Bunch of theoretical gibberish no one can understand. They all lap it up. Did I want to strangle him? I lost count. It wasn't personal."

Before Planchette could ask his next question, Dunn burst forth, "Mr. MacGrory, I have to say this. What you do is very important. Please remember that we want the people who live in this city always to feel that New York is their home, and not a machine built to process numbers. Please remember that."

Planchette and MacGrory stared at Dunn. She reddened and drew back in her seat. "I just needed to say that."

Planchette cleared his throat. "They didn't want to use the underground system. But you use the underground system."

MacGrory was still watching Dunn. "Yeah, well," he widened his eyes at Planchette, "on a limited basis, just to redistribute and maintain the pods."

"Could Friedman have been involved with a plot to sabotage your underground facilities?"

The question surprised MacGrory. He drew his chin in. "I don't see that, no. It was the one bone he threw me. That was the only thing he was onboard with me on."

"What do you think happened down there?"

"I don't know. Like I told the other detective, I'm not sure it *was* sabotage. Looked more like some freak accident to me. Something heavy had to fall on just the right spot. Pulling on it, like with a wheel loader, I don't see how that would have done it. That stuff's temporary, yeah, but it was installed by *my* people. No volunteers in the tombs we don't vet. We don't build stuff you can just blow on."

"If a big alligator fell in the right spot, would that do it?"

MacGrory blinked. "Crocodile. I don't know. I guess if it was big enough. It'd have to be really huge."

Planchette felt Dunn's surprise.

"How big *are* these things?" MacGrory asked. "I mean, I'm talking a couple of tons. They're that big?"

Twelve conveyed an approximate average weight. "Somewhere between a quarter to half that, maybe," Planchette said. "I'm just guessing."

MacGrory stared at him. "Oh, great. That's just fucking wonderful."

"Where were you night before last, Mr. MacGrory, between ten P.M. and three A.M.?"

"I worked late. Here. I think I got home around midnight."

"Can anyone verify that?"

"No."

"You live alone?"

"My bond mate got fed up with New York. And me. Moved west last year."

Planchette nodded. "How often did you meet privately with Friedman?"

MacGrory shook his head. "Never. That time at the college I was giving a talk. I took advantage of being there."

"What did you argue about?"

MacGrory raised his hands and dropped them. "This. Infrastructure. I think in particular the transit system."

"And you got mad."

"I did."

"Why?"

"I don't respond well to being patronized."

"Did you argue about the Temple Trust?"

MacGrory stared, again. "What's that got to do with anything?"

"You and Friedman are members."

MacGrory shifted uncomfortably. "I guess maybe I should have mentioned that. I didn't see it was relevant."

"It indicates another circle of involvement between you and the murder victim."

MacGrory sighed with exasperation. "The Trust is a give-back thing. The membership is anonymous; no one takes credit for anything. The objective is to beautify the city—'create visual events of an inspiring nature.' On that Friedman and I saw eye-to-eye. But it was *not* another 'circle of involvement' between us. We both contributed expertise, in my case resources. I only went to a couple of meetings. He wasn't present at either of them."

MacGrory was lying about something; Planchette was sure of it now. "What was your involvement with Olivetta's mural?"

"The thing that freak did? Nothing. I signed off on it on the advice of the others. I've never seen it. Personally I found the project a little iffy. I guess people like it."

"You wouldn't know anything about a hidden office behind the mural? A private office Friedman used for research?" Mac-Grory was a good liar but Planchette was certain his surprise was feigned.

"I don't know what you're talking about."

"I don't believe you."

"I'm offended and my feelings are hurt."

"We're going to need a list of the other members who belong to the Trust."

MacGrory squinted at Planchette and wagged a finger at him; "You didn't *know* I'm a member, did you?" When Planchette didn't answer, MacGrory shook his head. "I don't know everybody. Just the people who recruited me. And I'm going to consult with counsel before I give you their names."

"That's your prerogative. In the meantime some officers will go through your desk and files, here. We'll need your keys so we can search your residence."

"You can't do that."

"I can do many things. If you block me you won't block my Captain."

MacGrory rubbed his face, spread his hands, palms out, in surrender.

Planchette had been experiencing discomfort in his abdomen and groin, realized he needed to expel bodily waste. He asked MacGrory where the restrooms were, was directed back by the elevators. "Get the names," he told Dunn. Strain made the journey back across the bullpen longer. Each body was different. He hadn't had a moment, not a single moment, to accustom himself to this one.

He hurried into the restroom, started toward a urinal, changed course and took a stall. He dropped his trousers and undershorts— the latter, he noticed, had a lead-lined pouch for his genitals—and sat. The experience of evacuating his bowels and bladder was shocking and magnificent. He marveled at the efficiency of his human body; the entire process lasted mere seconds.

Spoon schooled him on the procedure for cleaning himself. Planchette finished wiping, stood and examined his waste. The solid component was compact, grey and cylindrical. A bluish-grey residue of post-natal slurry confused the color of his urine. Morph conveyed yellow to be the customary hue.

Planchette flushed and called Haliel on his sheet. No answer.

He returned to the bullpen. Across the room, in MacGrory's office, Dunn was still taking information from him. Planchette decided to leave her to it. He wanted MacGrory off-balance; the man had lied to him. He wandered among the draftsmen. Two worked at old-fashioned tables, sans digital surfaces, drawing on large sheets of paper with anachronistic implements. There was a warmth in their art that was absent from the rest. Here it was again, the unstated pact to honor the past. The peripheries of their tables were littered with small, inexpert drawings on forms labeled 'Independent Dome Application and Amendments—' what Mac-Grory had irreverently referred to as 'bumps,' the mosaic-surfaced mounds Planchette had seen scattered about the city. The substructures for them were prefabricated, Morpho conveyed, provided with assembly guidelines to colonists who wanted to build their own dwellings.

One of the draftspersons looked at Planchette and smiled. He nodded to her and moved to the window. The plasti-glass was photo-reactive—dark-tinted, at present, against the glare of the day. There wasn't a cloud in the sky; the afternoon would be searing. There was elegance in the twisted chaos of this city. Planchette watched pedestrians and passengers negotiate its whorls in the climbing heat.

He'd lost cognizance of the urgency of his circumstances, that morning, and been brought back to it by the cheers and applause he'd suffered entering the briefing room, everyone laughing when he shielded his face. Never had he experienced such adulation. Officers shook his hand and gripped his shoulders as he went forward. Incomprehensible sensations toppled through his body. By the time he reached the front he was shaking. This display just for him—nothing to do, however obliquely, with his purpose. The outpouring was overwhelming. The captain pumped his hand, again welcomed him to the force—with earnestness, this time. Schnitke had his bowler, which had been repaired. The dent had been smoothed and a tear in the crown rejoined, a seam faintly visible. Somehow it made it more precious. The formerly antagonistic detective embraced him.

Bewildered as he was, Planchette understood that these people wanted him to know they regarded his acts in the tunnels as valorous and heroic. He feared how they would feel when they learned the truth about him, hid his agitation with sheepishness, the sanguine plateau he had briefly inhabited rocked to pieces. He *was* moved, deeply moved, which confused him most of all. Shame, guilt, remorse, grief—life was stunted by such forces. Somewhere Frisa was hiding and alone, and even hope seemed extravagant. But hidden in expedience was a terrible truth: life moved on.

Looking out at the city through the running windows of the Planning Department bullpen, Planchette recognized that his faculties were destabilizing yet further. He'd become subject to fluctuations of mood that he had been designed to perceive, not experience. Then again he'd always felt everything, just with greater detachment.

There was a sequence to his destabilization. And there was a sequence to the events leading to and from the murder. The sequences overlapped, both with gaps, but things had to have happened in a specific order for the gaps to exist.

Planchette contacted Processing and requested a warrant to search MacGrory's residence, clicked off, stared out the window, unsure what to do next. He wanted to talk to Haliel. His sheet vibrated. It was Claire.

"I've been thinking I'd hear from you." Her voice was edged with distance.

Planchette felt unaccountably contrite. "Sorry." There was a sustained pause in which it seemed she might want him to say something that was beyond him. He held the silence.

"No, I'm sorry." Her voice softened. "You must be wiped."

"I slept."

"How's it going?"

He told her about the crocodiles, absurdly, trying to impress her, made a mess of it, stopped.

Again she was quiet. The distance had evaporated when she said, "Remind me never to imagine what your day is like."

He *could* feel her, even so removed. Her warmth brushed an aching cord in him, bolstered his hopes. He promised to come by when he could.

"Be good to see you. Not why I called."

Planchette listened.

"I remembered something Michael said. Keeps nagging me that it might be important."

"What did he say?"

"That he can't trust anyone who understands his work."

"He doesn't trust you?"

"He doesn't think I understand. Not really. He knows I appreciate what he does but he doesn't think I understand it. And I do think he trusts me."

"When—" Planchette's sheet vibrated—"hold on Claire." He opened the holoscreen. It was Perls, upset about something. Planchette told Claire he would call her back. "What's going on?" he asked Perls.

"Those two uniforms we left guarding Friedman's hidden room yesterday, you get their names?"

"They're not in the log?"

"No."

Planchette took that in. "Martin Delgado and Giffort Smith."

"You're sure?"

"I'm sure."

Perls repeated the names to someone. "Got that?" To Planchette he said, "I'm here with Al. I wanted him to see this room. Join us over here. You're gonna love this."

"On my way."

Planchette noticed a cloud of shapes swirling near the northern perimeter of the re-colonized part of the city. Taking distance into account the gathering was enormous. Morph conveyed that the swarm was massed above the building where they had found the murdered shapes.

Chapter Twenty-eight

"Do you believe in 'the moment?'" Dunn asked.

There was no point pretending he didn't know which 'moment' she meant. "Is it a matter of belief? It happened all over the world." Twelve perched on Planchette's left shoulder, his other supraliminal companions on his right. It rested heavy with all of them, the shape of measure's decision to inform the Cloud of the location of their murdered fellows.

Dunn steered the cruiser around a small flock of starlings. They watched the birds swirl by. "But we weren't there," she said. "Maybe they made it up, spread a rumor to get everyone to cooperate."

"Given the circumstances that seems unlikely." No rumor could have done what she suggested, though it was pointless to tell her so. There seemed nothing helpful he could convey to his other assistants either. Twelve, in a kind of outburst, had leaked the information about the missing shapes at the café that morning. The others were upset not to have been consulted. As a result they were shunning Twelve—behavior unprecedented, to Planchette's knowledge, among shapes anywhere in the Galaxy.

"Unlikely is not the same as impossible," Dunn said.

"So, you don't believe it?"

She hesitated. "See, you're asking me what I believe, not what I know."

That's not what you did? They were closer to the frenetic mass of shapes. Planchette did not think he had ever seen shapes so agitated, even in anticipation of global disaster.

He looked at Dunn. "Why are you bringing this up?"

Framed in profile against the sky, her inner self was so evident it called to the male in Planchette. "The histories," she said, "even the church litanies, all use the same words: 'unexplainable loss.' Not 'inconsolable,' 'unexplainable.' We've never been able to explain how, all at once, everyone in the world felt they'd lost something important that they couldn't identify. Have you ever experienced anything like that, 'unexplainable loss?'"

Had he? He'd witnessed oceans of failure at a clockwork remove, and now, in one day, all his barriers had failed him. "I don't know. Maybe."

Dunn glanced at him. "And you don't want to talk about it."

"Not much." How would he describe the distress he felt now were Frisa not absent to anchor it?

"Because it's private, right? Unexplainable loss is something you feel inside, privately. Even if you tried, you couldn't share it with anyone. Except this wasn't private. Everyone felt it. How did they know, if they couldn't talk about it?"

Pointing out the leaps in her reasoning would trivialize her earnestness. "Maybe they didn't have to," he said. "Maybe they just looked at each other and knew." Planchette conveyed that he wanted his assistants to accept Twelve's decision. They would take the Cloud's reaction as it came. Planchette's concerns had not been divulged, only the whereabouts of the dead, which was fitting. Nothing was served by being divided.

Dunn nodded to herself. "Maybe that's what trust really is. When you don't have to explain."

Planchette didn't know what was going on with her. It felt like the entire exchange was about something she hadn't said.

She brought the hover down into the alley where Friedman had been murdered. Return and return. This little aisle was the place on Earth Planchette knew best; he'd been here even in sleep. And still its defining aspect was mystery. Several cruisers and a C-tech van were already parked there. Planchette got out and was assaulted by heat. The stacked cruisers lifted and Dunn parked. A dozen uniforms were gathered near the mural, clinging to narrow shade on the left side of the alley. Outdoors in New York one suffered on days like this. Make them lightweight as you would, there was no way to make lead-lined garments cool. Planchette hung his badge from the breast pocket of his greatcoat. On the stairs, inside the disguised doorway, a C-tech scanned the right-hand wall. Planchette and Dunn edged by, following the course dictated by forensic markers. Planchette hung his badge from his shirt pocket and took off his coat. What they found in the hidden room did not surprise him. It had been in the atmosphere surrounding this case, a leading rationale in what remained unclear. Things having developed as they had, an escalation of intrigue had been inevitable.

The desk was gone. Schnitke, Hasker and Perls stood inside the room, to the right of the doorway. Planchette went in next to them. Dunn stayed in the hall.

"Oxgarten and Li will be disappointed," Hasker said.

They watched two C-techs scan the floor. Planchette recognized one of them—Randall Fry, the technician he had turned away disgruntled from Friedman's apartment, two nights ago. "When did this happen?" Planchette asked.

"Sometime between when we left, yesterday, and about six this morning," Perls said. "No one was here when the relief watch came on. They didn't report it until Al and I found this and questioned them."

Hasker grunted. "Didn't want to get their fellow officers in trouble."

"I believe them on that, Chief," Perls said.

Hasker grunted again.

"Where were Delgado and Smith?" Planchette asked.

"Delgado was deep in his grave," Schnitke said. "Smith, at the time, was probably asleep with his thumb in his mouth. Right now I imagine he's wracking his brain, trying to remember where he lost his badge."

"I sent you a file," Perls told Planchette.

Planchette opened his sheet, viewed two photographs. One labeled, 'Delgado, Martin, retired, deceased,' was of an elderly person, the other of an officer so youthful that he looked like a cadet in the wrong uniform. He was not the Giffort Smith Planchette had seen yesterday. Planchette conferred with Graph.

Fry came over, made a point of not acknowledging Planchette. "They were careful," he said. "We haven't found a print or a fiber. They had to dismantle the desk to get it out. There are a couple of scratches on the floor where they pulled it away from the wall. That's all I've got so far."

Hasker nodded. "Repeat that for Detective Chron."

Fry drew back.

"I got it, Chief," Planchette said.

Hasker glared up at Fry. "You disrespect my officer in front of *me?*" The senior technician looked away. Hasker lifted his chin at the door; the detectives and he went out. Back in the alley, they moved out of earshot of other personnel. Hasker started to speak, looked at the sky. "Life, it's hot." He pointed at the bar. "This place open?"

"No, but I think we can go in," Planchette said.

It was mercifully cool inside. The same worker Planchette had encountered yesterday was vacuuming the carpet. Hasker spoke to him; the man grimaced and left to some other chore. They all took off their coats and hats, got water from the bar, pulled cushions into a circle. "Oughta get this set-up at the station." Hasker situated himself.

The others laughed, except Planchette. He rued the snares of crime and procedure.

Hasker drained his glass, put it down. "Talk to me."

"Got a problem with Processing," Schnitke said.

"Let me handle that," Hasker said.

Dunn frowned at Planchette. "Someone altered the log," he told her. Shock spread on her face.

"Delgado and Smith were imposters, obviously," Perls said.

"They had to be," Planchette said. They all looked at him. "Something bothered me about them. It hit me in there, Martin and Giffort aren't Utilitarian names."

Perls' head rose. "I told them to take off their pins."

Planchette nodded. "They weren't cops. They didn't know it was against regulations to wear their pins on duty. So, without meaning to, probably, they showed us their credentials."

"Credentials?" Schnitke frowned. "You're saying Utilitarians are behind all this?"

Planchette shrugged. "The person who cut through the door at Friedman's," he asked Perls, "was he wearing a pin?"

"I think he might have been." Perls nodded. "Yeah, he was."

"And by his clumsiness, or *apparent* clumsiness, that desk was destroyed."

"What are we talking about, here?" Hasker scratched his forehead. "A plot by Utilitarians? A plot *involving* Utilitarians? A plot a couple of Utilitarians happen to be involved *in?* We can speculate ourselves crazy with that."

"Maybe," Perls said. "I'm curious, now, though, if Friedman was Utilitarian. 'Victor'—that could go either way, couldn't it?"

"Can Utilitarians always be identified by their names?" Hasker asked. "Does anyone know?" No one answered. Even the shapes were unsure. The Captain shook his head. "That's like chasing smoke. We're not turning a fifth of this city's inhabitants into suspects based on conjecture. A fifth with no history of criminality."

"We need to keep going after the Temple Trust," Perls said. "It was a big job, putting that room together. It took a lot of people and no one's come forward. People that shy engage my interest."

"We've got something on that." Planchette told them about the interview with MacGrory. "I applied to Processing for a warrant for his residence."

"I'll kick it through," Hasker said. He made a call on his sheet.

"He admitted belonging to the Trust?" Perls asked Planchette.

"I let him think we knew and he fell for it. Friedman was a member, too."

"Friedman—big surprise."

Hasker finished his call. "What else? Let's review everything."

"Forensics has compiled an edited holo-scan of the hidden room," Perls said. "With your permission, we're ready to submit it with a query into the knowledge pool."

"That'll alert the people we're looking for," Schnitke said.

Perls shrugged. "They know we're looking for them."

"Send it to Li and Oxgarten, too," Hasker said.

Perls nodded. "That whole building is wrong. It's about half occupied, storage and homesteaders. Front entrance is at the dead end of a street on the other side. No back entrance and no shortcut—you gotta go the long way around. All we have from Processing is when it was built—about twenty years ago. No permits, no inspection certificates, no blueprints—even the homestead applications are missing. They're registered but the forms are gone."

"Which means," Schnitke said, "we don't know who handled permits, applications, inspections—"

"Right."

"From what MacGrory told us," Planchette said, "they're way out of sync with oversight. I doubt it would be difficult to hide alterations to an existing structure."

"Dunn, I'm giving this to you," Perls said. "I want you to go back to the Planning Office, look through their records, the hard copies—don't go through Processing for anything unless you have to. Look for notifications of work to be done, anything that sticks out. Find out when the mural was proposed and exactly when it was painted. That will give you a time frame."

"Claire Fontaine will know," Planchette said.

"Okay," Perls said, "start with her. We want names, directions to look in. Al, you take Dunn back to the Planning Office, sweat MacGrory again while you're there. Don't tell him about the search warrant, just let him feel our eyes on him. Then start knocking on the doors he gave up."

Schnitke nodded.

"I'll go after our bogus cops. Start at the Utilitarian Lodge Majeure, see if I can scare up someone who recognizes them from my description. Chron, soon as the warrant comes through, take a couple of uniforms from outside and crack MacGrory's place."

"Where are we with finding Olivetta?" Hasker asked.

"Neighborhood door-to-door came up empty. I've got about twenty people canvassing the snag dens and known collectors of his art. The grazers have his pattern. There are a lot of places he can hide but we'll find him. The man has no friends."

"And P.C.?" Hasker asked.

"What about them?"

Hasker stared at Perls.

"They surveil us with no explanation and you want me to *trust* them?"

"Nate—" Hasker sighed.

Perls groaned.

"You think they're not looking for him anyway? You don't coordinate with them you lose half the eyes looking for this guy," Hasker said. "You also fail to establish he's our collar. Let *me* handle the politics. I should not have to keep telling you this."

"All right."

"What about the killer?"

"Same on all counts. No match to known offenders with Olivetta's pictures or the composite the Fontaine woman gave us. No hits from the global database, yet, either. I've got people looking through resident IDs. Our files are not comprehensive. She's the most confusing part of this, to me."

"Second that," Schnitke said.

"What we're looking for is the right question about her," Perls said. "We don't even know, for sure, that she exists. She could have been Olivetta in drag."

"I don't think so," Planchette said. "For that to work, Olivetta would have had to have some way to circumvent the proximity detectors in his apartment as well as the tracking device in his button. If he could do that, why didn't he do it when he ran away?"

Perls shrugged. "Maybe he didn't have time. Maybe, after dealing with Wright, he panicked, or didn't see the point. He knew as soon as we found Wright, we'd know."

Planchette cast Perls a skeptical look.

"Whoever this person is," Perls said, "our killer is the strangest part of this case. We have no motive, other than maybe she's involved with a person or group who, for some reason, wanted Friedman silenced or killed because of his work. No one can tell us what that work was. His students seem to know just enough not to be helpful. Pretty much the same with Oxgarten and Li, which is possibly suspicious. According to the witness, Friedman seemed to know the perp, yet no one else we've talked to recognizes her or remembers ever seeing them together. We have three wildly different pictures of her, a presumed 'her,' consistent only in what she was wearing."

"Has forensics gotten anywhere identifying that fabric?" Planchette asked.

Perls expression became complex. "Not really. It's strange stuff, apparently. The lab tech said it's not woven, it's grown."

"What does that mean?" Hasker asked.

Perls shrugged. "He said it's organic, more like skin than fabric. He doesn't know of anyone making anything like it."

"Can they tell if the piece from the alley matches the fibers we found in the tunnel?"

"Seems to, yeah," Perls said. "Everything about this person is bizarre. And yet no one's seen her and we can't find her."

"Maybe she's bizarre on purpose, or being made to seem bizarre. To confuse us," Planchette said. He wasn't sure if he was trying to help or mislead his human colleagues. Everything they learned about their prime suspect led him to the same reckoning.

Until he knew otherwise, he had to assume that Frisa was the person they were looking for, or was connected with her. He didn't want the police to find her any more than he did the shapes.

"It's not just what was she doing in the tombs," Schnitke said, "it's how'd she get *down* there? Either she used an unregistered entry point or had some way of opening those access panels from the outside."

"Maybe she had help," Dunn said. "Someone in the city engineer's office."

"Or Processing," Schnitke suggested.

"Go on, Dunn," Perls said.

"Maybe she works in the tunnels. Like you said, her dress could be a disguise. That doesn't have to be Olivetta. She might be someone professional or highly skilled, but otherwise ordinary. If she's a manual laborer it could account for her strength."

"Or a man disguised as a woman," Schnitke said.

"Okay, that's yours, too, Dunn. Take Olivetta's pictures and the composite and compare them with ID photos of tunnel and transit workers, anyone connected with city maintenance, construction, planning, so on."

Dunn kept nodding, as if the assignments were routine. But Planchette saw the tightening of her face, the way she swallowed and would not look at him. "She's going to need help with that," he said.

Dunn asked for Baranski and Hockurt.

"I want the Utilitarian question kept to the five of us, for now," Hasker said. "Leave it out of any dealings you have with Processing. Understood?"

Everyone nodded.

"Okay, we've got our assignments, let's get to it," Perls said. "Have another briefing at four this afternoon, at the station."

They all got up. Dunn looked around as if unsure where to go.

"Hockurt?" Planchette asked her.

She smiled evasively, left with Schnitke. The Captain gave

Planchette a nod and followed them. Planchette had dreaded this, a heightening of complexity that could drag the investigation out indefinitely. And he was back on his own.

"Sorry about Dunn," Perls said. "She's part of the inner circle on this thing, now. I have to allocate my resources."

Planchette nodded. "What do you want me to do while I'm waiting for the warrant?"

"Think," Perls said. "You're good at it. And Chron—" he gripped Planchette's shoulder and looked him in the eyes—"Your first day was for the records. You're no good to me fried, much less dead."

Planchette nodded and they left the bar.

Schnitke's cruiser rose out of the alley. Planchette saw Dunn look down at him. Sometimes seemingly unrelated communications answered each other, like ripples in a group mind. 'The moment' she'd asked him about—it was the answer to Haliel's question. The Ixilian had been correct; Planchette did need a great many people to die in order to do his work. Not just people, shapes. Whether in dream or an esoteric version of reality, he had renewed his vow to the ghosts of his ancestors never to let such loss be wasted. It took the deaths of billions of shapes for their parents to notice that they were gone. Even then they didn't know *what* was missing, just that something significant, something they had overlooked or failed to perceive, was no longer present. But when they noticed, it always hit all of them at once, a commonality which made it possible for world societies to rise from the ashes of world wars. Then they were ready for the message Planchette and Frisa had been made to deliver.

Planchette watched Dunn until she was gone from sight.

Chapter Twenty-nine

He stood in the alley with his hands on his hips, unsure what to do. He checked with Processing to see if the warrant had cleared. Not yet.

Think, Perls had said. There seemed nothing in Planchette's mind but void and confusion. He didn't want to put his greatcoat back on. He went again through the disguised doorway, down and up to the hidden room. Fry and his assistant were scanning the hall.

"All right if I go in?" Planchette pointed at the room.

Fry glanced back, nodded.

Planchette scrutinized the non-equilateral metal triangles that covered the walls. Twelve counted twenty-seven variations. Graph confirmed that the patterns on them were mechanical, not linguistic.

"Fry?"

The taciturn technician's arrival in the doorway was less than prompt.

"Has a metallurgical analysis of these panels been done?"

Fry looked at the walls.

"If we can't trace the tech, maybe we can trace the material."

Fry's eyebrows rose.

Planchette went back outside. From the officers in the alley he picked two who least resembled each other. Dancla was tall, dark and muscular, Grie, short, fair-skinned and lean. Planchette contacted Processing for MacGrory's address, drew the two aside. Dancla's skin had a reddish hue Planchette had not seen on a human. "I want you to locate a locksmith named Pick Sutton," he told them. "Collect him and meet me at this address. In about half an hour." He wanted more time to himself. Dancla copied the address on her sheet.

Planchette managed to take Dunn's cruiser out of the alley without scraping the side, though his ascent was less than graceful. He keyed MacGrory's address into the autopilot. The cruiser turned and the massed shapes came into view, again, on his left. They had dispersed some. Clusters of them swirled erratically, here and there above the city. The full impact of strange events on this world would not soon be known.

He remembered his interrupted conversation with Claire Fontaine and called her. She didn't answer. He contacted Processing and asked to be connected to the officer standing post outside her apartment. The officer sounded like the same one who had been there yesterday.

"Has Miss Fontaine left her apartment?" Planchette asked her.

"No, sir. She's in there."

"I just called and she didn't answer."

"I think she's working, sir. A woman came by about an article she's writing. I think she's interviewing her."

Planchette nodded. "Notify me when they get done."

"Yes, sir."

MacGrory lived about five kilometers northeast of the crime scene, a few blocks from the flooded zone by the river. The street was lined with domes and three and four-storey assemblage structures. MacGrory lived in a dome pyramid, which surprised Planchette. The engineer hadn't seemed to regard 'bumps' favorably. Planchette reviewed the information from Processing and determined that MacGrory occupied the entire building—one of the perks of office he claimed not to enjoy? This pyramid was unusual in being composed of four domes—three down and one raised—rather than the customary five, or occasional twelve or fourteen. The lot it stood on was bordered by poplars and stands of bamboo, none healthy-looking. It was the first independent domicile with defined grounds Planchette had encountered in the re-colonized city.

He got out and walked the perimeter. There was a stark iconoclasm to MacGrory's pyramid. He had not utilized salvaged materials in its construction. It was composed of bare concrete, no paint or mosaic embellishing its surface. The upper dome had a raised cap, beneath the flared overhang of which a ring of windows showed. Behind the pyramid was the only lawn Planchette had encountered outside of Old Pine Park. The grass here was in about the same state. Bamboo was taller behind the house.

Planchette returned to the street. He lifted his hat and wiped sweat from his forehead. Like the wider avenue where Claire lived, this section of road went straight for an anomalous distance, extending east, to the right, only a couple of hundred feet but to the west for perhaps a quarter of a mile. Empty the whole way of persons or vehicles. No one ventured out on days like this unless they had to. Planchette started back to the air-conditioned sanctuary of the cruiser, but noticed someone who hadn't been there a moment ago. Down where the street curved from view, to the east, stood a large person, broad and tall, in a black greatcoat and wide-brimmed fedora. Not moving, watching Planchette. His stillness felt odd.

Planchette registered that the person was not human, strode toward the Tehfoloran, who waited without moving. It was the environment suit that made it seem statue-like. Just as its clothing made it seem male.

"Is it you?" Planchette asked, "from the tunnel?"

The mask the Tehfoloran wore poorly imitated a human face. The color was too uniform, the features generic, lacking animation. When it shook its head the movement was mechanical.

"Is he all right? The one who saved me?"

The pause was longer this time, the lag probably due to translation. The creature nodded.

"Can you talk? A human language? I could not understand your associate, last night."

With a humanoid hand that was obviously artificial, the Tehfoloran pulled a disc-shaped device from its pocket. "I can," the device said, after another lag. The two words the device had produced sounded like they'd been spoken by different voices. Collated recordings, probably.

Planchette nodded. "Why are you here?"

The wait was longer, this time. In yet another voice, soft and feminine, the device said, "Danger."

Danger? Across the street, in a dome encrusted with blue fragments, a curtain parted and a little girl peeked out at Planchette. She pulled the curtain closed and open, closed and open. "Danger from what? From whom?"

The Tehfoloran pointed at Planchette's head. "Your mind."

The 'flesh' of the creature's mask looked real. The static lack of expression gave it away. Corpse-like, Morpho reflected. "Something's messing with my memory, is that what you mean? It's going to get worse?" Planchette felt the being's linguistic frustration, the stride through tar.

"Your mind is ... singularity. Danger to all ... world."

Planchette frowned, shook his head. "I don't understand." The Tehfoloran seemed to be referring not to a danger Planchette faced but one he posed. It seemed unable to clarify.

Planchette tried a different tack. "That ship, orbiting the planet next farthest from their star, here, is it yours?"

"Yes."

"It's heavily armed. Does the Galactic Council mean to attack Earth, or interfere with me in some way?"

Again the Tehfoloran took a long time responding. Finally it said, "Galactic Council does not exist."

Planchette heard a hover approach, watched another cruiser park by his. When he turned back the Tehfoloran was gone. The curtain in the blue dome was closed and did not part again.

'All world?'

Planchette looked at MacGrory's pyramid. The windows were all up high, like sky lights, none at eye-level.

Grie and Dancla got out of their cruiser. Dancla's head drooped in reaction to the heat. Planchette had been delivered another warning he couldn't make sense of. Pick Sutton emerged and squinted at the sky, extended the shade of his cap with his hand.

Planchette looked at his own right hand, turned it palm up, palm down. This was his flesh, now; he felt the fit complete, like a latch clicking into place. He had inhabited it to the depth of cell replacement. He walked back toward MacGrory's house, where his new assistants and Sutton stood waiting by the cruiser. Every jar and jangle would be experienced, now, seamlessly, as native to this body. Confidence possessed him, too, that he could function as a competent investigator. He had integrated his human persona much faster than he had any other.

And yet his inner, elder self was increasingly remote, and things that mattered most kept slipping from his grasp. He had the gnawing sense that he was missing something obvious. Not among the questions he was trying to answer, but hidden in their thicket.

He checked with Processing. The warrant had cleared. "Mr. Sutton." Planchette extended his hand.

"Detective Chron." They shook hands. "Good to see you again."

Planchette noted that Sutton wasn't wearing his Utilitarian pin. "Hopefully I won't present you with any impenetrable obstacles, today." He motioned towards MacGrory's front door.

"I doubt you'll come across another lock like that, anytime soon." Sutton accompanied Planchette up the walk.

"It so happens we have," Planchette said.

Sutton stopped and stared at Planchette. "Really?" His surprise did not seem feigned, though his reaction had an edge to it. He gazed down the street.

"Why does it surprise you so much?"

"I'm not sure," Sutton said, "but it does."

They continued to MacGrory's front door, which was locked. The lock operated by a magnetic panel. "Oh, this," Sutton said to himself. He rummaged in his kit, produced a hand-held device to which a small disc was connected, via leads. He attached the disc to the lock, inserted his sheet into the device, and keyed in a numerical code. With a sharp click, the lock disengaged.

Sutton removed his apparatus and stepped aside. Planchette turned the knob and pushed the door, let it swing open on its own. Cool air poured out. A vast-seeming, beshadowed space presented, arrayed with furniture. Planchette stepped inside. The three ground-level domes had been joined, interior walls omitted, the combined enclosure supported by pillars. Light from the high windows lanced the dimness.

The door closed and electric lights came on. Sutton had found the switch.

"Don't touch or move anything," Planchette said. It was at once apparent that both MacGrory's skills and aesthetics had found application in the design of his home. The furniture, most of it, with the exception of a few chairs and small tables, was built in, formed of concrete and joined to the floor and walls—sofas, armchairs, tables, counters, cabinets. Here and there wooden shelves rested in cement casements. As in Friedman's apartment there were some old books.

Planchette took off his coat and draped it over the back of a sofa custom-fitted with rust-colored cushions. The concrete was burnished, smooth as polished wood. He set his hat on his coat. Sutton put his coat and hat next to Planchette's. MacGrory's artfulness was most evident in the walls. Embedded in the concrete, arrays of small, salvaged objects swirled high and low across the domes' interior curves and decorated much of the furniture. In the nearest wall it was wristwatches, minus their straps, hundreds of them, those that still had hands showing 1:17. The time the first nuclear bomb detonated in the city, Morph conveyed.

A comment on the absurdity of fixation, Planchette thought, translated into a flowing display that came alive as the eyes moved. The ceiling was flat under the raised dome, the floor clear of furniture beneath it. Planchette didn't see a staircase. He went to the center of the space under the raised dome and looked up. There was a circle incised in the middle of the ceiling.

"Officer Dancla, go back out and look around the house, see if there are stairs or any kind of access to the upper dome."

Dancla and Grie had removed their helmets and hung them on hooks by the door. Dancla put hers back on and went out. Grie started to remove his tunic, looked to Planchette for permission. Planchette nodded.

Grie hung his tunic on a hook and came over to Planchette. His grey undershirt was streaked with sweat. "It's weird. Isn't there a way up?"

Sutton, looking around, drifted toward the kitchen. Planchette watched him. "Doesn't seem to be," he answered Grie. He returned to the objects embedded in the walls. In addition to wristwatches there were pendants, medallions, cameos, coins, innumerable small, polished stones. A random exhibit of specimens. Precious samples. Around the sleeping area, curtains hung gathered by cords to columns. The bed was unmade, the only evidence of disorder in the entire dwelling. It was apparent which side Mac-Grory favored; the sheets had not been changed in some time. Planchette looked about at the flowing walls. It had been a labor of love, making this home, and MacGrory's wife had left him. It must feel empty to live here, now. Empty everywhere, while he filled her absence with work. How long would he miss her before resentment overtook longing?

It shocked Planchette to think that prolonged separation from Frisa could result in alienation, even in him, even after all they'd been through. He didn't want to believe it but he could feel it already, the beginnings of disaffection. It seemed he'd hardly thought of her since the briefing that morning. His desire to find her was a pale shadow of the desperation he'd felt last night.

He was scaring himself again. He shook his head; this was design. Not his true condition. He was experiencing emotions as a human might, inflated and accelerated, more like a child than an adult, certainly not as one whose years spanned aeons.

Grie was watching him. The shapes cautioned Planchette that he should find a moment to let them reduce his mnemonic patch, which had thickened considerably.

Dancla returned, reported no visible access to the upper dome outside. Seeing Grie she took off her tunic. Her sweat molded her undershirt to her chest and she wasn't wearing a bra. Her breasts were small and firm, with pronounced nipples. She lifted the cloth away from her skin, shook and released it, to little effect.

She cast a diagonal glance upward. "What are we looking for, sir?"

Spoon conveyed that Planchette was being impolite. He returned his own attention to the ceiling. "A way into the upper dome, for now." He'd been distracted by reflex, which was not like him—yet another deviation. His nature was to know the distractions of others, not render his own.

"What do you want me to do?" Sutton asked.

Planchette answered with deliberate dismissiveness; "Wait 'til we're sure we don't need you."

He scrutinized the incised circle in the ceiling. Twelve verified that the cut went deep, and related to a concealed mechanism. There had to be a switch or lever somewhere. Planchette studied the pillars situated around the central space. Objects were embedded in them, too. Buttons and pins and bits of fused glass. An item caught his attention, a utilitarian pin amid a swath of buttons. His gaze slid to Sutton, who met it with placid incomprehension.

The pin sank into the pillar when Planchette pressed it, as he'd anticipated it would. With a soft, fluttering whir, a spiral staircase unwound from the ceiling. It was a marvel of craftsmanship, both in mechanical elegance and visual grace. Not a composite, something fashioned anew in echo of bygone aesthetics. White steps, centered by a burgundy runner secured with brass stair rods. Decorative brass mounts of stylized foliage on the sidewalls of the risers. Brass handrail and balusters, brightly polished. It all bespoke reverence for what lay above.

The opening was dark. Planchette told the others to wait and climbed up. As he neared the top a ring of faint illumination came into view on the roof of the upper dome. He climbed through the entry. It was dark. He made out a series of large, identically sized rectangles or partitions of some kind, vertically suspended and equidistantly spaced around the periphery of the chamber. Centered up high a large disc hung horizontally, around the perimeter of which the luminance shone. Planchette recalled the ring of windows he had seen outside, and the overhang that shaded them. Between that overhang and this suspended disc, any natural light penetrating the chamber was twice impeded.

Only indirect light was allowed here, Planchette saw. He noticed a hinged hatch and lowered it, shutting out light from below, and then began, as his eyes adjusted, to discern what the faint light revealed.

MacGrory had lied about much more than Planchette had guessed.

Chapter Thirty

Planchette counted sixteen paintings, all about eight feet tall by five wide, hung by cords from hooks high on the dome wall, spaced about ten feet apart, in a circle. He had known that Olivetta was a genius, possessed of a confounding vision, but he had not guessed the clarity of that vision, nor the full extent of the artist's skill.

Each canvas depicted a figure that hovered between symbol and artifact—or, in another way, between life form and idea. One looked like the head of a hammer with a leaf and a feather for a handle; another resembled an egg inset with a compass. Others bore, in varying mixtures, the combined aspects of snowflake and ideogram, teacup and life preserver, fountain and spray of flowers. One looked like a hexagonal nut with a fur-lined hole. Several had no clear, analogous aspects.

Planchette opened the hatch and called to Pick Sutton. The locksmith climbed the stairs and stopped, shoulder-high through the portal, holding the handrail and staring about. He came up the rest of the way and Planchette closed the hatch again.

Sutton studied the suspended disc, as Planchette had, before looking at the paintings. Planchette watched him. The locksmith went to a picture of a star-like figure, a kind of wreath of crystals.

"What are these things?" he asked.

"I thought you could tell me."

Sutton turned. "Why would I—"

"You haven't asked why I called you up here."

Sutton's bewilderment was genuine. But there was deception, too, in the way he twisted, drawing back—a kind of dodge.

"Why aren't you wearing your Utilitarian pin?" Planchette asked.

Sutton touched his lapel, opened his mouth but didn't answer.

"You're already facing obstruction; don't make it complicity. Who told you not to unlock the door at Friedman's apartment?"

"I—I *couldn't* unlock it."

Planchette sighed impatiently, stepped closer.

"No—it's not—" Sutton backed away. "There was a call."

"Yes."

"He told me not to open the door, to keep you out. But I couldn't—"

"Who?"

"I don't know."

"Mr. Sutton—"

"You don't understand. He said the words."

"What does that mean?"

"We have—secret ways of—the community—we're very deliberate. People think we're silly but we *are* dedicated—"

"Secret ways."

Sutton swallowed. "Handshakes. Phrases, like from Pre-C. So we know each other. Commands—"

"Commands?"

"Only in special—in emergencies. When something might be lost. Or undone. Something that could send us backwards. There are phrases, and the person has to do it, whatever you're asked. We commit to that."

"You're saying someone called you and, using a key phrase, ordered you to hinder us?"

"Not hinder, just not to open the door. Which I couldn't anyway."

"Would you recognize their voice if you heard it again?"

Sutton's eyes widened. He nodded.

Planchette glanced around at the paintings. He'd come nearer, here, to what he needed. He opened the hatch and called to Dancla and Grie, "Mr. Sutton is coming down. He's under arrest."

Sutton started back down, stopped. "Detective, I wasn't meant to hinder you. Not the way you think. We want you to find this killer. Friedman was our hope."

"Explain that."

"He found something important, that's all I know. A way forward." Sutton held Planchette's gaze, then continued down the stairs.

Planchette called Schnitke, told him what he'd discovered. "Have you talked to MacGrory? He didn't just lie, he deceived me."

"Yeah, well, that's another one we're gonna have to hunt down. He wasn't in his office. Didn't tell anyone he was going. And the people he named are all whereabouts who-the-fuck-knows, so far. He didn't give us anyone major, is my guess."

Planchette thought a moment. "We need to question the people in the Planning Office."

"Already happening. Dunn's in charge."

Planchette shook his head. "That's too much for her."

"Nate's sending help. You can go yourself, if you want. When you finish where you're at."

Planchette called Perls, who was at the Utilitarian Lodge Majeure. Planchette again relayed what he'd learned. Perls was silent. Planchette heard him mumble. "What?"

"No, I just want to know what's going on."

"Want me to report to Hasker?"

Perls was silent again. "Yeah, you better. That shouldn't go second hand. You done at MacGrory's?"

"I think so." Planchette stared at a painting of a spherical cloud. He went close, shined his flashlight on the lower left-hand corner, found Olivetta's signature.

"Chron?"

"I'm looking at something." He went behind the painting. A date was marked in black ink on the back of the canvas. It indicated that the picture had been painted over six years ago. Planchette went to the next canvas; it was a couple of weeks older. "I want to question Claire Fontaine again about Olivetta," he told Perls. He would have thought of this sooner if he'd had his full mind.

"Now?" Perls asked.

Planchette nodded, looking at the back of the next painting. It was dated slightly later than the other two. "I can go help Dunn, afterwards." He missed Dunn. They shared energy, working together. He was steadier with her.

"All right. We ought to have someone with rank over there, anyway."

Planchette didn't want to get trapped by more extraneous procedure. "Unless I think of something else," he added.

"Understood," Perls said. "Stay in touch."

Planchette looked around at the paintings. There was no question that they were depictions of shapes. They were like portraits. Olivetta had visualized them with remarkable clarity, each every bit as unique as a person. Illuminated brightly, they would appear sickly and necrotic. Here his skill was most evident, and his fear, as well. In this precisely restrained light, reserved for the shades between night and day, the subjects in the paintings acquired ethereal grace. Demons indeed—they bore the exalted character of angels.

They are not *like* portraits, Morpho conveyed. They *are* portraits.

Chapter Thirty-one

Once back in the hover and underway to Claire's, with the driving turned over to the autopilot, Planchette leaned back, closed his eyes and let his assistants go to work peeling his human memories away from his obstructed inner mind. Their gentleness soothed him, though he felt their anxiety. They were disturbed to have recognized the shapes depicted in Olivetta's paintings. Secrets had been kept by elements in the Cloud much longer than any of them had supposed.

It was increasingly evident to Planchette that he had been presented with a sequence of events that did not make sense. Olivetta had been able to see and depict shapes much longer than he had claimed. He had both lied and misled, for reasons unknown, though it certainly had something to do with that ability. Haliel said Frisa had been in New York, in common time, for five years. But for her to have activated Olivetta's bizarre acuity she had to have been here longer than that. Which could mean that Haliel also had lied, or simply did not know. The Ixilian agent was reliant, for much of his information, upon the beacon that monitored Frisa and $\frac{1}{4}$=ca.85 during hibernation. But the beacon had shown a significant lapse in analytical function when it followed Frisa to Earth without registering clearly that it was leaving $\frac{1}{4}$=ca.85 behind—abandoning surveillance, thereby, of what, according to Haliel, constituted half of the organism it was tasked to monitor. So the beacon's data was suspect, and Haliel might, unknowingly, have arrived later, in relation to Frisa, than he thought. Assuming, of course, that Haliel was telling the truth.

Again Planchette had the feeling that he was missing something obvious. He was not used to looking backward, trying to unravel sequences of events. For him the past had always been a unified quantity that informed the present. Analyzing it like this, parsing out strings of cause and effect, was wearying. Between that and the ministrations of the shapes, an urge to sleep crept over him and he dozed off. Again he dreamed, though more, now, in the manner common to him, entering the flow state of his psyche, letting go of events and interpretations. He fell awash of a purling pink mist, through which blue and grey streams slipped like eels. Close, here, to the condition in which he hibernated—to peace, of a kind, at its penultimate extreme. But there was an abnormality within the flow, a dark emergence, rising from the mist at an abstract of distance. It acquired features—black voids for eyes, a mouth that stretched and stretched to scream—

Planchette startled awake to the wail of the cruiser's siren. Twelve conveyed that the autopilot had been re-directed. Planchette rubbed his face, contacted Processing.

"Handler 42, Ganeel."

The name and voice were familiar; Planchette couldn't remember when he'd spoken with this person before. He cleared his throat, ran his hand through his hair. "What's going on?"

"Officer needs assistance at the Utilitarian Lodge Majeure, Detective Chron. Distress call from Detective Perls."

Planchette remembered talking to Ganeel before going down into the transit bay with Dunn. Graph conveyed that Planchette could countermand the re-direct. He didn't know if he should do that. Again he missed Dunn's faith and steadiness. He wanted to see Claire, needed to see her. At the same time he didn't want to experience, again, the void in her recognition of him. It was hard to think with so much competing for his attention. The clarity that had visited him at MacGrory's retreated into shadows. Only Spoon had counsel: that perhaps, lacking a more certain course, it might be as well to go where he had been asked.

Planchette surrendered to the will of Processing, told himself he was as likely to find answers pursuing trouble as he was questioning Claire. And Perls needed him. He could do worse than go where he was needed, if only to keep up appearances.

He brushed the shapes away.

The Utilitarian Lodge Majeure looked like a toppling wave of angles, less a product of assemblage architecture than an enormous sculpture. The corners of many buildings had been salvaged, to varying degrees up-ended and joined in an immense representation of change. The plaza in front of the Lodge was a divot in a field of chaos, so dissimilar were the jig-saw tenements defining the rest of its perimeter. A crowd had massed there, and a smaller group blocked the Lodge entrance at the top of a broad flight of stairs, near the foot of which several police cruisers were parked. Perls, accompanied on the stairs by uniformed cops, argued with a person in brightly-colored clothing who stood in front of the entrance-blockers.

Planchette brought his cruiser down by the others. Uniformed cops moved civilians back. He got out, nodded at the officers. A lot of shapes had been drawn here, too—at least a couple of hundred flitted about above the crowd. The human gathering numbered in thousands. Those Planchette could see all wore Utilitarian pins. They weren't doing anything, just standing there. He could smell their sweat.

Something very important to these people had to be at stake for them to subject themselves to this day's heat in lead-lined clothing. Most made do, like Planchette and the other detectives, with overcoats, probably protecting their genitals with lead-lined undergarments. Relatively few opted for the more comprehensive shielding of jump suits, similar to what street cops wore, in which one swam, figuratively, in one's own water—'fish suits.' It would be hotter amid the press of bodies. People would start passing out before long.

A young blonde-haired woman in a light brown overcoat and

floppy beret met Planchette's gaze. There was no hostility in her, just calm and steady defiance. She did not blink. A furrow formed between her eyes. She wanted Planchette to understand something. He found others looking at him, men and women, young and old. It seemed the full spectrum of society was represented here, every profession and racial variation, adolescents and elders side by side.

They were all here because of him, Planchette thought. Ever since arriving on this world, he had been confronted with his failings. Disregard for Frisa's suffering, false assumptions, ignorance of his own vulnerabilities—and now, it seemed, he had become a catalyst for strife among people he was meant to help. Morpho objected: The impression of social consensus veils discord. It is always there, Morph agreed. Yes, Planchette acknowledged, but my actions helped this discord to manifest. I was not made to do that. Nor to take undue responsibility for the actions of others, Spoon countered.

Planchette noticed fledgling shapes peaking from the crowns of many hats. An unusual percentage of these demonstrators were on the verge of giving birth. It seemed they all watched him, now, stolid folk in drab clothing, colors other than grey muted to inconsequence. Except in one case—high on the steps of the Lodge Majeure, the person with whom Perls argued shone like a beacon.

The remnant corner of a yellow brick building, upended and stabilized at about a sixty-degree tilt, framed the Lodge entrance with a tent-like hood at the top of the stairs. Demonstrators, presenting the same intractable demeanor as those in the plaza, blocked six pairs of glass double doors centered by a glass revolving door. A mosaic stone spiral with the Utilitarian symbol at its center filled the triangular space over the doors. At the base of the spiral, above the demonstrators heads, an inscription read, "NO DOCTRINE CAN DECIDE HUMAN FELLOWSHIP."

Perls argued with a woman of massive build nearly as tall as he. She wore a spectacular robe that was a patchwork of primary colors, and a similarly multi-hued skull cap. Her features were smooth and deep-hewn, her skin, sheened with perspiration, the color of coffee. She listened to Perls with her chin raised imperviously.

"No judge will grant a hold in a homicide investigation," Perls told her. "One way or another, we're coming in."

"Nevertheless, we will wait for our attorneys to advise us, Nathan."

"Oh, I think your attorneys have made their views known, Caster." Perls gestured at the crowd.

"I insist that we adhere to the formalities."

Perls wagged his sheet at the tall woman. "Just 'cause you won't look at it doesn't make my warrant not exist."

"I cannot confirm the authority of a document I have not seen. We are under no obligation to submit to a hypothetical edict."

"You go on and play games; you're endangering these people. *That*—" Perls aimed his sheet at her, "will send you to a reservation."

"If it does, so be it." Caster crossed her arms and fixed her gaze to the distance.

Perls stared in amazement. "You've got *kids,* woman! They'll never *see* you!"

Planchette snagged Perls' attention, drew him aside. "What happened?"

Perls looked back at Caster, shook his head. "I'm in here questioning people, this one comes out of her office. Caster's Lodge Steward right now—head asshole. Tells me she saw our phony Delgado and Smith run off before I got here. I follow her outside, because I'm mentally deficient, so she can show me where they went—that's what she tells me. I turn around, her crew is blocking the entrance. Back and side doors are sealed, mob starts showing up. Haven't been able to get hold of Hasker but—" he wagged his sheet again—"I *got* the warrant."

The crowd, ominous in its stillness, filled the plaza, now, and was massing down side streets. More shapes had come, too.

Planchette saw a cluster descend in a flurry. Someone had given birth.

"This was planned," Perls said.

Planchette heard hovers incoming, looked up. "Maybe not for us."

Perls followed his gaze. "What the—?"

A phalanx of hovercrafts—black government sedans and personnel carriers—approached from the north, flanked by four platform hovers. Pillbox-hatted P-techs rode the latter, standing. P.C. had arrived in force.

A voice Planchette recognized boomed from loudspeakers: "This assembly is hazardous, and will be dispersed in accordance with mandated procedures. By judicial order, all present will submit to evaluation and treatment. Repeat, this gathering is hazardous …"

"Aw, bullshit," Perls growled. He whistled and signaled the cops in the plaza to come to him.

The hovers dropped into the plaza. The crowd was slow to give way. Planchette watched demonstrators put plugs in their ears and don blindfolds. One of the platforms broke toward the steps, stopped a few feet from Perls, just high enough for its rider to look down at him. P.T. Birns now wore a crimson capelet, and there was a red bar on his hat. Spoon conveyed that he had been promoted.

"You heard the order, Perls," Birns said. Hot air that tasted of metal blew from beneath his platform.

"That hyphen doesn't count with me, Birns," Perls said. "You've got no authority over my people."

"The order is judicial."

"You pricks keep a deck of those on file. They might work with a grim in the sex zone or a drunk taking a dump in the street but you know damn well they don't fit cops. And quit doing that!"

Birns was more skilled than Planchette had taken him to be. He mirrored Perls, out of sync, to throw him off, and it was working. Perls was not good at marshaling his emotions. Planchette made a loud honking noise to disrupt the P-tech's concentration. Birns glared at Planchette in shock.

It was enough for Perls to regain his composure. He clicked his sheet into record mode and held it up for Birns to see. "Everything within a quarter mile of the Lodge is evidentiary—the plaza, all of it. These people are witnesses—" Perls pointed at the demonstrators. "They need to be interviewed by police investigators before P.C. takes action towards them of any kind."

"You can't claim that!" Birns cried.

"Back your agents out of here."

Birns nostrils flared. "I don't think so."

"Outside the perimeter. You interfere in any way, you're obstructing and perverting. I'll go to court on it. I'll sequester myself and refuse medication. Same goes for all my people here. They're witnesses to my decision, which is official."

Birns fumed, dead-eyed on Perls, but Planchette felt the bulk of his heat coming his way. The P-tech's voice went flat; "No need for dramatics. Your investigation takes precedence."

Planchette felt an inner shift, like a toxic wave, pass through him. He squeezed his eyes shut and took a deep breath, focused on his physical center of balance. The vertigo subsided. Maybe he would just fall apart at some point—hands, arms, legs, head, plopping in a heap around his defunct torso. Like Haliel's version of a construct popping its bolts. He peered at the sky, took another long breath. Did Haliel have bolts?

A noise rose from the demonstrators in the plaza. P-techs had started loading them onto transports, carrying those who wouldn't walk. In response, the demonstrators had commenced to moan, with the obvious purpose of further disrupting the P-techs' efforts to manage them.

Perls pointed at the scene. "Release those people."

"You'll take responsibility for containing this situation?" Birns said.

"Yeah, we'll handle it, thanks." Perls pocketed his sheet, spun about and climbed the stairs toward Caster.

"Will that hold him?" Planchette asked, keeping abreast. His limbs felt heavy and sluggish.

"It'll slow him down." Perls glanced at Planchette. "You come in handy."

"That man should not have authority. 'Dramatics!'"

Perls grunted, turned his attention to the Lodge Steward, who, it was clear, had observed developments closely. The others blocking the entrance behind her now had on blindfolds and earplugs like those in the plaza. "What's it going to be, Caster? Us or them, those are your options."

Caster scanned the plaza, where P-techs were guiding demonstrators back off of transports. "You don't understand the circumstances, Nathan."

"I'll give you that. You really want all these people to get their eggs scrambled by those sons-of-bitches?" Perls asked.

"You place our future in danger, Nathan," Caster said. "You don't mean to, but you do."

"See, it *bothers* me, you say things like that. Which means I have to take you in for questioning. But one thing at a *time?*"

Caster sighed. "I should not be the one making this decision." She turned to a man behind her, touched his hand in a communicative way. The man frowned but let Caster guide him down a step and aside. Planchette looked back at the scene in the plaza and witnessed something he didn't think he'd seen before. Scores of demonstrators gave birth simultaneously. Shapes poured into the plaza. Meanwhile the P-techs made slow work of releasing demonstrators and did not withdraw. Additional black hovers appeared at the mouths of two side streets. Planchette tugged Perls' sleeve and pointed at them. Caster moved through the people blocking the entrance, creating an aisle. Perls picked six uniforms to stay behind, with instructions to let no one pass. Then he, Planchette and the rest of the uniformed cops went up the stairs and into the Lodge. Caster followed, guiding the people she'd moved, who had joined arms, back to their blocking positions.

Planchette experienced another spasm as he went through the door. The shapes could not identify the cause. He didn't know what he would do if he did break down.

Immediately commanding attention inside the building, at the far end of a vast entry hall, a gigantic sculpture of a man appeared to be climbing out of the floor. He was rendered half emergent, from his abdomen up, one hand flat on the ground, supporting his rise, the other outstretched, reaching for something—an unseen potential. His expression conveyed pain and hope.

Perls tried to make a call on his sheet, muttered.

"Still can't get Hasker?" Planchette asked.

He shook his head.

The entry hall was cool and surprisingly dark. Windows once vertical, now horizontal, at varying tilts, were all fitted with photo-reactive glass. Bookshelves, supplied with ranks of ladders, scaled jagged heights on an upper level, which was bordered by a brass balustrade. The staggered vault, assembled from the remnant corners of fallen towers, echoed, on a mammoth scale, the turning pages of a book. This library is part of the Continental Archive, Graph conveyed. Planchette noticed that, where sunlight hit them directly, the shelves were shuttered. An automated system, Twelve conveyed. Here it was again, the determination to keep old ways functional.

Planchette found Caster watching him.

"You're wondering if anyone ever reads those old books," she said.

Planchette had wondered nothing of the kind. He was caught by the solidity of the Steward's persona. She was a natural anchor for those around her.

"We do," she answered her own question. The furrows between her eyes smoothed. She seemed to see something about Planchette that surprised her.

Perls picked six officers to search the library. "Assume anyone you find is of interest. Grab them." The officers broke into groups of three, headed towards curving flights of stairs at the far corners of the hall, past the sculpture.

Caster gave Perls a weary look.

"How did you think this was going to work?" He picked four uniforms to stay with him, assigned four to Planchette, told four to stand post in the entry hall and the remaining eight to fan out. Several archways around the hall's perimeter at ground level gave access to other parts of the Lodge.

"Keys?" Perls asked Caster.

She shook her head. "We don't lock our offices."

Perls led the cops he'd picked to the central archway on the right; Planchette went with his group to an opposite corridor on the left. The floor of the entry hall was a polished amalgam of stone and fused glass, laid in a mosaic of intersecting rounds describing the orbits of the planets around the sun and the major constellations. Echoes of their footfalls swelled and diminished. The corridor extended only a few yards before opening onto a high-ceilinged lounge furnished with old arm chairs and wooden tables, and bordered by more shelves of books. Above the latter hung Pre-C portraits, most showing damage, and tapestries so patched and faded it was hard to make out what they depicted—a vague impression of a castle, ghostly revelers beneath ghostly trees, pale oxen pulling a cart through a void of countryside. The focus here was on conservation, not combining damaged materials. Beyond the reading room they came to a curved hallway lined with doors. Planchette signaled his officers to start searching. His sheet vibrated and he touched his ear.

"Open your video link," Perls said.

Planchette took out his sheet and opened the holoscreen. A view of the plaza showed, shot from an elevated angle. P.C. had resumed rounding up demonstrators. One of the cops on the steps was video-graphing the scene.

"You want us to try and stop them, Detective Perls?" the officer asked.

Perls cursed. "No, don't interfere. Continue recording. Tell the others to do that, too. But don't comply if they try to take you. Record everything. Chron, you better come back—"

The holo-feed died. Planchette tried to re-contact Perls but couldn't. Twelve conveyed that the signal had been blocked.

Planchette hurried back to the entry hall. Sounds of shouting roiled up the corridor. Caster's composure had shattered. Hand over mouth, she stared in horror at the scene outside. The demonstrators had gone limp in a pile, blocking entry. P-techs, trying to climb over them, struggled with cops. Perls emerged furious from the opposite corridor. "I am going to *eat* that son-of-a-bitch. They can send me to a reservation; I am going to cook him in a pot and *eat* him!"

An explosion at the rear of the building rocked the floor.

Chapter Thirty-two

Caster shouted to get Perls' attention. He glared at her.

"I know what they're after," she said.

"What, you're gonna trust me now?"

Caster spread her arms helplessly.

Perls studied the melee outside. Caster gestured for him to follow her. "Been better if you'd started this way," he told her. The officers who'd gone up to the library came to the balustrade. Perls told them to come down and help the others hold the entry hall. He minced no words making it clear that he wanted P.C.'s agents kept out of the building.

The four cops he'd picked earlier Perls signaled to stay with him. He, they and Planchette followed Caster to the statue of the reaching man. She stopped by the giant hand splayed on the floor and tried to get her sheet to work. The hand's knuckles were nearly as tall as Planchette. Much of the sculpture's torso, head and arms had been fashioned from molded plastic. Wire and circuitry glimmered in a dark, composite mix. Old technology recycled, Twelve conveyed. The stuff of dreams. Load-bearing parts were metal.

A second explosion rumbled from the depths.

"What are we doing, here?" Perls asked.

Caster cursed, put her sheet in her pocket and beckoned Perls and Planchette. They helped her lift a panel from the floor. Underneath was a lever, which Caster pushed counter-clockwise. Latches clanged open, and the hand's thumbnail, revealed to be a trap door, popped up about an inch along its inner edge.

Caster tried but couldn't move it. Perls and two officers, lifting together, raised the door until it locked into an upright position. There was a sharp click and the tip of the thumb sank into the floor. A stairway led down into darkness.

Caster went first and turned on lights. Another spasm, more pronounced than the previous two, hit Planchette as he followed Perls down the stairs. He leaned on the handrail, pretended to watch the passage above and waved the officers behind him by. His vision shifted repetitively; he grew nauseated. Graph conveyed that the patch had thickened, as before, but evidenced no further abnormality. The others confirmed the assessment. Then Morpho detected an instability in Planchette's core. What kind of instability? Planchette asked. It is expanding, Morpho conveyed. It seems to be an autonomic reaction to the containment of your elder psyche. Is it serious? Planchette asked. No criteria exists to evaluate severity, Morph answered, but it seems very slight.

Planchette rubbed his forehead, took deep breaths, swallowed several times. A dread arose for which he had no name.

"Chron!" Perls called from the bottom of the stairs, "you coming?"

Planchette continued down. His feet were weights at the ends of his legs. The stairs ended at a round chamber, from which several passages diverged through stone archways.

"You okay?" Perls asked.

"Where are we going?" Planchette asked Caster. His desire to lead was spent. Caster took them into the passage straight across from the stairs.

"I think we've found the Temple Trust," Perls muttered.

Planchette nodded but his thoughts were elsewhere. *Your mind is singularity,* the Tehfoloran had said. *Danger to all world.* He needed Frisa to help him understand. He knew in a basic way what she and he were, how they had been made—just enough to be frightened by the implications in the Tehfoloran's warning. His core was a compressed nodule of what Friedman and his colleagues and students would have called dark energy, the same stuff shapes were made of. Planchette had no idea what might happen if the nodule lost coherence, how much energy would be released, or in what manner. He could not dismiss the possibility that, unbeknownst to himself, it might contain the power to destroy an entire planet. He pushed the notion aside. He was scaring himself. The shapes were quick to agree, though they were worried, too. If his core did come apart—and *this* was the dread—what would remain of *him?*

It was the second time on this world that he had been confronted with the prospect of his own mortality. The death suggested now was no gradual decline; it was an unforeseeable, sudden end.

Vertigo overwhelmed him. He staggered to his knees and vomited. The taste was horrid.

Perls knelt beside him, put his hand on Planchette's back.

How did people cope with this? ¼=ca.85 had thought that he understood. But his understanding had been insulated by the presumption that he, himself, was invulnerable. Others rose from bed each day to the knowledge that a terrible end might befall them, without warning, at any moment. A hovercraft might sever a cable and bring an unstable building down on their heads. In his case he was cable, building and vehicle, all three, and didn't know if he was driving toward disaster or away from it.

"Hey, pal, you all right?" Perls' deep voice reverberated comfort. Comradely warmth issued from his hand.

Planchette's vision steadied. He encountered Caster's panicked stare and waved Perls on. "I'll catch up."

They left him and hurried down the passage. Perls glanced back at him.

Planchette had forgotten to eat or drink or take supplements again. Dunn hadn't been there to remind him. Maybe he was experiencing a recurrence of the effects of physical neglect. Perls and the others sank from view down another flight of stairs.

It came to Planchette, the obvious thing he'd been missing.

Frisa and he weren't the only ones under attack. A steady, secret campaign was being waged against the inhabitants of this world, which was incredible. They posed no threat to anyone in the galactic community. Their space travel technology wasn't just rudimentary, it was inconsequential. There was no reason to attack them. Unless—a thought brought Planchette to his feet. Unless there was something about them that was different from the other species he'd met.

Unless they were like his creators.

Echoes of distant explosions stuttered up the corridor. Planchette forced himself to move on, jogged, stumbled, ran, took stairs three at a time down to another junction. Faint shouts echoed from the left. At the end of another corridor he found a glass door that opened with resistance. Cool air poured out and Planchette entered a vast, climate-controlled vault, sped past rows of shelves crowded with artifacts—machines and appliances, furniture, art, file cabinets. More noise drew him right, between shelves, through another passage and a vault full of musical instruments. Beyond that and yet another corridor he entered a chamber that housed a great stockpile of weapons. Planchette slowed, taking in rack after rack of projectile firearms.

Bangs and staccato bursts sounded ahead, and more shouting. Planchette saw Perls and the others, ran to catch up. An acrid smell stained the air. Planchette gagged, breathed deeply through his mouth, spit several times. He was pouring with sweat.

"You're restoring *Pre-C* weapons?" Perls shouted at Caster. "Are you in*sane?*"

"What are *they* using?" she shouted back.

The next junction was strewn with broken masonry and debris, the air hazy with smoke. A metal door had been blown down. The intruders had entered here. More gunfire sounded from a corridor diagonally to the right. Planchette shrugged out of his greatcoat, left it on the floor. Perls and he ran together, leading the others. Caster fell back. Morph and Morpho flew ahead.

Another odor stung Planchette's nostrils—some ignited propellant. Possibly cordite, Twelve conveyed. They were nearing the fight. Bright flashes accompanied sounds of gunfire through the archway ahead.

"This is the police!" Perls barked and drew his O-bow. "Drop your weapons!"

The shooting stopped. Twelve conveyed that Perls might not fully appreciate the dangers of Pre-C firearms. Planchette grabbed Perls' shoulder, raised his chin forward and backward at the tunnel. Perls' eyes widened with the understanding that they were exposed.

Somewhere beyond the end of the corridor a chaos of gunfire and explosions erupted. Morph and Morpho raced back, their warnings incomprehensible. Something slid down the hall behind them. Twelve conveyed that it was a stun grenade. Before Planchette could warn his colleagues, everything went white and he was deaf again. He stumbled against the wall, faintly heard Perls shout. Another grenade went off. Planchette squeezed his eyes shut and shook his head, clung to the wall. Someone shoved him and he fell down. People ran by. Planchette groped air and caught hold of a coat, was dragged a distance before being kicked loose. He kept blinking, saw shadowy figures exit the archway they'd come through, heard Caster yell.

A moment later she ran by with an agonized howl. Planchette, Perls and the other officers helped each other up as their equilibrium returned and their senses cleared. Planchette and Perls staggered after Caster.

Past the next junction, at the end of a short corridor on the right, a makeshift barricade of crates and metal cabinets had been breached, and the glass door beyond it smashed. Inside the vault the door had sealed a fire blazed, fought by two men with extinguishers.

Caster stood by the barricade, staring down at a figure slumped on the floor. One of fire fighters turned and Planchette recognized the Delgado imposter. "Get more extinguishers!" he yelled. "They shut off the water!"

Perls crouched by the body of Gable MacGrory and checked for a pulse, shook his head. He sent his officers to look for more extinguishers. The vault housed thousands of paintings. Most were filed vertically but a few faced outward. Through fire and smoke Planchette recognized the works of Michael Olivetta.

Chapter Thirty-three

The vandals had set off two incendiary devices at the near end of the vault and six more down the center aisle. The fire spread rapidly, blocking access to paintings not yet burning. Soot blackened the arched ceiling; flames grew higher and brighter. The vault was turning into an incinerator.

Friedman's desk had been a distraction. It should have been obvious. What person of his intelligence does not back-up their work? No doubt his enemies would hunt for those back-ups tirelessly. But they'd achieved their main objective by killing him. After that the target had always been Olivetta, to erase him from the record. Planchette felt an urgency in Perls as keen as his own. They both knew this was at the heart of everything, though Perls less knew why.

The uniformed officers, who had stripped off their tunics, returned bearing two extinguishers each. Planchette grabbed one and ran into the vault. The others followed. He attacked the near end of the fire at its center, trying to break through to the aisle. Perls, Caster and the imposters joined their sprays to his. Whatever accelerant the arsonists had used defied the retardant. When they directed their sprays away from a spot, it burst back into flame.

The contest was over in minutes. The ventilation system couldn't clear the air fast enough; smoke forced them out before the fire could. They clustered at the doorway, reluctant to quit. "Aw, life!" Perls cried, and dragged Planchette after him. Planchette's final glimpses of Olivetta's paintings seared his memory. Broken souls amid ruins, children playing with bones—the sufferings of survivors, internal and external realities entwined. All burning, as if in final torment or release. Everywhere their agonies witnessed by shapes, who flickered between beauty and grotesquery in the shifting brightness and smoke-shadow. Just before he turned away Planchette noticed one picture, mounted up high, in which the shapes retained grace brightly lit: abstract angels at play above a ring of children holding hands in a cemetery. Maybe Olivetta had painted it before he'd felt the need to mask his vision.

The surface of the painting blistered and flared.

Perls and Planchette herded the others back to the weapons vault, closed the door, watched smoke fill the glass.

"They won't stop here," Perls said. He held Planchette's coat out to him.

Planchette shook his head in agreement, taking the coat. "Thanks."

Perls pointed at Caster and the imposters. "You're under arrest." He addressed his men: "Hold them here until someone comes down and tells you the situation in the plaza has been resolved. Under no circumstances do these people get turned over to P.C."

"You have a photographic record of Olivetta's paintings?" Planchette asked Caster. "You documented his work?"

She nodded.

"Think you better check on that?"

Caster's eyes widened; she bolted away with a moan.

They all ran after her, back through the passageways and archives, up to the main entry hall of the Lodge. "Let her do what she needs to," Perls told his officers, "then take them all to the station and put them in separate rooms. I don't want them talking to each other." Caster led the imposters and their escort through an archway on the left; Perls and Planchette continued to the main entrance. Perls' inside team had remained where he'd left them. Outside, the doors were guarded by uniformed cops paired with white-suited officers from Judicial Branch. Obviously the situation had changed.

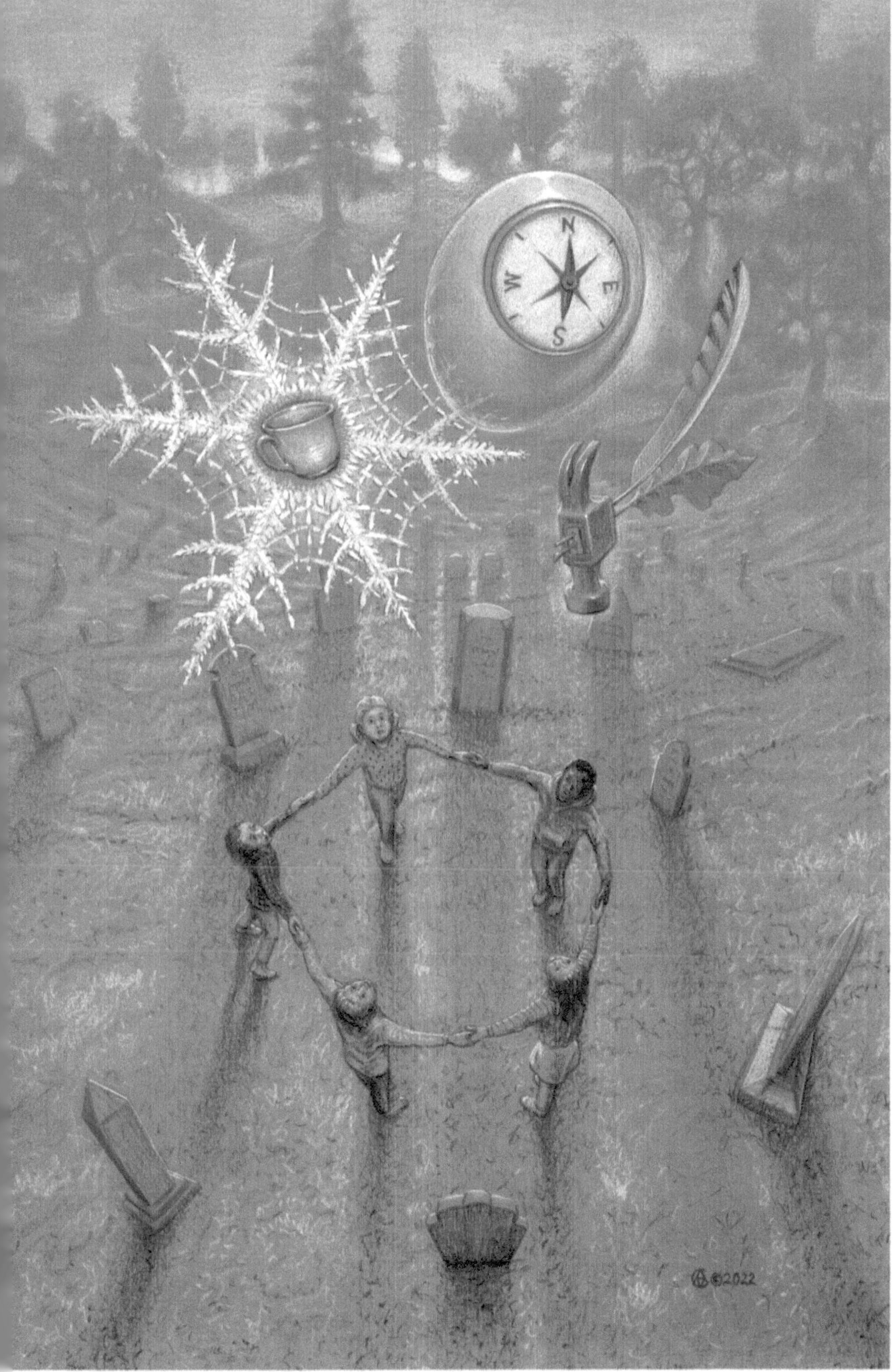

Perls contacted Processing and reported the fire and the water cut-off, then headed toward the doors. "Whatever we got out here, I'll deal with it," he told Planchette. "You keep going. Get fire-fighters and crisis response to Olivetta's studio and the engineer's place. Send Al to one, you go the other."

Reluctantly, Planchette pulled his greatcoat back on. He was dehydrated and his mouth tasted like he didn't want to know what. The plaza had been cleared of demonstrators. P.C.'s agents had departed as well—all but two, who were engaged in a heated exchange with Hasker at the bottom of the stairs. Officials from Judicial Branch and Processing stood by, observing.

Perls headed toward Hasker, and Planchette made for his cruiser.

Hasker spotted them. "Hey!" he shouted at Planchette.

Perls emphatically waved Planchette on. "Let him go, Chief!"

Planchette took the hover up. To the northeast, toward Mac-Grory's house, a plume of black smoke curled into the sky. Farther north, in the approximate direction of Olivetta's studio, there was a distant plank of haze that could have been fire-related as well. Planchette contacted processing and relayed Perls' instructions.

Response teams were already on site at MacGrory's house. Someone else must have reported the fire. Smoke streamed from the ring of windows in the upper dome. Fire-fighters in two positions directed water from hoses up through the windows. Cops and emergency personnel milled in the street. Grie, his arm in a sling, talked with another officer. Planchette circled the scene, looked for a reason to go down.

He called Grie for a report. Armed assailants, dressed like agents from Judicial Branch, had shown up with a warrant. Once inside they'd attacked Grie and Dancla and restrained them. Dancla was in hospital, unconscious. Pick Sutton had tried to help fend off the intruders and been injured, too.

Someone else was calling. Planchette signed off with Grie and answered.

It was Schnitke. "Olivetta's studio is gone."

"Burned?" Planchette asked.

"To ashes."

Planchette sighed. "Tell Perls."

If he had followed his original impulse would things have gone differently? Probably not, and he would not know what he knew now. That knowledge had come at a terrible cost, not just in the loss of Olivetta's legacy. The shapes were absorbing the impossible reality that they, along with their human parents, were under attack. The understanding visited their moods with a shadow the likes of which $\frac{1}{4}$=ca.85 had never before encountered in their kind. Or so it seemed; Planchette could trust his elder memories for little. If their feelings were unprecedented, no less the circumstances that inspired them—of that he *was* sure.

Planchette contacted Perls, filled him in on the situation at MacGrory's, told him what he suspected and meant to do. He turned the cruiser towards Claire Fontaine's, without engaging the autopilot. Reports came in while he drove—break-ins, thefts, further incidents of arson. It would be happening in other cities, too. Olivetta's censors were cleaning up, destroying private collections of his work.

Frisa must have stumbled into this intrigue, maybe when she first arrived. The danger she'd encountered had been so great it had driven her into hiding. Which meant that Planchette was likely at risk himself in ways that he did not recognize. The confounding thing was that there seemed to be a collaboration taking place between humans and aliens. But in all the humans could only be pawns. Planchette had to drive his real enemies into the open. The humans were doing their work for them. He needed to give the puppeteers a reason to reveal themselves.

He had to push the buttons and wind the gears he could see, until the larger mechanism was exposed. He needed Haliel's assistance and still didn't know if he could trust him.

Haliel answered his sheet this time. Planchette tried the ploy he'd used on MacGrory, pretending to know both more and less than he did. "Why does your boss want Olivetta's paintings destroyed?"

The inscrutable Ixilian was silent a moment. "My *boss?*"

Twelve cautioned Planchette. Planchette looked at his sheet, glanced about the interior of the cruiser. Of course his communications were being monitored. With all that had happened it would be a shock if they weren't. Planchette sighed audibly, feigned a fatalistic tone; "Who *knows* what we're talking about."

"Who knows . . ?" Haliel paused. "Oh. Wait."

Planchette tried to remember his previous long-distance communications with Haliel. It would raise eyebrows that the two of them knew each other. Beyond that he didn't think they'd revealed much. Twelve was sure Planchette's previous calls had not been monitored.

"You're right, Processing has an open link to your sheet, and the video feed inside your cruiser is being recorded," Haliel said. "I've interrupted both."

"Will they know?"

"It will seem like an internal glitch. They won't trace it to either of us. What's this about Willbury?"

"Him, P.C.—they just bombed their way into the Continental Archive and set fire to Olivetta's life work. They burned down his studio, too, and they're mopping up right now, going after private collections."

"You're telling me things I know nothing about. Willbury's in a closed meeting. P.C. is claiming it had nothing to do with the bombings at the Utilitarian Lodge."

"They're lying. Or Willbury is. He and some others."

"I believe you. Why does it matter?"

Planchette sighed. He had not the slightest sense if Haliel was representing himself truthfully. "I've been trying to call you. I've had two encounters with our friends from Mars."

Haliel was silent again. "What did they want?"

"They told me the Galactic Council has been dissolved."

"What? That …"

Something in the way Haliel stopped caught Planchette. His human instincts told him the Ixilian had raised his guard. "That *what?*" Planchette asked.

"That doesn't make sense."

"Could it be true?"

"I don't know. I have to check."

"How long will that take?"

"At least a couple of days. But I don't believe them. It's nonsense. They're trying to confuse you. They're the ones who are behind everything."

"I don't think so."

"Why not?"

"Because I wouldn't be talking to you right now if they were. Not as Planchette Chron."

"I don't understand."

Planchette told Haliel what had happened in the tunnel, described how the Tehfoloran had saved his life.

"That's—remarkable."

Again Planchette had the sense that Haliel was withholding something.

"Then it's someone else," Haliel said. "Someone we don't know about."

"And humans are working with them."

"How do you know that?"

Planchette couldn't think of a better way to test Haliel's trustworthiness than giving him an opportunity to fail. "Because Friedman was going to prove Olivetta could see shapes."

Again a long pause. "I'll talk to our Martian visitors."

"Let me know what you learn."

Back-up units beat Planchette to Claire Fontaine's. A dozen uniformed officers waited in the hall outside her apartment. Planchette would have preferred to handle this on his own but the risks were too great. The same officer stood post at the door.

"The woman who came to see Miss Fontaine," Planchette asked her, "is she still here?"

The officer, Gloria Spinotta, was nervous, furtive in her glances at the other cops. "Is there going to be trouble, sir?" she asked Planchette. She was scared.

A couple of nearby officers snickered. Planchette sobered them with a look.

"No trouble, Gloria, just tell me. Is she in there?"

Gloria nodded. "Yes, sir."

Planchette rang the doorbell. Claire answered. She glanced into the hall and blanched, stepped back for him to enter. "It's— good to see you."

Planchette squeezed her hand, whispered, "It's all right." He asked for water.

A slim, young, blond-haired woman with elfin features sat on the sofa in the sunken living room, her hands folded primly on her knees. In a grey pencil skirt and matching blouse she was the picture of feminine poise. Without looking at Planchette she said, "I'm glad you came, Detective Chron."

Claire brought Planchette a glass of water, which he drained. Morph conveyed that his core was expanding again. Planchette took a breath with his eyes closed. At least the sourness in his mouth was less.

He went down into the living room. To the person on the sofa he said, "I need you to come with me, Michelle. We have to ask you some questions."

Olivetta presented him with a philosophical smile. "You can call me Michael, Detective. It won't sound like an insult coming from you."

Chapter Thirty-four

Uniformed cops stood post down the crooked, dim hallway, murmured and nodded as Planchette went by. He did not relish their deference. Through a two-way window on the right he saw Caster, weary with sadness, awaiting questioning in the first interview room. Mason Dial and Skip Leroi, the imposters who had posed as officers Delgado and Smith, were sequestered farther along. Dial was a concrete cutter, Leroi a waste management engineer.

Hasker, Perls, Schnittke and Dunn stood at the end of the hall by the last interview room. Relief spilled through Planchette when he saw Dunn. His elder memories were so muffled he was sure of nothing from his former lives. In her eyes he found an anchor in the present.

She turned away, embarrassed. The others were watching them.

Hasker cleared his throat. "He'll only talk to you. Why is that?"

Planchette waited for Natalie to look back at him. He wanted her to see the steadiness in his regard for her. She did.

"I don't know," he answered Hasker. "Maybe because I asked him about his paintings. I don't know."

"Nathan says you're good with him, thinks we should roll with it."

Almost by reflex, Planchette nodded. Even with a broken mind he played his part. These people, his nominative colleagues, wanted him, without being asked, to do what he needed to do. Meanwhile, somewhere, records were being searched, fingers flipping through files, the moment drawing inexorably nearer when the searchers would realize that they were looking for someone who did not exist. It would not be long before his ruse was exposed.

And no one would ever understand that it wasn't a ruse.

"He insists on not being recorded," Hasker said.

"He hasn't asked for an advocate, Chief," Perls interjected. "Time's against us. He's not who we're after."

"That business you told me about your memory," Hasker asked Planchette, "is it true?"

Planchette wasn't sure of anything where his mind was concerned. "I remember conversations clearly." He hoped he still did.

"You come out of here, you're with a witness right then, recording every word."

Planchette nodded.

Hasker drew him aside. "You think I'm not watching you?"

Planchette met his Captain's gaze with pure persona.

"You dance into town, a beat and a half later you're the guy with the news. Maybe you're that smart. Maybe you just stumbled in the right direction. It's on my mind Friedman's death and your arrival were damn near synchronized. That's one hell of a stumble."

Planchette swallowed before he could catch himself. (He had not been made so vulnerable to reflex.) "Just trying to do my job, Chief."

Hasker peered at him a moment longer, relaxed his scrutiny. "I got a call from MacGrory's widow. She didn't leave him, he sent her away. Which means he knew something was coming." The Captain pointed through the window at Olivetta. "You try to convince that winder to give us a statement. I know he's a victim but that does not make him innocent. He could have helped and he ran."

Planchette nodded.

"And Chron, you know something you haven't told us, *now* would be the time."

Planchette feigned incomprehension. Hasker lifted his chin at the interview room.

Planchette went in. Grey walls, grey floor, grey ceiling—a room for the suspension of alternatives. Olivetta's hair was mussed. He'd been deprived of wig and wig cap, along with the rest of his clothes. He looked much diminished in a white paper jumpsuit. Planchette was glad no one had told him that his paintings had been destroyed. Questioning him would be hard as it was.

"Michael." Planchette sat down across the grey, oblong table from Olivetta.

"Detective Chron." The artist's voice was frail in the anechoic chamber.

"You can call me Planchette."

"I prefer 'detective.'"

"You asked to speak to me."

"Are we being recorded?"

Planchette shook his head.

"Overheard?"

Planchette glanced back at the two-way glass. He looked weary, too, in his reflection. He pushed a black button on the table's surface, cutting the intercom. The light next to the button went out.

Olivetta watched him. "I think it's better if you ask questions."

Planchette liked Olivetta and admired him, but none of that mattered. "You're a very good liar."

Olivetta chewed his lip, looked away, mumbled.

"What?"

"You have to be or they own you."

"P.C.?"

Olivetta nodded.

"Tell me about Friedman."

The façade dissolved and Olivetta's wretchedness showed.

"He was more than a customer," Planchette prodded.

"We kept it secret."

"Why?"

"Victor thought we should. To protect me. My work. It's complicated."

"Explain it to me."

"Could you ease up? P.C.'s probably ripping through my studio right now, and I can't do anything about it. I am cooperating."

Planchette didn't have time to be patient. He waited but did not soften his demeanor.

Olivetta stared at him. "Did you know, detective, that in some early societies there were individuals whose responsibility it was to interpret reality for the group? Sometimes those individuals claimed to see or talk to spirits. Civilization came along and discredited them, said they were delusional, dishonest, hallucinating under the influence of drugs. I think maybe they were impugned unjustly."

"Is the history lesson going someplace?"

Olivetta sighed, glanced around, sucked his teeth. "It goes back to my childhood—"

"You've known Friedman since—"

"*No*. This is about my *art*, not *me*. It's about what I *see*. That's why Victor became interested in me."

"All right."

"I've always been able to draw. An unkind person might call me a savant or a freak or something. I could render with a high degree of binocular accuracy when I was four, without any training. My foster parents—I never knew my birth parents. I don't know what happened to them; no one would ever tell me. Maybe they don't know but you might see why I'd wonder.—My foster parents were well-meaning but didn't understand me. My drawings scared them. I've always interpreted things, looked underneath. If you're not doing that, what's the point? But it scared them.

"I'm sure they talked with people in P.C. about me a lot. I

turned twelve, took my first long-form DAT. We lived in The Angels on Cemetery Bay, in a scratch called Town Number Three. Things went slowly, there—no technology. It was beautiful. I miss that water. Still, usually you'd get a response in ten or twenty days; but this went months with nothing. Then this person shows up, high-ranking, no uniform. I'm not even there. I'm a specimen in a beaker. He questions me like he's testing chemicals, puts me on all this medication—"

Morph conveyed an anomaly. "They didn't give you behavioral therapy, first?" Planchette asked.

Olivetta shook his head. "Not then, no, just the drugs. But I'd had a lot of treatment before that. On and off low-doses. Stopped me dreaming, sometimes, or made them weird, which for me was saying something. Meditation drills, behavioral exercises. Wake up in the morning, empty the trash before you pee. Short-form DATs are usually given to kids every couple of years. By the time I was ten I was being tested every other month. At the time I did not know that was unusual."

"Go on."

"For three years I'm a cabbage. Wipe my chin, stare at nothing. The courts lowered the Right-of-Refusal age to fifteen, so on my birthday I went off of everything. They don't *tell* you how hard that is. But it was like getting my life back. Maybe two weeks I started drawing, again, which *I* found telling. *He* shows up."

"The person from three years earlier?"

Olivetta nodded. "Gives me another DAT, tells me I'm Class One. I refuse to go back on pills so this little girl's off to the reservation. Shit mummy and shit daddy don't even wave bye-bye. Four hundred miles in a closed container to be dumped at a hut in the desert. With other huts nearby—lots of them. Inadequately supervised. I'm young and pretty so from my first night I get toyed around. Which wouldn't have been so bad if I'd been able to draw. Two years more to get a court to provision my banishment with art supplies.

"I bury myself in my work and shut out the world. Start painting, which became my drug. Every couple of months some mouthless uniform from P.C. takes everything. I'm sure they destroyed it all. But I'd moved into a private world and didn't care. Everything that wasn't painting was background noise.

"One day a woman from the Continental Archive shows up and wants to *buy* my stuff. Which is a shock, but I don't have to think about it. Sure, *honey*, take it *all.* Anything's better than painting for the crematorium. But it was around then I got the sense something else was going on. A struggle behind the scenes. With me in the middle.

"Fifteen years, I'm shuffled from one reservation to another. With the money from the Archive I could afford better materials. Couple of places I even had a studio separate from my living quarters. I still get visits from P.C. —less frequent—once a year. They don't take anything, now, just make a show of re-testing me. I paint and Utilitarians cart it away.

"Then Victor shows up. How he became aware of me I don't know. He never admitted to being a Utilitarian, but he was one. Absolutely. And he had the clout to visit me, in person and unsupervised.

"I was up north in the islands. Which was okay. I wish I was there now. The XTs police it better up there; you're left alone. One day this big, square-headed lump comes ashore. Gives me a hug and sort of beams at me, like I'm precious. No one'd looked at me like that before." Olivetta tossed his head, dismissing emotions. "In other circumstances we might have had something. We tried a couple of times—to Victor, sex was exercise. He didn't care who he did it with so long as you were fit. He was in love with his mind."

Like all of Frisa's recipients.

"Maybe I'm that way."

"Wright told us you prefer women."

Olivetta smirked. "*Wright.* Confirmation P.C. is fallible: Terrence Wright is my CA. He's infatuated with me. How do you think I got him tied up? He doesn't understand me. If it's just for sex, yeah, I prefer women. More specifically snags. Like a dose, or a good beating, and I fly away. I'm not unpleasant about it. But if I ever got involved with someone it would have to be a man."

"Why was Friedman interested in your paintings?"

Olivetta was silent a moment. "I'm not sociopathic, Detective. I've never hurt anyone. The only provocation they've had for classifying me as a black hole is that some of the things I paint are hard to look at. But there's nothing I've painted that isn't inside all of us. Nothing. And that is *not* why they've done this to me."

"Why, then?"

Olivetta peered at Planchette, clearly wanting him to answer his own question.

"You're talking about your demons."

Olivetta's expression twisted with irony. "They're not demons."

"It's your word—"

"I know—"

"What, then?"

"I don't know. I call them semaphores. They're like little, living signals. Always trying to tell me something. I've never met anyone else who can see them. Maybe one of the XTs up in the islands—I wondered about that one. But even I can't hear them. If they do actually speak."

"You told us you acquired the ability to see them recently."

Olivetta shook his head.

"You said the woman you painted showed them to you."

"No. That was, I don't know, an instinct."

"Instinct? To mislead us about a prime suspect in a murder inquiry?"

Olivetta goggled Planchette. "I didn't know she was a suspect. Nobody told me that!"

"Then why bring her up? Why tell that story?"

Olivetta was at a loss.

"You gave us two very different pictures of her. Aside from the clothing, no one recognizes her, in either the portrait or the holograph."

"There's no holograph. I thought you'd catch that. They're both paintings—"

"So, Wright is not entirely stupid. You *were* playing with us."

"Is it playing when you're afraid for your life?"

It was hard for Planchette to craft reactions with so much rising in himself. "Maybe not." He rolled his fingers on the table. The trail continued to lead both to and away from Frisa.

"They're trying to make it look like *I* killed Victor."

"How so?"

Olivetta stopped himself. He'd said more than he'd meant to.

"You can't expect me to let that go."

Olivetta swallowed, looked away. "The knife."

"Knife? You mean from your surgical tools?"

Olivetta nodded. "The one that's missing. Someone took it."

"You said it was gone when you got them."

"Someone took it."

Planchette became irrelevantly irritated. "When did you notice it missing?" It was an intrusion of emotion exclusive to his human persona.

"I don't know. A couple of weeks ago, maybe."

"Tell me about the woman." A face Frisa had worn in a far-off life came to Planchette, all quills and convoluted flesh and too many eyes, so foreign it frightened him. He swallowed. His partner of ages had become so distant her echo was a cipher, his feelings for her a pain of vacancy.

"Friedman brought her to my studio. All I can remember is there was something wrong with her. They're not supposed to but I know they've got cameras in there. I found one; it was gone the next day. They knew he was there, and they knew she was with him."

"P.C. again."

Olivetta nodded.

"How long ago was this?"

"A few months. I can't remember exactly. They pulled me in for an unscheduled DAT and did something. There's a gap. It's happened before." He closed his eyes and shook his head. "They've fucked with my mind so many times."

"Not a year and a half ago."

Olivetta shook his head.

"I still don't understand why you lied. In that way."

Olivetta sighed in exasperation. "It was the first thing I thought of when you told me Victor was dead. That woman—I painted her. *Twice*. Why can't I remember? What did they do to me? That was the last time I saw Victor. It's all intrigue with P.C. You can't go at anything with them in a straight line. And I *know* what they care about."

"What does that mean?"

Again, Olivetta answered with a questing gaze.

Shapes. "Semaphores."

Olivetta nodded.

"You're telling me that agents of P.C. knowingly mis-classified you as a black hole because of little figures in your paintings."

"You're catching on."

"Which would mean they somehow find those figures problematic."

"But you're skeptical."

Planchette replied with silence.

"I'm forty years old, detective. I took my first DAT when I was five. In all the testing and questioning and counseling and therapy and treatment and outright fucking torture I've endured since then, not once has anyone from P.C. asked me about those curious little figures. It's never become a question on my personalized DAT, and no agent, analyst or test giver has ever made reference to them. Not one single time. In thirty-six years, detective, not once. You asked me about them three minutes after we met. They were the *first* thing you asked me about."

"You never brought them up yourself?"

Olivetta shook his head. "I don't remember when I first realized no one else saw them, but I must have been really little because I only remember keeping it to myself. *Seeing things* is not conducive to smooth relations with others. Someone asks I'll talk about them, to whatever extent I can satisfy myself they really want to know. I'm careful. Very, very careful. But someone intrudes into your life, makes themselves a fixture, year after year, exerts complete control over your circumstances, and they *never* ask? What does it say?"

"And the semaphores were Friedman's interest as well."

"Yes, they were."

"In what way?"

"He recognized them for what they are. Somehow, through his science, he understood them."

"He didn't think they were hallucinatory?"

"Sometimes I wondered if he needed to believe they weren't. He was looking for an explanation for 'the moment.' Sort of. He had a lot of passions. He wasn't spiritual, really. He wanted to give everything to everybody, which was the extraordinary thing about him. He wanted humanity to fly to the stars, and believed we could do it. He'd say things like, 'Darkness is faster than light,' like that explained everything. And then blah, blah. I didn't understand most of it."

"Space flight had something to do with your paintings?"

"No. Or maybe. With Victor everything was connected. I thought maybe what he really wanted was to prove the existence of the soul. Which—why you need to *prove* that. Except if your bedrock faith is empiricism, there's no point. I've got no wound to stick your finger in that you don't make yourself. I told him that. I said disbelief in the soul is an excess of empiricism. An excess of *faith* in empiricism. He just smiled."

"He thought your semaphores are souls?"

"No. Neither do I. It doesn't matter because they're alive. They're all around us and we can't see them. Most of us. I mean I hate to think I'm the *only* one. They don't function the way we do. Not at all. But we're related."

"And you think P.C. wants to suppress that information."

"I think they want me to stop painting pictures of them."

"Why?"

"Evidence of things unseen, detective. Beyond what we know or believe. Victor said the purpose of science is to examine reality, not decide it. We're all trapped in a box with our awful history and the viciousness of time. We need a future." Olivetta held Planchette's gaze, smiled faintly. "You're wondering why, if what I say is true, they haven't just killed me. It *is* P.C. we're talking about. Not supposed to be their thing. Although some of them seem to have gotten past that."

"Some of them."

"Show me two people who agree on everything. Any impression of consensus at *that* level? Is false. To some degree, it's false. Victor couldn't have gotten me off of the reservation without help from someone in P.C."

For a moment Olivetta's dignity surfaced, out of his hard circumstances and wounds. He was like a twisted branch, all soft tissue, no bark. "Why me?" Planchette asked.

Olivetta lifted his chin, right and left, at the spaces above Planchette's shoulders. "The company you keep."

"My demons?" Planchette smirked. "They're still with me?" Pretense felt pointless with Olivetta but imposture won out.

Again, the sad smile. "Would you like me to describe them?"

Planchette shook his head.

"Victor had one that followed him around like that. Just one but I think it was special."

A question he should have thought of sooner came to Planchette. "And you? They're always around *you,* right?" That was the core inconsistency. It had eluded him.

"Well," Olivetta made a face and bobbed his head, "*that* was the thing. Why'd I make a story up about that woman? Did you ask Terry to come with you, or did he just show up? *I* know they're listening; *I* know they're watching. *Always.* The day before Victor brought her to see me the semaphores stopped coming around. First time in my life. I see them in the distance but it's like they're avoiding me. Then P.C. pulls me in and my memory's fucked with. And no semaphores. From then until you show up with your little entourage, they don't come near me. Did P.C., or *someone,* do something to *keep* them away? That's a fun thought. Is it something about my circumstances? And why are *you* here? Oh, I see, Victor is *murdered.* These things can't possibly be connected. Don't kid yourself. It's all intrigue. Massive. It is *not* coincidence."

There was only one more question Planchette wanted to ask. It was a formality, for the record, for the cop in him. He knew the answer.

"Why kill Victor, detective?" Olivetta asked. "Why kill hope?"

Because they don't want you to be hopeful.

The door opened and Perls leaned in. "We've got a situation."

Planchette nodded and stood up.

"Thank you for treating me like a regular person, detective," Olivetta said.

Planchette wanted to tell Olivetta that he knew he wasn't crazy. But there was too much to think through, so he kept silent, and regretted it, even before he closed the door.

Chapter Thirty-five

Hasker glared down the hall. Schnittke, calm and ready, stood next to him. Dunn looked worried.

"Highballs in the building," Perls explained, "headed this way."

Willbury and a contingent of P-techs rounded the bend and pressed up the corridor.

"You're in no position, Mathias," Hasker said.

"You have evidence of my complicity?"

"Not yet."

"That sounds prejudicial. Stress may be compromising your professional aplomb. I can prescribe something—"

"Stow it."

"You've been watching old movies, again."

"Just me?"

Willbury glanced aside.

"Olivetta's ours 'til we complete our investigation. Unless you have a judicial warrant, an uncontested decision from Processing, and can demonstrate cause, your route's the other direction."

Willbury was unruffled. Planchette noticed Clarence Tythe and Randall Fry bringing up the rear, behind Willbury's escort. Tythe looked uncomfortable. Fry saw Planchette and grinned. Planchette closed his eyes and hoped this wasn't what he feared.

"This isn't a jurisdictional dispute, Captain," Willbury said. "Your investigation has been compromised."

"How's that?"

"We're not here for Olivetta. Though we would appreciate being notified when you're through with him."

"State your business."

"Detective Chron. I shouldn't say 'detective,' really, just 'Planchette,' although I don't know either if that's his name. I don't know *who* he is. More to the point, neither do you. I know he is no detective."

"What the hell are you talking about?" Hasker glanced back at Planchette.

"You overstepped, Captain, logging him in without confirmation."

Hasker, somehow more formidable under fire and half a foot shorter, closed on Willbury. "I didn't overstep one bit. No one conducts himself as this man has without advanced training and experience."

"Be that as it may, Angels Academy has no record of him, nor do any of the departments in which he purports to have served. I have the Academy's report." Willbury opened his hand over his shoulder and one of his escorts put an envelope in it. He gave it to Hasker. "Whatever his training, he's not who he says he is."

Hasker removed a document from the envelope, unfolded and scanned it, held it at Planchette. "What's this?"

Planchette didn't answer. Dunn stared at him. Perls went blank.

Schnittke wasn't buying it. "I don't know what you think you've got, highball, but that man saved my *life*—"

"And we're all glad he did, detective. I've read the report, however, and note it was also he who led you into danger. However commendable some of his actions may have been, it does not alter the fact that he has misrepresented himself."

Hasker shook his head, folding the document and putting it back in its envelope. "I have to confirm this through my channels."

"I anticipated that." Willbury gestured to Tythe and Fry. "Mr. Tythe has something to tell you."

Tythe shook his head, nodded at Fry, who became a picture of professional dispassion. "The sealed room at Friedman's apartment," he told Hasker, "Detective Chron was in there before we cut through the door. Lead investigator Rouse noted in his site report that he witnessed Detective Chron pick up a couple of shards of the shattered desk with his bare hand, and that the resulting prints should be eliminated. We found Chron's prints on two shards, fingers on one side, thumb on the other, consistent with him picking them up like that, and eliminated those prints. But in reassembling the desk we also found, on a group of shards, a full palm print of his left hand, exclusive to the upper surface of the glass, that could only have been made when the desk was intact. Which means that, at some point before we cut down the door, Detective Chron was inside that room."

Hasker looked at Schnittke, Perls and Dunn, stared at Planchette. "If all this is true," he said to Willbury, "we need to question him."

"As you no doubt will, in due course. Prior to a full psychological evaluation, that's beyond the capacity of your department. He has demonstrated unusual skill with subterfuge, and I can personally attest that his persuasive powers extend beyond that. It's likely that he suffers from a disorder of some kind, possibly resulting from trauma or fatigue. But the disorder could be anything from stress-induced amnesia to schizophrenia to homicidal psychopathy. He has to be assessed before we can determine how to manage him."

"Yeah, well, think what you want of our capacities, we're investigating a homicide," Hasker said. "We get him first."

Willbury gestured at two of his escorts, who held forth sheets exhibiting holographic documents. "I am presenting you with a judicial warrant and a decision from Processing, both witnessed and confirmed, dated today, superceding your investigative priority over the person calling himself Planchette Chron, and authorizing me to arrest him on behalf of the Constabulary Triumvirate. We're taking him." Willbury flicked his hand and two of his men advanced on Planchette. "We will of course provide you with any information relevant to your inquiries that we uncover."

Willbury's men handcuffed Planchette. He did not resist. Hasker argued with Willbury, threatened repercussions. *"Say something, Chron!"* Dunn wouldn't meet Planchette's gaze. She looked like she'd been gut punched.

If his mind had been functioning normally he could have stopped them all, interrupted their cerebral functions and walked out of the building unhindered. In his current state he didn't know what would happen if he tried to do that. Morpho suggested that the shapes might be able to stabilize his core long enough for him to escape. But Morph had conveyed earlier that Planchette's core was not merely expanding, it was unraveling. Neither of the shapes of change could diagnose the severity of the instability, nor predict what would happen if he tried to access his core's power in its unstable state. He would not risk harming these people, least of all Dunn. He had harmed her enough.

As they were leading him away he called to Perls, "Nathan! Ask Olivetta who gave him his first DAT."

"Yes, yes, Mr. whoever-you-are," Willbury said, "all very interesting. Come along."

"*Ask* him who's kept him on the reservations all these years!"

Spoon conveyed that it might not be a bad thing to damage Willbury a little bit. The cops in the hall were shocked. Planchette drew confused stares all down through the station.

The main floor was buzzing with activity, officers in light armor assembling in groups. Baranski lumbered near and Planchette asked what was happening.

"They're sealing the tunnels around those alligators. We have to set up a perimeter—" Baranski registered Planchette's restraints. "Hey!" He stared after him.

Everything was falling apart. Frisa would be trapped, now. They had both failed this world.

Once outside the building, Willbury went off on his own. His escort loaded Planchette into a black, departmental van. The ride was brief. Planchette never saw the outside of P.C.'s operational complex. The side of the carrier opened in an underground parking facility, from which Planchette was led through a series of secured doors down a long corridor to a holding cell.

The cells were enclosed by bars, following the old tradition. Seven Days Grace, weeping with his head in his hands, occupied one across the corridor. P.T. Birns had the cell to Planchette's right. Evidently he'd been promoted to the rank of scapegoat. He met Planchette's gaze with a flat, bitter stare.

Planchette was too low himself to find satisfaction in Birns' downfall. The only way out now was to abandon his human body, which he prepared to do. The shapes did not argue. They accepted his decision with mute resignation.

But Planchette sensed another presence. In the cell beyond Birns, Thaddy Myers stood watching him. It angered Planchette to see the boy incarcerated. Thaddy, for his part, met Planchette's gaze with his chin high in somber defiance.

Chapter Thirty-six

Willbury's office was a spacious, white, windowless room, square and regular, with a large black desk. On one side of the desk was a comfortable, high-backed swivel chair, on the other a grey, metal stool. Inset in the wall opposite the door were long, glass shelves, on which a multitude of small wire objects were displayed—stick-figure representations of humans in myriad postures.

Planchette was led in by two P-techs, who directed him to sit on the stool and wait. Planchette did as directed and the P-techs left. He sat calmly, looking at the wire figures. Twelve confirmed his impression about them. Planchette shook his head.

He didn't need his memories to know that he had never been so cast from his purpose. But he would not run away. Thaddy Myers had changed his mind. He would not abandon the people who had put trust in him without first exhausting alternatives. He would see this life through, however it unfolded. His bond with his assistants had deepened.

"I see you've taken an interest in my homunculi." Willbury came in, sat in the comfortable chair on the opposite side of the desk, and regarded Planchette with a bemused smile.

"They characterize emotional states," Planchette said. "You have them arranged by primacy, with the least complex at the front right of every shelf, nearest whoever sits on this stool, the rest subordinated according to conflation of aspects."

"Very perceptive. I almost want to say, 'detective.' They're equipped with hologram emitters, so one can examine the physicality of each dynamic as well as its underlying posture. For instance, in your case, you've accepted your circumstances but are watching for opportunities to reassert your discretion. You also feel responsible for causing distress." Willbury tapped a spot on his desk and one of the wire figures became obscured by a hologram of a naked man with an agonized, enraged expression, in a posture of supplication. "I made these," Willbury said. "I suppose you might call them my art. Though without technological assistance I could never render so accurately."

"Feelings are not static. They flow."

"The skill is recognizing bends in the river, points of constriction."

Willbury spoke with mock civility, which was telling. He knew he was addressing an adversary. "I thought P.C. didn't endorse a mechanistic attitude toward consciousness." But who pulled Willbury's strings?

"What one endorses and what one knows are separate matters. We are responsible for maintaining civil equilibrium. Few people are easy with death."

Graph conveyed an inaccuracy. "Your responsibility is to coordinate with the other regulatory bodies and Processing to facilitate, with as little intrusion as possible, social stability."

Willbury smiled. "You say potato, I say potah-to."

"There's more than pronunciation distinguishing those statements."

Willbury shrugged wearily—a masquerade.

"You think things would go better if you had more authority," Planchette said. This, from the human end, had to be the core of the conflict.

"Most people, over ninety-nine percent of them, have no understanding whatsoever of their own neurology or neurochemistry. We can't help them so long as the courts tie our hands."

Planchette nodded. It was possible that not even Willbury's peers would have detected the artifice in his composure. "You think Right of Refusal should be rescinded."

"Not if we want to keep incarcerating people and banishing them to the reservations. No matter how good you get at testing, you'll never catch all of the sociopaths. Even if you could, you'd still have violent crime. If we were allowed to assess people properly and treat them, we could reduce it to almost zero."

It was Planchette's turn to sigh. "Regardless the cost to the human spirit."

"Well, I wouldn't want to put law enforcement out of a job."

Willbury's cynicism was bottomless. It concealed egomania, possibly even from himself. Planchette tired of the exchange. This was a turf war to Willbury. It was time to dispense with pretense. "Whatever they told you, you shouldn't help them."

"To whom are you referring?"

The obvious answer was Haliel and the Ixilians. But somehow, that didn't fit. The Tehfolorans? Or was another agency involved? Something about this whole business was upside down. "They have no interest in the fate of humanity."

"Ah, pardon me, I neglected messianic delusions." Willbury touched another spot on his desk, and another hologram, with lunacy in its eyes, came to life.

"How old were you, Mathias, when you first realized that your parents couldn't protect you?"

Willbury went blank.

There was no point in prolonging the game. It would end only one way. "I know you know I was born on another world."

Willbury nodded, almost imperceptibly. "Megalomaniacal and schizophrenic. You may have suppressed a former identity. You're functional, so I can't treat you without your consent, which I presume not forthcoming. Case in point: I have no alternative but to remand you to a reservation, effective immediately."

Chapter Thirty-seven

Planchette watched islands drift by in the liquid expanse below. Already they were several hundred kilometers north of New York. Morph conveyed that this had been a region of lakes before the waters rose.

P.C. had given little attention to comfort in the design of its long-range transport—not, at least, in the passenger compartment. The seat was a cushionless bench. The drone of the rotors would have made conversation impossible had Planchette's escorts wished to talk with him. The driver kept the transparent partition securing the forward compartment sealed, and neither she nor her partner ever glanced at Planchette.

He did not mind. For the moment he was resigned to the flow of circumstances, content to watch the world unfold. He still did not understand how doubt had so infected him, but recognized, again, as he had many times in the last two days, that it did not matter. All that mattered was how he reacted. Doubt served a deceptive impression, that vulnerability could be eliminated through a change in behavior. There was no immunity, within or without, from the vicissitudes of existence.

It were as if someone had emptied a great caldron of doubts into his psyche. Doubts invigorated by the unknown and fear of death, and thereby unanswerable. They had always been there, the doubts, and the fears too, but in weaker states, less substantiated. He wanted to object, which was an adolescent longing. His creators were dust; nature, the intractable conundrums of sentience, God, should one exist, inscrutable and impervious.

He turned his will to the immediate. Doubt and fear secured the margins, like andirons flanking a fire.

The sun sank toward the horizon. The hover descended to a splash of foliage that resolved into a small island. A tall man with long, dark hair stood by the water's edge and watched them land. By his red armband Graph identified him as a monitor—one of the Ex-Tribals who oversaw the reservations.

The door to Planchette's compartment slid open. His escorts remained silent and still did not look at him. Willbury had probably warned them not to interact with him. Planchette stepped out onto soft, moist earth and breathed in cool evening air. A mild breeze tousled his hair. The hover took off. He was glad to be quit of the noise.

The tall man regarded Planchette expressionlessly. He had a long face, deeply creased. He wore a grey shirt and faded blue pants patched on the left thigh. "I am Takiyok," he said. "They didn't say you're violent so I didn't bring the dogs. But there are sonics aimed at you."

Planchette sighed and nodded. Water lapped at the shoreline. The young sea spread away ageless under a sky flocked with itinerant clouds. Several other islands hunkered in the distance. Sunset tinted the whole scene amber.

"Your spirit shimmers," Takiyok said. "The old ones like you." He stepped forward and extended his hand.

Planchette shook it.

"We are one people," Takiyok said.

Spoon conveyed the appropriate response. "Of many ways," Planchette answered.

Takiyok released Planchette's hand. "You have no possessions?"

Planchette shook his head.

Takiyok led him along a path toward the interior of the island. A short way in they came to a clearing toward the far side of which stood a small plank cabin with a cedar-shingle roof and a narrow porch. The roof was mossgrown. "I'll bring clothes and supplies tomorrow." Takiyok went in ahead of Planchette and lit an oil lamp mounted on the wall inside the door. It was a single-room dwelling with a wood stove, a sink with a hand-pump faucet, a cot, a square wooden table and two straight-backed wooden chairs. Shelves above and below the sink bore a sparse assortment of plates, utensils and cookware. There were a couple of empty shelves along the far wall by the bed. "You will have to learn to fish. Tackle and nets are in the shed in back. Gardening tools, too. The garden has been neglected. You might find some potatoes. Dig them up and store them. I'll bring seeds and root stock in the morning, with manuals and growing schedules. The soil is good; you'll eat well. Twice a month I or one of the other monitors will take you hunting on one of the bigger islands. Whatever you kill is community use. But we have to teach you. If you don't hunt your share is smaller."

"I'll do what is required," Planchette said.

"Are you hungry?"

Planchette shrugged. "Thirsty."

Takiyok showed him how the pump worked. Planchette filled a clay mug and drank. The water was rich and crisp. He drained the mug.

Takiyok went to his boat and returned with a ruck sack. In front of the cabin was a pit banked with stones where he built a small fire. He placed a grill on the stones and laid out strips of red meat, cooked fern shoots, nettles and sliced potatoes in a pan. When the smell reached Planchette he located his hunger.

They ate in silence, and afterward sat awhile watching the fire. It was good to be quiet with someone.

A question occurred to Planchette. "Did Michael Olivetta ever stay on this reservation?"

Takiyok nodded. "The one who paints spirits." He raised his chin at the cabin. "He was here."

Planchette looked at the cabin. "On this island?" That couldn't be a coincidence. Someone must have arranged for him to come here. Or maybe it was coincidence. A small owl lit on the roof of the cabin and cocked its head at Planchette. Its eyes caught firelight.

"What did you think of him?" Planchette asked Takiyok. The owl flew away.

"He was sad. He did not belong here." Takiyok studied Planchette. "Spirits followed him. They follow you, too."

Without thinking Planchette said, "Yes." There seemed no point denying it.

Takiyok nodded. "They will keep you company. This is a lonely place." He cleaned the grill and left it by the fire pit, packed the rest of his gear and stood to go. "You do not belong here, either."

Planchette lifted his hands and dropped them. "Nevertheless."

He followed Takiyok to his boat, watched him start the outboard and motor away. Planchette went back to the cabin, collapsed on the cot and fell asleep to the music of lapping water and swaying branches.

Three hours later the shapes awoke him and conveyed that he had been called.

Chapter Thirty-eight

It cannot not be ruled out that shapes will evolve the ability to procreate. What, then, would become of their relationship with their parent species? The shapes here now in my study know these thoughts before they reach the page.

—Kum Laret, *The Fortieth Visitation*

The oil lamp had burned low. Planchette sat on the edge of the cot and stared across the room at the small flame. The shapes beckoned but he ignored them. They had labored on his mind while he slept, and he had his old memories back. Immersed in glue but accessible.

He had been a dentist, once. Many times a farmer, mechanic, repairman, clerk. He'd held a number of bureaucratic positions, operated small businesses. Never had he much distinguished himself in any occupation. The objective had always been to provide for his families and otherwise keep a low profile. On Sixaren he had been a raker of eggs, an honor of awkward prominence but necessary to achieve his purpose in the hive. $\frac{1}{4}$=ca.85 remembered amber light filtering through arching curtains of centuries-old wax, the sweet odor of the birthing pools, experienced a twisted ennui, like a reflection in a warped mirror. He had been offered a mastership, which of course he had declined.

Most of his recipients had been artists, for whom limelight was desirable. Many times $\frac{1}{4}$=ca.85 had felt drawn to express himself artistically. Frisa had often collaborated with her recipients. She had always been skilled at staying in her mates' shadows, and anonymity was easier in the sciences. But it had always seemed to

Gascot that any attempt to indulge his creative inclinations, collaboratively or otherwise, could too easily make him conspicuous, so he had suppressed the urges. Innumerable visions, stories and musical ideas had thereby gone unrealized, and he felt their losses, every one. It seemed the one thing his memory did not retain was any neglected progeny of imagination.

Memories spilled over him with a languor that invited regret. Leaves falling, light changing, beauties subtle and bold, scenes of strife and solace that wrenched the heart, the flow of lives, watching others watch. Times he'd been touched. Whatever their physical attributes, people needed closeness. They needed purpose, too. But where purpose thwarted intimacy it became a burden. His mates and spouses all had known who and what he was—at least in a conceptual, rudimentary way, often romanticized—but there was a gulf between knowing and understanding, and, truly though he had loved them, and they him, their relationships had all become practiced, over time. It was an unavoidable by-product of secrecy and the attenuated mingling of minds. Having to conceal his nature from his children rendered fatherhood bittersweet, as well.

Sometimes, in the course of a life, even his great purpose seemed insufficient to the drudgery of a staid existence. Even the knowledge that entire species might perish if he deviated from his course failed to assuage the oppression of ceaseless imposture. But Frisa helped him pack such thoughts down deep in his being, under the weight of logic, reason, and service to life. She knew when he was near crisis, and was always there to steady him, with a look or a touch, so that his depressions faltered half-formed, enduring mere moments. She had been his compass and his anchor.

And he had forgotten her.

The oil lamp went out as if cued by the thought. It was an indictment of his existence, that Frisa had receded not only from his mind but his feelings. He had no proof that he had succeeded at anything. For ninety-nine lifetimes he had fooled himself, suppressed fear of death and tricked himself into believing that he understood his purpose. Billions had died that he might live. Hundreds of billions. Frisa had supported his illusions, and he hers. She had betrayed him by doubting him, and been right to do so. Of course she thought he had abandoned her. It was exactly what he had done.

That is a lie, Morpho conveyed.

The precision with which the shape of change intruded upon his doubts startled Planchette. Echoes followed from the others: Is it meet, Spoon asked, to further subterfuge? *Falsehood is easy, truth so difficult,* Graph quoted. There is hidden design at work, Twelve conveyed. Purpose resolves in motion, Morph ventured, beyond veils yet unparted.

Planchette sighed. Fatigue made one more susceptible to depression.

He stirred himself and followed his assistants out the back of the cabin into a night gone still and deep with stars. In the absence of moonlight, broadly spaced chains of small clouds beaded the universe with gauzy voids. Foliage snagged his foot—the verge of the neglected garden. Beyond stood the dim rectangle of the shed, recessed in the trees. It was larger than Planchette had expected. Olivetta might have used it for a studio.

A filigree of gossamer lines etched the darkness around it, and the shed itself became obscured by a purling haze. The lines, in dark sight glistening, described a crinkled opening, like a crystal-line mouth to a cave. Planchette looked back. Only a few steps to reach the threshold of a supraliminal reality. The phenomenon might materialize anywhere on the planet; its substance had no name or analogy in the realms of matter.

The shapes went ahead, with Morpho in the lead, and vanished into the haze. Planchette followed. He met a barrier, felt around and found a latch, opened a door. The corporeal world streamed with voids and the haze cleared. It took a moment for his vision to adjust. In material reality he had stepped inside the shed. As he relinquished reflective vision and let dark sight take over, he found himself in a luminous, cavern-like space, by perceptual scale perhaps two hundred meters high and half as wide, extending tunnel-like into the distance beyond the range of sight.

He had never relied entirely on dark sight before, except in the inward way one does with one's eyes closed, in dreams or memory or imagining. Projecting the faculty outward to perceive an exterior, etheric reality required a kind of surrender. The walls had the appearance of stone, sculpted with semblances of house fronts, of myriad types and styles, all jumbled atop each other like a fantastic rookery. They met in the vaults, roof against roof, leaving no sky-like void, though the cavern's floor was sculpted with criss-crossing, overlapped paths and roadways.

His assistants had become his equals in size. He followed them into the cavern, propelled, now, by stream of consciousness, dependency upon legs and feet suspended. It struck him that he had always regarded shapes as somehow lesser. It was an attitude of which he had been incognizant, reinforced, no doubt, by their unwavering solicitude. Frisa and he had ever been saviors in their perception. But mostly it had been a reflex reaction to their diminutive, ambiguous physicality.

Another pattern ran across the sculpted façades, the nature of which eluded Planchette. And he noticed, here and there, cracks that faintly glowed, as if wrought by embers. Shareholds, like this one, had always existed outside of ¼=ca.85's concern. He'd known, in an abstract sense, that shapes spontaneously generated eccentric realities. But those realities had had no bearing on his purpose so he'd never taken an interest in them. As far as he could see they were random phenomena. This sharehold had not been made so much as accreted by the interplay of consciousness. It was a kind of inner sanctum of the shapes' Cloud mind. ¼=ca.85 had never been asked inside a sharehold before.

Other shapes drifted, high among the tiered house fronts. Planchette scrutinized the walls. Every surface—brick, board, knob and pane—was incised with other echoes of human ingenuity. All manner of implements and appliances, machine parts, furnishings. Stethoscopes strewn across a mass of bolts incised a sculpted door. The columns flanking an archway were carved with up-ended canoes amid clustered light bulbs. There was no categorization or hierarchy to the renderings, that Planchette could see. It was all a random reflection of the bond between the shapes of this world and their parent species.

Ninety-nine lives, ninety-eight adopted, and ¼=ca.85 had never familiarized himself with the separate realities of shapes. This sharehold echoed something within him that bespoke an unrealized potential, as if all he had done had been a digression. There was no stone tree, physical or etheric, to which he might affix new roots and branches. If the self he understood himself to be was coming apart, he could imagine no subsequent person who might emerge from its ruin.

The cant of the cavern veered right and downward, to an oval flat that centered an amphitheater-like surround of sloping stone. As the floor descended so did the vaults rise, and the character of the walls changed accordingly, from houses to towers and skyscrapers, retaining the look of sculpted stone. The pattern that had eluded Planchette revealed itself on the larger scale. Fanning all across the skyscrapers, like an elusive sheen, was a wild garden, the likenesses of flora and fauna—behemoth flowers crowded all about, dense as moss, by minuscule trees, blades of grass hundreds of meters high—it was a phantasmagorical exhibition of non-human life on Earth. The faces of animals, huge and impassive, feline, canine, simian, and on, peered out from subtle jungle. Below, overlaying the sculpted paths and roadways, were also rendered fish and sea life, and above, where the rooftops met, Planchette saw flights of birds.

He noticed a greater incidence of the glowing cracks in the walls around the amphitheater.

Many shapes drifted, high in these vaults, paying neither Planchette nor his assistants any heed. The sharehold, in its most essential aspect, was a sanctuary. Planchette felt his own burdens lighten, though for some reason was hesitant to embrace ease.

A gathering of elder shapes awaited them in the arena. Planchette recognized them from the paintings in MacGrory's house. The spherical cloud was there, the crystal wreath, the feather-handled hammer, the compass egg, the hexagonal nut with the fur-lined bore. These are the Stations of the Close, Morpho conveyed. The shapes' council of elders. Their number was nineteen, though only eighteen were present, hovering in a half-circle. They cast no shadows but their auras were bright and distinct. Against the mammoth backdrop of the sharehold, they emanated dignity and the power of seasoned intelligence.

Planchette felt them reach out to link with his mind and he let them. Five of them, the Stations of Continuity, Belief, Certainty, Inquiry and Tools, were hard to focus on. Their bodies lacked visual clarity, like indeterminate elements, wire or bricks or bits of glass, continually churning. It was a further testament to Olivetta's skill that he had managed to depict these entities at all, let alone so clearly as he had.

The Stations finished linking with Planchette's consciousness, and it became as if they were inside of his mind with him and his assistants. The spherical cloud, Station of Ambiguity, seemed to have a degree of primacy among the others. To Planchette it conveyed, Your mind is compromised. Planchette sensed a subtle accusation in the statement. There is a schism within your collective, he responded defensively. There is no schism, conveyed the crystal wreath, Station of the Known. On the wall behind the Stations, the giant face of a boar seemed to frown in consternation, a smoldering crack scarring its brow. Planchette wasn't sure how to interpret the elder shape's denial. Within his mind he felt the other Stations lend Known their agreement. Other potentials being exhausted, Graph paraphrased, what remains must be true. Planchette and his assistants arrived at the same conclusion together. Information has been withheld only from these five, he conveyed. They relinquished a portion of their memories, Ambiguity corrected, among them having done so. Planchette sought clarification. We wished that their impressions of you might coalesce without bias, Inquiry, one of the churning Stations, supplied. Which meant they had anticipated his coming, Planchette understood. More than that, they had prepared for it. He noticed the walls had changed, again. The surface imagery had shifted. To a lesser degree, the sculptural façades had too. Questions, the Station of Etiquette conveyed. It had the appearance of a gold ring spanned by a spider web. Somehow it did not impress Planchette as wiser or more formidable than Spoon. I have them, he conveyed. We are present, conveyed Ambiguity. I must know what transpired before I arrived, Planchette conveyed. Another off-worlder came to us, the Station of Continuity, another formless churner, responded. He knew of you and foretold your coming. He conveyed that you had been to his world, aeons past, that your intentions are benign but your result calamitous. He supported that assertion? Planchette asked. He had in his company a group of shapes from his world, conveyed the Station of Stone, a faceted gem of many colors; they were void, without consciousness. He claimed this a result of our efforts? Planchette asked. He did, the Station of Numbers, who resembled a faceless coin, conveyed. That is absurd, Planchette conveyed. Who is this person? Where is he? He concealed his origin and identity, conveyed Inquiry, and his consciousness kept closed to us, therefore we did not trust him. Neither could we ignore his warnings, nor the condition of the shapes in his consort. How long since my partner arrived? Three months and two days, conveyed Numbers. What happened to her? The Station of Passage, who resembled a chalkboard eraser, answered, We were aware, within the Cloud, of her coming. The mark of the empty ones was upon her. We discerned, in reflection, that her mark had also been upon them. As with you, we sensed no malice in her, no intention or inclination to harm, only to help. Therefore did emissaries venture to greet her. They presented with her and were gone. Gone? Planchette asked. We could not find them, answered Ambiguity. In the place where they met, all trace of both her and them vanished. Only technology could achieve such a thing, Planchette conveyed. Neither I nor my partner possess technology. Which is why we helped you to form, and supplied your assistants, conveyed Etiquette. We need answers as well, though we perceive you do not have them. Not yet, Planchette responded. He sensed, though, that the Stations were no longer interested in any information his investigations might yield. The walls had changed, again. It was all in flux, here. Fixity had been an illusion his mind had invented to give itself time to adjust. A disturbing impression crept over him that something had been concealed from him. Another aspect of the vast chamber they occupied revealed itself. It was not crossed by only a single passage, it was a hub of many passageways, the mouths of which Planchette now saw in the walls all around as well as the vaults above. And in all of the passageways were massed great hosts of shapes. That was what had been making him uncomfortable, the feeling that he was being watched. My partner and I answered your call, he conveyed, no others; you know the marrow of my thoughts and intentions. We acknowledge that you are open, your nature and intentions clear, conveyed Passage. And yet you doubt me. Do you not doubt yourself? asked Ambiguity. Your memories are vast and occluded. It would take long to know them. But you know from my current mind that my purpose is as it has ever been, and that my psyche has been seeded with doubt. The elder shapes did not respond. The shapes in the tunnels grew agitated. Some drifted out into the junction. Why did you call me here? Planchette asked. To assess the danger you pose, conveyed the Station of Shelter. In this place you can do no harm. The answer struck Planchette as disingenuous. He stared at the elder shape, who resembled a much used book. I have never known shapes to prevaricate, he conveyed. We do not deceive, conveyed the Station of Sentiment, who resembled a lichen-encrusted headstone. You withhold; it is the same thing,

Planchette answered. Have you not withheld? asked Change, who resembled a wooden doorknob with a round mirror in its face. Out of fear, responded Planchette. So it is with us, conveyed Shelter. Comprehension shocked both Planchette and his assistants. You mean to confine me here! After a moment's hesitation, the elders let Planchette see the extent of their intentions. That is madness! Planchette conveyed. Hoards of shapes poured out from the tunnels, massing within the vast junction. Survival, conveyed several of the Stations. Survival? As *what?* Planchette glanced about at the massing shapes. There were more than enough to hold him. You cannot create bodies like _=ca.110 and I possess, he told the Stations. It took the cooperation of an entire species, shapes and parents alike, to give us life. All of you would have to surrender your individuality to accomplish what you intend. Permanently. Even then you would lack more than half of the resources required. Nevertheless it may be that we must try, conveyed Inquiry. Among our parents are those who know of our existence and deny us. They betray our kind. Are we to resign ourselves to oblivion? Planchette saw how intelligence could work against itself, even among shapes. By 'our kind,' Inquiry had not meant humans and shapes alike. Desperation and wisdom made contentious bedfellows. You hope, in studying my dissolution, he conveyed, to learn how to procreate amongst yourselves. In the school of your unmaking we may learn alternatives, conveyed Change. It is not possible. It is not my function to understand the science but I know it is not possible. Planchette thought of Frisa. She had been here longer than he. If she had been experiencing effects from their separation similar to his, she might be in a more unstable state than he. What of my partner? he asked. The Stations did not respond, but Planchette deduced their intentions. You seek to *experiment* with her? Sacrifice some group of yourselves in a foolish attempt to bond with her core as it comes apart? These forces you do not understand. The massing shapes encroached everywhere, now. Planchette wanted to disengage from the Stations but it might trigger the masses to attack him. He didn't know if they really could trap him here, but they might destabilize him further in the attempt. They might even cause him to implode. Understanding exists within your partner, conveyed the Station of Belief, who resembled a shifting maze. We will extract it. We have also Victor Friedman's understanding. An absent member of our consort observed his work and shared it with us. You refer to the Station of Futures, Morpho conveyed to the elders. We have that one's death manna. Nowhere within it is there concurrence with what you propose. Planchette felt surprise spread through the shapes all around him. Just when it seemed they would abandon restraint and descend on him, they halted their advance. The enormity of what Planchette's assistants had revealed, the death and transfiguration of a Station of the Close, was a sobering slap in their collective faces.

A kind of rain fell on the arena, and a moment later ceased. The Stations conferred among themselves.

If you hinder me in my efforts, Planchette conveyed, you will hasten the outcome you dread.

We will release you, conveyed Ambiguity, but we will assist you no further. Tension among the massed shapes relaxed, and they began to withdraw, though they remained confused.

Provide me, at least, with the identities of those among your parents who conspire against us, Planchette asked.

We will assist you no further, conveyed the Known. The mark of the empty ones is also upon you. You must answer this or remain apart.

Planchette did not understand. He thought they must be referring to the dead shapes. I slept among their remains, he conveyed. Some trace may have adhered.

The mark is not of our kind, nor of this world, conveyed Inquiry.

Planchette was shocked anew. The elder shapes were conveying the truth as they understood it. He would have known if they lied.

We will assist him, Planchette's assistants conveyed.

We know all that you know, Certainty argued, and more.

You have not lived our quest with this one, Morpho conveyed.

He has not gifted you with names, Graph conveyed.

You have not known his will, Morph conveyed.

He adapts with elegance, Twelve conveyed.

He strives for all, to his own peril, Spoon conveyed. It is ill-mannered to abandon him.

The Stations again conferred inscrutably among themselves.

To Planchette's assistants the Known conveyed, We shall retain those memories you relinquished, and you shall receive no further assistance while you persist in this course. You go, as he, unhindered, but in all other ways declined.

The compass egg, Station of Hope, for the first time addressed Planchette: Our parents cannot see us and we cannot link with their minds. We can, however, observe, and to considerable degree interpret, the field of their consciousness. You behold it, all about you. Planchette gazed at the walls, again, and the unifying aspect in their phantasmagorical makeup became clear. Giant human figures, lent subtle definition by all of the other elements, sprawled naked across walls, floor and ceiling, engaged in a glacial ballet of passion, yearning, consternation and grace. He had been wrong to suppose the sharehold's character a result of accident. It was a living map.

The birth rate among our parents long ago fell below replacement levels, Hope conveyed. Despair, disillusionment, disaffection, loathing, conflict—when such motivations reach communicable levels they manifest here as anomalies. Planchette looked at the glowing cracks. They had a concentric orientation toward the apex of the hub. When they meet, Hope conveyed, the door of the future closes.

Your circumstances are difficult, Ambiguity conveyed, and your time short. Your partner is more unstable than you. We will not squander the opportunity to learn from her failure, neither permit her to commit further harm.

Chapter Thirty-nine

Takiyok showed Planchette how the wood stove in the cabin worked and put on coffee in a black-enameled metal pot. Among the clothes he'd brought for Planchette was a heavy, fur-lined coat, which Planchette donned immediately. The temperature had dropped overnight. But Takiyok told him it was not cold enough for that coat, yet, and said he should accustom himself to the seasons. "Winter is a long way off."

Planchette rummaged through the other clothes and slipped on a black and white pull-over sweater vest knitted with stylized deer and fish.

For breakfast Takiyok had brought strawberries and small, hard, sour apples, smoked fish and hearth bread. Planchette had difficulty with the taste of the fish. His body wanted it so he ate it. Takiyok's boiled coffee was unfiltered and the harshest Planchette had tasted.

Planchette had observed the operation of the outboard motor when Takiyok pulled in. Twelve supplied an estimate of its top speed and an assessment of its running condition and fuel level.

When they'd finished eating and were lingering with their coffee, Planchette asked Takiyok about the reservation, how far it extended and how it functioned.

"It is about three hundred kilometers south, by water, to the nearest maintained road that connects with the mainland," Takiyok answered, anticipating Planchette's interest. "The tank on my boat does not hold enough to make it that far. You would need to take extra fuel. The nearest place you can reach the road is a long way from anywhere motorized vehicles are used. The villages don't have much technology."

The significance was not lost on Planchette. Even if he stole Takiyok's boat, or Takiyok gave it to him, it could take weeks, even months, to reach New York by land.

"There are hot zones, too," Takiyok said, "and animals. And unregistered people."

Planchette wasn't worried about animals or people. But his lead-lined coat and hat had been taken from him. Of his radiation-proof clothing he retained only his lead-lined briefs. Hopefully he would still be able to perform, if he managed to get back to Claire.

Planchette asked if the reservation was self-sufficient or if supplies were flown in.

"There is a small airstrip on Ukoska, where I live," Takiyok said. "Supplies are flown in twice a month but we keep no aircraft on the reservation. The only hovercraft I've seen risk coming this far is the one that brought you."

"That was a risk?"

Takiyok nodded.

"Why?"

"Wind, weather, battery."

"They stopped to recharge."

"Still."

Willbury must have been desperate to get Planchette away, where no one could question him. Which meant that something else was going to happen, and that, whatever it was, Willbury, or those who controlled him, saw Planchette as a threat to its success.

There was no deception in Takiyok; Planchette was sure that his characterization of circumstances was accurate. Traveling south in Takiyok's boat, given or taken, would be pointless without a follow-up plan. The shapes, cut off from the Cloud, could not provide him with logistical information adequate to formulate one.

"If you were banished here," Planchette asked Takiyok, "and

needed to leave, how would you go about it?" There was no point in disguising his intentions.

"I would stow away on the next supply transport, two weeks from now."

"And if that was not soon enough?"

Takiyok shook his head. "Then I would pray."

Takiyok left, again, and Planchette, with a growing sense of futility, watched him shrink across the water.

It had still been dark when he'd returned to the reality of the shed. Tired as he'd been, he hadn't been able to go back to sleep.

Now it looked as if he would have to wait for someone to rescue him. The likelihood of that happening seemed infinitesimal. Among humans, Takiyok was probably the only one who might help him, which was ironic in some way Planchette didn't care to work out. Haliel was too much of a cipher to put any hope in. That left the Tehfolorans, and Planchette sensed they were more interested in his personal well-being than the fate of Earth. Their objectives extended beyond the scope of a single world; they were more likely to let him stay put until things calmed down. Planchette shook his head. He was not sure that even Frisa still wanted him to succeed, here.

More and more it seemed his only allies were his assistant shapes, whose capacities were greatly compromised, and did not include transporting him hundreds of kilometers back to New York. Which meant that, much as he appreciated their company, Planchette was essentially on his own.

He spent the rest of the morning working out with Twelve how best to disable the island's security system, the components of which were camouflaged as rocks and trees. He also found the outhouse, where he had his second experience with bodily evacuation. Around midday, Planchette recognized his hunger for the first time, and ate a few bites of bread and fish. Then he slept. He woke up mid-afternoon feeling listless.

Takiyok had left seeds, root stock and gardening manuals on

the table. Planchette sat down and scanned the manuals. He supposed he might as well do some gardening.

He went out to the shed. In daylight, even before entering, it was obvious that Olivetta had worked here. There were paint smudges on and around the latch, and on the right side of the frame. Inside, the floor was covered with paint spatter, the walls with overlapping sketches and rectangular outlines where canvases or paper had been tacked up. It was a pitiful testament to an epic body of work. One could only hope that Olivetta would not be too disheartened by the loss of all he'd done to keep going.

A shovel, a rake and a hoe leaned in the far left corner. Gloves and a hand trowel hung from nails nearby. On the opposite wall hung a creel, nets and a fishing rod.

Planchette stared at the gardening tools and shook his head. If he stayed on this island long enough to bring in a harvest, any reason for his continued existence as a human would be long passed. He wasn't here to take up residence.

He gathered wood for the stove and the fire pit, then sat in front of the cabin by the pit, not knowing what else to do with himself. He noticed shapes flitting about, high and far off. They were watching him.

He had never asked shapes how they viewed their own purpose. He'd always taken their servitude for granted. When his assistants didn't respond he assumed they were thinking. Certainly no one had asked them the question before. Then he realized that non-responsiveness was their answer. They held to a potential they felt self-evident; in their silence was faith and attention. Planchette did not ask them to explain. They expressed, in their quiet presence, a purpose too valiant to name.

He sat a long time without thinking, listening to the world. He sat until the sun set and it became dark. He made a small fire.

Watching the flames, ¼=ca.85 did something else that he had never done. He prayed. He did not know to whom or what but nevertheless he prayed. He prayed for himself and the universe, for Frisa, for all of his colleagues, for every member of every species he had ever known. He prayed for life, and for the existence of a kindly God.

Planchette went down to the shoreline. Out across the dark waters, that sparkled with reflected stars, faint lights shone on other islands, all isolate as his own. He wondered if the inhabitants of the reservation ever gathered together. This is a banishment zone, Morpho conveyed. The intent is to give criminals and sociopaths time apart to know themselves.

Something splashed to the northwest. Somewhere south someone started playing music, a violin, maybe, or electric guitar. It must have been a trick of distance, of the air and the water and the lay of the islands, because the music grew louder, and resolved into the sound of an approaching hovercraft.

Chapter Forty

Planchette sat in front of his cabin, stirred the little fire he'd made, and waited. He didn't know whether his facility with making and banking a fire came from his adopted human memories or some older experience or both. The shapes could not decide the matter one way or the other.

Planchette didn't have any particular expectations regarding who might have come to see him. He planned to take their hover, whoever they were. But when Perls and Schnittke stepped out of the trees he wondered if he had begun to hallucinate in some new way.

Graph conveyed the particulars of several statutes.

Trying to appear unsurprised, Planchette said, "I'm fairly certain you're violating protocol by being here."

"That concerns you, does it? Protocol?" Perls said.

Planchette shrugged in bewilderment.

Perls put his hands on his hips and studied a point near the treetops. Schnittke gave the perimeter a watchful scan.

"I asked Olivetta what you said."

Planchette looked up.

"He wouldn't talk to me."

Planchette made a face and returned his gaze to the fire.

"I don't know who you are or what you're up to," Perls said. "Nobody can figure this thing out. But none of us make you for a villain—"

"Hasker?" Planchette asked.

"Who do you think sent us?" Perls locked eyes with Planchette.

Planchette was surprised, not for the first time on this world, by his own emotions. He cared about his professional standing among these people. They were his peers.

"Whatever your deal is," Perls said, "Willbury and his lot are shady as …" Perls couldn't find a comparison. "We got farther following you than anything the rest of us did put together. But we got problems."

"You can't trust me," Planchette said.

"Kind of hard when we don't know who you are."

"How do we fix that?"

"You could start by telling me your name."

"Planchette Chron."

Perls took a breath and grinned impatiently.

"That's my name, Nathan. My legitimate, true name."

"Prove it."

"I can't. Or I'm not sure I should."

Perls took another breath, sans grin.

"Look," Planchette said, "I'm glad you're here. I'd make idiots out of us both trying to say how much it means to me that you want to trust me. I have other names, it's true. But if I explain that, you won't believe me. You're more likely to think Willbury got it right. What I can tell you is that we're in danger, all of us. You can't catch the people responsible on your own; you can't stop them. But, if you let me help, together we might be able to."

Perls stared at Planchette the way one might a rock. The silence dragged.

"What are you thinking?" Planchette asked. "I don't know what else to say."

"Here's what it is," Perls said. "You don't have to convince me." Without taking his eyes off of Planchette, he waved someone behind him forward. "You have to convince her."

Dunn stepped out from the trees. Planchette thought the look in her eyes—hope and consternation all mixed up with respect— might have been the most beautiful thing he'd ever seen. It was too much. He had to look away.

"Shoulda' heard what she had to say about this business," Schnittke said. "Sized us all down." Perls and he withdrew into the trees.

Dunn, hesitant and determined, sat on the log opposite Planchette. Her willingness to be vulnerable was humbling.

Planchette didn't know what to say, so he said, "Are you thirsty?" Water was all he had to offer her.

She shook her head.

"What, uh—" Planchette tilted his head in the direction Schnittke and Perls had gone—"what did you say?"

Dunn came around the fire and sat near him, eyes as open as the sea. "I told them," she said quietly, "that I've clung to hope my whole life, and that you're the first person who made me feel like I wasn't a fool for it. I told them that, whether they admitted it or not, they all knew what I was talking about, and could either listen to the hope in their hearts or obey the rules. I told them they could count on me to burn the rules down."

Planchette felt a tremor in his chest spread toward his extremities. Maybe he'd had it wrong from the beginning. Maybe Frisa and he both had. Maybe they had risked too little, trusted too little, loved too little. They'd had the weight of the living and the dead on their shoulders.

"What do you want me to tell you?"

"Everything."

"You won't believe me." He was trembling visibly. He couldn't control it.

She touched his hand. "You know what the most inspiring thing I've ever heard was, in my entire life?"

Planchette swallowed. "What?"

"That the lead investigator in a homicide investigation danced with his primary witness and took her to church."

Planchette was afraid to make a sound. His heart might break.

"Give me a chance," she said.

The sadness in Planchette was older than he was. He'd added to it, life after life, and walled it down. The wall broke.

When he finished sobbing he told her everything.

Chapter Forty-one

Dunn looked at the stars as if she'd never seen them before. In firelight, the encircling trees became the visible limit of the world. She smelled the pines and the water; it seemed she could smell the stars, like some rare, forgotten incense. The universe was moments, ticking away, more precious than anything, impossible to retrieve. The diamonds and gold of breath expired with each exhalation.

Had she seen anything as it was? Ever? The man before her said he'd lived a hundred lives that spanned millennia. He had been creatures beyond imagining, who slithered or rolled or swam beneath skies the wrong color. Creatures who had in common the mystery of their fall, their severed faith, the insufficiencies of their upbringings and inheritances.

He said he was three days old and that it was his job to save humanity.

All she saw was a man.

She wanted to believe him. It was not logical or provable. She believed him because she wanted to. She wanted to believe that the universe would make a being so selfless that he would spend forever in service to others.

She had grown up amid twisted beams and splintered concrete, the grime and detritus of ruin, the sick and their broken dreams, in the wake of a history of failure. Just once she wanted touch something greater than misery. She'd never met anyone who carried so much misery as he did, nor hid it so well. She didn't want to add to his pain. She wanted just once to see around the edge of things, to have a glimpse beyond the veil.

She wouldn't let herself think about what else she wanted. If she thought about that her heart would break.

The message he spoke of, his message, the message he had been made to deliver, it was too distant, too impossible. "You can only give it to Claire Fontaine? No one else?" She'd never been able to keep the quaver out of her voice when her heart was exposed.

"It's complicated."

Wasn't everything? Watch leaves blow across a road, watch the waves. All the victims and criminals.

"There are others. Somewhere. If we survive, Frisa and I, we might look for them."

And if not? Will you leave us here, to fall and keep on falling? Will you let the darkness swallow us? Confess you are a liar? While I weep and pray for your soul.

"Until I find her it doesn't matter. I'm not sure I can convey the message to another, though."

Planchette touched his head and his heart in a way that was so true and unaffected it cut Dunn with yearning.

"I've never imprinted one recipient and consummated with another. I don't know what would happen."

Dunn looked away. She couldn't see the water but heard it lapping. It carried her back before it rose, before the poison rain, when this had been a realm of lakes instead of islands. It carried her to her mother before she had hardened, to the kindness of her arms. Natalie felt the water spread, filling every nook of the land with its mystery. She wiped her eyes. "You couldn't give it to me."

Planchette shook his head. "It's genetics and the structure of your mind. The message is almost infinitely malleable, but a recipient has to be able to retain it. It's alive, in a way. It recognizes the mind it can survive in."

"Couldn't you show me a little of it?"

Planchette shook his head again. "It comes out all at once.

When the recipient is ready and willing. It's her decision, not mine. I don't control it."

Something in her eyes hurt him and he looked away. The scar on his chin, that was false too. Everything about the person before her was a disguise. She couldn't see him like that. He was real. However he'd come into being, he was real. Physically real. She wasn't just made of wishes and wonder.

"I might be able to show you something," he said.

Natalie watched him wrestle with himself. He was so full of hope and need, and she realized he didn't understand what was happening any better than she did.

His eyes locked with hers. "It would only be for a moment. You'd never be able to see it again. That might be—hard."

"Life is hard," she said softly. "Show me." Her answer came unbidden. "I want to see."

He held out his hand and she took it. From that point, until it happened, she couldn't let go of his eyes. The emotions they conveyed, the seasoned weariness of a person long embattled, the underlying anchor of indefatigable determination.

His eyes wavered, or shimmered, or oscillated, and some kind of energy radiated from them. She became aware of an ethereal glow emanating from his body, from a source within him. That part was not human, and it frightened her, until she understood that the rest of him truly was human, entirely human, purely human. His humanity was so plain that seeing it became a rediscovery of her own.

There was a kind of silent pop and the oscillations cleared. They were still there—she could feel them in her visual field but not see them. Not the way she was used to seeing.

A little silver spoon with an ornate handle swooped in front of her. She understood it was a living being, not an inanimate object. The spoon floated upright and twisted side to side, presenting itself, twirled in greeting. Dunn put her hand over her mouth. A tear left her eye.

Another creature flew before her, a complex geometric shape of many colors, and another that looked like a glowing symbol, and two that changed and changed.

"Natalie," Planchette said, "these are my other partners, Spoon, Twelve, Graph, Morph and Morpho."

The little creatures spun and danced and Natalie wept with delight.

And then they were gone.

"I dare risk no more," Planchette said, "it could harm your mind."

He appeared, again, as he had, and Natalie knew more than ever what it was to be a person. She leaned against him and he held her. No one knew where they were or what they were doing. Not even Perls and Schnittke, down by the water. They were in a private universe, and, just for that moment, he was hers.

Chapter Forty-two

About four hundred kilometers south of the island, Perls stopped at a vacant police barracks to recharge the cruiser's batteries. The trees around the box-like facility tossed in a rising wind. There were no lights or habitations anywhere nearby. The driveway was matted with leaves, strewn with fallen branches. The cedar plank walls were checked and weathered.

"This is on the grid?" Schnittke asked doubtfully.

"Moth-balled for future activation," Perls said.

"Why don't I think that's going to happen."

Perls had the door code. Inside, when he turned on the lights, it was obvious the place had never seen use—bunk beds with bare mattresses, offices empty of furniture.

They pulled the hover into the garage and hooked it up. Planchette understood better the risk his colleagues had taken when he saw that the charge on the backup cell was below five percent.

The winds grew stronger as they continued south. For over an hour it felt like the hover would at any moment spin out or go into a roll. Perls kept it on course. No one spoke.

Once the weather smoothed out, Planchette's memory patch, as if to deny him respite from anxiety, broke apart entirely. Both the scene inside the hover and the night view out the windows flooded with pale, colorless visions of other worlds, and his hearing rushed with absent voices. It was like traveling through a dimension of static. There was too much information moving too quickly for anything to be perceptibly distinct. Here and there a face or a building or a landscape flickered into focus but was swallowed before Planchette could recognize it.

The shapes clung to their connections with his psyche. They struggled to repair the patch but Planchette was too much in turmoil, and the breach in his mind had spread and become more complex. The patch had grown increasingly unstable since the ordeal at the Utilitarian Lodge Majeur. They took over as his eyes and ears.

Planchette wondered if the link he had briefly formed with Dunn might have contributed to this latest breakdown. He hoped he had not damaged her. Graph informed him they were nearing New York. Planchette saw the recolonized city as a radiance amid chaos.

"Where do you want to go?" Perls asked via Morph.

"I need to see Claire Fontaine," Planchette answered. Twelve conveyed that he had shouted.

Dunn, via Spoon, asked if he was all right.

She was next to him, in the back seat. He found the outline of her face. "I'm all right." Her eyes became iridescent blue pools in the writhing tangle of memories.

He could tell when they entered the city because a crush of phantom architecture again dominated his vision. They were less than a kilometer from Claire's apartment when Schnittke detected a vehicle in pursuit.

"P.C. or cops?" Perls asked.

"Can't tell," Schnittke said.

Perls said he'd try to draw off their pursuers, took the cruiser down to let Planchette out. Dunn went with him. Planchette couldn't tell which way to go. Twelve suggested they hide for a moment in a wedge-shaped space between two buildings. Planchette tried to follow directions but walked into a wall.

Graph conveyed that Dunn wanted to know what was wrong.

"I can't see," he confessed. He felt her hand on his arm. She guided him a few steps and stopped. Graph conveyed that she wanted him to stand still.

"If I'm slow to respond," he told Dunn, "it's because I can't hear, either. The shapes relay your words to me."

He didn't need the shapes to tell him that Dunn was distressed. He could feel it. He could feel everything, he realized, the entire city, every contour. He had been designed to understand through empathy, which was an extra-sensual extension of touch, in him of a highly developed order. There was no reason why he could not 'look' at the world through that perceptual aperture.

The phantom realities of memory molded themselves to the city that was and he could 'see' New York again, ironically with greater clarity than he could have in the dark with his eyes, though the surfaces of buildings flowed with ghosts. He thought he might apply the same approach to hearing and asked Dunn to say something and keep repeating it. It took a moment but he identified the vibrations of her voice and molded the contours of phantom noise to their pattern.

"Can you hear me?" she said.

He could 'hear' her words as wailing wreckage, tearing themselves to pieces. "I'm fine, now," he told her.

She put her fingers on his lips. They shrank back in the recess, pressed close together, as a hover went slowly by. The smell of her hair was a blossom of grace. The walls streamed with remembered flowers.

"P.C.," Natalie said, when the hover was gone.

"Which way is Claire's? We should get going."

They walked quickly. Planchette recognized Claire's apartment building and broke into a run. The phantom world raced by, crawling with bleached, distorted sights, all familiar, unrecognizable and alien to the present. It was terrible to think of things being always that way, though maybe, in the depths of the mind, they were, leaking up, now and then, to sting the spirit, stain the view.

At Claire's door, Planchette hesitated. "What time is it?"

"About three A.M.," Dunn said.

"She'll be asleep." The door strobed with a revue of entrances. Planchette didn't know what Claire had been told or how she would respond to him in his current state. Even if her will had cleared enough for her to recognize him, he didn't know if he was recognizable.

"Yeah, we should probably wait." Dunn knocked on the door.

Claire answered immediately. She had on a robe and her hair was mussed but she hadn't been asleep. The moment Planchette saw her his senses began to right themselves. His memories returned to their proper recesses. She told them both to come in, closed the door and seized Planchette in a strong embrace. The wave of warmth and well-being that swept through him was so powerful that it frightened him. Then he surrendered and everything was okay.

She still didn't recognize him, but she wanted him. For the moment, that was enough.

Chapter Forty-three

They sat silently around Claire's table. How they had found this silence was a mystery to Planchette. There was an awkwardness in it that was confounding. In particular to the emotions, which were as well the source of confusion. Desire was an elliptical frustration among them. Oh, yes, they all wanted. The room spilled with yearning.

Claire offered wine. Dunn responded with a dead stare. Morph conveyed that it was an intoxicant. Planchette shook his head.

Claire went to the kitchen, poured a glass for herself and returned. "What's going on?" she asked. "They told me you were off the case."

"It's complicated," Planchette said.

Dunn stood up abruptly and went down into the sunken living room, stood at the window looking out, with her back to Claire and Planchette.

Planchette watched Natalie, turned back to Claire. Maybe it had been a mistake to come here, though certainly Claire had steadied him. But the message would not be delivered this night. The desire in Claire's eyes was too mixed with confusion and fear.

"I was arrested," he said. Maybe frankness would weaken the barrier. "It's a mistake. But, yes, officially, I'm off the case."

"Then why are you here?"

Planchette wasn't sure how to answer. He wasn't there to seduce her or reason with her. If she couldn't see his purpose for herself, talking about it wouldn't help. And yet silence wasn't adequate either, and he didn't want to lie.

"You should trust him," Dunn said, without turning.

"What's that supposed to mean?" There was umbrage in Claire's tone; she did not like being told what to do.

Dunn turned. "It's supposed to mean you should fucking trust him. Am I speaking Chinese?"

The look Claire gave Natalie was not friendly.

Planchette stared back and forth at the two women. "I—what are you doing? I don't know what to say, Claire. I've never been in this situation. If I explain I might make it worse."

She didn't like that either. Claire drew so far inside herself it was like she left the room. Planchette winced. She saw it and only turned stonier. He knew he was trying too hard to say the right thing but her anger hurt. He started trembling, again, afraid of his own mind. In desperation he said, "I need you."

That reached her. Planchette felt a hint of warmth return. "For what?"

He could only stare, like a child seeking forgiveness.

"How do you need me?" she said more softly, "in what way?"

"In every way," he said.

She held his gaze, wavering. "That's quite a thing to say."

"I think it's all I *can* say."

"What the *fuck!*" Dunn jumped back from the window. "What the *fuck* is *that?!*"

Something clung to the outside of the window at its bottom edge, a prow of pale, undulous flesh, climbing the glass. Claire and Planchette stood up. Dunn backed out of the living room until she was stopped by the dining table. The fleshy thing climbed until it was fully in view. It was ovoid and tapered at both ends, taller than a man. Planchette knew what it was, and knew it could move much faster. Its slowness was a sign of hesitation. Or deliberation, maybe. He knew, too, why the shapes had been murdered, or at least the circumstances that had led to their deaths.

The fleshy foot constricted, clenching the plasti-glass until it broke, and Frisa fell forward into the room.

She had formed incorrectly. Her upper body resembled a human female, but her lower body bore the snail-like characteristics of her and Planchette's creators. Her head grew rhythmically firm and flaccid, like a respiratory bladder. Firm, her features agreed with the portrait of the attractive young woman Olivetta had said was a holograph, flaccid more the canvas he'd shown Perls and Planchette of a subject with frog-like features, and in between Claire's composite. Her 'gown' was actually flesh, composed of parti-colored skin tags, probably the result of being attacked by the shapes trying to subvert her formation.

"Gascot," she said, in a hollow monotone, without moving her lips. "You should not be here." A slit in her humanoid belly parted when she spoke. It must have been her mouth.

Planchette's human self was repulsed by her, his elder persona too removed to absorb the impact of her deformity. He couldn't speak.

"Where is she?" Frisa said. "You have to get away from her. Enemies—"

Frisa's enormous foot dragged across the jagged bottom edge of the broken window. Her gray-blue blood seeped across the carpet.

Planchette swallowed. "Frisa—"

"I thought you abandoned me, Gascot."

"I never did."

Frisa looked at him. "I know." Her real eyes were in her shoulders; her humanoid eyes were residual and sightless. It tore Planchette to see her so ruined.

"I surfaced and you were gone."

Feelings began to flow between them. Frisa looked at Claire. "Is that her, Gascot?" One of Frisa's tentacular pseudopods formed a humanoid hand and withdrew Olivetta's missing Liston knife from the folds of her flesh. "Is she your recipient?"

Dunn saw the blade and reacted before Planchette could stop her. She moved sideways, placing herself in front of Claire, who stood with her back to the wall, slack-jawed in horror and amazement, on the other side of the table. *"I'm* her," Dunn said. "I'm Claire Fontaine. I'm his recipient."

Frisa reared back, looking Dunn up and down. She lunged at her with the knife. Planchette leapt between them and took the blade through his heart.

Frisa recoiled in horror. Dunn caught Planchette as he crumpled to the floor.

"Accident," he told her. "She didn't mean it."

Dunn clicked her sheet three times to send a distress call. She pressed her hand to his breast, the blade between her fingers. "Hold on."

He shook his head but clung to life. "Promise you'll protect her. Both of them. Promise me."

Tears streamed from Natalie's eyes. She nodded. "I promise."

He touched her face. She was beautiful in sorrow. "I think—" His throat constricted.

She clutched him. "What?"

He could not leave without telling her. "I think you're the only friend I've ever had."

Shapes flooded into the room through the broken window and descended upon wailing, grief-stricken Frisa. All Planchette could do was die.

Chapter Forty-four

The moment he left his human body two things became clear to ¼=ca.85. First, that his core self had become severely destabilized. Second, that it had been designed by his creators to do so in certain circumstances. He could not tell, though, whether the destabilization had occurred per that design or through its disruption, for the latter had most certainly occurred as well.

He saw also that he had identified with his human self more than he ever had any other. Sinister influences had played a part in that. Watching Dunn cradle his lifeless, human body, he could not regret it had happened.

Claire remained backed to the wall in abject shock, a wan caricature of herself. It was strange how detached he now felt from her—her and the others, the entire drama at play. An instant ago they had defined his existence.

He missed those feelings, which was in itself remarkable, because he never missed anything about a life he left behind. He lived, he died, he moved on—such was his nature.

But this was the first time he had died without fulfilling his purpose. He looked at Dunn and knew it was more than that. He had always instilled trust in others. No one had ever instilled trust in him—except for Frisa and his recipients, and in their cases trust had always been consequent, at least in part, to the work of his creators. Natalie was the one exception.

The damage to his core self would take time to repair. An impurity he hadn't detected had insinuated itself into his composition. He wouldn't be fully himself until it was purged.

All of these observations he made in barely more than a

second. Then he remembered that he was in danger. As was Frisa. The attacking shapes were reacting to them the way anti-bodies would a virus. If enough of them constricted tightly enough about him, he might implode, with uncertain results for everyone. But the shapes were on automatic. There would be no reasoning with them.

His assistants were still with him, taking extraordinary measures to defend him. They had joined and smeared themselves across the intervening space to form a barrier between ¼=ca.85 and the swarm, beseeching their fellows to cease hostilities. The latter effort was failing and the former could not hold long.

The attacking shapes were desperate to keep ¼=ca.85 from escaping. They feared what he might do if he did. Frisa was effectively trapped in her body. She could abandon it but in the process would almost certainly be captured by the massing shapes.

And she didn't want to abandon her body. She wanted to fulfill her purpose.

If he could escape, ¼=ca.85 might draw the majority of the attacking shapes away from her. He would have to leave the planet, which was what he needed to do.

His assistants forged a way through the swarm inside the apartment for him. Outside, ¼=ca.85 veered skyward and told his assistants go back and protect Frisa. He would have to leave it up to them to pacify the Cloud.

He didn't get far before it became apparent that he wouldn't make it. Thousands of shapes clustered around him, jostling to cling to him. As his core self, ¼=ca.85 was almost immeasurably small, and nimble enough to dodge his way through them, so long as they didn't merge. Soon, though, they would bunch so tightly that, even in their disorderly panic, they would merge and he would be trapped.

Then Spoon was there, spinning like a rotor, blowing its fellows out of the way, smearing itself into a bubble around ¼=ca.85. The shape of etiquette pressed on, drilling a passage upward through the milling shapes.

The outer reaches of space, beyond the upper atmosphere, were no danger to shapes. But they were progeny of human perception, and limited in how they saw themselves. The higher Spoon went, the more the attacking shapes fell off and dropped back toward the planet, until ¼=ca.85 was free of danger. He realized too late what the shape of etiquette was doing. Spoon expended itself, letting itself be stripped apart, to see ¼=ca.85 to safety.

Go back, Spoon, ¼=ca.85 beseeched, but it was too late. The attacking shapes receded in a collapsing plume. Spoon, in a final gesture of defiance, bore ¼=ca.85 high into the planet's exosphere.

Come back to us, it conveyed, and died, a shredded silhouette of itself manifesting in farewell before disintegrating into mist.

¼=ca.85 lingered motionless and empty of thought in respect for the gentle entity who had given its life to save him. He drew Spoon's remains into himself. He would bear them back to the Cloud to be shared as they should be.

He repaired himself. The breach was worse than his assistants had perceived, and he discovered its source. Tucked away ever so discretely in the composition of his nuclear being were the remains of thirty or so dead Ixilian shapes. How they had penetrated his core he had no idea. But he saw now what should have been obvious earlier. The Ixilians had had millennia to study Frisa and him. Of course they knew everything about them. Haliel had been more than disingenuous to imply otherwise. Ixil excelled in the development of technology. They had found a way to do what had been done.

¼=ca.85 had returned, as Planchette, to the wrong beginning. It was not the triangular intersection in recolonized New York where this intrigue had begun. It had begun in the depths of space, where Frisa and he had last hibernated. ¼=ca.85 was sure the Ixilians had long since mapped the locations of sentient species in the galaxy, and projected how they might develop. Somehow they must have predicted the call from Earth.

¼=ca.85 remembered rousing from hibernation in response to the call from another world: a nest of minds, shrill with alarm, somewhere near the outer rim. Reflexively he sought the call's source, attuned his senses to the subtle undercurrents of darkness that traveled faster than light, in which the signatures of life were borne along, their voices faint, hard to distinguish. That was what their creators had designed them to do, Frisa and he.

But then he realized that he was alone. He reached out with his senses but found no response, no trace of Frisa in any direction.

Having only known panic in others, he had not recognized it in himself. He had never been alone. Frisa had always been with him. Now she was gone, and he had no idea where, why or when she had left him. 'When' in particular was a liquid caliper to one who had drifted aeons among the stars, contemplating nothing. But time flowed in one direction only.

His anchor was the message, his purpose, the thing that always restored him. Composure returned. This was some accident, or maybe a game. Yes, a game. Frisa's purpose was the same as his; all he had to do was follow the call and he would find her. She must have gone ahead. Out of playfulness—of course. She would be unhappy to learn she had distressed him.

He located the source, sorted its string from the weave of darkness and wiped away the film of distance. He could see his objective as many eyes and senses might, but, with an inimitable instinct not even Frisa possessed, saw it as it's inhabitants did: a lovely blue globe poised on the brink of calamity. World number ninety-nine. (He always counted their birth world as number one.)

And so he had begun his quest there, on that world, and not here, in the void, where the intrigue really began. The plan had been intricate. Conceal ¼=ca.85 so that Frisa would think he had left her. Then let him wake and be so distracted by her absence that he would chase after her and rush to adopt a human construct without first examining himself. Once he was human it would be too late. Immersed in his human perceptions and circumstances he would be blind to the pollutants in his elder mind.

There was another remarkable factor in the case, which was impossible to evaluate. Effecting the destabilization of ¼=ca.85's psyche had cost the lives of many Ixilian shapes. Ixilians did not take lives, nor did they sacrifice them. That they had done so now indicated an ominous shift in the character of their kind.

Or maybe not. Maybe it only indicated a change in one. ¼=ca.85 examined the remains of the Ixilian shapes closely, searching for a sense of who they had been, and how they had regarded their mission. The remains had been very well preserved inside his core self. But there was nothing, not the slightest echo or residue of thought or consciousness.

¼=ca.85 could see only one way to persuade the shapes of Earth that Frisa and he could be trusted. They would never help him create another body. Any blank he might contrive would be sterile and unconvincing, a mere costume. He would never be able to consummate, in such an incarnation, delivery of the message to Claire or any other potential recipient.

He would have to reanimate the corpse of Planchette Chron. It might cost him everything to do it. The self he knew now, his true self that had been there from the start, might disintegrate in the process. He did not know if any self that remained would be him, if any self remained at all.

He couldn't think about it. He did not know if he possessed the courage to do what he was contemplating. The thought would never have come to him had he not been separated from Frisa. It could destroy her too, or leave her unpartnered, which amounted to the same thing. He needed answers that he could not get on earth before he made his decision. He turned his attention to Mars, and again parted space.

Chapter Forty-Five

From the perspective of his core self, the ship was its own cosmos. That was one way of seeing it. In his core state ¼=ca.85 did not rely on a relativistic perspective. He could see things many ways. He looked at the ship differently, now, and saw it as a dense and complex composition of matter in a less dense composition of 'space.'

Like all interstellar vehicles he had encountered, with the exception of Ixilian ships that not only parted space but compressed it, this one had attracted a field of particulate matter rich in its molecular makeup. ¼=ca.85 gathered some of the matter and composed a body from it, the only one he could render accurately without assistance. He resurrected his original self. Only a model he could propel by will, not an organism that would die in space with the first breath it tried to take.

Through the optics of the model, the ship acquired spectacle and relative dimension. It was gigantic. ¼=ca.85 guessed it could accommodate the current population of New York several times over. Its lack of aerodynamic design was more obvious than it had been in Haliel's small hologram. This ship did not sail or fly, it moved. Its central structure was more or less spherical, but thousands of massive compartments protruded from it without regard for symmetry.

It was an excursion and exploration vessel. Certainly it had not been designed for combat. The 'armament batteries' Haliel had pointed out, if indeed such they were, ¼=ca.85 suspected were most likely for clearing obstacles, like asteroids, out of the way.

A light shone near the forecastle of the ship. ¼=ca.85 slipped down to investigate and found an open portal. Someone had detected his presence. ¼=ca.85 entered the portal. It closed, and the chamber filled with breathable atmosphere. ¼=ca.85 indulged himself in activating the full complement of his organs and senses.

It felt good to stretch real eye stalks and see through the eyes he'd been born with, to reach out with pseudopods unhindered by skeletal constraints. There was never a more stable base upon which to stand than the giant, undulous foot he had been given by his parents. He reached up and touched the residual shell on the back of his head. All was in order. Outside of his imagination, only twice before had he worn this body, addressing the Ixilian Galactic Council and in the early times following his birth. And yet, it felt like he had always lived in this form, that no other body had truly been his. The ironies and contradictions of his existence were manifold.

When the inner airlock opened, what confronted him on the other side was the greatest surprise of his many lives. Cheers and applause thundered down on him in a crashing wave. The floor of the vast bay and tiers of decks that lined the walls were crowded with beings from an indeterminate number of worlds, all, in their varied voices, hailing him. The space was hundreds of meters high, at least a thousand wide, its farthest reaches lost in distance, and yet it was all full of people who, though they had never seen him before, seemed to know who he was and what he did, and hold him in high esteem.

It was impossible. Frisa and he had always preserved their anonymity with great care. There was no reason for their memory to have survived with such intensity. Their families should have filtered in with the rest of their respective kinds, and their own outwardly unremarkable lives been lost to the records.

A cloud of shapes milled through the vast chamber, above and between the cheering throng. Understanding overcame ¼=ca.85 and humbled him.

It was the shapes who had remembered them. On every world they had preserved their memories, over time conveyed them to their parents, and made certain they were kept alive.

His focus had always been on the importance of the message, and the species he had been tasked to serve. He had never thought how revered Frisa and he might become if what they'd done were known. Frisa should have been there to experience this with him. It was hard to endure on his own.

A group of Tehfolorans came down the aisle to meet him. Outside of their containment suits their movements were quite graceful. ¼=ca.85 remembered what it was to have segmented limbs. Among the greeters ¼=ca.85 recognized the individual who had helped him escape the giant reptiles in the tunnel. With the assistance of an elder shape, the Tehfoloran introduced himself as Rus the eighty-seventh, and presented ¼=ca.85 with a small, pale-orange sphere. When he accepted it and held it in his pseudopod it played an audio recording of his ancient Tehfoloran self telling a bedtime story to his son.

He would learn that his bedtime stories, which he had composed extemporaneously, had affected his children on many worlds in ways he could never have foreseen.

He learned that and a great deal else, much from his hosts and more by deduction. He lingered an Earth day, meeting the citizens of many worlds, to whom he was presented like royalty. The passengers of the ship hailed from about twenty of the worlds Frisa and he had visited. He learned of the great impediment to their interstellar society, and showed them on star charts where some of the other worlds they had visited were located. He told them Frisa would be able to help them find more. And then, after he had tasted the pleasures of a dozen worlds, and reveled in a community diverse beyond his dreams, he prepared to return to Earth.

Many shapes offered to intercede for him with the shapes of Earth. He declined their help, saying he did not want to risk compromising the designs of his parents.

He did not tell his hosts his true intentions or fears. They would have tried to stop him from carrying through with his plans, and he was not going to give them an opportunity to do that. It was not in him to leave a job undone, or Frisa unable to complete even part of it. It was not in her either, though she would not welcome his decision. He did not like it himself. Histories lost, cultures laid waste, the dead beyond counting—it was too much. It was too big a job for two handmade beings.

Chapter Forty-six

¼=ca.85 had never reanimated a corpse before. It was perhaps ironic that his core self, which would do the work, was so small as to be imperceptible, without great magnification and other optical enhancement, to the visual faculties of every species he had encountered, while the physical self he sought to reanimate was, by comparison, a titanic lumbering behemoth. It became clear immediately that it was simpler to assemble a body from inanimate matter than it would be to return to life one that was dead. He did not have thousands of shapes to help him with the details, either.

The biggest problem was that he was not building a life form around himself, he was reaching out into a highly complex and eccentric organism that was in a state of incipient decomposition. He had to open himself—the self that had become the core of every entity he had ever been—and extend connective tendrils of such multiplicity that he had to entrust the bulk of the process to unconscious art.

He started with his brain, which was dead flesh that retained nothing. All of the memories had to be re-installed. It was like entering a vast labyrinth of rooms in darkness, without any notion where the light switches might be.

But he had supposed rightly. His core self did have the capacity for this. It had collaborated in the making of this being and retained the map, knew where things went. Gradually the dead brain warmed, synapses re-activated and the person who had been Planchette Chron moved back into the whorls and creases of his former home.

Then he worked his way into the rest of his body. The effort was interminable. Flaccid muscles did not want to flex, lungs did not want to breathe, blood did not want to flow. But gradually he restored viability and function to each molecule, cell and organ.

It was nearly as laborious to restore his heart as his mind, especially with all the torn tissue that had to be knitted back together. Its first pump would have made him scream had his throat not been too constricted to allow it. Cramps cascaded through his muscles. He became aware of confinement—remembered, fleetingly, his minuscule self finding a flaw in the seal around a steel door, reentering this body through its right nostril.

He was on his back in a space too narrow to sit up in or even raise his arms. The surface he lay on rocked back and forth—some kind of rolling platform. The door was at his feet. He focused his convulsions there, put the force of his core behind them and kicked.

The door flew off its hinges and clanged against a far wall. Planchette wheeled the platform forward. Light stabbed his eyes. Tangled in the sheet that covered him, he fell off the platform onto a hard, cold floor. His heart stopped and started several times. He found his voice and screamed for mercy. A million tiny, clawed hands wrung his veins and arteries. White pain stabbed behind his eyes, and again at the base of his skull. He was attacked all over by saw-toothed spikes, writhed in agony.

The seizures subsided and his vision cleared. Through a dash-line of high transoms, pale light filtered in upon a white-tiled chamber and a wall of cadaver closets. The center closet on the bottom row was open, the drawer protruding like a tongue sticking out.

A generator or ventilation unit kicked on outside, the drone loud even through the wall. The air smelled of disinfectant and death. Something rattled on the platform he'd fallen from. Planchette wrestled free of his shroud, struggled to his knees, steadied himself on the edge of the extended drawer. A vibrating sheet skipped across the metal surface. Planchette grabbed it, dropped back on the floor, sat up against the wall.

It wasn't the sheet the shapes had helped him make. It did not bear their psycho-kinetic signature. Someone must have left it by accident. Unless they had expected his body to revivify.

Without thinking he opened the holoscreen. Haliel's face appeared. They stared at each other without speaking. Even with all he now knew Haliel had done, Planchette couldn't see him as a villain.

"I suppose you'd like someone to come get you," Haliel said.

Planchette nodded, coughed and wretched. "I'm in—"

"The morgue. You're in the morgue."

Planchette nodded again. The connection terminated. He hoped Haliel would bring clothes.

A flicker of movement drew his eyes up. Morph, Morpho, Twelve and Graph were there. Planchette's joy at seeing them was pursued by grief. They read his recent memories, and he suffered with them, afresh, over Spoon's death.

More for the first time, which made it worse. ¼=ca.85's relationship to Spoon had been distant, of historical record, more so due to the occlusion of Planchette's mnemonic functions. It was Planchette whose relationship with the shape of etiquette had been intimate. He had not really been able, as his elder self, to mourn Spoon. The gentle little shape's sacrifice weighed terribly. It had devoted its obscure, diminutive existence to grace and consideration, and thrown down its life for truth and forbearance. Planchette thought of the adulation he had received aboard the Tehfoloran vessel and was ashamed of himself. He'd had a great many friends, throughout his many lives, that he had not recognized. Four of them were with him now.

He let them connect with his core and extract Spoon's remains.

There was something on his foot. The middle toe of his right foot had a tag tied to it. He pulled it off and squinted at what was written. Under the date and time it read, *"John Doe, AKA Planch-ette Chron, no autopsy without perm. Hasker."*

Planchette took a long, deep breath. He was alive, again, in this body, by more than one agency, not least providence. He was glad to return to this life. At the same time he was deeply afraid. He could tell that he would not be able close his core again, having opened it. Already his elder self was destabilizing. He had no way of knowing how long it would hold together, nor what would happen when it failed. Whatever he was going to do, he needed to do it soon.

Chapter Forty-Seven

Pale, wavering light limned strange accumulations of objects in Haliel's dome. Stacks of neatly folded clothing, hammers, plates, hats, things Planchette couldn't identify. Artifacts Haliel had taken from the veldt and restored. There would be no simple answer to why he had done that. Long, curving shelves on the walls displayed a vast and varied assortment of cups and teapots.

Planchette huddled under a mound of blankets, curled up in a patched leather armchair. Haliel's dome was the rear left ground unit in a pyramid of five, the other four of which were unoccupied. In the courtyard, under the raised dome, an illuminated swimming pool rippled from the agitations of an automated pool cleaner. The only light on inside was in the kitchen, over the stove. It reflected off the counter and uplit Haliel's face. He was chopping something and putting it in a steaming pot.

Planchette stared at the water and wanted to float. His body was fragile.

He had died and brought himself back to life. That was one perspective. Another was that the person who had performed the resurrection, and made the decision to do so, his original self, who retained the memories of his many lives, was different from the person he had been and was again now. All the other people he had been were dead. Surviving death did not negate loss of life.

Though love echoed on.

Haliel set a tray bearing a white cup and teapot on a low table by Planchette's chair. "Ginger with a little ginseng in it." He poured Planchette a cup. "It will calm your stomach and help you get your strength back."

The taste was prickly and vaguely sweet. It felt good in his throat. Planchette's hand shook, putting down the cup. The self he had always been, who had watched ninety-eight civilizations collapse and warily return to existence, had always been itself, collector of memories, observer of lives, never the one who lived.

"No one comes here, do they?" he asked Haliel.

Haliel had been prattling on about reconfiguring his replicator to extrapolate complete objects from the fragments he found. He stopped and stared at Planchette. "Why would they?"

It was the thing Planchette had failed to register—Haliel drinking tea, when he first encountered him in the veldt. Haliel's automaton possessed no biological functions. *His* inner self, *his* observer, *was* the one who lived. But he'd had no life for at least seven millennia. His existence had become as unique, in its own way, as Frisa's and Planchette's, only with no commensurate purpose to anchor him. Neither the watcher nor the watched of Haliel had lived, only waited in fear.

"How long have you been here?"

"In this house?" Haliel glanced around like one imprisoned. "No."

Haliel's expression became wistful, flawless in composition. "Oh." His gaze turned low and inward. "About thirty years."

"Miscalculation?" Frisa had been here only a few weeks.

"I'm not sure."

Planchette believed him. "I need to hear you say it, if I'm going to trust you."

Haliel sighed. He actually sighed. "I deceived you."

"You tried to stop me."

"Do you understand why?"

Planchette looked at Haliel's shapes. They drifted about the dome in disarray, like scattered, forgotten memos. They were not conscious. Planchette was not certain they were even alive. It would be a stretch to characterize destroying some of them as killing. They were just memory bags. They did not communicate with other shapes because they couldn't. Which meant that Ixil, for all of its technological sophistication, could never participate as an equal in a galactic society, and explained why Ixilians had tried so hard to prevent one from forming.

Planchette asked Morpho to convey what they had learned to the Stations of the Close. The shape of change departed and Planchette's thoughts returned to Frisa. Haliel was sure no one in P.C. or the police force knew where she was, or even that she existed. If there had been awareness of a creature half human and half giant snail at large in the city, he was sure he would have heard about it. She must have fled. She could move swiftly on the foot of her original body, even on vertical or inverted surfaces. Planchette touched the place where the knife had entered his heart. The flesh had knitted but it was tender.

His legs cramped when he tried to stand. Haliel helped him up. Planchette wanted to wash the morgue off of himself.

Columns of glass shelves in the bathroom displayed soaps and toiletries like artifacts in a museum. The shower, though, was an affirmation of the body. He moaned under the warm spray, let go of the cares of the universe. This flesh, however it had come into being, possessed validity. If all the stars were peopled, nothing would be worth more than consciousness held in a single chalice of flesh. This was what labor and pain were for, moments of ease and mercy, known one by one, that not only secured the past and redeemed the future but distinguished loss from forgiveness.

Haliel had sorted his salvaged clothing by size, separate stacks for each type. Morph made a couple of tentative suggestions. Planchette missed Spoon's counsel. He found a pair of dark pants and a grey shirt.

"I'll never really understand that, will I?" Haliel leaned against the kitchen counter, watching Planchette with his arms folded.

"What?"

"What it feels like to dress a body not my own."

Planchette shook his head. What a sad question. "This *is* my body, Haliel." Pulling on pants left him breathless. He collapsed into a chair at a round table by the glass doors that looked onto the courtyard, watched the glowing water until he was calm. Then he called Dunn on Haliel's sheet.

He didn't open the holoscreen. His voice would be shock enough. There was relief in hers, once she believed it was him. More than relief, in the quaver of her voice and the way her breath caught between words.

Haliel sat at the table when Planchette clicked off. "She'll come?"

Planchette nodded.

"How much have you told her?"

"Everything."

Haliel was quiet a moment. "That must have been a relief."

Planchette watched the water. The existence of moments was fiction. Time passed and became memory. "What does Willbury have planned?"

"Not just him. It's a network. Planet-wide."

"What do they want?"

"I don't know all of it. They want to repeal Right of Refusal. Which means they have to purge opponents from positions of authority."

"How will they do that?"

"I don't know. They're P.C. Probably accuse them of dissociative tendencies. Diagnose them. I think what they're doing here is a kind of experiment."

"Why go after Olivetta?"

Haliel's automaton shrugged, too naturally to be anything other than reflex. "I've never understood that. As long as I've known him, Willbury's been obsessed with Olivetta."

Planchette remembered paintings in flames, all the beautiful portraits of shapes, never mentioned, never discussed, consigned to soot and ash. Morpho's oscillations quickened at Planchette's thought. "I know why," Planchette said. He looked at Haliel.

"Olivetta is no sociopath."

"Was no sociopath."

"What?"

"He's dead. Was no sociopath. He killed himself."

"Oh—" Planchette's gaze rose and his eyes closed—"how is that possible? He was in lockup."

"He bit through the veins on his wrists. After Willbury went to see him."

A knock at the door interrupted the bloom of outrage. Dunn stood backlit by streetlight, her face obscured. Planchette made himself walk normally to her. She only met his gaze for an instant, enough for him to see hope and fear bound up in unanswerable bewilderment.

She had Frisa in her cruiser, strewn suffering across the back seat like a mound of guts. Frisa recoiled from Haliel's touch.

"It's all right," Planchette told her. His human revulsion at her deformities was gone. They got her out of the cruiser and helped her inside. Haliel suggested Planchette tend to her injuries in the swimming pool. Her massive foot would never fit inside the shower stall. Planchette told Dunn to go get some things, realized too late that he had spoken to her as if she were still his subordinate. Before he could correct himself Haliel said he had everything they needed.

Planchette got undressed and helped Frisa into the pool. She slumped across the steps in the shallow end and surrendered to his ministrations. He probed the wounds on the bottom of her foot. Dunn had tended them as she could. Planchette caught her eye and gave her an appreciative look. She turned away. The defensive systems of Frisa's birth body were functional; the bleeding had stopped. But her connection with her core was compromised, like his had been, though differently. She was not healing as she should. Two deep gashes, both over a meter long, needed to be closed.

Haliel provided medical adhesive and an applicator. The eyes in Frisa's mock-human shoulders followed his movements. Her false human head sank and inflated. That was still hard to watch.

"Do you know what he did?" she said softly to Planchette.

"He's helping us now," Planchette answered.

"You didn't have to hide from me." Haliel came back.

"Looking like this? I had to hide from everyone!"

"I didn't mean that to happen."

"How can you think anything you meant matters now?"

"He was trying to stop me," Planchette said.

"Both of us."

"Me more than you, I think."

He felt her probe his mind, his core. "Gascot, what have you done?" He knew she understood. He stroked her shoulder, tended her wounds.

"No! Gascot!"

But he knew she understood. It was too much for two hand-made beings. Too much death. They'd never been meant to live as long as they had. The work needed to be passed on to others. He closed her wounds. She convulsed. Some terrible pain tore through her.

"Oh, Gascot, I want to die."

"You don't want to die."

Chapter Forty-eight

Processing relayed video of the Tehfoloran vessel, now in Earth orbit, to the large holoscreen in the briefing room at the police station, and confirmed it to be no hoax. After that, known for imposter, alien and reanimated corpse though he was, by default the case became, again, Planchette's. No one else had any idea how to proceed. He met no objection when he asked Perls to shrink the picture from Processing and connect with Haliel's sheet.

The briefing room had been cleared of extraneous personnel. Its eccentric asymmetry seemed fitting, now. Frisa had been brought up in a secured elevator, adjacent corridors sealed off. Planchette stood with her near the right rear corner of the room, by the slanted windows. Hasker, hands on hips, watched the screen from the room's center, glanced back at Planchette with exaggerated skepticism. Pretense failed him when he looked at Frisa. Planchette was sorry to see his former Captain diminished, a bewildered spectator to his own investigation. Perls connected with Haliel's signal and the face of Mathias Willbury, transmitted, unbeknownst to him, from his own office, dominated the screen.

"You don't think we should be worried?" Haliel said.

"What do you have to worry about?" asked Willbury.

"More than you."

Willbury laughed.

Frisa's false head was hooded, the rest of her bulk swaddled in blankets, with a narrow gap for her mal-placed eyes to see through. She was the largest and tallest person in the room. She sneaked out a hand-like pseudopod and Planchette clasped it.

Dunn kept to the far side of the room, left haunch on a desk top, arms crossed, remote as another country. Planchette watched her, an impossible, nameless longing refusing to be denied. Which was as well; he had lied enough.

Schnittke and Perls stood together in their customary spots up front. Perls glanced back at Planchette, disappointment in his eyes. Schnittke remained fixed on the holoscreen in an attitude of wry vindication.

"They know you're behind the fires."

"They don't *know* anything. Let them prove it. It'll never reach this office."

"If they catch the ones who did it? That's foolhardy, Mathias."

"None of my people will dare implicate me. They'll let themselves be banished, first."

Also present were two high-ranking justices from Judicial Branch, both women, one of whom Planchette recognized as the elder who had presided at the church, and two representatives from Processing, a heavyset woman and a lean, dark-skinned man, the latter Ganeel Godbole, Senior Supervisor and no mere handler. Processing had watched Planchette more keenly than he had supposed. Of the Stations of the Close, only the feather-handled hammer, Station of Furniture, had come to bear witness. It hovered near Hasker like an invisible colleague. A gaunt, inscrutable woman, current Chair of the Neural See, had flown in from Europe by emergency jumper, with her personal translator, to represent P.C. But to Planchette the most surprising member of their company was Frederick Bash, full name Frederick Milliner Bash, who turned out to be High Steward of the New York Chapter of the Society of the Useful, the highest ranking Utilitarian in the district. Among the native humans in attendance he seemed least troubled by the presence of aliens. He seemed, in fact, quite pleased.

The Mayor and the District Regent had not shown up and their whereabouts were unknown. A number of high-ranking P.C. officials were missing as well. Hasker suspected they would be found where Planchette had been incarcerated, in the bowels of P.C.'s operational complex. Just outside the briefing room, cops backed up by agents from Judicial Branch and observers from Processing prevented a squad of P-techs from coming in to arrest Hasker. Everyone inside the room had been briefed about who Planchette and Frisa were and why they were there.

Willbury's eyes darted and gleamed as he indulged his evident fondness for his own voice. Haliel got him to reveal everything—enough that the blanks were easy to fill. The global plot, the test-ground strategy for New York, even the names of conspirators. The Chair of the See's face went slack, hearing the latter.

Planchette was sure that Willbury was the principal architect of the plot. Rushing things as he had, in all likelihood it would have fallen apart on him. Olivetta had said it: consensus at that level is an illusion. Probably there was a counter-plot within P.C. to remove Willbury quietly, the sort of strategy people hold in reserve, secret even to themselves. Even in failure he'd left his mark. He was an embarrassment, a disturbingly smart and clever man who had outwitted the inviolate testing system.

Planchette noted the skill with which Haliel extracted information from Willbury. He did it with subservience, both learned and practiced, and vengeful in its underlying character. It was no guise Haliel presented but a fully actuated persona. The elder psychologist was distracted, failed to recognize his own presumption of control being used against him.

Meanwhile, Planchette continued to come apart inside. The self he knew as $\frac{1}{4}$=ca.85 was losing coherence. Thusfar to a minuscule degree. Of the billions of tendrils his core had extended to reanimate his corpse, only a handful had broken. But the deterioration would quicken as it increased. The broken tendrils shrank and retracted like lies. They would never re-integrate with his core.

Frisa knew he was dying. She felt what was happening and squeezed his hand. It was a strained show of support. She was angry, grief-stricken and afraid. It was a ghost of reunion they suffered now, an opportunity to haunt each other. Their time of long communion had expired. She could not give him the sympathy he craved. He would have to die without it.

Arrests were made; Willbury, shaken but defiant, was brought to the briefing room. Planchette felt caught between reluctance and the inevitable. Once he finished here, there would be nothing to keep him from fulfilling his purpose, and what would come after. But that would come, fulfillment or no. He was determined to have a say in the design of his end.

The escorting cops sat Willbury down with his hands cuffed behind him. Planchette told them to remove the restraints and sat in front of Willbury, regarded him without expression.

Willbury scoffed at Hasker, "You're condoning this charade?"

Hasker said nothing.

The psychologist was formidable. Nostrils flared, lips tight, chin raised, he narrowed his eyes in challenge. It would not be enough to demonstrate his culpability. His hidden attitudes would have to be exposed. Given time to fester and brood, even in exile, Willbury would hatch another scheme. It was ones such as he who had engineered the fall of Planchette's forebears.

Planchette thought of Olivetta's destroyed work and the manner of his death and did what he had never done—never permitted himself to do—as any other person he had been. He channeled his aura into the psychologist's brain and opened his core to Willbury's mind's eye. Not long enough to do irreversible damage, just enough to break his resistance. A little over a second. Perhaps longer than was absolutely necessary. He gave Willbury a glimpse of the underside of consciousness, a brief wade in a minor tributary of a lesser dark stream.

Willbury paled.

"Reveal," Planchette quietly commanded.

Willbury's features set with resistance.

"More?" Planchette asked.

Willbury sneered and looked away. His head drooped in defeat. "Hope," he muttered, and glared at Planchette; "What's it for? Friedman's shining future, yours. What a blessing. How precious."

Planchette met Willbury's vitriol impassively.

The psychologist scowled. "Other worlds, new Earths, new Edens, unsullied by the corruption of humanity, waiting to be ravaged by civilizations that reach the stars and a future millions or billions of years in duration—what *for?* It will be the same. We'll hurt and kill and destroy and deceive and pervert, suffer and die without end until it all comes to nothing. Nothing, nothing and more nothing. Endless nothing. No purpose, no meaning, no one left to remember or care about anything. Because we can? That's a *reason?* Giving birth is an act of murder." The psychologist's forehead beaded with sweat and a wildness entered his eyes. "The organism—" he waggled his hands to either side of his face— "desperate to prolong its existence, creates another—" he threw his arms wide—"in utter denial that it is consigning its progeny to misery, futility and death. Any beneficial characterization is a *lie.* Better to find peace and go to sleep, all of us, and we *know* it. We're just afraid. Which is irrelevant because it is inevitable. Let all of this senseless matter and energy wear itself out as it will, in accordance with its nature. It doesn't care about us. We have no fit reason to treat with it. Prolong the agony? Avoid the nothingness a little longer? Let the plants and the dumb beasts *have* it. Release ourselves from this incessant pestilence of intelligence."

"That's why you killed Friedman?"

"I didn't kill Friedman."

Planchette studied Willbury. He hadn't lied. Not overtly—by omission in some way. Planchette's assistants lit on his shoulders. Willbury suppressed a reflex, masked it but Planchette caught it.

"You can see them, can't you?"

Willbury avoided his gaze.

"See what?" Hasker asked.

Morph and Morpho lunged at Willbury and he flinched, brought his hands up to shield his face. When he lowered them he had turned sullen.

Planchette nodded and shook his head. Willbury had always been able to see shapes, just like Olivetta. Like Olivetta, he'd hidden it. What it must have been to discover a child who saw what he did. What a relief, and how terrifying. A thousand scenarios must have run through Willbury's head of what the world would be like if people knew they gave birth with their minds. But Planchette suspected it was the tyranny of his ego—the inability to accept proof of his own sanity from a lesser intellect, least of all a mere artist—that had ultimately decided the course Willbury took.

Willbury's eyes had gone dead. Planchette didn't want to understand him anymore, he just wanted to be done with him.

"How you must have disliked his paintings."

Willbury met Planchette's gaze dully. "Michael Olivetta committed suicide."

"Less than an hour after you muscled your way in to see him."

Willbury looked at the Chair of the See, found his ruin confirmed in her attitude. After that he didn't look at anyone.

There was still a piece Planchette did not understand. He'd known it, surrendered his reasoning to a facile conclusion because he was weary and frightened. But he didn't need to do anything. They would all have the answer soon enough. He sat and waited and not even Frisa came near. He waited and accepted the singularity of his life. There was little left of a personal nature that he could do for any of those he cared about. He was being reduced to his purpose, a tool of the future.

He did not know how long it was before they brought in Thaddy Myers. The boy still trusted him. He ran to Planchette and hugged him. The room fell quiet. Planchette caught Dunn watching them.

Gently, he broke the embrace. Thaddy looked around at the others. His gaze settled on Frisa. He stared at her as only a child could, without fear or revulsion, only curiosity. The connection between them was palpable to Planchette. Frisa might have been able to convey the intellectual component of her message to the boy right then. But it would have stolen his childhood and she would not do that.

"Thaddy, we need to ask you something," Planchette said.

"About the night that man was killed."

Planchette nodded. "Someone ran out of the alley, shouting that something terrible had happened, and the men at that table in the park and I followed him back into the alley. Do you remember that?"

Thaddy nodded.

"Before that, did you see anyone else come out of the alley?" Planchette signaled Perls.

Thaddy nodded again.

Planchette pointed at the holoscreen, where, among pictures of the registered black holes living in the city and a random sampling of cops, Perls had brought up shots of Olivetta, Gable MacGrory, Claire Fontaine, the depictions of Frisa that Olivetta and Claire had provided, and Mathias Willbury.

"Do you see that person there?"

Thaddy scanned the pictures carefully, looked back and forth, with clear dislike, between Willbury's image and the psychologist himself, but shook his head.

"You saw *none* of them?"

"No," Thaddy said, "but I saw him." He pointed at Haliel.

Frisa cried out in fury and disbelief. Planchette had thought his capacity for surprise exhausted. Graph reiterated the truism that what remains after alternatives have been exhausted must be true.

"He didn't look like that at first," Thaddy said. He pointed at Claire's composite rendering of Frisa. "He looked like that. But it was a hologram. He turned it off and went to the hover where that man was waiting for him." Thaddy pointed at Willbury.

Chapter Forty-nine

Haliel's automaton, which had become, by every perceptible measure, Haliel himself, or at least, in its now thirty years of uninterrupted operation, his authentic persona, sat across the oval table from Planchette in the chair Olivetta had occupied. He hadn't brought many of his memory bags with him. Only three.

"How's your body?" Planchette asked.

"I could ask you the same." When Planchette didn't respond Haliel said, "I'm aging." Like Olivetta, his voice had acquired a frail character.

"You're all right, though." Maybe it was only the room.

Haliel nodded. "I'm all right."

"What are you doing?"

Haliel smiled faintly. "What do you mean?"

"Here, in custody, letting yourself be questioned."

"I killed a man, Eighty-five."

Planchette opened his mouth and closed it. He had misunderstood this person from the start. All the aeons and reaches of their acquaintanceship would be summed up in what happened in the next few minutes, here in this small, grey room.

"Aren't you going to interview me? Play your part, Detective Chron."

Planchette sighed. They had both buried themselves in their roles. "Tell me how you got involved with Willbury."

Haliel nodded at the Station of Furniture, who clung to the front corner of the room opposite the door. "Ask it."

Planchette looked back.

We knew the psychologist could see us, Furniture conveyed,

and of his antipathy toward the physicist; he contrived against him. It created an anomaly in the field. The Station of Futures was with us then, and sought to evaluate this one so we informed him of the polarity.

Evaluate how? Planchette asked.

Through observation of the anomaly.

What was his impact on it?

We could not determine that he had one.

Haliel laughed. "Story of my life. I was never here."

The understanding that he killed the physicist, Furniture added, has informed the assessment. His efforts to remedy his acts inform it further. The anomaly is in flux.

Haliel sobered, went blank and still as stone. He became animate again. "I would like to explain."

Little stings pricked Planchette, inside and out, more tendrils of his core breaking loose. The deterioration was accelerating. He was determined to see both of his assignments through to their ends. This was the last time he would see Haliel.

"I want you to understand. What it's been like for me. How far I've come from the life I knew."

"I've been to Ixil, Haliel. You've told me many times."

"Have I? I don't remember. Not like this. And you've been to *one* of our worlds. I don't think you saw it. Not really."

"I looked."

"With disdain."

Planchette remembered taking in the view of Idria, Frisa and he, from the observation deck of the mammoth administrative center that had been represented to them as the seat of the 'Galactic Council.' The Ixilian city had been an idyllic environ of spires and terraced communes built of smooth, banded stone and living wood, aflow with streams and waterfalls and bowered by leafy canopies that grew from the buildings themselves. Its pale, eel-like denizens seemed, in their ethereal grace, to glide along its avenues, content in all they did. Something about the placidity of the scene had struck both Frisa and him as a veneer.

Possibly it had had something to do with the ranks of identical pale white ovoid shapes scudding about everywhere in formation.

"When I was born," Haliel said, "my mother did not nurse me. She laid me in the warm loerl stream that ran through our home. The flow vines held me, and tanea leaves fed wine to my lips. I was surrounded by shapes that were already relaying to my mind the history of our people.

"Life in Ixil is kind, Eighty-five. There is no government—not like what they have here—no police. Everyone knows what to do. There's no struggle or strife. No crime, no want, no infirmity, no ignorance. Our cities grow themselves. Our science arises organically from what we require. We have five habitable planets in our system that share a vast envelope of oxygen in space. We can travel between them with the windows down."

"Your shapes aren't conscious."

"They're part of us. They arose from the primordial substrate with us. We remember it all. The ascent to consciousness, everything. There's no division. We do not separate experience into moments. It's all one event—one shared event. Birth, life, death—we have no reason to expect less of death than life. We know we will be remembered.

"We look out onto the rest of the galaxy and see perpetual conflict, violence, chaos that consumes worlds. Other species are defined by their struggles. They will never understand us. We do what we can to prevent them finding each other. Or us. Especially us. Distort the structure of space, divert communications, cultivate impressions that they are each alone. Space itself resists our efforts. We can only do so much.

"You amazed us, when we found you. Your creators made a magnificent leap that was beyond our understanding. All these thousands of kerns later it still is. We know what you are but not how you were made. In your infinite adaptability is an echo of our perfect existence. We hoped you might influence other species toward similar states."

Planchette doubted it was the how of his creation that stumped the Ixilians. More likely they couldn't understand the sacrifice his ancestors had made, surrendering everything to an uncertain end. They would not understand regret. "Your Galactic Council was a fraud."

"We did that, yes. Made simulacra, like this one, of members of other species. But you wanted to be fooled."

"Why do you say that?"

"Ask yourself when we're done and make up your own mind. At the time, you were the only non-Ixilian life form, if life form you are, with whom we had communicated directly."

"I should feel honored."

"You should. And you would, if you knew us better. Or maybe not. Few of my people had ever used constructs before. The technology was developed in anticipation of rare instances when we might need to interact with other species. We'd never put on a show like that. We only wanted to create an appearance of—"

"Superiority."

"Authority. We hoped you would defer to us. But you didn't like us."

"We didn't feel one way or another. You diverted us from Fixot. We needed to go. Galaxy Prime was a fiction, too, I suppose."

"I had to make up a story of some kind."

"You're a good liar."

"Who do you think taught me? We wanted you to succeed. But we had to assess the danger to ourselves. I was chosen, from among volunteers, to be your monitor because I favored intervention. I thought you should be stopped. But I was not meant to pursue you indefinitely, only to Fixot."

"To Fixot? You never told us that."

"The decision to extend the mission came later. I followed you there and watched the Olot tear themselves apart. It was like watching a chemical reaction go wrong. I was too shocked to feel anything. That was the only time I went easily into stasis. My perspective changed when I woke to discover that the planet had made more than two hundred revolutions around its sun.

"My replicators generated an Olot construct, which was my first experience of interfacing with a construct. It was … terrible. I went down to the planet to observe your interactions with the descendants of the survivors. Almost immediately I became uneasy. I say that now; at the time I could not have named the feeling. It wasn't the devastation or the suffering of those creatures, it was being an impostor among them. For the first time in my life I felt vulnerable. It was an irrational reaction; I was entirely safe. But that feeling separated me from everyone.

"Or maybe it was the long silence. Two hundred plus Fixot years in stasis. I wasn't dealing with the same people. The decision was made that I should continue monitoring you. There was a moment, I think, when I wanted to kill myself. Surely I'm the first of my kind to have that thought. I went back into stasis, which was a kind of an end. Interruption resumed."

"This was all your own doing, Haliel."

"Better than you can imagine, I *know*. The next three worlds you went to I could hardly bear to leave stasis long enough to monitor your transitions. The violent events I avoided. I became farther and farther removed from my people. Again, I have to name my emotions in retrospect. 'Resentment,' I'll call it—a festering in my mind that fed on its own futility. Everyone I knew was dead. The language changed so much I couldn't understand the people with whom I communicated. My shapes had to osmose translation modules. It was humiliating.

"I disciplined myself to making observations. Tried to interact with you. Hoped, here and there, that we might become friends but you would not allow it. I watched you live lives, raise families, took it as much as I could and went back into stasis.

"I think I did my job too well. Before the call came from Earth,

I was awakened to find instructions waiting. It was the first time that had happened. They wanted me to interfere with you. I knew then that I had become a tool. What they proposed meant sacrificing some of my shapes. I'd already lost over half of the ones I'd started with to old age. I couldn't take them all into stasis with me. But my users didn't care about that. My kin were part of the grey memory of antiquity to them, and I had acquired the status of implement."

"What did they want you to do?"

"They were concerned you might manifest a reaction we hadn't seen. Something final."

"Because, like my parents, humans were beginning to develop the ability to see shapes on their own."

Haliel checked out a moment, came back. "There was a second matter."

Planchette rubbed his face. "How shapes communicate."

Haliel nodded. "Across distances, particularly between planets far removed from each other. Once an initial connection is made it becomes more a quantum exchange than a transmission. We can't interrupt it—not by any acceptable means—and we're deaf to what is relayed. It was thought that something might be learned by interfering with you.

"My instructions had three parts: separate you and One-ten, cause the shapes of Earth to mistrust you, and interfere with your development of human bodies and personas. The purpose was to see how you functioned as individuals, clarify how you interact with shapes in the creation of your personas, and how they communicate with each other, particularly as a shared mind.

"There's a lag, when you receive a distress call from shapes. It takes awhile for you to rouse. You don't, always, I'm sorry to tell you. The calls are diffuse, omni-directional and extremely faint in the hidden streams. Our beacon has detected some that you didn't. Clearly my users had anticipated that you would respond to the call from Earth. I made preparations, conditioned some of my shapes to interfere with your mental processes and insinuated them into your cognitive core." Haliel looked at Planchette beseechingly. "I did not like doing that. I hope you believe me."

Planchette rested his forehead in his hand, closed his eyes. "I suppose so." He was coming apart, inside. The shapes were doing their best to slow it down. He sensed Haliel watching him, straightened and took a deep breath. "Go on."

"The idea was to create a distraction, so that you might, in haste, generate a construct without first examining yourself—"

"I figured that part out. The strategy seemed conditional on our survival. It could only work if we didn't die."

"That was never—I never saw that as a possibility."

"Your instruments tell you we're one entity, but cutting us in half won't kill us?"

Haliel looked away, went away. His throat performed a reflex of swallowing.

"Go on." Planchette tried to keep irritation out of his tone.

"One-ten always roused before you. I masked my bio-rhythms and enclosed you in a nullification field so that she would think you'd left without her. The instant I did that she burst awake, parted space and was *gone*. The ferocity of the reaction shocked me. I withdrew the nullification field, terrified that I had hurt you. Your reaction was calmer—"

"You'd interfered with my mind."

Haliel nodded. "But you hurried to Earth without detecting what I'd done. In that respect the initial phase of the experiment was a success."

"My compliments."

"We might do without sarcasm."

Planchette was fairly certain they didn't have sarcasm on Ixil but forbore pressing the point.

Haliel let silence draw a moment before continuing. "I followed you, in a panicked state myself. If I'd damaged you I would be more isolated than ever. From orbit I watched you observe the destruction of London and New York. And then you jumped, just as always, except this time alone.

"My next task was to sow distrust towards you among the shapes of Earth. To do that I had to come out of stasis before you returned to what you call common time. That meant not relying on the beacon. My users had made an estimate, which I think incorporated a degree of leeway to which I was not made privy. I keyed their settings into the nullification system. When I came out of stasis the beacon did not detect your presence so I knew I was ahead of you. I had a feeling that I was in for a long wait.

"The worst thing was being restricted to my ship and the neural hammock. I didn't want to go back into stasis but boredom became a torment. I tasked the replicators to generate a human construct with heightened sensual acuity, and suppressed, as I could, aware-ness of my body when I interfaced with it.

"For years I wandered this world. I wondered if I would end my days here. I found beauties that gave me comfort. Skies colored by the sun, storms and mountains. I spent long periods by rivers and seas, watching water roll and flow.

"It preyed on me, what I'd done to you, not knowing what I'd done. I think it was inevitable that I wind up here, in the last city you came to. I liked the veldt, which I explored a great deal. I restored a few, small broken things I found there, developed a fondness for cups, which humans make in endless variety. It turned into something of an obsession. Eventually I homesteaded that abandoned dome and began to assemble a collection. It extends through all five domes, now.

"One day the shapes noticed me. A couple of them made contact and delivered a greeting from the Stations. It had been a long time since I'd thought about my users and their instructions. I wiped a few of my dwindling complement of shapes and met with the Stations, told them about you and One-ten, that your inten-tions were benign but your effect destructive, showed them the blanks as evidence, planted that seed. I told them I didn't know when you would arrive but that you were coming.

"They didn't trust me but they couldn't ignore me. It bothered them that they couldn't see inside my mind, but they were more concerned, obviously, about their relationship with humans. I professed ignorance of the specifics of your message. I told them a piece of the truth, that I knew it was intended, in part, to open a door for humans and shapes to communicate. The lie I told them was that, somehow, in the process, new shapes would eventually be born without self-awareness or the ability to think. They conveyed to me that there had always been a few humans who had been aware of them, and that once in a great while they were able to communicate with them, which confirmed the worries of my users. Futures was convinced that Friedman was aware of its presence, and that eventually they would communicate. Perhaps, it was suggested, you might be dissuaded from your mission if you believed your help was not needed. I rendered no opinion."

A deeper fatigue bore down on Planchette. He had always found his own deceits cumbersome. The duplicity Haliel related was of another order.

"Before we parted, the Stations told me about Willbury and the enmity he bore Friedman. I didn't understand why they did that but it was clear they had a reason. We engaged, I understand now, in a mutually surreptitious exchange. I instilled doubt in them and they curiosity in me. They did not *tell* me Willbury could see shapes."

You sought to deceive us, Futures conveyed, and fault our omission?

Haliel shrugged. "We were all set up. Friedman I did not approach directly. My scans showed that he could be a recipient for One-ten; his neurology was sympathetic. That made me more interested in Willbury, which was clearly what the Stations intended. How they foresaw that might occur I do not know. There seems little doubt they possessed an instinct." Haliel eyed Furniture but the Station did not respond.

Haliel had never communicated much with conscious shapes. To Planchette it was plain that he had not appreciated the extent of their intelligence.

Haliel paused a moment before continuing. "An opportunity to meet Willbury presented itself when he issued a notice for a personal assistant. I applied for the position and he called me in for an interview." Haliel stopped. He looked like a doll that had turned off. Then he sighed. Planchette wondered if he simulated, for himself, the sensation of air entering and leaving physical lungs in his automaton's chest.

"We talked for awhile and he offered me the job," Haliel continued. "I hadn't expected that. I'd only meant to meet him, get a sense of what he was like. I wondered about his motives. I'd found my construct to be inconveniently attractive to humans of both sexes. But it was something to do, so I accepted the job. Of course, I'd misread him entirely. Foolish of me, to think I could fool someone like him. He knew I was artificial from the start, and hid it. Hid, too, that I scared him. He's very good at hiding.

"I think I'd been working for him about two weeks when he told me he could see that I was isolated and troubled and offered to help. No one had ever offered to do that before, *help* me. That sounds worse than I mean it to. No one *needs* help on Ixil. Life is a pleasant collaboration, with each other and our environment. We don't really have a concept of work. What needs doing is obvious and we are all pleased to do it.

"But I was no longer part of that event, and hadn't been for a very long time. I hadn't realized how lonely I'd been until that moment. I was so overcome by emotions that I lost the interface. When I re-established it I could tell Willbury had seen me shut down. A panic took hold of me, a desperation to be understood. It translated into an irrepressible need to reveal myself. Once I started I couldn't stop. It was intoxicating to be heard so intently. He made me feel safe and important. I told him everything—who I was, why I was here.

"Nothing I said surprised him. He knew that I was alien, that I was here for a reason, and alone. He said I was suffering from anxiety. He said he couldn't prescribe anything for me, but that he might be able to help me in some other way. He told me he was honored to be the first human to greet an emissary from another world, said he had no idea what to make of my mission but could think of no better way to represent humanity than to be my friend. I needed help and he would do his best to help me. I would be his patient, too, so anything I told him would be held in confidence.

"'Friend' is a powerful word, especially to one isolated as I was. I've reflected a great deal, during the years, about things we take for granted on Ixil. There are ironies in our perfect existence. It's difficult to know if you really care about someone if you never have cause to be concerned about them. Willbury ensured my cooperation with that enchanting word—'friend.' To have a friend, to *be* one—Willbury would be my friend, someone with whom I could be at ease, to whom I could unburden myself. He was a savior.

"The course of treatment he suggested was essentially that I learn to be human. He praised my 'parody'—his word—of human behavior, but said it lacked nuance and perspective. He suggested that by examining and correcting the flaws in my performance we would both learn about my emotions, my psychology and neurology. I would gain a dispassionate perspective on myself, and he a context for counseling me.

"And so, being human became my special study. Willbury explained human emotions to me and taught me how to portray them. I, in turn, described my reactions, identified the emotions that seemed foreign or incomprehensible. I watched movies in the clubs of Insomnia, read books and continued my explorations of the veldt. And I watched people. Watched and watched and watched. Meanwhile acting as Willbury's personal assistant. I drove him, managed his appointments, travel, wardrobe, diet. His routine became mine. I was more involved than his wife with his daily affairs. More, too, his confidant. He told me who he trusted, who he regarded as enemies. He complained incessantly about the restrictions on P.C.'s authority, especially Right of Refusal. Railed against those within P.C. who did not share his views. There was no reason for people to suffer, he insisted. If P.C. were allowed to medicate them properly, violence and criminal behavior could be eliminated. I have to say that seemed reasonable to me.

"Friedman was a frequent object of ridicule. He was a proponent of Right of Refusal, and effective in defending it. Willbury called him a weekend psychologist, made fun of his interests in space flight, chaos architecture, and philosophical inclusivism. A few years ago Friedman went to visit Olivetta on his island. Willbury found out about it and was furious. He took it as a personal attack. He was convinced that Friedman was spying on him, and had somehow learned of his personal interest in Olivetta. When Olivetta was granted an indulgence to move to New York, Willbury was sure Friedman was behind it. He knew some of his colleagues were, too, but the decision was sealed and he couldn't find out who they were, which infuriated him further. Willbury often used Olivetta as an example of someone the legal system had failed, who should be receiving enforced medication. Olivetta's sociopathy, he argued, drove him to create art that traumatized the viewer and thereby kept him personally isolated. If he were medicated properly, his talents might benefit society and he might develop healthy relationships. Willbury said Friedman was trying to discredit him by making Olivetta look harmless.

"He became obsessed with watching Olivetta. Friedman visited Olivetta regularly and Willbury wanted to know what they talked about. Legally, he could not install surveillance cameras inside of Olivetta's studio. So I did it for him. That was the first time I saw Olivetta's artwork. I didn't really understand it, but I could see why Willbury might find it disturbing.

"I knew he did not tell me everything. He was far more secretive than I imagined. Plots and intrigues he kept to himself. I sensed, sometimes, that he was manipulating me, told myself it was for my own good. I questioned him about it, once, and he became immediately distant. It was painful, like having some intangible thing I'd become dependent upon suddenly taken from me. It was terrifying. I didn't question him about it anymore after that.

"I continued to work with him in a therapeutic context. He was very interested in you and One-ten. Then I think he began to doubt that you existed, maybe wondered if I'd made you up. I attributed it to what I'd told him about shapes, which he never seemed to take seriously. He never said so but I thought he must have believed I imagined them, invisible beings flying around everywhere that only I and two ancient beings could see. Eventually he stopped asking about you. Not before reviving my apprehensions about your quest. I don't know if he meant to do that. He said my people had had ages to analyze the information I'd given them, and had likely discovered dangers I'd failed to perceive, but which might well validate my instinctive misgivings. It was a thought I'd had myself many times. But hearing it from a member of another species, who had, to all indications, a sincere interest in my well-being, lent it added credence.

"One-ten arrived nine weeks ago, in the same place you did. Any reluctance I'd felt to proceed with the next phase of the experiment had long since faded away. The beacon alerted me in time to get to her before she could complete a construct. I did not tell Willbury. In that omission, I think, was an instinct I failed to note. It was late and the street was empty. A massive gathering of shapes had answered her call, and she was already making herself within their sphere. I took a position where you found the dead shapes, in the unfinished apartment at the top of that building, cloaked myself and extended a capturing field. Immediately I found out that shapes are more sensitive than I knew. They detected the field and most of them escaped before it closed. More unexpected was what happened next. I couldn't tell what was going on inside the field but clearly it wasn't good. It should have been entirely quiescent, but some instability made the enclosure wobble and bulge. I didn't want to create a spectacle, so I transferred the nullification bubble to the apartment before retracting it.

"I think I understand, now, what happened. The shapes and One-ten were in conflict. I think they thought she had created the capturing field. Inadvertently, I made things worse. *I* was cloaked but, in my panic, I hadn't thought to cloak my shapes. Remember that I presented some of them, blanked, to the Stations as evidence against you. The Earth shapes in the apartment mistook my shapes, I think, for their fellows somehow changed by One-ten, and attacked her in a frenzy. Some of my shapes got caught in the fray, which frightened them more. One-ten was in mid-formation, too far along to stop. I could do nothing. She defended herself, killing the shapes and becoming … what she became. She, too, recognized my shapes and fled.

"The incident left me in chaos. I was afraid to contact my users on Ixil. I called Willbury. He came to my dome. I was incoherent, couldn't explain what had happened, kept losing the interface with my construct. I ran the visual record for him, showing One-ten's grotesque malformation. It terrified him; that was the first time I saw him show fear. He demanded to know why I had not informed him that one of my fabled messengers had arrived. He shouted at me, said I'd betrayed his trust in me.

"I was so distraught I lost the interface completely and passed out. When I came to he was sitting there, watching me. He offered a cursory apology, completely devoid of warmth, for speaking as he had, told me to let him know when I had found One-ten, and left.

"I can't exaggerate the disorientation I experienced. It was hours before I calmed down enough to leave the dome. I was desperate to regain Willbury's trust. I searched for One-ten, but I—" Haliel checked out again.

Planchette was left alone with the clustered detachments taking him apart inside.

Chapter Fifty

Nothing conquered Time, the erstwhile behemoth.

—Unknown

Planchette thought he might have sacrificed himself for nothing. He wanted to run away, to Dunn, to the Tehfolorans and their medical experts. He knew he would do neither of those things. He sighed. The longer this exchange went on, the harder it was to watch Haliel's lapses. It was too clear that they were caused by emotions, cascades of synaptic complexity overloading the interface. Inside the compressed space of his ship, the real Haliel was suffering.

Haliel's construct reanimated, looked embarrassed. "How long was I gone?"

"Not long. I think you were about to tell me you couldn't find _=ca.110."

Haliel averted his gaze. "Our instruments show you to be a single entity—"

"Which interferes with your ability to track us not at all." Planchette wondered if Haliel understood the irony in his own prevarication. "You were afraid of the alligators."

"What? They're no threat to me."

"To you, no. Your construct, though, they would tear to pieces."

Haliel shrugged, still avoiding Planchette's gaze. "Eighty-five, you keep forgetting that I have technology—"

"I haven't forgotten that at all."

"Even—even if there were some fluke accident, I can make another construct—"

"That's the question, isn't it? Would it be the same? It's hard to give up a body you've grown accustomed to. Especially when the line between where you end and it begins has blurred."

Haliel's response was barely audible. "Willbury trained me well."

Planchette shook his head. The giant, voracious reptiles epitomized everything Ixilians feared most. "My partner went down there to hide from the shapes. But when she found the alligators she stayed close to them, because she knew they would scare *you* away."

Haliel's strained smile saddened.

"There's no shame in it, Haliel."

"Is that what I'm feeling? Shame?"

Planchette sighed. "I don't know. What did Willbury do, when you told him you couldn't find her?"

"He didn't believe me. Stopped talking to me. Suspended our therapy sessions. But everything changed when Friedman showed up with One-ten at Olivetta's studio. I have to say I didn't see that coming. I never imagined that One-ten would seek out her recipient in the state she was in. But she did. Friedman's scientific objectivity must have overridden his visceral reactions to her appearance.

"They went to Olivetta's at night. Willbury didn't see the record until the following morning. He called me to his private office at his home to look at it. One-ten wore a shroud when she entered Olivetta's studio. Friedman told Olivetta to prepare himself and uncovered her. When Olivetta got past his initial amazement, Friedman whispered something and Olivetta went straight for the monitor I'd installed and disabled it. Which showed he'd known where it was. But Friedman made a mistake, there, that probably cost him his life. He wanted Willbury to see One-ten. He wanted to slap him in the face with her. It was a mistake.

"Willbury became dispassionately methodical. He sent agents to bring Olivetta in for questioning. He asked me if I could really inhibit memories. I'd told him many things about myself. All those hours and days answering his questions, and he'd posed a great many about my technological capabilities. I couldn't believe, though, that he, too, would regard me as a tool. I did as he asked and suppressed Olivetta's memories of his encounter with One-ten.

"I didn't like doing that. I did it out of friendship, you see. The memories were precious to Olivetta. One-ten had given him the first concrete proof he'd ever had that his visions were not hallucinations.

"I installed new monitors in his studio and stole the knife. I didn't know why Willbury wanted that, just did as I was told. I wanted Willbury to look at me as he had, with admiration and respect. I was as gentle with Olivetta as I could be. I hadn't counted on the tenacity of his mind. He fought my intrusions into his psyche, painted those portraits of One-ten. Willbury saw that and showered me with rebuke. I was an imposter and a dullard; I couldn't be trusted with anything. More in that vein.

"It was horrible. I don't have words for what went on inside of me, to be spoken to like that by the person I had come to regard as my one true friend. I begged him to relent and he said I disgusted him.

"And then he changed. He didn't just apologize, he begged *my* forgiveness. He said the fate of humanity was on his shoulders, and that he would have to do terrible things no one else had the courage to do. I was the only one who could understand, the only one he could trust. I knew he was lying but I needed to believe him."

"Why did he want to kill Friedman?"

"He didn't. He wanted to kill Olivetta. But there were too many records of their involvement. Diagnoses and treatments. All the banishment orders. Too many actions he'd taken that might be questioned if they were examined closely. Which they absolutely would be if Olivetta were to die in suspicious circumstances. So he'd devised an alternate plan: Kill Friedman and make it look like Olivetta did it.

"He'd been planning for years. I think his training had restrained him from doing it himself."

Or maybe just fear of getting caught, Planchette guessed. Things weren't always complicated.

"He had proof that Friedman and Olivetta had been lovers—pictures of them together on an island where Olivetta had lived during his banishment. And he had other pictures, lots, of Friedman with other lovers, male and female, in New York. The idea was to make it look like Olivetta had killed him out of jealousy. It would serve two purposes—discredit Friedman and get Olivetta banished for good. It would also bolster Willbury's arguments for rescinding Right of Refusal.

"I assured him that he could count on me. I would have agreed to anything. I didn't need a reason."

"He asked you outright to kill Friedman?"

"No, I offered." Haliel watched Planchette's reaction. "You're incredulous."

Planchette didn't know what he felt. Weary bones suffered the weight of another dispelled illusion.

"Willbury had someone to do the actual killing," Haliel said. "He wanted me to disable Olivetta's monitoring button and make it look like he'd done it himself. He also wanted me to eliminate any evidence of the real killer's involvement.

"I wanted to please him, you see; I was desperate to please him. I said it would be easier to erase my own tracks than someone else's. I think, in that moment, I was the most *in* this construct I've ever been, completely dissociated from my body in the ship. Maybe I went a little insane. It was like a door opened and I split in two. One of me thought my usual thoughts and went the way I normally go, down the course I always have, but without my participation. I watched from a detached perspective, the way you might a discharge of energy. Not without alarm—it was me walking away from me, and I knew it. But I was incapable of doing anything about it. Willbury was talking but I didn't hear him. His mouth formed speech but his body said something else, pointing me along that other way, where it was obvious that my people had sent me out to experience a violent act. So I argued, not hearing my own voice, only feeling its texture, like liquid bent to a channel, persuading him to let me do exactly what he meant me to do."

Planchette nodded grimly. "That's called coercion."

Haliel continued as if he had not heard. "He knew Friedman was a regular at that bar, came and went alone. He thought an opportune moment should avail itself late at night in a dimly lit alleyway. I followed Friedman there a couple of nights. He had a high tolerance for alcohol. The third night I was surprised to see him meet One-ten in the unlit stretch of the alley. I followed them but when I rounded the corner they were gone. Friedman was formidable. He knew he was being watched.

"I searched for them. When I came back where I'd lost them, they were there. I had no idea where they'd gone. A bit embarrassing to be fooled by that door. One-ten went back down the dark end of the alley. I was cloaked, standing at the bend. She went right by me, inches away. She's never been as sensitive to my presence as you. For an instant I thought she noticed but she kept going."

Planchette stopped listening. He remembered the night of his arrival in recolonized New York. He had seen Friedman go by in a pod. There was no way Frisa could have been there and made it to the alley before him. But Planchette had seen her silhouette, backlit in a room with no electricity. Something else had happened. A kind of phantasm, a spark ignited by their psyches, calling to each other. He could feel it, now, feel *her*, like background radiation from intangible depths. He'd never noticed because they'd never been so far apart. The connection was unbreakable; it had only been stretched. It had led him here, to this city and this time. It would have led him to her across the universe. Too late he'd recognized it, now, just as he was about to go much farther away than that.

Haliel was watching him. "You're seeing it, aren't you?"

Planchette swallowed. "You were telling me how you killed Friedman."

Haliel grimaced. "That woman showed up, Claire Fontaine. I was going to wait but I was impatient. It occurred to me that it might not be bad to have a witness, particularly if I distorted her memory. Willbury wanted me to disguise myself as Olivetta. But I had an inspiration and disguised myself as One-ten, the way she looked in Olivetta's grotesque depiction of her. I would make it look like he'd donned his holo-suit to disguise himself, and leave the knife by the body with his fingerprints on it. Something went wrong, though. I left the knife but it must have been lost or something. It never showed up in any of the investigation reports."

"_=ca.110 took it."

"Ah, so she did sense me."

"She sensed something. It bothered her and she went back. She found Friedman dead and Claire in a trance. Claire came around and went in the bar for help, and _=ca.110 took the knife."

"Smart of her."

Planchette peered sidelong. "I don't know how smart it was. An instinct, maybe. Or a reflex."

"We could probably still have assembled enough circumstantial evidence to banish Olivetta without that. If you hadn't turned up and flipped the universe on its head." Haliel again stared pointedly at Planchette. "Do you see it?"

Planchette stared back.

"You will." Haliel looked away. "Something in me broke. I doubt it will mend. The real horror of murdering someone is that you become someone else. It makes your life a pretense until you confess. Either way the person you were is gone."

"You did something else, didn't you?"

"What?"

"To Claire Fontaine, when you 'distorted her memory.'"

Haliel sighed and nodded. "My ship's instruments had alerted me that she was a potential recipient. I interfered with her ability to read you."

"How?"

"Just altered a few neural pathways. The effect will wear off."

"When?"

"Probably the next time you see her. Your presence weakens it."

Planchette took a long breath. "What happened then, after you killed Friedman?"

"I left Willbury at home and drove out into the veldt, parked and wandered through the unmarked necropolis of that place. It's always comforted me. Sometimes I perform a little ritual, take one of my cups, make a tea and drink it. I can't taste it but it gives me a sense of participating in life. I did that, out near Insomnia, and you found me.

"I couldn't ignore the coincidences piling up. I try to discredit you with the shapes and wind up involved with a man plotting to kill One-ten's recipient. Later I find my witness is *your* recipient. You show up the very night I kill Friedman, disguised as a police detective. Cum lead investigator, no less. You must have noticed this."

Planchette knew where Haliel was going. It didn't matter. "Let's just finish."

Haliel grunted and shrugged his eyebrows. "Well, here you were, badge and everything, and I hadn't even looked for you. If you don't see a telling peculiarity in that I don't know what to say. We had our less-than-gratifying tete-a-tete, which is a fair characterization of every exchange we've ever had. Until maybe last night. I don't think it was an hour later that the beacon alerted me to the arrival of the Tehfoloran ship. A veritable windfall of coincidence, wouldn't you say? Disparate agencies, inexplicably drawn together. By what?

"That morning I told Willbury of your arrival, and that you were pretending to be a cop. My loyalties were, you understand, divided. He contrived to meet you at the College. You shook him up, particularly in your competence with human behavior. There was no lack of nuance in your performance, as there had been in mine. As far as he could tell, you *were* human—"

"Because I am."

Haliel shrugged. "It scared him. He said you had to be stopped. I left him at a meeting and called you. I was still in an emotionally detached state, going through the motions of being someone who cared, who wanted to conceal his wrongs and spare others, without knowing how to go about it. Simple curiosity prodded me along more than anything. I'd detected a shielded room in that building with the hidden door and I wanted to know what Friedman had in there.

"His work exhibited incredible leaps in reasoning. I suspect that was another part of what my users feared. There was an echo in it, or perhaps a foreshadowing, of the science in your making. The question remains whether such leaps are more common than we know, or if the qualities this world's inhabitants share with your creators are as rare as they seem.

"I had no more time to investigate. Your presence was a threat to Willbury's ambitions—an insult to them, the way he took it—so he hurried to propel his long-nurtured schemes into motion. I raced him around from meeting to meeting, wheels within wheels. Paintings were burned, opponents quietly rounded up, the Utilitarians in the Psychology Council exposed, you were arrested and banished. I watched shapes dart about above the city in a frenzy I'd never seen.

"Then you escaped banishment and a few hours later word came through that you'd been killed. No details about the circumstances of your death, which distressed Willbury. And me, though I hid it. Tried to. It kind of woke me up, shook me out of my daze. He had me drive him to the place where Claire Fontaine lives.

"It was still dark. A giant mass of shapes circled the towers high up in a state of hysteria. I caught Willbury watching them. It was unmistakable, his shock at the spectacle. His expression changed to something like hatred. I couldn't get my mind around it, the enormity of what he'd concealed. From everyone, his whole life. He looked at me and knew that he had exposed himself, gave me the most cutting look imaginable.

"Nothing had been what it seemed. Even now I'm not sure what his true motives are. It was more about the shapes than Olivetta. Willbury hates them. He sees them as vermin, the illegitimate spawn of dysfunctional consciousness. I'd never understood him. I still don't."

"He's mad at a god he doesn't believe exists," Planchette said.

Haliel frowned. "I don't know what that means."

"It doesn't matter."

Haliel was momentarily confused, recalled his thread, went on. "What he didn't know, Willbury, and what I know now, is that, no matter how intricate or careful his plans, failure was inevitable. All the coincidences—you must see, I know you do. When I insinuated my shapes into your cognitive core, I unwittingly became part of your organism, part of what you and One-ten are. From that point on, no matter what I did, I couldn't divert anything from ultimately going your way."

"I wouldn't call this my way, Haliel."

"Maybe not from your individual perspective, but from that of your creators? Look at the impact you'd had, Eighty-five. You drop a pebble and the ripples change everything, world after world. I'm not sure you haven't communicated that change to Ixil. All consciousness and intelligence is drawn inexorably into alignment with the dual singularities of your psyches. The will of your creators imposed on all you touch. The entire galaxy is becoming part of your organism."

"You don't believe that."

"I'm not even sure that I'm sane, Eighty-five, let alone what I believe. But I had that question from the beginning. When do we all become servants of your pattern?"

"When do we own awareness that consent is required for our actions? You see what you look for. You see the imposition of a pattern and disregard the underlying design. There's no imperative in my message, no requirement to believe or accede to anything. It's an offer, an invitation, based on a simple premise, that when people have hope and see a future for themselves they tend to prosper and cooperate, and when they lose hope and see no future, the inclination to conflict and despair increases."

Haliel smiled and for a moment remained silent. "Thank you, my friend," he said quietly. "I wanted to hear that from you. I wanted very much to hear you say that."

Planchette became exasperated. "Why *do* this, Haliel? Follow us, world after world. You could have turned the job over to someone else. I understand it must have been terrible to realize that all of the people you knew were dead. But the living ones are still your people. You could have lived a life. Why bring yourself to this? What have you accomplished?"

Haliel checked out again. When he came back his attitude was much changed, distilled, somehow, to a purity of philosophical acquiescence. "I'm sorry, Eighty-five, I thought I'd made it clear. I couldn't go back."

"What?"

"After my first interface, on Fixot, I wanted to go home immediately and erase the experience from my memory. I discovered that my navigation systems had been scrambled, and that a signal from Ixil had caused it. I requested an explanation, expressed my need to return. They responded with a request for clarification. I clarified in every way I could think of. Further information required, they said. What information? Observations of you and One-ten. I returned to Fixot, observed, clarified. So it went until the truth became evident. My people would not let me come home. I'd been sacrificed. I was no longer part of the event."

Planchette felt sickened. "We didn't know."

"Why would you? You didn't want to know about me. And I didn't want you to, either. Not then. Most especially I did not want to become any more trivial in your estimation than I already was.

"Every time I came out of stasis, I sent home an appeal, and every time it was rejected. My status as a pariah reinforced its own precedent. My ship docks inside the beacon. From that point on I was bound to you. Where you went, I followed."

"If you'd told us, we could have led you back to Ixil."

"I wonder how they would have reacted if we'd done that. I'm going to tell you something, Eighty-five, that I do not think you want to hear. Irritating as it has been to have me follow you around, secretly you have been reassured by it, by the existence in the galaxy of a species that is entirely non-violent.

"Willbury persuaded me, it's true. But how does one understand danger if one has never experienced it? How does one recognize one's own capacity to be dangerous? We have lied to ourselves, you see. There is a great darkness in Ixil. I think it amused Willbury to awaken it in me. He knew it was there. Even as Friedman approached me, in the alley, deep down I counted on my instincts to restrain me. But I slashed his throat without hesitation, and what I felt was not shock but release. *Elation.* It was buried so deep in me that I didn't believe it existed, held down by the certainty that my people never argued or struggled in any way, that the environment I grew up in made me incapable of wrath. But the *universe* is our environment, Eighty-five, not just Ixil. And the universe is very violent indeed."

Planchette glanced back at Furniture, who returned his regard with solemnity. The sadness of creation haunted the room with them, ghost of an explosion.

"We had to know, you see? We tell ourselves that we are benign and defenseless by nature, that we could never do things, terrible things, that we possess the power to do. But we *developed* those powers. We can enclose an entire world in a nullification field,

Eighty-five, hold it in place while its system, its star, the entire galaxy moves on. Do that for a moment, just a few seconds, remove the field, and everything dies. Such are the unacceptable means. How could we develop such a thing if it is beyond our capacity to use it? Why is that part of our event?

"I had to know what it felt like to kill, so that I could recognize and understand the nature of my restraint. Was it truly inherent, or merely cosmetic, a story I told myself so that I could imagine myself immune? No, I cannot put the blame on Willbury. Nor entirely on myself. This was what my users wanted me to do. *I* was the true experiment, Eighty-five. Not you, not One-ten, not the shapes, not the people of this world. Could I kill, you see? I'm not sure they even admitted to themselves what they were after. But the question was there. Asked and answered."

Planchette closed his eyes and rubbed his forehead. Haliel had said it, he was only a pebble. He would have to leave the ripples to their own designs. "So, you're going to stay like this."

Haliel went dead again, came back. "I—I don't really understand why I'm alive. I don't think I know myself very well, Eighty-five. I'm not connected to anyone but you."

"I'm sorry that I was mean to you."

Haliel nodded. "By now Ixil has my report and they know what I've done. I'll serve my sentence." Haliel took his ship from his pocket, placed it on the table in front of Planchette. "Give that to whomever you think best."

Planchette looked at Haliel's three memory bags. "Where are the rest of your shapes?"

"I wiped them. I don't need to remember much, anymore, that isn't in my mind." He pointed at the three survivors. "That one's my childhood, that's you, and the other is … private."

Planchette cleared his throat. "The Tehfolorans have established a rudimentary interplanetary council. I told them I think you should represent Ixil."

"You're probably right. They'll know where to find me."

Planchette looked at the ship.

"I've disconnected volitional functions," Haliel said. "Except for the link with my neural tree, my body is in suspended animation. I can't disconnect myself without permission. Official *human* permission. The ship will know if that happens."

"You'll be more alone than ever."

"Maybe you'll come visit me." Haliel smiled, but only with his mouth. His surrogate eyes were bleak as craters. "It's all right, Eighty-five. I'm part of the event again."

Chapter Fifty-one

Hasker, Perls, the two judges and Ganeel Godbole stood huddled in the hallway. Hasker heard Planchette, stepped away from the others and confronted him.

"What's that supposed to mean, he'll 'serve his sentence?'" The Captain was himself again, ferocity intact.

"What it means."

"Bullshit. About point-oh-five percent of what you two said in there made any sense at all. And I didn't appreciate the blackouts."

Planchette had disconnected the intercom intermittently when Haliel and he talked about shapes. "Chief—"

"Hey, *you* don't work for this department."

"What do you want me to call you?"

"Say what you were going to say."

Planchette shook his head. "I'm tired. I don't have the energy to argue. Haliel—Halbert Leal—is the killer, but Willbury was behind it and everything else, including the fires, Gable MacGrory's death and Olivetta's suicide. You have more than enough evidence to prosecute both of them and provide the courts with grounds for indefinite banishment." He watched Hasker's features soften. Planchette still didn't understand what it was in him that elicited sympathy from others.

"You're telling me that whatever that is in there is going to stay where we put it."

"Yes."

"It's not even a person."

Planchette glanced back through the glass at Haliel. "Close enough." He gave Hasker Haliel's ship.

"What's this?"

"It's him. The real him. Don't try to figure it out, just keep it safe. And don't mess with it. It's important that his people see him submit to your judgement, and see you treat that with respect. When you're ready to let him go, give it back to him."

Hasker frowned at the cube, put it in his pocket. "You're keeping things from us. Important things."

"It's not my place to reveal them. Haliel—Leal—is bound by similar constraints."

Hasker peered aside as if the world had moved beyond him.

"Willbury, on another hand—" Planchette let the thought hang.

"What about him?"

Planchette held Hasker's gaze.

"He's bound to us."

"If anyone. Right of Refusal is rescinded when complicity in a homicide has been established, if memory serves."

Hasker grunted. "You and that memory."

Planchette made his exit down the jagged hall, avoided eye contact with those he passed. It was time to go. He wanted to see Dunn but didn't look for her. He didn't want to see Frisa, and she didn't want to see him. The house of his identity was a shambles.

Schnittke waited at the end of the hall with Planchette's greatcoat, helped him into it, patted him on the shoulder. Planchette didn't use the elevator. No more hidden doors, no more masquerades. He would live his last moments in the open. He went down the central staircase, through the bull pens, drew stares all the way.

"Wasn't he *dead?*"

The air was cool outside, the sky overcast. At the bottom of the steps in front of the station Frederick Bash sat on a concrete bollard. He slid to the sidewalk and held Planchette's hat out to him.

Planchette didn't want to talk. Something about Bash still irritated him.

"You've got an audience." Bash gestured up the steps.

Planchette didn't look.

"Do you know where you're going?"

Planchette turned the hat in his hands. It had been better repaired; the tear was invisible. Both it and the coat bore the taint of grave goods, now. He put the hat on—"Thanks—" crossed the street, and headed across the narrow plaza, with its reedy, crooked saplings and withered grass. The universe was a mess. The whole thing was held together with duct tape and bailing wire. A gathering of shapes attended his passage. He ignored them too.

"Remember the poem," Bash called after him.

Crumpled buildings bordered the far perimeter of the plaza, interspersed with narrow streets that all curved or bent too soon to see down. Planchette didn't know how to get to Claire's.

His assistants were re-connected with the Cloud, now. His trustworthiness had been established, at last. Graph began to suggest a route but Planchette stopped him. He wanted to be alone, find his own way. He didn't need assistants anymore. He couldn't carry their pain, left them there, ducked a fan of stabilizing cables.

The street wound among empty lots, rubble, domes, improbable multi-level tenements. Planchette wandered like one lost and abandoned. He was not ready to surrender. He let the currents of sense and reflection draw him. He walked for miles. He loved his body, this body, his last. All he had not appreciated lay behind him in the present. The physicality he had loved and failed to cherish. The cryptic existence of his core self, too, for even in its null state of jettisoned emotions he had been located among the stars.

It began to rain. He loved the broken, jagged, half-built abstraction of New York. A word inscribed on the riser of a stoop read "Library" upside down, remnant of an absent repository. No one could help him find the piece that was his. Around the next bend, three Tehfolorans waited by the road. One of them, no doubt, his distant descendant. Perhaps all three. Planchette stopped. This was what they'd feared, the 'danger to all world,' that he would destroy himself. He had nothing to tell them, either.

He walked until his legs ached, relished the feeling. Buildings became shadows in the hard fall of rain. The pinpricks of disintegration cascading inside of him were muted by the pelting of droplets. He stopped, held his hand up, palm down, blade to eyes. He couldn't distinguish his trembling from the rain's oscillations on his skin. He loved the rain, loved it, the sweet roar, took his hat off and let it batter his face.

He heard a voice, drifted toward it, blinking, came to the steps of a three-storey jigsaw with a wrap-around porch on the ground floor. Several women and men, some in see-through garments, sat in chairs on the porch. Two stood and beckoned him, leaned down from the railing. Planchette put his hat back on. Their words were noise. A skinny young man came down and pawed him, spoke unintelligibly. Planchette sought help from Graph, remembered he'd sent his assistants away.

He drifted on, here and there glimpsed figures in windows. A woman pushed her naked breasts against the glass. He was in the sex zone. Olivetta's studio was somewhere nearby. Had been. Nothing looked familiar. Two women dashed into the street and pulled at him. He couldn't tell what they were saying.

"Did you know him?" he asked.

They didn't understand.

"Michael Olivetta. Michelle. Did you ever see his paintings?"

It might have been English or anything they spoke. The language of enticement. They didn't know they were propositioning a corpse.

A dark form settled to the street in front of him. The passenger window rolled down.

"Get in," Dunn said.

The snags tried to hold him. Planchette stared at the one who tugged his sleeve. Her hair was matted against her forehead by the rain. She had on a transparent jumpsuit. "That doesn't protect you," he told her. He looked in her brown eyes and saw everything, the pain and yearning, all the way to the stars. She saw him, too, for an instant, let go and ran away. The other went after her.

When he was inside Dunn rolled up the window. The rain became a muted thrum.

"What are you doing? You're soaked."

"I can't stay."

"What?"

"Hasker will have to wait."

"You think Hasker sent me?"

He was afraid to look at her but he did. "You came looking for me."

She didn't have to answer.

This wasn't fair to either of them. "I have to go to Claire's."

She inhaled sharply and faced the rain. "You're miles in the wrong direction."

Planchette watched the blurred city drop below. He would have liked to drive again, without the autopilot. Dunn kept asking him questions he couldn't process. His lives pressed at the doors of his consciousness, but he only cared about this one. The others had been lived by other people. This one had been lived by him.

He recognized Claire's tower and told Dunn to take the hover down.

"You're soaked."

"I want to walk."

She opened her mouth to argue.

"I can't help you," he told her. "I'm not real. I'm a simulation. Everything that happened between us was artificial. You served your purpose, Officer Dunn. I can't be with you, now. I need to finish my job."

She took the hover down. He hated hurting her more but didn't say goodbye, just got out and closed the door. He'd gone about twenty steps when he heard her running after him.

She threw her arms around him, held his face. "Not like this."

She kissed him.

Her face streamed with rain. He gave in and held her. The rain became shelter, a sanctuary with a time limit.

"You're real," she breathed in his ear. "Everything was real."

He watched her walk away.

Chapter Fifty-two

Claire clicked off her sheet. Dunn had said that Planchette was coming. "The report of his death was inaccurate." The word hung there: *inaccurate*. Claire didn't know what to do with it. You died or you didn't. The report was true or false, not inaccurate.

She recognized his knock, stared at the door. He was waiting on the other side. He wasn't human. Or he was, and wasn't. They'd let him go out on his own. They trusted him. Maybe they couldn't control him.

He wasn't what she'd thought he was. He wasn't a person. No one had explained anything to her. He was someone she had watched communicate with a monster—not an aberration, not an unaborted mutation, something much more distorted than that. A monster.

He'd taken a sword through the heart for his partner.

Don't open the door, she told herself.

But she wanted to.

He came in. She'd seen old film clips of kings and queens, everyone bowing. Not an association she could account for but she had that thought—royalty. She bowed herself, felt ridiculous.

He had died inaccurately, however one did that, and here he was.

He put his sopping coat over a chair at the dining table, the same one he had the first time he'd come, his hat on the table as he had before. He didn't speak, didn't look at her. There was so much sadness in him. Resignation.

He was afraid of her. The realization frightened her in return. She watched him go to the window and stare out into the rain. He stood so still, not succumbing to his burdens, not defying them, head neither raised nor bowed, facing the unavoidable, straight on. He made a gesture with his hand—not to her, to himself—a sideways toss of the fingers, like dismissing regret and all that could not be changed.

He sat on the sofa, leaned forward with his hands clasped, finally looked at her.

She sat down, hesitantly, on the other sofa, held his gaze.

There was something in his eyes that she wanted. She wanted to be sure but that was the child in her protecting the adolescent in her. Nothing was ever sure. Except that all he really wanted was to give her something.

And he was broken; that was sure, too. He could no more repair himself than she could the world. He wouldn't stop looking at her. Not meek, not beseeching. He had been ravaged by everything, pulled under, surfaced now like a corpse from the water. Inaccurately dead.

She wanted to comfort him.

She put a drink in front of him, didn't remember pouring it. He drank it, turned the glass in his hands. A strange thought came to her. She might have had the thought before. She didn't know but its texture was familiar.

Something unstable in her wanted to fall apart. She let go, trembling, and an inner wind took the shambles. Everything that worried her, that she had been told to fear, was shouldered aside by a question: What if she lived not just in this world but the universe, not just this time but eternity?

He changed, deepened, opened, like a door. Inside, he was a world. Worlds. Everyone was. But something about his world was familiar.

She remembered, when she was a child, finding a ring in the sand. A gold ring, pitted and bent. Her mother was nearby, picking through piles of stone and concrete that a scrubber had scoured, looking for bits of things for their dome. Her father was farther off, doing the same.

"Put that down, Clairey. It doesn't belong to you," her mother said.

Claire looked around at the rubble and ruins. "Who does it belong to?"

"Hope," her mother answered wearily, picking on. "The hope that died."

That night her father sat on the edge of her cot, in their lead-lined tent, and smiled down at her while wind rattled the flaps.

"We're going to make a beautiful home, Clairey. A work of art."

"Life is a work of art, right Daddy?"

"That's right," he nodded. He'd said so many times. He held his hand out, palm down, fingers closed. She opened her small hand beneath it. He placed the ring in her hand. He'd worked the bend out and polished it. "There's always hope, Clairey. Always."

Claire stared at Planchette, into his kind, tired eyes. He smiled, a faint, gentle smile, like her father had, and she recognized him. Not who he was but what he was:

Hope.

He was hope.

He was the living personification of hope.

She understood what he wanted. He would never ask for it. It was up to her. If she told him to go he would go. She was still afraid, but she knew what she wanted, too. She wanted to drop her defenses and give him a gift. She wanted to give him permission to give her his gift.

She sat beside him, touched his hand.

Time stopped.

How they found their way to her bed she did not know. They lay down naked together and she was not afraid. They found each other in the darkness. He was breaking apart, like a raft against rocks, the universe silvered by infinite moons, stars, places he'd lived, people he'd been, in her arms, this person, this time, constant and never the same. He was a universe of waves in her arms, in a place completely their own. They could have been on stage, surrounded, exposed to everyone, and invisible. He was so close her very substance was bound to the moment, that came and went, came and went, impossible to hold, unrepeatable.

They found a sanctuary deep in that private place where they could break apart together, and as they reached it a light like none she'd known beamed from his mouth and eyes, and her mind and being were bathed in the light, possessed by ecstacy and the understanding that consciousness could neither be created nor destroyed, that there was a future beyond this world for both the living and the dead, that in that future all things were possible, and beauty and purpose lived at its heart.

The light dimmed and failed. He had ruined himself, giving her everything. She felt the infinite break loose in him and depart in a great flurry, and she held him and wept.

Planchette fell back against the pillows and surrendered to the collapse of his core. He watched, inside and out, as the billions of shapes that had bonded to form it burst forth, free again, after countless millennia, to be themselves. He had not known they were alive in him. Frisa had never told him.

"Open the window," he breathed.

Claire, weeping, lurched to the sash window by the bed and threw it open, swept back to hold him. She couldn't see what was happening but he knew she could feel it.

The shapes of his parents poured out into the sky of a new world. They would mingle with the shapes of Earth, and the quest would be carried on, as it had always been meant to, not by two handmade beings, but by an entire species, an interstellar society.

He had expected to die but he did not. The shapes of his parents left him his human self, with great longevity and a working memory of the lives he had lived, a further flicker for the winds of time.

He would keep this hundredth life, live once more. Tears slipped from his eyes down the sides of his face.

Finally he could tell Frisa that he loved her.

Epilogue

There was a knock at the door and Claire got up from her work to answer it. It was Sybil, bringing back Thaddy from their afternoon walk.

Claire always felt uncomfortable around Sybil, the shy, reticent person Planchette's partner of millennia had become. She was small, dark-haired, and hardly ever looked Claire in the eyes. Not what Claire would have expected. She could not reconcile this woman with the thing that had burst through her window.

She felt no animosity toward Sybil but wished she would firm up. It was unseemly for an ancient being to have a mousey personality. She seemed always on the verge of apologizing. Sometimes Sybil stared at Claire's belly in a way that was disquieting. Claire was in her fourth month of pregnancy, and beginning to show.

"Won't you come in?"

Sybil shook her head. She and Thaddy nodded to each other and Sybil left without a word. Claire did not take offence.

Thaddy went to his usual place on the floor by the window in the living room, took out his journal and began to write. He did not frown but his concentration was absolute. The light through the window made a nest in his hair.

Claire sat back down at her dining table, which was also her desk. She was writing a tribute to Michael Olivetta. His self portrait hung in the hall, now, where the photo of the crash site had. So far as she knew, it was the only painting of his that survived. Apart from the mural, which Claire considered an abomination. Even the digital records of his work had been erased. It was small consolation that Willbury and his confederates had been banished, one and all.

She'd had to put off writing about Michael. She'd had to give up writing altogether for several weeks. Even now she couldn't go long without needing to stop. She tapped open the holo-monitor and typed:

> I can't reclaim the loss, all I can do is describe the wound. I refuse to do it gracefully or prettily. I will not scour my phrases. Let them be torn and bleeding. As you tread across them, know he buoyed up the stars. That's what he gave us, burnt offerings for the stars.

She closed the monitor. She needed to write about his history but kept going on like that. She wanted it printed word for word. In red ink.

Sometimes her attention drifted and her thoughts were not her own. She spent long periods looking up. Until something opened, and life came a bit more clearly into focus. She found herself noticing how light touched surfaces and people, how things felt in the dark.

And sometimes, as now, a small figure floated into view, pale and translucent, that she knew to be real, and no hallucination. She knew also that it was alive, and wanted to talk to her, and that one day she would understand what it wanted to say.

This one looked like a golden ring encircled by silver leaves.

Thaddy had stopped writing, too, and was looking out the window. He'd only been with Claire a couple of months but she couldn't imagine life without him.

"Can you see them?"

He nodded. "They never talk."

Claire went over and looked. Sybil and Planchette walked down the street, hand in hand. He still had that ridiculous coat.

"Are you mad at him?" Thaddy asked.

She shook her head. "He's not who he was."

Thaddy frowned. "Yes he is. He just can't be anyone else."

Claire didn't have anything to say to that. She went back to her desk.

"We have a strange family," Thaddy said.

"Yes, we do."

Thaddy studied the building across the street, which was covered, now, in a flame-like mosaic. "It's good. We need something different."

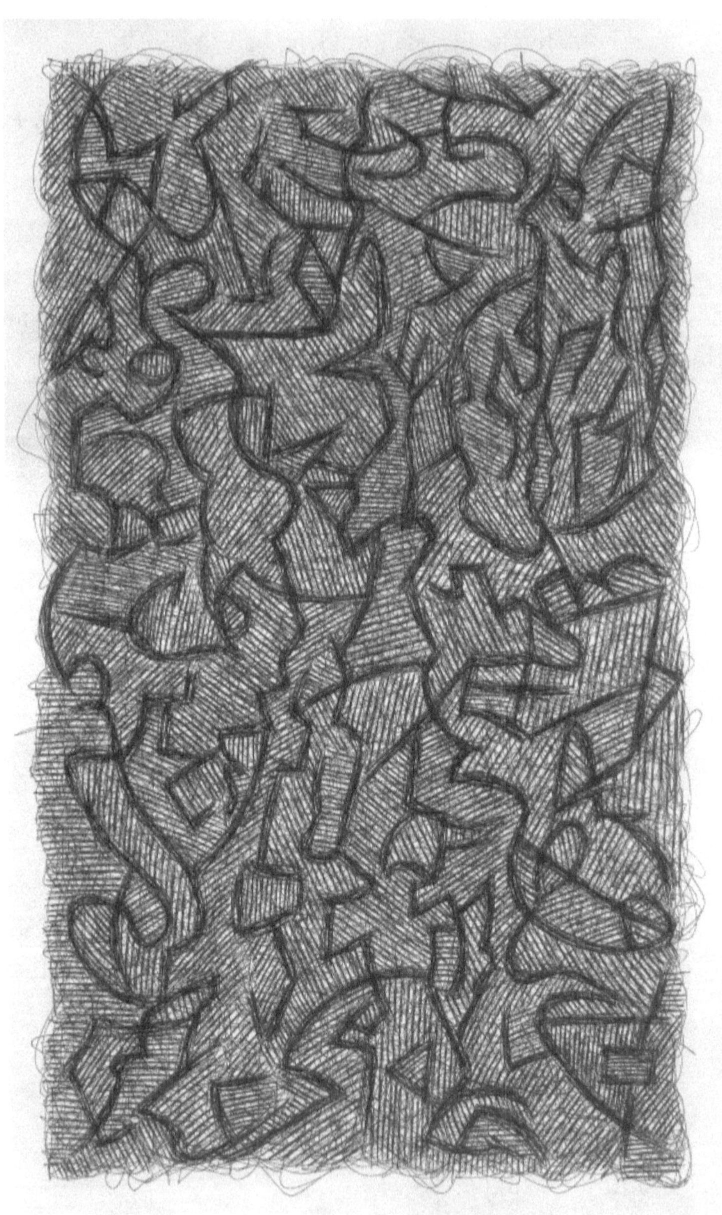

About the Author

Stephen T. Vessels is a Thriller Award nominated author of science fiction, dark fantasy and cross-genre fiction. His previous novels, *The Door of Tireless Pursuit* and *The Ruptured Firmament*, were released by Shadow-Spinners Press. His stories have appeared in *Ellery Queen Mystery Magazine* and collections from Grey Matter Press and ShadowSpinners Press. His story collection, *The Mountain & The Vortex and Other Tales,* was released by Muse Harbor Publishing. He has written art and music reviews for the Santa Barbara Independent and is a published poet and visual artist. An exhibit of his ballpoint pen drawings was on display at the Andre Zarre Gallery in New York City during August of 2016.